"Lovely and brilliant ... a highly whimsical kind of picaresque tale that puts one in mind of both Faulkner and Camus."

Joyce Carol Oates,
The Nation

"It is Walker Percy's triumph that he is able to sustain a comic surface while his darker intentions gather below."

Newsweek

"Breaks your heart in the midst of laughter."
Philadelphia Inquirer

"A rich book ... brilliant."
The New York Review of Books

THE
LAST
GENTLEMAN

Walker Percy

IVY BOOKS • NEW YORK

Ivy Books
Published by Ballantine Books
Copyright © 1966 by Walker Percy

Library of Congress Catalog Card Number: 66-18861

ISBN 0-8041-0379-8

This edition published by arrangement with Farrar, Straus & Giroux, Inc.

Manufactured in the United States of America

First Ballantine Books Edition: April 1989

For Bunt

If a man cannot forget, he will never amount to much.

Sören Kierkegaard, Either/Or

. . . We know now that the modern world is coming to an end . . . at the same time, the unbeliever will emerge from the fogs of secularism. He will cease to reap benefit from the values and forces developed by the very Revelation he denies . . . Loneliness in faith will be terrible. Love will disappear from the face of the public world, but the more precious will be that love which flows from one lonely person to another . . . the world to come will be filled with animosity and danger, but it will be a world open and clean.

Romano Guardini, The End of the Modern World

The characters in this novel are fictional. No real persons are portrayed. The places do not necessarily correspond to geography. That is to say, New York is New York, but localities in Alabama, Mississippi, and Louisiana have been deliberately scrambled. For example, the Southern city herein set forth bears certain resemblances to Birmingham. But the nearby university is more like the state institution in Mississippi. The town of Shut Off, Louisiana, is not across the Mississippi River from Vicksburg. These liberties are taken as a consequence of my impression that this region as a whole, comprising parts of Alabama, Mississippi, and Louisiana, shares certain traits which set it apart from much of the United States and even from the rest of the South.

I

1. ONE FINE DAY IN EARLY SUMMER A YOUNG MAN LAY thinking in Central Park.

His head was propped on his jacket, which had been folded twice so that the lining was outermost, and wedged into a seam of rock. The rock jutted out of the ground in a section of the park known as the Great Meadow. Beside him and canted up at mortar angle squatted a telescope of an unusual design.

In the course of the next five minutes the young man was to witness by chance an insignificant, though rather curious happening. It was the telescope which became the instrument of a bit of accidental eavesdropping. As a consequence of a chance event the rest of his life was to be changed.

He was an unusual young man. But perhaps nowadays it is not so unusual. What distinguished him anyhow was this: he had to know everything before he could do anything. For example, he had to know what other people's infirmities were before he could get on a footing with them.

Most people would have forgotten the incident in question in a week's time. But he did not. His life had come to such a pass that he attached significance to it. For until this moment he had lived in a state of pure possibility, not knowing what sort of a man he was or what he must do, and supposing therefore that he must be all men and do everything. But after this morning's incident his life took a turn in a particular direction. Thereafter he came to see that he was not destined to do everything but only one or two things. Lucky is the man who does not secretly believe that every possibility is open to him.

It was a beautiful day but only after the fashion of beautiful days in New York. The sky was no more than an ordinary Eastern sky, mild and blue and hazed over, whitened under the blue and of not much account. It was a standard sky by which all other skies are measured. As for the park, green leaves or not, it belonged to the animal kingdom rather than the vegetable. It had a zoo smell. Last summer's grass was as coarse and yellow as lion's hair and worn bare in spots, exposing the tough old hide of the earth. The tree trunks were polished. Bits of hair clung to the bark as if a large animal had been rubbing against them. Nevertheless, thought he, it is a good thing to see a park put to good hard use by millions of people, used and handled in its every square inch like a bear garden.

A 35-millimeter camera had been fitted to the telescope in place of the in-line ocular, but a lateral eyepiece allowed him to lean over from time to time and take a squint. There sprang into view a section of the cornice of a building, no doubt one of the hotels along Central Park South. But so powerful was the instrument that it was hard to say which building was being looked at. It was as if the telescope created its own world in the brilliant theater of its lenses.

He was waiting for the peregrine.

The day before, he had seen it but not photographed it. The falcon had abandoned its natural home in the northern wilderness and taken up residence on top of the hotel. From this eyrie it preyed on the fat pigeons of the park. Along the cornice it would strut, cock a yellow eye down at the great misty rectangle (the eye sunk and fierce in its socket and half eclipsed by the orbit of bone), and down it would come smoking, at two hundred miles an hour, big feet stuck out in front like a Stuka, strike the pigeons in mid-air with a thump and a blue flak-burst of feathers.

The peregrine did not return to his perch. As the young man made ready to unlimber his telescope, he loosened the thumbscrew and the barrel dropped to the horizontal. He took another look. Being of both a scientific and a superstitious turn of mind and therefore always on the lookout for chance happenings which lead to great discoveries, he had to have a last look—much as a man will open a telephone book and read the name at his thumbnail.

There in the telescope sat a woman, on a park bench, a white woman dark as a gypsy. She held a tabloid. Over her shoulder he read: ". . . parley fails."

But when he looked up he couldn't find her. The telescope was pointed toward the southeast, where a thicket of maples bordered the Great Meadow. She could only be there. Yes, now he saw: the telescope looked toward a leafy notch and through it to the summit of one of the little alps which overlook the Pond.

There she was, not twenty feet away and shimmering slightly in the pressed optic air as if she sat at the bottom of a sunlit ocean. Her coarse hair gave off rainbows. One arm was flung along the back of the bench, the hand smudged with newspaper ink. She was a neat stocky woman with a shock of hair and a handsome if somewhat meager face, like the face of an athlete, as if all strength and beauty had gone first to her body.

The woman was doing something. The soiled left hand dropped behind the bench, where by any calculation of hers it could not be seen, for the bench sat on the slope of an alp and there was nothing behind it but treetops. The blue hand felt its way down along a partition. It was an old-style bench, the sort built many years ago of a porous tufalike concrete in which pebbles had been set like raisins in a cake. A sad yellow 1901 concrete it was, enough to strike a pang to the heart. The seat was divided into thrones by scroll-shaped partitions which arched up and over to the rear, where they fastened the back into the bench. At the bottom the scroll was mortised into the bench by an ornamental tenon. Down crept the hand along the scroll. As he watched, the hand shattered into rainbows and disappeared. In another second the woman herself was gone, vanishing into the blue nimbus which rimmed the circle of light.

It did not take him long to act. Often nowadays people do not know what to do and so live out their lives as if they were waiting for some sign or other. This young man was such a person. If a total stranger had stopped him this morning on Columbus Circle and thrust into his palm a note which read: *Meet me on the NE corner of Lindell Blvd and Kings Highway in St. Louis 9 A.M. next Thursday—have news of utmost importance*, he'd have struck out for St. Louis (the question is, how many people nowadays would not?).

The hillock was easy to find. The bench overlooked the Pond and, beyond, the Grand Army Plaza. To the north the slope fell away abruptly into a screen of privet and poplar. Below, workmen were setting out folding chairs in the plaza and draping bunting over scaffolding in preparation for a patriotic ceremony.

Setting down his case, he explored the rear of the bench. The tenon which fastened the scroll between the third and fourth thrones, counting from Fifth Avenue, was loose. It could be slid back a way in its mortise, opening a recess into the blind bottom of the scroll. The cul-de-sac so formed was the sort of place which only neighborhood boys know of (and here there were no neighborhood boys), a time-niche where one leaves a note addressed to oneself: to be opened May 20, 1995. But today there was only a scrap of tin, a disc cut from the top of an orange-juice can, folded to a semi-circle, and sealed with chewing gum. He pried it open with a fingernail. It contained a slip of paper like a supermarket receipt upon which was written in violet script:

> *Some say thy fault is youth,*
> *some wantonness;*
> *Some say thy grace is youth*
> *and gentle sport;*
> *Both grace and faults are lov'd*
> *of more and less*
> *Thou makest faults graces*
> *that to thee resort.*

It was eleven thirty. He replaced note in tin, tin in cul-de-sac, and returned to his rock in the Great Meadow where he set up his telescope, and waited.

At fifteen minutes after twelve a girl came to the bench, set down a brown paper bag, and, making no secret of it, slid back the tenon and got her note. She read the note without expression as she ate her sandwich.

His heart gave a leap. He fell in love, at first sight and at a distance of two thousand feet. It was not so much her good looks, her smooth brushed brow and firm round neck bowed so that two or three vertebrae surfaced in the soft flesh, as a certain bemused and dry-eyed expression in which he seemed to recognize—himself! She was a beautiful girl but she also slouched and was watchful and dry-eyed and musing like a thirteen-year-old boy. She was his better half. It would be possible to sit on a bench and eat a peanut butter sandwich with her and say not a word.

But before he could think what to do, his love had finished

her sandwich, wiped her mouth with Kleenex, and vanished. By the time he reached the alp, there was no sign of her.

Taking the gravel path which skirts the pond, he crossed Central Park West, entered the Y.M.C.A., and went straight up to his room, which was furnished with a single bed and a steel desk varnished to resemble wood grain. Carefully stowing away his telescope under the Val-Pak which hung in the closet, he undressed to his shorts and lay on the bed. After gazing at the ceiling for some minutes, he fell asleep and slept soundly for five hours.

2. HE WAS A YOUNG MAN OF A PLEASANT APPEARANCE.

Of medium height and exceedingly pale, he was nevertheless strongly built and quick and easy in his ways. Save for a deafness in one ear, his physical health was perfect. Handsome as he was, he was given to long silences. So girls didn't know what to make of him. But men liked him. After a while they saw that he was easy and meant no harm. He was the sort whom classmates remember fondly; they liked to grab him around the neck with an elbow and cuff him around. Good-looking and amiable as he was, however, he did not strike one as remarkable. People usually told him the same joke two or three times.

But he looked better than he was. Though he was as engaging as could be, something was missing. He had not turned out well. There is a sort who does well in school and of whom much is heard and expected and who thereafter does less and less well and of whom finally is heard nothing at all. The high tide of life comes maybe in the last year of high school or the first year of college. Then life seems as elegant as algebra. Afterwards people ask, what happened to so and so? And the answer is a shrug. He was the sort who goes away.

Even now he made the highest possible scores on psychological aptitude tests, especially in the area of problem-solving and goal-seeking. The trouble was he couldn't think what to do between tests.

New York is full of people from small towns who are quite content to live obscure lives in some out-of-the-way corner of the city. Here there is no one to keep track. Though such a person might have come from a long line of old settlers and a neighborhood rich in memories, now he chooses to live in a flat on 231st Street, pick up the paper and milk on the doorstep every morning, and speak to the elevator man. In Southern genealogies there is always mention of a cousin who went to live in New York in 1922 and not another word. One hears that people go to New York to seek their fortunes, but many go to seek just the opposite.

In his case, though, it was part of a family pattern. Over the years his family had turned ironical and lost its gift for action. It was an honorable and violent family, but gradually the violence had been deflected and turned inward. The great grandfather knew what was what and said so and acted accordingly and did not care what anyone thought. He even wore a pistol in a holster like a Western hero and once met the Grand Wizard of the Ku Klux Klan in a barbershop and invited him then and there to shoot it out in the street. The next generation, the grandfather, seemed to know what was what but he was not really so sure. He was brave but he gave much thought to the business of being brave. He too would have shot it out with the Grand Wizard if only he could have made certain it was the thing to do. The father was a brave man too and he said he didn't care what others thought, but he did care. More than anything else, he wished to act with honor and to be thought well of by other men. So living for him was a strain. He became ironical. For him it was not a small thing to walk down the street on an ordinary September morning. In the end he was killed by his own irony and sadness and by the strain of living out an ordinary day in a perfect dance of honor.

As for the present young man, the last of the line, he did not know what to think. So he became a watcher and a listener and a wanderer. He could not get enough of watching. Once when he was a boy, a man next door had gone crazy and had sat out in his backyard pitching gravel around and hollering out to his enemies in a loud angry voice. The boy watched him all day, squatted down and watched him, his mouth open and drying. It seemed to him that if he could figure out what was wrong with the man he would learn the great secret of life.

Like many young men in the South, he became overly subtle and had trouble ruling out the possible. They are not like an immigrant's son in Passaic who decides to become a dentist and that is that. Southerners have trouble ruling out the possible. What happens to a man to whom all things seem possible and every course of action open? Nothing of course. Except war. If a man lives in the sphere of the possible and waits for something to happen, what he is waiting for is war—or the end of the world. That is why Southerners like to fight and make good soldiers. In war the possible becomes actual through no doing of one's own.

But it was worse than this in his case. It was more than being a Southerner. For some years he had had a nervous condition and as a consequence he did not know how to live his life. As a child he had had "spells," occurrences which were nameless and not to be thought of, let alone mentioned, and which he therefore thought of as lying at the secret and somehow shameful heart of childhood itself. There was a name for it, he discovered later, which gave it form and habitation. It was *déjà vu*, at least he reckoned it was. What happened anyhow was that even when he was a child and was sitting in the kitchen watching D'lo snap beans or make beaten biscuits, there came over him as it might come over a sorrowful old man the strongest sense that it had all happened before and that something else was going to happen and when it did he would know the secret of his own life. Things seemed to turn white and dense and time itself became freighted with an unspeakable emotion. Sometimes he "fell out" and would wake up hours later, in his bed, refreshed but still haunted.

When he was a youth he had lived his life in a state of the liveliest expectation, thinking to himself: what a fine thing it will be to become a man and to know what to do—like an Apache youth who at the right time goes out into the plains alone, dreams dreams, sees visions, returns and knows he is a man. But no such time had come and he still didn't know how to live.

To be specific, he had now a nervous condition and suffered spells of amnesia and even between times did not quite know what was what. Much of the time he was like a man who has just crawled out of a bombed building. Everything looked strange. Such a predicament, however, is not altogether a bad thing. Like the sole survivor of a bombed building, he had no secondhand opinions and he could see things afresh.

There were times when he was as normal as anyone. He could be as objective-minded and cool-headed as a scientist. He read well-known books on mental hygiene and for a few minutes after each reading felt very clear about things. He

7

knew how to seek emotional gratifications in a mature way, as they say in such books. In the arts, for example. It was his custom to visit museums regularly and to attend the Philharmonic concerts at least once a week. He understood, moreover, that it is people who count, one's relations with people, one's warmth toward and understanding of people. At these times he set himself the goal and often achieved it of "cultivating rewarding interpersonal relationships with a variety of people"—to use a phrase he had come across and not forgotten. Nor should the impression be given that he turned up his nose at religion, as old-style scientists used to do, for he had read widely among modern psychologists and he knew that we have much to learn from the psychological insights of the World's Great Religions.

At his best, he was everything a psychologist could have desired him to be. Most of the time, however, it was a different story. He would lapse into an unproductive and solitary life. He took to wandering. He had a way of turning up at unlikely places such as a bakery in Cincinnati or a greenhouse in Memphis, where he might work for several weeks assaulted by the *déjà vus* of hot growing green plants.

A German physician once remarked that in the lives of people who suffer emotional illness he had noticed the presence of *Lücken* or gaps. As he studied the history of a particular patient he found whole sections missing, like a book with blank pages.

Most of this young man's life was a gap. The summer before, he had fallen into a fugue state and wandered around northern Virginia for three weeks, where he sat sunk in thought on old battlegrounds, hardly aware of his own name.

3. A FEW INCIDENTS, MORE OR LESS AS HE RELATED THEM to his doctor, will illustrate the general nature of his nervous condition.

His trouble came from groups. Though he was as pleasant and engaging as could be, he had trouble doing what the group expected him to do. Though he did well at first, he did not for long fit in with the group. This was a serious business.

His doctor spoke a great deal about the group: what is your role in the group? And sure enough that was his trouble. He either disappeared into the group or turned his back on it.

Once when he was a boy his father and stepmother put him in a summer camp and went to Europe. Now here was one group, the campers, he had no use for at all. The games and the group activities were a pure sadness. One night as the tribe gathered around the council fire to sing songs and listen to the director tell stories and later ask everyone to stand up then and there and make a personal decision for Christ, he crept out of the circle of firelight and lit out down the road to Asheville, where he bought a bus ticket which carried him as far as his money, to Cedartown, Georgia, and hitchhiked the rest of the way home. There he lived with his aunts for several weeks and with the help of a Negro friend built a tree house in a tall sycamore. They spent the summer aloft, reading comics while the tree house tossed like a raft in a sea of dappled leaves.

Later there was trouble with another group. Like his father and grandfather and all other male forebears, save only those who came of age during the Civil War, he was sent up to Princeton University. But unlike them he funked it. He did very well in his studies, joined a good club, made the boxing team, but funked it nevertheless. It happened this way. One beautiful fall afternoon of his junior year, as he sat in his dormitory room, he was assaulted by stupefying *déjà vus*. An immense melancholy overtook him. It was, he knew, the very time of life one is supposed to treasure most, a time of questing and roistering, the prime and pride of youth. But what a sad business it was for him, this business of being a youth at college, one of many generations inhabiting the same old buildings, joshing with the same janitors who had joshed with the class of '37. He envied the janitors. How much better it would be to be a janitor and go home at night to a cozy cottage by the railroad tracks, have a wee drop with one's old woman, rather than sit here solemn-and-joyous, *feierlich*, in these honorable digs. On this afternoon, some of his classmates were standing just outside in the hall, a half dozen young Republicans from Bronxville and Plainfield and Shaker Heights. They too knew it was the best years of their lives and they were enjoying themselves accordingly. They had a certain Princeton way of talking, even the ones from Chicago and California, and a certain way of sticking their hands in their pockets and settling their chins in their throats. They were fine fellows, though, once you got used to their muted Yankee friendliness. Certainly this was the best of times, he told himself with a groan. Yet, as he sat at his desk in Lower Pyne, by coincidence in the very room occupied by his grandfather in 1910, he said to himself: what is the matter with me? Here I am surrounded by good fellows and the spirit of Old Nassau and wishing instead I was lying in a ditch in Wyoming or sitting in a downtown park in Toledo. He thought about his father and grandfather. They had been very fond of their classmates, forming relationships which lasted through the years. One had only to mention the names, Wild Bill (each had a Wild Bill in his class), the Dutchman, Froggie Auchincloss the true frog the blue frog the unspeakably parvenu frog, and his father would smile and shake his head fondly and stick his hands in his pockets in a certain way and rock back on his heels in the style of the class of '37.

His classmates used words in a distinctive way. That year they called each other "old buddy" long before this expression was heard at Tulane or Utah State, and they used the words "hack" and "go" in an obscure but precise way: if you made a good run in touch football, somebody might say to you, "What a hack." At other times and out of a clear sky, even in the middle of a sentence, somebody might say to you, "Go!", a command not to be confused with the argot of disc jockeys but intended rather as an ironic summons to the speaker to go forth. It was a signal to him that he was straying ever so slightly from the accepted way of talking or acting, perhaps showing unseemly enthusiasm or conviction. "Go!" he would be told in the obscure but exact sense of being sent on a mission.

The fall afternoon glittered outside, a beautiful bitter *feierlich* Yankee afternoon. It was the day of the Harvard–Princeton game. He felt as if he had seen them all. The ghost of his grandfather howled around 203 Lower Pyne. He knew his grandfather occupied room 203 because he had seen the number written in the flyleaf of Schiller's *Die Räuber*, a dusty yellow book whose pages smelled like bread. After a moment the young Southerner, who still sat at his desk, tried to get up, but his limbs were weighed down by a strange inertia and he moved like a sloth. It was all he could do to keep from sinking to the floor. Walking around in old New Jersey was like walking on Saturn, where the force of gravity is eight times that of earth. At last, and despite himself, he uttered a loud groan, which startled him and momentarily silenced his classmates. "Hm," he muttered and peered at his eyeballs in the mirror.

"This is no place for me for another half hour, let alone two years."

Forty minutes later he sat on a bus, happy as a lark, bound for New York, where he lived quite contentedly at the Y.M.C.A.

The following summer, in deference to the wishes of his father, who hoped to arouse in him a desire to complete his education and particularly to awaken a fondness for the law, he worked as a clerk in the family law firm. There was no place to sit but the library, a dusty room with a large oval table of golden oak which also served as a conference room and a place to read wills and pass acts of sale. The fragrant summer air thrust in at the window and the calfskin of the law books crumbled and flew up his nostrils. Beyond the glittering street, the oaks of the residential section turned yellow with pollen, then a dark lustrous green, then whitened with dust. He contracted dreadful hay fever and sat all summer, elbows propped on the conference table, tears running down his cheeks. His nose swelled up like a big white grape and turned violet inside. Through the doorway, opened at such an angle that he might overhear without being seen, he heard his father speak with his clients, a murmurous sound compounded of grievance and redress. As the summer wore on, it became more and more difficult to distinguish the words from the sound, until finally they merged with the quarrels of the sparrows under the window sill and the towering sound of the cicadas that swelled up from the vacant lots and filled the white sky. The other members of the firm were cordial enough, but he could not get on any other footing with them save that of the terrific cordiality of their first greetings, to which he responded as best he could while holding his great baboon's nose in a handkerchief.

At the end of summer his father died. Though his death was sudden, people were less surprised than they might have been, since it was well known that in this particular family the men died young, after short tense honorable lives, and the women lived another fifty years, lived a brand new life complete with a second girlhood, outings with other girls, 35,000 hearty meals, and a long quarrelsome senescence.

For another month or so the young man, whose name was Williston Bibb Barrett or Will Barrett or Billy Barrett, sat rocking on the gallery with six women: one, his stepmother, who was a good deal older than his father, was nice enough but somewhat abstracted, having a way of standing in the pantry for minutes at a time and whistling the tunes of the Hit Parade; three aunts; a cousin; and a lady who was called aunt but was not really kin—all but one over seventy and each as hale as a Turk. He alone ailed, suffering not only from hay fever but having fallen also into a long fit of melancholy and vacancy amounting almost to amnesia. It was at that time that he came near joining the ranks of the town recluses who sit dreaming behind their shutters thirty or forty years while the yard goes to jungle and the bugs drone away the long summer days.

Managing to revive himself, however, he concluded his father's affairs, sold the law library to the surviving members of the firm, reapportioned the rooms of the house in the fashion best calculated to minimize quarrels, had drawn in his favor a letter of credit in the amount of $17,500, his inheritance—and, again losing the initiative, sat rocking on the gallery with his aunts. He considered farming. But all that remained of Hampton, the family plantation, was two hundred acres of buckshot mud long since reclaimed by canebrakes.

As it turned out, his mind was made up for him, for he was drafted shortly thereafter. He put Hampton in the soil bank and served two years in the United States Army, where he took a large number of courses in electronics and from which he was honorably and medically discharged when he was discovered totally amnesic and wandering about the Shenandoah Valley between Cross Keys and Port Republic, sites of notable victories of General Stonewall Jackson.

Once again he found himself sitting in the television room of the Y.M.C.A. in Manhattan, a room done in Spanish colonial motif with exposed yellow beams and furniture of oxidized metal.

As he surveyed his resources and made allowance for his shortcomings—for he was, in some respects, a cool-headed and objective-minded young man—it seemed to him that two courses of action were called for. There was something the matter with him and it should be attended to. Treatment would take money and therefore he needed a job. Transferring his inheritance to a savings account at the Chemical Bank New York Trust Company, Columbus Circle branch, he engaged a psychiatrist, whom he consulted for fifty-five minutes a day, five days a week, for the following five years, at an approximate cost of $18,000. He joined therapy groups. Toward the satisfaction of the second requirement he discovered, after careful study of the classified columns of *The New York Times*, that a "maintenance engineer" earned $175 a week. In order to qualify as a maintenance engineer, who was, as it turned out, a kind of janitor, it was necessary to take a six months' course at Long Island University, where he specialized in Temperature and Humidification Control. Upon graduation, he had no trouble securing a position since he was willing to take the night jobs no one else wanted. For the past two years he had been employed as humidification engineer at Macy's, where he presided over a console in a tiny room three floors below street level. Since automatic controls gauged the air outside and regulated the store accordingly, there was little to do but make sure the electrical relays were working properly. His hours were between 12:00 a.m. and 8:00 a.m., a shift no one else wanted. But he liked it. Not only did he have ample time to read and ponder, the job also offered excellent health and retirement benefits. After twenty-three years he could retire and go home, where, if the ranks of old ladies had thinned out, he could let out rooms and live like a king. The dream even came to him as the subway trains thundered along close by that he might restore Hampton plantation to its former splendor.

Even with this job, there came a time when his inheritance ran out, and it became necessary to find extra work now and then. Again he was lucky and hit upon congenial employment. A medical student who had flunked out of school and joined the Macy's staff put him onto it. For weeks and months at a time he served as companion to lonely and unhappy adolescents, precocious Jewish lads who played band instruments and lived in the towers along Central Park West. It meant removing from his congenial cell in the Y.M.C.A. to an apartment, a dislocation true enough, but it was the sort of thing he did best: tuning in his amiable Southern radar to these rarefied and arcane signals which until he came along had roamed their lonely stratosphere unreceived. Strange to say, he got onto the wave lengths of his charges when their parents could not. Best of all, it fitted in with his regular job. He worked at Macy's at night, slept in the middle of the day, and was ready for his "patient" when the latter came home from school.

4.

HIS TROUBLE STILL CAME FROM GROUPS.

It is true that after several years of psychoanalysis and group therapy he had vastly improved his group skills. So thoroughly in fact did he identify with his group companions of the moment, so adept did he become at role-taking, as the social scientists call it, that he all but disappeared into the group. As everyone knows, New York is noted for the number and variety of the groups with which one might associate, so that even a normal person sometimes feels dislocated. As a consequence this young man, dislocated to begin with, hardly knew who he was from one day to the next. There were times when he took roles so successfully that he left off being who he was and became someone else.

So well did he adapt that it always came as a surprise when two groups who got along with him did not get along with each other. For example, he had fallen in with an interracial group which met at a writer's apartment in the Village on Friday nights. It did not strike him as in the least anomalous that on Saturday night he met with the Siberian Gentlemen, a nostalgic supper club of expatriate Southerners, mostly law-yers and brokers, who gathered at the Carlyle and spoke of going back to Charleston or Mobile. At two or three o'clock in the morning somebody would sigh and say, "You can't go home again," and everybody would go back to his Park Ave-nue apartment. One night he made the mistake of bringing a friend from the first group to the second, a Southerner like himself but a crude sort who had not yet mastered group skills and did not know the difference between cursing the governor of Virginia, who was a gentleman, and cursing the governor of Alabama, who was not. Thereafter the Siberians grew cool to him and he dropped out. Nor did he fare much better with the interracial group. On his way home from the Village, he was set upon by Harlem thugs in the park and given the beat-ing of his life. When he related the incident at the next meet-ing, his friends frowned and exchanged glances.

He fared a little better with the Ohioans. Some winters ago, he found himself at a ski lodge near Bear Mountain in the company of seven other employees of Macy's, three young men and four young women, all graduates of Ohio State University. Like him, they purchased their outfits complete from cap to boots at a discount from the sports department. They all smelled of new wool and Esquire boot polish and were as healthy and handsome as could be. He hadn't been in their company a week before he became one of them: he called a girl named Carol *Kerrell*, said *mear* for mirror, *tock* for talk, *ottomobile*, *stummick*, and asked for *carmel* candy. The consonants snapped around in his throat like a guitar string. In April he went to Fort Lauderdale. In short, he became an Ohioan and for several weeks walked like a cat with his toes pointed in, drank beer, forgot the old honorable quarrels of the South, had not a thought in his head nor a care in the world.

It did not last. As they sat this night around the fire in the ski lodge, he and his fellow Ohioans, eyes sparkling, cheeks rosy, Tom and Jerries in hand, heads on laps, the Southerner felt a familiar and disastrous sinking of heart. The little scene, which was pleasant in every respect and which any normal person would surely have found to his liking, suddenly became hateful to him. People seemed to come to the point of flying apart. Though his companion was an attractive and healthy brunette named Carol (Kerrell) Schwarz and though he had reason to believe she liked him and would not repel his advances, the fact was that he could think of nothing to say to her. She was long of leg and deep of thigh and he liked having his head in her lap, but he experienced a sensation of giddiness when she spoke to him. Once he took her for a walk in the park. She picked up a cat. "Hello, cat," she said, looking into the cat's eyes. "I can see your name is Mehitabel. I'm Kerrell and this is Billy. Billy, say hello to Mehitabel." Try as he might, he could not bring himself to speak to the cat.

Now at Bear Mountain he lay with his head on her thigh and she leaned over him and said: "I'm a people-liker and I think you're my kind of people. Are you a people-liker?"

"Yes," he said, his cheek going stiff, and thought what a pity it was he might not have sport with her without talking to her.

His knee began to jerk involuntarily and at the first opportunity he extricated himself and rushed out of the lodge. Outside, he ran through the snowy woods and threw himself into a brierpatch like a saint of old. Shivering with pain and cold, he gazed up at the shadowy knoll associated by tradition with

Mad Anthony Wayne. He muttered to himself: "Barrett, you poor fellow, you must be very bad off, worse than you imagined, to have gotten things so mixed up. Here you are lying in a brierpatch when you could be lounging with young people like yourself, people against whom no objection can be raised, your head pillowed in the lap of a handsome girl. Is it not true that the American Revolution has succeeded beyond the wildest dreams of Wayne and his friends, so that practically everyone in the United States is free to sit around a cozy fire in ski pants? What is wrong with that? What is the matter with you, you poor fellow?"

When he was with Ohioans, he found himself talking like an Ohioan and moving his shoulders around under his coat. When he was with Princetonians, he settled his chin in his throat and stuck his hands in his pockets in a certain way. Sometimes, too, he fell in with fellow Southerners and in an instant took on the amiable and slightly ironic air which Southerners find natural away from home.

It was shortly after the weekend at Bear Mountain that he lapsed into a fugue state which was worse than the last.

But now he had developed an even more alarming symptom. He began to get things backward. He felt bad when other people felt good and good when they felt bad. Take an ordinary day in New York. The sun is shining, people live well, go about satisfying their needs and achieving goals, work at creative jobs, attend cultural attractions, participate in interesting groups. This is, by every calculation, as it should be. Yet it was on just such a day as this, an ordinary Wednesday or Thursday, that he felt the deepest foreboding. And when his doctor, seeking to reassure him, suggested that in these perilous times a man might well be entitled to such a feeling, that only the insensitive did not, etc., it made him feel worse than ever. The analyst had got it all wrong. It was not the prospect of the Last Day which depressed him but rather the prospect of living through an ordinary Wednesday morning.

Though science taught that good environments were better than bad environments, it appeared to him that the opposite was the case.

Take hurricanes, for example, certainly a bad environment if ever there was one. It was his impression that not just he but other people too felt better in hurricanes—though it must be admitted that he had studied only four people and one hurricane, evidence hardly adequate to support a scientific hypothesis. One real robin does suggest a spring, however.

The summer before, he had got caught in hurricane Donna. A girl named Midge Auchincloss, none other in fact than the daughter of his father's old friend, had invited him to drive her up to a jazz festival in Newport. During the same weekend a small hurricane was beating up along the coast but giving every sign of careening off into the North Atlantic. Nobody took much notice of it. Friday afternoon, nothing was very different. The old Northeast smelled the same, the sky was hazed over, and things were not worth much. The engineer and his friend Midge behaved toward each other in their customary fashion. They did not have much to say, not as a consequence of a breakdown in communications such as one often hears about nowadays, but because there was in fact not much to say. Though they liked each other well enough, there was nothing to do, it seemed, but press against each other whenever they were alone. Coming home to Midge's apartment late at night, they would step over the sleeping Irishman, stand in the elevator and press against each other for a good half hour, each gazing abstractedly and dry-eyed over the other's shoulder.

But a knoll of high pressure reared up in front of Donna and she backed off to the west. On the way home from Newport, the Auchinclosses' Continental ran into the hurricane in Connecticut. Searching for Bridgeport and blinded by the rain, which hit the windshield like a stream from a firehose, the engineer took a wrong exit off the turnpike and entered upon a maze of narrow high-crowned blacktops such as crisscross Connecticut, and got lost. Within a few minutes the gale winds reached near-hurricane strength and there was nothing to do but stop the car. Feeling moderately exhilarated by the uproar outside the snugness within, dry as a bone in their cocoon of heavy-gauge metal and safety glass, they fell upon one another fully clothed and locked in a death grip. Strange Yankee bushes, perhaps alder and dogbane, thrashed against the windows. Hearing a wailing sound, they sat up and had the shock of their lives. There, standing in the full glare of the headlights, or rather leaning against the force of the hurricane, was a child hardly more than a babe. For a long moment there was nothing to do but gaze at him, so wondrous a sight it was, a cherub striding the blast, its cheeks puffed out by the four winds. Then he was blown away. The engineer went after him, backing up on all fours, butt to wind like a range pony, reached the ditch and found him. Now with the babe lying as cold as lard between them and not even shivering, the engineer started the Continental and crept along, feeling the margin of the road under his tire like a thread under the fingertip, and found a diner, a regular old-style streetcar of a restaurant left over from the days before the turnpikes.

For two hours they sat in a booth and cared for the child, fed him Campbell's chicken-and-rice soup and spoke to him. He was not hurt but he was round-eyed and bemused and had nothing to say. It became a matter of figuring out what to do with him. The phone was dead and there was no policeman or anyone at all except the counterman, who brought a candle and joined them. The wind shrieked and the streetcar swayed and thrummed as if its old motors had started up. A window broke. They helped the counterman board it up with Coca-Cola crates. Midge and the counterman, he noticed, were very happy. The hurricane blew away the sad, noxious particles which befoul the sorrowful old Eastern sky and Midge no longer felt obliged to keep her face stiff. They were able to talk. It was best of all when the hurricane's eye came with its so-called ominous stillness. It was not ominous. Everything was yellow and still and charged up with value. The table was worth $200. The unexpected euphoria went to the counterman's head and he bored them with long stories about his experiences as a busboy in a camp for adults (the Southerner had never heard of such a thing) somewhere in the Catskills.

Even the problem of the lost child turned into a pleasure instead of a chore, so purgative was the action of the hurricane. "Where in the world do you come from?" Midge asked him. The child did not answer and the counterman did not know him. At last Midge turned up a clue. "What a curious-looking ring," she said, taking the child's hand.

"That's not a ring, that's a chickenband," said the counterman.

"Is there a chicken farm near here?" the engineer asked him.

There was, and it was the right place. When they delivered the babe an hour later, wonder of wonders, he had not even been missed. Ten children were underfoot and Dad and Mom were still out in the chickenhouses, and sister, a twelve-year-old who was also round-eyed and silent, received the prodigal as if it were nothing out of the way. This was the best of all, of course, returning the child before it was missed, him not merely delivered from danger but the danger itself cancelled, like Mr. Magoo going his way through the perilous world, stepping off the Empire State building onto a girder and never seeing the abyss.

Breakfast in the diner and back to the turnpike and on their way again. Down and out of the storm and into the pearly light of morning, another beautiful day and *augh* there it was again: the Bronx all solid and sullen from being the same today as yesterday, full of itself with lumpish Yankee fullness, the bricks coinciding with themselves and braced against all comers. Gravity increased.

Down into the booming violet air of Park Avenue they crept, under the selfsame canopy and into the selfsame lobby and over the sleeping Irishman and into the elevator where they strove against each other like wrestlers, each refusing to yield an inch.

5. ONE DAY THE NEXT WEEK, A RAINY THURSDAY AFTER-noon, he stood in a large room in the Metropolitan Museum of Art. Somewhere in the heights a workman was rattling the chain of a skylight. Happy people were worse off in their happiness in museums than anywhere else, he had noticed sometime ago. In here the air was thick as mustard gas with ravenous particles which were stealing the substance from painting and viewer alike. Though the light was techni-cally good, illuminating the paintings in an unexceptionable manner, it nevertheless gave the effect of descending in a dis-mal twilight from a vast upper region which roared like a conch shell. Here in the roaring twilight the engineer stationed himself and watched people watch the paintings. Sometime ago he had discovered that it is impossible to look at a paint-ing simply so: man-looking-at-a-painting, *voilà!*—no, it is necessary to play a trick such as watching a man who is watching, standing on his shoulders, so to speak. There are several ways of getting around the ravenous particles.

Today the paintings were there, yes, in the usual way of being there but worse off than ever. It was all but impossible to see them, even when one used all the tricks. The particles were turning the air blue with their singing and ravening. Let everything be done properly: let one stand at the correct distance from a Velázquez, let the Velázquez be correctly lighted, set the painting and viewer down in a warm dry museum. Now here comes a citizen who has the good fortune to be able to enjoy a cultural facility. There is the painting which has been bought at great expense and exhibited in the museum so that millions can see it. What is wrong with that? Something, said the engineer, shivering and sweating behind a pillar. For the paintings were encrusted with a public secretion. The harder one looked, the more invisible the paintings became. Once again the force of gravity increased so that it was all he could do to keep from sinking to all fours.

Yet the young man, who was scientifically minded, held himself sufficiently detached to observe the behavior of other visitors. From his vantage point behind the pillar he noticed that the people who came in were both happy and afflicted. They were afflicted in their happiness. They were serene, but their serenity was a perilous thing to see. In they came, smiling, and out they went, their eyes glazed over. The paintings smoked and shriveled in their frames.

Here came a whole family weaving along, sunk in their happiness, man, woman, teen daughter and son, and child, all handsome as could be. But they were bogging down. When all at once: *KeeeeeeeeeeeeeeeRASH*, first a rusty clank from above like a castle drawbridge, then a cataclysm (it got on the front page of *The Times* the next morning). As the dust cleared, he made out that it was not so serious, though serious enough. The skylight had fallen down at his feet, frame, glass, wheel, chain, worker, and all. For there he was, the worker, laid out and powdered head to toe like a baker. Some seconds passed before the engineer realized that it was glass that turned him white, glass powdered to sugar. It covered the family too. They stood for an age gazing at each other, turned into pillars of salt; then, when they saw that no one was hurt, they fell into one another's arms, weeping and laughing. Suddenly everyone remembered the worker. They knelt beside him and bore him up like mourners of Count Orgaz. The workman, an Italian youth with sloe-black eyes and black mustache who was as slight as Charlie Chaplin in his coveralls, opened his eyes and began stretching up his eyebrows as if he were trying to stay awake. Others came running up. The workman was not bleeding but he could not get his breath. As they held him and he gazed up at them, it was as if he were telling them that he could not remember how to breathe. Then he pulled himself up on the engineer's arm and air came sucking into his throat, the throat just grudgingly permitting it.

It was at this moment that the engineer happened to look under his arm and catch sight of the Velázquez. It was glowing like a jewel! The painter might have just stepped out of his studio and the engineer, passing in the street, had stopped to look through the open door.

The paintings could be seen.

6. HE HAD, OF COURSE, GOT EVERYTHING TWISTED around. Though he took pride in his "objectivity" and his "evidence," what evidence there was, was evidence of his own deteriorating condition. If there were any "noxious particles" around, they were, as every psychologist knows, more likely to be found inside his head than in the sky.

There were other signs that all was not well. The next morning he bought a $1,900 telescope and wiped out his bank account. The afternoon of the same day he broke off his analysis.

Some weeks earlier the telescope had been set up in the window of an optical store on Columbus Circle. Chunky as a mortar, it had a rough crackled barrel and a heavy nickel mount. The lens cup had been unscrewed and hung by a leather strap, exposing the objective lens, which had a violet cast and glowed in its recess like a great jewel. He inquired inside. As a consequence of the recent discovery of a new optical principle, he was told, it had become possible to do away with the long, mostly empty barrel of old-fashioned telescopes and to fit lenses and prisms together like the lamina of an onion. What the telescope amounted to was a canister jampacked with the finest optical glasses and quartzes, ground, annealed, rubbed and rouged, tinted and corrected to a tenthousandth millimeter. It was heavy and chunky, a pleasant thing. It was German.

It must be admitted that although he prided himself on his scientific outlook and set great store by precision instruments like microscopes and chemical balances, he couldn't help attributing magical properties to the telescope. It had to do with its being German, with fabled German craftsmen, gnomic slow-handed old men in the Harz Mountains. These lenses did not transmit light merely. They penetrated to the heart of things.

The conviction grew upon him that his very life would be changed if he owned the telescope.

This morning he emerged from the control room under Macy's into the thundering morning twilight of Seventh Avenue. All at once he had to own the telescope. Not another hour must pass without it. As if his life depended on it, he plunged underground again, sat on the edge of the subway seat drumming his fingers on his knees, emerged at Columbus Circle, hopped around to the Chemical Bank New York Trust Company, withdrew the balance of his inheritance and soil-bank money, a sum of $2,008.35, stuffed the money into his coat pocket, skimmed back around the Circle and whisked into the optical store, but not before casting a single fearful glance at the window. Ah, there it was, a low-down mean mortar of an instrument, a somehow military thing. Another five minutes and the telescope plopped like a walnut into its case, a kind of hatbox of blue leather which exhaled an intricate German smell and was strapped, bradded, buckled, and bulged out in front like a toilet bowl, a wicked unlovely and purely useful thing. The interior of the case was molded into irregular recesses like hollow viscera and lined in chamois and fitted with a little rack containing prisms, eyepieces, sun plate, clock drive, and a tiny camera of satiny metal which lay invested in the chamois like a platinum clip. He turned the neck of the telescope, which was knurled and calibrated with a black spiderlash in the nickel: it turned like a gear socketed in oil.

Sweating like a field hand, the engineer climbed the steps of the Y.M.C.A. with his prize, doing his best to look like a young Christian come to bowl. In his room, he sat at his desk drumming his fingers on the varnished metal and presently jumped up and undid the straps with trembling fingers. But suddenly the corner of his eye was filled with shooting sparks and he felt dizzy. Falling upon his narrow bed, he lay perfectly still for some minutes. He felt his forehead; it was cold and greasy with sweat. Ah, I've forgotten to eat again, he thought. Jumping up again, he threw a few punches: his arm, developed by five years' work on the Y.M.C.A. sandbag, felt as strong as ever. When he lay down again he was seized by a rigor, shook for a full minute, and fell fast asleep. When he awoke, he felt refreshed but weak and hungry. It was growing late. The light in the window was yellow and from the park there drifted up the four-o'clock sound of sparrows.

After washing his face in cold water, he clamped the telescope to the window jamb, selected a terrestrial eyepiece, and screwed it in place. He focused on a building clear across the park and beyond Fifth Avenue. There sprang into view a disc of brickwork perhaps eight feet in diameter. Now stripping to his shorts, he drew up a chair, made himself comfortable, and gazed another five minutes at the bricks. He slapped his leg. It was as he had hoped. Not only were the bricks seen as if they were ten feet away; they were better than that. It was better than having the bricks there before him. They gained in value. Every grain and crack and excrescence became available. Beyond any doubt, he said to himself, this proves that bricks, as well as other things, are not as accessible as they used to be. Special measures were needed to recover them.

The telescope recovered them.

7. HE DRESSED AND PAID HIS LAST VISIT TO DR. GAMOW, his psychoanalyst.

For the thousandth time he took his seat in a reclining chair that had been purposely set in a position that was neither up nor down, neither quite faced the doctor nor faced away. Dr. Gamow, who had had it specially designed and constructed, called it his "ambiguous" chair. He learned a great deal about a patient from the way he sat in the chair. Some would walk in and sit straight up, swivel around to face the doctor across his desk like a client consulting a lawyer. Others would stretch out and swivel away to face the corner in conventional analytic style. It was characteristic of the engineer that he sat in the ambiguous chair ambiguously: leaving it just as it was, neither up nor down, neither quite facing Dr. Gamow nor facing away.

For the thousandth time Dr. Gamow looked at his patient—who sat as usual, alert and pleasant—and felt a small spasm of irritation. It was this amiability, he decided, which got on his nerves. There was a slyness about it and an opacity which put one off. It had not always been so between them. For the first year the analyst had been charmed—never had he had a more responsive patient. Never had his own theories found a readier confirmation than in the free (they seemed to be free) associations and the copious dreams which this one spread out at his feet like so many trophies. The next year or so left him pleased still but baffled. This one was a little too good to be true. At last the suspicion awoke that he, the doctor, was being *entertained*, royally it is true and getting paid for the privilege besides, but entertained nevertheless. Trophies they were sure enough, these dazzling wares offered every day, trophies to put him off the scent while the patient got clean away. Sourer still was the second suspicion that even the patient's dreams and recollections, which bore out the doctor's theories, confirmed hypotheses right and left, were somehow or other a performance too, the most exquisite of courtesies, as if the apple had fallen to the ground to please Sir Isaac Newton. Charged accordingly, the patient of course made an equally charming confession, exhibited heroic sweats and contortions to overcome his bad habits, offered crabbed and meager dreams, and so made another trophy of his disgrace.

The last year of the analysis the doctor had grown positively disgruntled. This one was a Southern belle, he decided, a good dancing partner, light on his feet and giving away nothing. He did not know how not to give away nothing. For five years they had danced, the two of them, the strangest dance in history, each attuned to the other and awaiting his pleasure, and so off they went crabwise and nowhere at all.

The doctor didn't like his patient much, to tell the truth. They were not good friends. Although they had spent a thousand hours together in the most intimate converse, they were no more than acquaintances. Less than acquaintances. A laborer digging in a ditch would know more about his partner in a week than the doctor had learned about this patient in a year. Yet outwardly they were friendly enough.

The engineer, on the other hand, had a high opinion of his analyst and especially liked hearing him speak. Though Dr. Gamow was a native of Jackson Heights, his speech was exotic. He had a dark front tooth, turned on its axis, and he puckered his lips and pronounced his *r*'s almost like *w*'s. The engineer liked to hear him say *neu-wosis*, drawing out the second syllable with a musical clinical Viennese sound. Unlike most Americans, who

24

speak as if they were sipping gruel, he chose his words like bonbons, so that his patients, whose lives were a poor meager business, received the pleasantest sense of the richness and delectability of such everyday things as words. Unlike some analysts, he did not use big words or technical words; but the small ordinary words he did use were invested with a peculiar luster. "I think you are pretty unhappy after all," he might say, pronouncing *prĕtty* as it is spelled. His patient would nod gratefully. Even unhappiness is not so bad when it can be uttered so well. And in truth it did seem to the engineer, who was quick to sniff out theories and such, that people would feel better if they could lay hold of ordinary words.

At five o'clock, the Southerner's hour, the office smelled of the accumulated misery of the day, an ozone of malcontent which stung the eyes like a Lionel train. Some years ago the room had been done in a Bahama theme, with a fiber rug and prints of hummingbirds and Negresses walking with baskets on their heads, but the rug had hardened and curled up at the corners like old skin. Balls of fluff drifted under the rattan table.

"I—suggest—that if it is all right with you—" began Dr. Gamow, jotting a note on a smooth yellow pad with a gold pencil (this is all you really need to set your life in order, the patient was thinking, a good pad and pencil), "—we'll change Monday from five to five thirty. How is that for you, bad, eh?"

"No, it's not bad at all."

Dr. Gamow pricked up his ears. "Did you say mad?"

"No, I believe I said bad: it's not bad at all."

"It seemed to me that at first you said mad."

"It's possible," said the agreeable patient.

"I can't help wondering," said Dr. Gamow shyly, "who is mad at who." Whenever he caught his patient in a slip, he had a way of slewing his eyes around as shyly as a young girl. "Now what might it be that you are mad about?"

"I'm not really."

"I detected a little more *m* than *b*. I think maybe you are a little mad at me."

"I don't—" began the other, casting back in his mind to the events of the last session, but as usual he could remember nothing. "You may well be right, but I don't recall anything in particular."

"Maybe you think I'm a little mad at you."

"I honestly don't know," said the patient, pretending to rack his brain but in fact savoring the other's words. *Maybe*, for example, was minted deliberately as a bright new common coin *mebbe* in conscious preference to *perhaps*.

Dr. Gamow put his knees exactly together, put his head to one side, and sighted down into the kneehole of his desk. He might have been examining a bank of instruments. His nostril curved up exposing the septum of his nose and imparting to him a feral winged look which served to bear out his reputation of clinical skill. His double-breasted suit had wide lapels and it was easy to believe that, sitting as he did, hunched over and thick through the chest, his lapels bowed out like a cuirass, his lips pursed about the interesting reed of a tooth, that he served his patients best as artificer and shaper, receiving the raw stuff of their misery and handing it back in a public and acceptable form. "It does sound to me as if you've had a pretty bad time. Tell me about it." And the unspeakable could be spoken of.

He told Dr. Gamow he had reached a decision. It seemed plain to him that he had exhausted the resources of analysis— not that he had not benefited enormously—and in the future he thought he might change places with the analyst, making a little joke of it, heh-heh. After spending almost five years as an object of technique, however valuable, he thought maybe he'd go over to the other side, become one of them, the scientists. He might even have an idea or two about the "failure of communication" and the "loss of identity" in the modern world (at it again, throwing roses in the path, knowing these were favorite subjects of Dr. Gamow's). Mebbe he should strike out on his own.

For another thing, said he, he had run out of money.

"I see that after all you are a little mad at me," said Dr. Gamow.

"How's that?" said the patient, appearing to look caught out.

"Perhaps it might be worthwhile to look into whatever it is you are mad about."

"All right," said the patient, who would as soon do one thing as another.

"Yesterday," said the analyst, leafing back through his pad, "we were talking about your theory of environments. I believe you said that even under ideal conditions you felt somewhat —hollow was the word I think you used."

"Yes." He was genuinely surprised. He had forgotten that he had spoken of his new theory.

"I wondered out loud at the time what you meant by hollow—whether it referred to your body or perhaps an organ,

26

and it seemed to me you were offended by the suggestion."

"Yes."

He remembered now that he had been offended. He had known at the time that Dr. Gamow had thought he meant that he had felt actually hollowed out, brain or spleen emptied of its substance. It had offended him that Dr. Gamow had suggested that he might be crazy.

"I then made the suggestion that mebbe that was your way of getting rid of people, literally 'hollowing them out,' so to speak. A pretty thoroughgoing method of execution."

"That is possible."

"Finally, you may recall, you made a little slip at the end of the hour. You said you had to leave early—you had jumped up, you may recall—saying that you had to attend a meeting at the store, but you said 'beating.'"

"Yes."

"I couldn't help but wonder who the beating was intended for. Was it you who got the beating from me yesterday? Or am I getting a beating from you today?"

"You could be right," said the other, trying to straighten the ambiguous chair and face the doctor. He meant to signify that he wished to say something that should be listened to and not gotten at. "Nevertheless I have decided on a course of action and I think I'd better see it through." For some reason he laughed heartily. "Oh me," he said with a sigh.

"Hnhnhn," said Dr. Gamow. It was an ancient and familial sound, so used between them, so close in the ear, as hardly to be a sound at all.

The Southerner leaned back and looked at the print of hummingbirds. They symbolized ideas, Dr. Gamow had explained jokingly, happy ideas which he hoped would fly into the heads of his patients. One bird's gorget did not quite fit; the print had been jogged in the making and the gorget had slipped and stuck out like a bib. For years the patient had gazed at this little patch of red, making a slight mental effort each time to put it back in place.

"I notice now that you use the phrase 'run out'—'I have run out of money,'" said Dr. Gamow. Lining up his feet again, he sighted along his knee like an astronaut. "The idea suggests itself that you literally ran out of your own money—"

"Figuratively," murmured the other.

"Leaving it behind? I could not help but notice you seem to have acquired what seems to be a very expensive possession."

27

"What is that?"

"The handsome leather case." Dr. Gamow nodded toward the reception room. "Camera? Microscope?"

"Telescope," he said. He had forgotten his recent purchase! He was, moreover, obscurely scandalized that the doctor should take account of something out in the waiting room.

"A telescope," mused the analyst, sighting into the farthest depths of the desk. "Do you intend to become a seer?"

"A seer?"

"A see-er. After all a seer is a see-er, one who can see. Could it be that you believe that there is some ultimate hidden truth and that you have the magical means for obtaining it?"

"Ha-ha, there might be something in that. A see-er. Yes."

"So now it seems you have spent your money on an instrument which will enable you to see the truth once and for all?"

The patient shrugged affably.

"It would be prĕtty nice if we could find a short cut and get around all this hard work. Do you remember, the last time you left you stood up and said: 'Look here now, this analysis is all very well but how about telling me the truth just between ourselves, off the record, that is, what am I *really* supposed to do?' Do you remember that?"

"Yes."

"And do you still think that I am spoofing you?" Dr. Gamow, who liked to be all things to all men, had somewhere got the notion that in the South you said "spoofing" a great deal.

The patient nodded.

"You also recall that this great thirst for the 'answer,' the key which will unlock everything, always overtakes you just before the onset of one of your fugue states?"

"Not always."

"Always in the past."

"Not this time."

"How much did it cost you?"

"What?"

"The telescope."

"Nineteen hundred dollars."

"Nineteen hundred dollars," repeated the analyst softly.

"Which leaves me with the sum of fifty-eight dollars and thirty cents," said the patient. "According to my calculations, I owe you for eight sessions this month, including this one." And arising from the ambiguous chair, he placed two twenties and a ten on the desk. "Now I owe you one fifty. I'll pay you at the end of the month."

Dr. Gamow gazed at the money. "May I review for you one or two facts. Number one, you have had previous fugue states. Number two, you give every indication of having another. You always quit the analysis and you always buy something expensive before taking off. The last time it was a Corvette. You still have a defective ego structure, number three. Number four, you develop ideas of reference. This time it is hollow men, noxious particles, and ultimate truths."

It always seemed strange to hear Dr. Gamow speak of him clinically. Once, when the analyst was called away from the office, he had ventured out of the ambiguous chair and stolen a glance at the file which lay open on the blotter. "... a well-developed and nourished young white male," he read, "with a pleasing demeanor, dressed in an unusual raglan jacket." (This description must have been written at the time he had fallen in with the Ohioans, become one himself, and bought a raglan jacket so that he could move his shoulders around freely.) "When asked why he had chosen this particular article of apparel, he replied that 'it made me feel free.'"

Seeing himself set down so, in a clinical quotation, gave him a peculiar turn. His scalp bristled.

But now he nodded equably and, leaning back, gazed at the dusty little hummingbird.

"Very well," said Dr. Gamow when he did not answer. "You have made your decision. The question is, what is to be done next."

"Yes sir."

"May I make a suggestion?"

"Certainly."

"Next week I am starting a new group in therapy. It will be limited to ten persons. It is a very good group and my feeling is that you could profit by the experience. They are people like yourself who are having difficulty relating to other people in a meaningful way. Like yourself they find themselves in some phase or other of an identity crisis. There is—let me see—a novelist who is blocked, an engineer like yourself who works with digital computers and who feels somewhat depersonalized. There is an actress you will recognize instantly, who has suddenly begun forgetting her lines. There is a housewife with a little more anxiety than she can handle, psychiatrically oriented but also success-oriented. There is an extremely sensitive Negro who is *not* success-oriented—a true identity problem there. And four social workers from White Plains. It's a lot better than the last group you were in—these are some very highflying folks and I don't think you'll be able to snow them quite as successfully."

That's what you think, said the Southerner to himself; these are just the kind of folks I snow best.

"We shall meet here three times a week. The fee is nominal, five dollars."

"I certainly do appreciate it," said the other earnestly. "It does indeed sound like an interesting group, but for the present my salary will not permit it. Perhaps when my soil-bank check comes through—"

"From the old plantation?" asked Dr. Gamow.

"Yes. But I assure you I feel quite well."

"Euphoric, in fact," said Dr. Gamow ironically.

He grinned. "Mebbe I could join y'all later."

"This is not a catfish fry," said the analyst testily.

At the end of the hour they arose and shook hands pleasantly. The patient took a last look at the dusty hummingbird which had been buzzing away at the same trumpet vine for five years. The little bird seemed dejected. The bird, the print, the room itself had the air of things one leaves behind. It was time to get up and go. He was certain that he would never see any of them again.

Before leaving, he obtained from Dr. Gamow a prescription for the little blue spansules which he saved for his worst times. They did not restore his memory, but when he was at his hollowest, wandering about some minor battlefield in Tennessee, he could swallow a spansule, feel it turn warm, take root, and flower under his ribs.

So it was that Williston Bibb Barrett once again set forth into the wide world at the age of twenty-five, Keats's age at his death, in possession of $8.35, a Tetzlar telescope, an old frame house, and a defunct plantation. Once again he found himself alone in the world, cut adrift from Dr. Gamow, a father of sorts, and from his alma mater, sweet mother psychoanalysis.

Though it may have been true that he gave every sign of a relapse of his nervous condition, of yet another spell of forgetfulness and of wandering about the U.S. and peering into the faces of Georgians and Indianians, for the present at least he was in the best possible humor and alert as a cat. In the elevator he set down the telescope and threw a few punches:

his arm was like a young oak, he could have put his fist right through the steel of the Otis cab. Each of his five senses was honed to a razor's edge and attuned like the great Jodrell Bank antenna to the slightest signal of something gone amiss.

I am indeed an engineer, he thought, if only a humidification engineer, which is no great shakes of a profession. But I am also an engineer in a deeper sense: I shall engineer the future of my life according to the scientific principles and the self-knowledge I have so arduously gained from five years of analysis.

II

1. IT WAS THE DAY AFTER HE BROKE OFF HIS ANALYSIS that the engineer received a sign: he set up his telescope in the park to photograph the peregrine and had instead and by the purest chance witnessed the peculiar behavior of the Handsome Woman and her beautiful young friend. Every morning thereafter the engineer returned to the park and took his position beside the same outcropping of rock.

The peregrine returned to his perch. Every morning he patrolled the cornice, making an awkward sashay in his buff pants, cocked a yellow eye at the misty trees below, and fell like a thunderbolt, knocking pigeons out of the air in all directions. The engineer took a dozen photographs at magnification one fifty, trusting that at least one would catch the fierce eclipsed eye of the falcon.

Every morning after work he set up his Tetzlar. After taking his two bearings, one on the eyrie of the peregrine, the other on the park bench, he had then only to lock the positions into the celestial drive, press a button, and the instrument would swing in its mount and take aim like a Navy rifle.

The Handsome Woman came four days later, left a note, but the girl did not come. Again he prized open the semicircle of tin and again he found a verse.

> *From you have I been absent in the spring,*
> *When proud-pied April, dressed in all his trim,*
> *Hath put a spirit of youth in every thing,*
> *That heavy Saturn laugh'd and leap'd with him.*

32

After that, neither one came.

At night he sat at his desk in the Y.M.C.A. casting about in his mind and drumming his fingernails on the steel top, which had been varnished to represent wood grain.

For two weeks he spent every spare moment at his vigil, coming to the park directly from work, forgetful of all else, sometimes forgetting to change his engineer's smock.

What had become of his love?

Emerging one morning from Macy's sub-basement, the engineer stood blinking in the sunlight at Nedick's corner. It was the most valuable spot on the entire earth, having been recently appraised, he had read in *The Times*, at ninety dollars per cubic inch. It gave him pleasure to stand in Nedick's and think about the cubic inch of space at the tip of his nose, a perfect little jewel of an investment.

For a minute or so he stood watching the bustle of traffic, garment porters pushing trucks of dresses, commuters from Penn Station pouring down Thirty-fourth Street.

Then, and for several mornings running, he experienced a hallucination which, however, he did not entirely recognize as such, a bad enough sign in itself. When he got sick, his sense of time went out of kilter, did not quite coincide with the ongoing present moment, now falling behind, now speeding ahead: a circumstance that no doubt accounted for the rich harvest of *déjà vus*. Now, as he stood in Nedick's, it seemed to him that the scene which took place before his eyes was happening in a time long past. The canyon of Seventh Avenue with the smoking rays of sunlight piercing the thundering blue shadow, the echoing twilight spaces as dim and resounding as the precipice air of a Western gorge, the street and the people themselves seemed to recede before his gaze. It was like watching a film of bygone days in which, by virtue merely of the lapsed time, the subject is invested with an archaic sweetness and wholeness all the more touching for its being exposed as an illusion. People even walked faster, like the crowds in silent films, surging to and fro in a wavelike movement, their faces set in expressions of serious purpose so patent as to be funny and tender. Everyone acted as if he knew exactly what he was doing and this was the funniest business of all. It reminded him of a nurse he had in the South. Once his father took some movies of him and his nurse in a little park. Ten years later, when on Christmas Eve the film was shown and D'lo, passing in the hall behind the projector, stood for a moment to see herself with the others, the black nurses whose faces were underexposed and therefore all the more inscrutable but who nevertheless talked and moved and cocked a head with the patent funniness of lapsed time—D'lo let out a shriek and, unable to bear the sight of herself, threw her apron over her head. It was, he reckoned, the drollness of the past which struck her, the perky purpose of the people who acted for all the world as if they knew what they were doing, had not a single doubt.

Still no sign of the women in the park, and he cut short his vigil, watching only during the noon hour. There was more time now to attend to his physical health. He took pains to eat and sleep regularly and to work out in the Y.M.C.A. gym. He punched a sandbag an hour a day, swam forty laps in the pool, or, on cool days, jogged three times around the reservoir in the park. After a cold shower and a supper of steak, milk, vegetables, and wheat germ, he allowed himself a half hour of television and spent the remaining three hours before work seated bolt upright at his desk trying to set his thoughts in order.

He began the day by reading a few lines from *Living*, a little volume of maxims for businessmen which he had come across in Macy's book department. It made him feel good to read its crisp and optimistic suggestions.

On your way to work, put aside your usual worries. Instead keep your mind both relaxed and receptive— and playful. The most successful businessmen report that their greatest ideas often come to them in such intervals.

Yes. And it was in fact very pleasant walking up Broadway instead of riding the subway every morning, one's mind wiped clean as a blackboard (not that it was necessary for him to try to "put aside your usual worries," since he forgot everything anyhow, worries included, unless he wrote them down).

Cheerful and sensible though his little book of maxims was, it was no match for the melancholy that overtook him later in the day. Once again he began to feel bad in the best of environments. And he noticed that other people did too. So bad did they feel, in fact, that it took the worst of news to cheer them up. On the finest mornings he noticed that people in the subway looked awful until they opened their newspapers and read of some airliner crashing and killing all hundred and seven passengers. Where they had been miserable in their happiness, now as they shook their heads dolefully at the tragedy they became happy in their misery. Color returned to their cheeks and they left the train with a spring in their step.

Every day the sky grew more paltry and every day the ravening particles grew bolder. Museums became uninhabitable. Concerts were self-canceling. Sitting in the park one day, he heard a high-pitched keening sound directly over his head. He looked up through his eyebrows but the white sky was empty.

That very night as he sat at his console under Macy's, his eye happened to fall upon the Sunday *Times*, which lay in a corner. There on the front page of an inner section was a map of Greater New York which was overlaid by a series of concentric circles rippling out to Mamaroneck in the north, to Plainfield in the south. He picked it up. It was one of those maps illustrating the effects of the latest weapon, in this case some kind of nerve gas. The innermost circle, he noted idly, called the area of irreversible axon degeneration, took in Manhattan Island and Brooklyn as far as Flatbush, Queens as far as Flushing, and the lower Bronx. The next circle was marked the zone of "fatty degeneration of the proximal nephrone," and the third that of "reversible cortical edema."

He frowned at the flickering lights of the console. Was it possible, he wondered, that—that "It" had already happened, the terrible event that everyone dreaded. He smiled and socked his head: he was not yet so bad off as to believe that he was being affected by an invisible gas.

Then, after looking at the map another ten minutes, he saw it at last, and his heart gave a big bump in his neck. Like a funnel, the circles carried his eye plunging down into the heart of Manhattan Island to—there, just inside the southeast corner of Central Park; there the point of the compass had been stuck while the pen swiveled, there just north of the little amoeba of the Pond.

The bench, where the Handsome Woman had sat, was exactly at ground zero.

He smiled again. It was a sign. He knew he would see the two women again.

He resolved to resume his vigil.

2. HE NEEDN'T HAVE BOTHERED. THE VERY NEXT MORN-
ing, an unmemorable day neither cloudy nor clear, hot
or cold, the engineer, who had emerged from Macy's only to
plunge immediately underground again, caught sight of the
Handsome Woman on the subway level of Pennsylvania Station. It was not even necessary to follow her. She took his
train. When she did not get up at Columbus Circle, he stayed
on too.

The train burrowed deep into the spine of the island and
began a long climb up into Washington Heights, where they
emerged, she taking an elevator and he a flight of steps (but
why? she didn't know him from Adam), into a gray warren of
a place which descended in broken terraces to the Hudson
River. From the moraine of blackened gravel which covered
the rooftops below, there sprouted a crooked forest of antennae and branching vent pipes. A perpetual wind pushed up the
side streets from the river, scouring the gutters and forcing the
denizens around into the sunny lee of Broadway with its sheltered bars and grills and kosher groceries and Spanish hair-
dressers.

He followed the Handsome Woman into a great mauve pile
of buildings. Inside he took a sniff: hospital.

This time, when he saw her bound for an elevator, he entered beside her and swung around behind her as she turned.
Now, eight inches in front of him, she suddenly looked frail,
like a dancer who leaves the stage and puts on a kimono.
There arose to his nostrils the heavy electric smell of unper-
fumed hair.

She got off at the tenth floor, so up he went to the eleventh
and back down the steps in time to catch a glimpse of her foot
and leg disappearing through a doorway. He kept on his way,
past the closed door and other doors, past a large opening into
a ward, and to the end of the corridor, where he cocked a foot
on a radiator, propped his mouth on a knuckle, and looked out
a sooty window. As usual, he had forgotten to put on his
jacket when he left Macy's, and his tan engineer's smock gave

him the look, if not of a doctor, at least of a technician of sorts.

Directly a man came out of the room into which the Handsome Woman had disappeared, and, to the engineer's astonishment, made straight for him.

At first he was certain he had been found out and someone had been sent to deal with him. His imagination formed the picture of a precinct station where he was charged with a misdemeanor of a vaguely sexual nature, following a woman on a subway. His eyes rolled up into his eyebrows.

But the stranger, an old man, only nodded affably. Lining up beside him, he rubbed himself against the vanes of the radiator and began to smoke a cigar with great enjoyment. He cradled one elbow in the crook of the other arm and rocked to and fro in his narrow yellow shoes.

"It looks like Dr. Calamera is running late." The stranger screwed up an eye and spoke directly into the smoke. He was a puckish-looking old fellow who, the engineer soon discovered, had the habit of shooting his arm out of his cuff and patting his gray hair.

"Who?" murmured the engineer, also speaking straight ahead since he was not yet certain he was being addressed.

"Aren't you assisting him in the puncture?"

"Sir?"

"You're not the hematologist?"

"No sir."

"They suspect a defect in the manufacture of the little blood cells in the marrow bones, like a lost step," said the stranger cheerfully, rocking to and fro. "It don't amount to much."

Two things were instantly apparent to the sentient engineer, whose sole gift, after all, was the knack of divining persons and situations. One was that he had been mistaken for a member of the staff. The other was that the stranger was concerned about a patient and that he, the stranger, had spent a great deal of time in the hospital. He had the air of one long used to the corridor, and he had developed a transient, fabulous, and inexpert knowledge of one disease. It was plain too that he imputed to the hospital staff a benevolent and omniscient concern for the one patient. It amounted to a kind of happiness, as if the misfortune beyond the door must be balanced by affectionate treatment here in the corridor. In hospitals we expect strangers to love us.

An interne passed, giving them a wide berth as he turned into the ward, holding out his hand to fend them off good-naturedly.

"Do you know him?" asked the old man.

"No sir."

"That's Dr. Moon Mullins. He's a fine little fellow."

The illness must be serious, thought the engineer. He is too fond of everyone.

The stranger was so wrapped up in cigar smoke and the loving kindness of the hospital that it was possible to look at him. He was old and fit. Ruddy sectors of forehead extended high into iron-colored hair. Though he was neatly dressed, he needed a shave. The stubble which covered his cheeks had been sprinkled with talcum powder and was white as frost. His suit, an old-fashioned seersucker with a broad stripe, gave off a fresh cotton-and-ironing-board smell that pierced the engineer's memory. It reminded him of something but he could not think what.

The engineer cleared his throat.

"Excuse me, sir, but are you from Alabama?" He had caught a lilt in the old man's speech, a caroling in the vowels which was almost Irish. And the smell. The iron-washpot smell. No machine in the world had ever put it there and nobody either but a colored washwoman working in her own backyard and sprinkling starch with a pine switch.

"I was." The old man took a wadded handkerchief from his pocket and knocked it against his nose.

"From north Alabama?"

"I was." His yellow eye gleamed through the smoke. He fell instantly into the attitude of one who is prepared to be amazed. There was no doubt in his mind that the younger man was going to amaze him.

"Birmingham? Gadsden?"

"Halfway between," cried the old man, his eye glittering like an eagle's. "Wait a minute," said he, looking at the engineer with his festive and slightly ironic astonishment. "Don't I know you? Aren't you—" snapping his finger.

"Will Barrett. Williston Bibb Barrett."

"Over in—" He shook his hand toward the southwest.

"Ithaca. In the Mississippi Delta."

"You're Ed Barrett's boy."

"Yes sir."

"Lawyer Barrett. Went to Congress from Mississippi in

38

nineteen and forty." Now it was his turn to do the amazing. "Trained pointers, won at Grand Junction in—"

"That was my uncle, Fannin Barrett," murmured the engineer.

"Fannin Barrett," cried the other, confirming it. "I lived in Vicksburg in nineteen and forty-six and hunted with him over in Louisiana."

"Yes sir."

"Chandler Vaught," said the old man, swinging around at him. The hand he gave the engineer was surprisingly small and dry. "I knew I'd seen you before. Weren't you one of those fellows that ate over at Mrs. Hall's in Hattiesburg?"

"No sir."

"Worked for the highway department?"

"No sir."

"How did you know I wasn't from Georgia? I spent many a year in Georgia."

"You don't sound like a Georgian. And north Alabama doesn't sound like south Alabama. Birmingham is different from Montgomery. We used to spend the summers up in Mentone."

"Sho. But now you don't talk like—"

"No sir," said the engineer, who still sounded like an Ohioan. "I've been up here quite a while."

"So you say I'm from somewhere around Gadsden and Birmingham," said the old man softly in the way the old have of conferring terrific and slightly spurious honors on the young. "Well now I be damn. You want to know exactly where I come from?"

"Yes sir."

"Anniston."

"Yes sir."

"He don't even act surprised," the old man announced to the hospital at large. "But hail fire, I left Anniston thirty years ago."

"Yes sir. Did you know my father?" asked the engineer, already beginning to sound like an Alabamian.

"*Know* him! What are you talking about?"

"Yes sir."

"We used to hunt together down at Lake Arthur," he cried as if he were launching into a reminiscence but immediately fell silent. The engineer guessed that either he did not really know his father or they were on different sides of the political fence. His cordiality was excessive and perfunctory. "I got my youngest boy in there," he went on in the same tone. "He got sick just before his graduation and we been up here ever since. You know Jamie?" For all he knew, the engineer knew everything.

"No sir."

"Do you know Sutter, my oldest boy? He's a doctor like you."

"I'm not a doctor," said the engineer, smiling.

"Is that so," said the other, hardly listening.

Now, coming to himself with a start, Mr. Vaught took hold of the engineer's arm at the armpit and the next thing the latter knew he had been steered into the sickroom where Mr. Vaught related his "stunt," as he called it.

It seemed to be a roomful of women. There were only three, he determined later, but now with Mr. Vaught gripping him tight under the armpit and five pairs of eyes swinging round to him and shooting out curious rays, he felt as if he had been thrust onto a stage.

"And listen to this," said Mr. Vaught, still holding him tightly. "He didn't say Gadsden and he didn't say Birmingham, he said halfway between."

"Actually I didn't say that," began the engineer.

"This is Ed Barrett's boy, Mama," he said after pointing the engineer in several different directions.

A pince-nez flashed at him. There was a roaring in his ears. "Lord, I knew your mother, Lucy Hunicutt, the prettiest little thing I ever saw!"

"Yes ma'am. Thank you."

The women were taken up for a while with tracing kinships. (Again he caught a note of rueful eagerness in their welcome: were they political enemies of his father?) Meanwhile he could catch his breath. It was a longish room and not ordinarily used, it seemed, for patients, since one end was taken up with medical appliances mounted on rubber casters and covered by plastic envelopes. At the other end, between the women, a youth lay in bed. He was grinning and thrashing his legs about under the covers. The Handsome Woman stood at his bedside, eyes vacant, hand on his pillow. As the engineer looked at her he became aware of a radiance from another quarter, a "certain someone" as they used to say in old novels. There was the same dark-browed combed look he remembered. Again a pang of love pierced his heart. Having fallen in love, of course, he might not look at her.

"—my wife, Mrs. Vaught," Mr. Vaught was saying, aiming him toward the chunky little clubwoman whose pince-nez flashed reflections of the window. "My daughter, Kitty—" Then Kitty was his love. He prepared himself to "exchange glances" with her, but woe: she had fallen into a vacant stare, much like the Handsome Woman, and even had the same way of rattling her thumbnail against her tooth. "And my daughter-in-law, Rita." The Handsome Woman nodded but did not take her eyes from the patient. "And here all piled up in the bed is my bud, Jamie." The patient would have been handsome too but for a swollen expression, a softening, across the nosebridge, which gave his face an unformed look. Jamie and Kitty and Mrs. Vaught were different as could be, yet they had between them the funded look of large families. It was in their case no more than a blackness of brow, the eyebrows running forward in a jut of bone which gave the effect of setting the eye around into a profile, the clear lozenge-shaped Egyptian eye mirroring the whorled hair of the brow like a woods creature.

He sized them up as Yankee sort of Southerners, the cheerful, prosperous go-getters one comes across in the upper South, in Knoxville maybe, or Bristol.

"Where're you from," cried Mrs. Vaught in a mock-accusatory tone he recognized and knew how to respond to.

"Ithaca," he said, smiling. "Over in the Delta." He felt himself molt. In the space of seconds he changed from a Southerner in the North, an amiable person who wears the badge of his origin in a faint burlesque of itself, to a Southerner in the South, a skillful player of an old play who knows his cues and waits smiling in the wings. You stand in the posture of waiting on ladies and when one of them speaks to you so, with mock-boldness and mock-anger (and a bit of steel in it too), you knew how to take it. They were onto the same game. Mrs. Vaught feasted her eyes on him. He was *nice*. (She, he saw at once, belonged to an older clan than Mr. Vaught; she knew ancient cues he never heard of.) She could have married him on the spot and known what she was getting.

It was just as well he hadn't pretended to be a doctor, for presently two doctors came in. One, a gaunt man with great damp hands and coiling veins, took the patient's arm and began massaging it absently. The doctor gave himself leave not to talk and not to focus his eyes. The hand was absent-minded too, felt its way into the boy's armpit, touched the angle of his jaw. What I am doing is of no importance, said the hand. Nothing was important but an unfocused fondness which seemed to hum and fill the room. Now, while the hand went its way, browsing past bone and artery and lymph node, the doctor leaned over to read the title of the book the boy had closed on his finger.

"Tractatus Log—" he began, and exchanged glances with his assistant, a chesty little house physician with a mustache and a row of gleaming pencils and penlights clipped in his pocket. The doctors gazed at each other with thunderstruck expressions which made everybody laugh. Again the youth's eyes narrowed and his legs began to thrash about. Again the big damp hand went about its business, this time gliding to the youth's knee and quieting him. Why, he's seriously ill, thought the sentient engineer, watching the monitory hand.

"It's not too hard to read," said the patient, his voice all squeaks and horns. "Sutter gave it to me," he told the Handsome Woman, who was still gazing dry-eyed and had taken no notice even of the doctors.

"What a wonderful man," cried the engineer when the doctors left. "I envy you," he told the patient.

"You wouldn't envy me if you had to live in this room for five weeks."

"I wouldn't mind at all," said the engineer earnestly.

They looked at him. "How long have you been up here?" Mrs. Vaught asked.

"Five years. Seven, including my two years at Princeton. All my immediate family are dead. Do you know this is the first time I have talked to a, ah, family in years. I had forgotten—" he broke off and rubbed his forehead. He saw that he was expected to give an account of himself. "No, really. I don't think it is bad to be here. It reminds me of a time I was in the hospital—for three months—and it wasn't bad at all! In fact I felt better in the hospital than anywhere else."

"What was the matter with you?" Jamie asked him.

"I had a nervous condition, nothing very serious, an episode of amnesia, if you want to know the truth."

"Amnesia," said Kitty, looking at him for the first time.

"Yes. I didn't know my own name, but I knew enough to put myself in the hospital. It was caused by a toxic condition."

"You committed yourself," said Mrs. Vaught.

"Yes ma'am. I went to a very expensive place in Connecticut and was soon much better."

"How did you recover your memory?" Kitty asked him curiously.

"That was the strangest thing of all. For two months I remembered nothing. During this time I had gotten into the habit of playing Chinese checkers with another patient, a girl with a more serious condition than mine. She had not spoken to anyone for two years—she had not uttered a single word—even though she had received shock treatment. There was something familiar about her. Perhaps that was why I was attracted to her—that and the fact that I too was shy about talking and since she—"

They all laughed and he looked startled. "Yes, it's true. I was shy! I don't know why I'm not shy now. Anyhow she said nothing and I remembered nothing, and so it wasn't bad. You asked me how my memory came back. It was very simple. One night as we played Chinese checkers I looked at her and remembered who she was. 'Aren't you Margaret Rich?' I asked her. She said nothing. 'Didn't your family have the cottage next to ours in Monteagle ten years ago?' (That was before we started going to Mentone.) Still she said nothing. 'Why, I remember the dress you wore to a dance,' I told her (I always remember the remote past first). 'It was an orange-colored cotton twill sort of material.' 'That was my piqué,' says she as normally as you please." For some reason he flushed and fell silent.

"Do you mean that she spoke normally after that?" asked Kitty presently. She had swung around and was searching his face with her bold brown eyes.

"No, not normally, but it was a beginning," he said, frowning, feeling irritated with himself for being garrulous.

"I don't understand why she didn't speak before," said Jamie, thrashing his legs.

"I understand it!" cried Kitty. But then she blushed and turned away.

The others were not as amazed by the engineer's somewhat disconnected story as one might expect. For, strange to say, it was understood that it was open to him at that moment to spin just such a yarn, half-serious and curious.

"Yes, I know why your stay in the hospital was not so bad," said Jamie. "You weren't really sick."

"I'll trade with you any time," said the engineer. "Believe

me, it is a very uncomfortable experience to have amnesia."

At that moment the Handsome Woman whispered something to Kitty and the two of them kissed the patient, said their goodbyes and left. He waited for another brown-eyed look but Kitty had lapsed into vacancy again and did not seem to notice him. The talkative engineer fell silent.

Presently he roused himself and took his leave. The patient and his mother asked him to come back. He nodded absently. Mr. Vaught followed him into the hall and steered him to the window, where they gazed down on the sooty moraine of Washington Heights.

"You come on up here and see Jamie again, you heanh me," he said, drawing him close and exhaling his old-man smell of fresh cotton and sour breath.

"Yes sir. Sir?"

"What's that?" said the old man, giving him a hairy convoluted ear.

"The lady who just left. Now is that Mrs. Rita Sutter or Miss—"

"Mrs. Mrs. Rita Vaught. She married my oldest boy, Sutter Vaught. Dr. Vaught. They're divorced. But I'm going to tell you, we're closer to her than to Sutter, my own flesh and blood. Oh, she's a fine woman. Do you know what that woman did?"

"No sir," said the engineer, cupping a hand to his good ear and straining every nerve to get the straight of it.

"Why, she's the one who went up to his school when he got sick this time and got him into the hospital. When there was no room. That's not even a regular hospital room!"

"And, ah, Kitty?"

"Kitty is Jamie's sister. You want to know what she's done for Kitty?"

"Yes sir."

"She invites Kitty to come up here to New York not for a week but a year, to take ballet. She's taking her to Europe next month! And she's not even kin! What are you going to do with a woman like that," cried the old man, taking the engineer by the blade of muscle at his shoulder and squeezing it hard.

"All right," said the engineer, nodding and wincing.

"And she's second in command to the third largest foundation in the world!"

"Foundation," said the engineer vaguely.

"She's executive secretary. She can pick up the telephone and spend five million dollars this afternoon."

"Is that right?"

"You come on up here in the morning and see Jamie."

"Yes sir."

3. HE DID GO SEE JAMIE BUT KITTY WAS NOT THERE.

"What about Kitty?" he asked Mr. Vaught in the hall. It was not really a bold question since Mr. Vaught had once again set a tone of antic confidence, as much as to say: here we are two thousand miles from home, so it's all right for me to tell you about my family.

"Do you know what they've had that girl doing eight hours a day as long as I can remember?"

"No sir." The other, he noticed, pronounced "girl" as "gull," a peculiarity he last remembered hearing in Jackson, Mississippi.

"Ballet dancing. She's been taking ballet since she was eight years old. She hopes to try out for the New York City Center Ballet Company."

"Very good."

"Lord, they've had her studying up here, in Chicago, Cleveland, everywhere."

The engineer wondered who "they" were. Mrs. Vaught? "She must be very good."

"Good? You should see her prizes. She won first prize two years in a row at the Jay Cee Festival. Last year her mama took her up to Cleveland to study with the world's most famous ballet teacher. They lived in a hotel for nine weeks."

"It must require a great deal of self-sacrifice."

"Sacrifice? That's all she does." The other's eye glittered through the billowing smoke. Yet there was something unserious, even farcical, about his indignation.

"Even now?"

"I mean all. She dudn't go out to parties. She dudn't have, just as to say, dates. If a young man paid a call on her, I swear I don't think she'd know what to do."

"Is that right," said the engineer thoughtfully.

"I don't think it's worth it, do you?"

"No sir," he said absently. He rose. "I think I'll go in and see Jamie. Excuse me, sir."

"That's all right!"

4. WITHOUT QUITE KNOWING WHY HE DID SO—FOR NOW he had the Handsome Woman's name and had looked her up in the telephone book and now knew where Kitty lived —he kept up his vigil in the park.

Once he went to look at the house they lived in. They had, Kitty and Rita, a charming cottage in a mews stuck away inside a city block in the Village. He had not imagined there could be such a place in New York, that the paltry particles, ravening and singing, could be so easily gotten round. But they were gotten round, by making things small and bright and hiding them away in the secret sunny center of a regular city block. Elsewhere in New York—wherever one stood— there was the sense of streets running a thousand miles in either direction, clear up to 302nd Street and petering out in some forlorn place above Yonkers or running clean to Ontario, for all he knew. They, Kitty and Rita, got out of the wind, so to speak, found a sunny lee corner as sheltered as a Barbados alley.

Then why not pick up the telephone and call her up and say, what about seeing you? Well, he could not exactly say why except that he could not. The worst way to go see a girl is to go see her. The best way is not to go see her but to come upon her. Having a proper date with a girl delivers the two of you into a public zone of streets and buildings where every brick is turned against you.

The next day Rita came to the bench and Kitty joined her. It was not until he saw them through the telescope that he knew why he had kept up his vigil: it was because he did not know enough about Kitty.

When they left, they turned west. He waited. After five or six minutes they came through the maples and crossed the meadow toward the Tavern-on-the-Green. There they sat not half a mile away but twenty feet, outlined in rainbows and drifting against each other weightless and soundless like mermaids in the shallow ocean depths. Packing his telescope, he walked south past the restaurant and turned back. He found a table against a peninsula of open brickwork where by every calculation—yes: through a niche he caught a glimpse of the gold chain clasping the hardy structures of Kitty's ankle. He ordered a beer.

Like all eavesdroppers, he felt as breathless as if the future of his life might depend on what was said. And perhaps, he being what he was, it did.

"It's no use," Kitty was saying.

"It is use," said Rita. Her hair stirred. She must be turning her head to and fro against the bricks.

"What do you think is the matter with me, Ree?"

"Nothing that is not the matter with all of us."

"I am not what I want to be."

"Then accept yourself as you are."

"I do!" Kitty had a trick of ending her sentences with a lilt like a question. It was a mannerism he had noticed in the younger actresses.

"What is it?"

"Everything."

"Ah."

"What's wrong with me?"

"Tell me," said Rita, turning her head to and fro.

"Do you want to know?"

"Yes."

"The truth is, I'm stupid. I'm the stupidest person in the world."

"I see."

"That doesn't help."

"What would help?"

"I'm serious. Val and Jamie and you and Sutter are all so smart."

"You're the best of the lot," said Rita idly, turning her head against the bricks.

"Sometimes I think other people know a secret I don't know."

"What secret?"

"The way they talk—"

"People, what people? Do you mean a man and a woman?"

"Well, yes."

"Ah."

"Do you know, before I meet somebody—"

"Somebody? Who is somebody?"

"Before I meet them—if I know I'm going to meet them —I actually have to memorize two or three things to say. What a humiliating confession. Isn't that awful? And it is getting worse. Why am I like that?"

"Why say anything?"

"I keep thinking that it must be possible to be with a person with things natural between us."

"A person? What person? I'm a person. Aren't things easy between us?"

"Yes—because you've spoiled me."

"Like hell. Finish your sandwich and get back to work."

"Ree, I'm not even a good dancer."

"You're good, but you're lazy."

"No, Can Can." Or did she say *Quin Quin*?

"So now I'm getting old."

"No, Ree. But in a particular relationship do you think it is one's attitude or the other person who counts?"

"Who is this other person?"

"Do you remember what Will said yesterday?"

"Will?"

"Will Barrett? You know, the boy Poppy brought in."

"So now it's Will."

"Didn't you like him?"

"You make him sound like Cousin Will from Savannah."

"Well."

"Honey, I've got news for you."

"What?"

"That boy is not well."

"Not really."

"Really. And I can assure you there is nothing romantic about mental illness."

"But he isn't—"

"Wait. I suddenly begin to get it. I do believe that it is his symptoms which interest you."

"No, I think he's very nice."

"Yes, I see it! You're the girl who can't talk. And he can't remember. That makes you a pair."

"No."

"So you're going to remember for him and he's going to talk for you."

"No."

"Only it's more than that, isn't it? You also believe you can help him."

"Help him? Why does he need help?"

Rita's reply was not audible. They had gotten up and were moving away.

He sat deep in thought until he finished his beer. My need for eavesdropping is legitimate enough, he said to himself, screwing up an eye. What with the ravening particles and other noxious influences, when one person meets another in a great city, the meeting takes place edge on, so to speak, each person so deprived of his surface as to be all but invisible to the other. Therefore one must take measures or else leave it to luck. Luck would be this: if he saw her snatch a purse, flee into the park pursued by the cops. Then he would know something and could do something. He could hide her in a rocky den he had discovered in a wild section of the park. He would bring her food and they would sit and talk until nightfall, when they could slip out of the city and go home to Alabama. Such a turn of events was unlikely, however.

5. THE VAUGHTS LIKED THE ENGINEER VERY MUCH, EACH feeling that he was his or her special sort of person. And he was.

Each saw him differently.

Mr. Vaught was certain he was a stout Southern lad in the old style, wellborn but lusty as anyone, the sort who knows how to get along with older men. Back home he would have invited the younger man on a hunt or to his poker club, where he was certain to be a favorite. The second time Mr. Vaught saw him, he took him aside ceremoniously and invited him to Jamie's birthday party.

Jamie—who, he was told, had a severe and atypical mononucleosis—saw him as a fellow technician, like himself an initiate of science, that is, of a secret, shared view of the world, a genial freemasonry which sets itself apart from ordinary folk and sees behind appearances. He lent the engineer a tattered offprint of a scientific article which was written by his brother and which he kept under his pillow. It was titled *The Incidence of Post-orgasmic Suicide in Male University Graduate Students*, and divided into two sections, the first subtitled "Genital Sexuality as the Sole Surviving Communication Channel between Transcending-Immanent Subjects," and the second, "The Failure of Coitus as a Mode of Reentry into the Sphere of Immanence from the Sphere of Transcendence." The engineer read the article twice and could not make head or tail of it, except a short description of technical procedure in which Dr. Sutter, following some hunch or other, had examined the urethral meatus of some thirty male suicides for the presence of spermatozoa.

To Mrs. Vaught elder he was as nice as he could be. His manners were good without being too ceremonial. There was a lightness in him: he knew how to fool with her. They could even have a fuss. "Now you listen to me, Billy Barrett, it's time you buckled down," etc. So acute was his radar that neither Mrs. Vaught nor her husband could quite get it into their heads that he did not know everything they knew. He *sounded* like he did. She would speak allusively of six people utterly unknown to him—"So I took one look at her when she got home from school and of course her face was all broken out and I said ho-*ho*—"

"Who is that now?" asked the engineer, cupping a hand to his good ear and straining every nerve.

"Sally, Myra's oldest."

"Myra?"

"My stepdaughter."

She was much as he remembered other ladies at home, companionable and funny, except when she got off on her pet subject, fluoridation or rather the evils of it, which had come in her mind to be connected with patriotic sentiments. Then her voice became sonorous and bell-like. She grew shorter than ever, drew into herself like a fort, and fired in all directions. She also spoke often of the "Bavarian Illuminati," a group who, in her view, were responsible for the troubles of the South. They represented European and Jewish finance and had sold out the Confederacy.

"You know the real story of Judah P. Benjamin and John Slidell, don't you?" she asked him, smiling.

"No ma'am," he said, looking at her closely to see if she

50

was serious. She was. In her smiling eyes he caught sight of fiery depths.

Rita, however, paid no attention to him. She looked through him.

Kitty? Twice she was in Jamie's room when he came up, but she seemed abstracted and indifferent. When he asked her if she wanted a Coke (as if they were back in high school in Atlanta), she put her head down and ducked away from him. He couldn't understand it. Had he dreamed that he had eavesdropped?

On his fourth visit to Jamie he had a small amnesic fit, the first in eighteen months.

As he climbed into the thin watery sunlight of Washington Heights, the look and smell of the place threw him off and he slipped a cog. He couldn't remember why he came. Yonder was a little flatiron of concrete planted with maybe linden trees like a park in Prague. Sad-looking Jewish men walked around with their hands in their pockets and hair growing down their necks. It was as far away as Lapland. A sign read: *Washington Heights Bar and Grill*. Could George Washington have set foot here? Which way is Virginia?

He sat down under a billboard of Johnnie Walker whose legs were driven by a motor. He put his hands on his knees and was careful not to turn his head. It would happen, he knew, that if he kept still for a while he could get his bearings like a man lost in the woods. There was no danger yet of slipping: jumping the tracks altogether and spending the next three months in Richmond.

It was then that he caught sight of Kitty coming from the hospital, head down, bucking the eternal gale of the side streets. He knew only that he knew her. There were meltings of recognition about his flank and loin. He wished now that he had looked in his wallet, to make sure of his own name and maybe find hers.

"Wait," he caught her four steps down the IRT.

"What? Oh." She smiled quickly and started down again.

"Wait a minute."

"I've got to *go*," she said, making a grimace by way of a joke.

"Please come over here for a moment. I have something to tell you." He knew that he could speak to her if he did not think about it too much.

She shrugged and let him guide her to the bench.

"What?"

"I, ah, thought you might do me a favor." He looked at her hard, groping for himself in her eyes. If he could not help her, hide her in Central Park, then she could help him.

"Sure, what?"

"You're going in the subway?"

"Yes."

"I just came out. To see, ah—" He knew he would know it as soon as she thought it. She thought it. "—Jamie."

"Good. He'll be glad to see you." She eyed him, smiling, not quite onto whatever roundabout joke he was playing and not liking it much.

"I changed my mind and decided to go back downtown."

"All right." But it was not all right. She thought he was up to some boy-girl business. "What's the favor?"

"That I ride with you and that you give me a punch if I miss my station."

"What?"

"Do you know where I live?"

"Yes. At—"

He touched her arm. "Don't tell me. I want to see if I know when I get there."

"What's the matter—oh"—all joking aside now, eyes black as shoe buttons. She saw he was sweating.

Oddest of all: strange as he felt, having slipped six cogs, the engineer knew nevertheless that it was a negotiable strangeness. He could spend some on her. "Nothing much. Will you do as I say?"

"Yes."

Above them, Johnnie Walker's legs creaked like ship's rigging.

"Let's go." He started straight out, not waiting on her.

"That's the wrong subway," she said, catching up with him. "I'm taking the IRT."

"Right." It was like a *déjà vu*: he knew what she was going to say as soon as she said it.

They rode in silence. When the train came to the first lights of the Columbus Circle platform, he rose. "This is it," he said.

"Yes," she said, watching him sloe-eyed.

"Thank you," he said, taking her hand like a man's, and left quickly.

He stopped at a gum-machine mirror to see how he looked. There was nothing much wrong. His face was pale but intact. But when he straightened, his knee gave way and he stumbled to the edge of the platform. The particles began to sing.

A hand took his. "This way," said Kitty. Her hand was warm and grubby from riding subways.

She led him to a bench on an arc of the Circle. It is strange, he thought, musing, but love is backwards too. In order to love, one had not to love. Look at her. Her hand was on his thigh, rough as a nurse. She made herself free of him, peering so close he could smell her breath.

"Are you all right?"

"Yes."

"You're pale. Your hand is so cold." She made a slight movement and checked it. He knew she had meant to warm his hand in her lap.

"As long as you are here, will you go over there and buy me a glass of orange juice?"

She watched him drink the juice. "Have you eaten anything today?"

"No."

"Did you have supper last night?"

"I don't remember."

"You don't remember to eat?"

"I eat when I get hungry. I don't remember that I have eaten."

"Are you hungry now?"

"Yes."

They walked to the automat on Fifty-seventh Street. While she drank coffee, he ate four dollars' worth of roast beef and felt much better. I'm in love, he thought as he drank his third glass of milk.

"I don't think there is anything wrong with you," she said when he finished.

"That's right."

"What will you do now?"

"Go home and go to bed."

"You work at night?"

"Yes."

"Oh, for heaven's sake."

"There's one more thing—" he said.

"What?"

"Write your name and telephone number on this."

She smiled and did so but when she looked up and saw him she grew serious. "Oh."

"Yes, I need somebody to call. Is that all right with you?"

"Yes."

The sicker I am, the more I know, he thought. And the more she loves me. "Suppose I need to call you at three o'clock in the morning and say come to Weehawken."

"Call me." Her face clouded. "What about next month?"

"What about it?"

"I'll be in Spain. In Torremolinos."

"Write it down." After she wrote it, he asked her. "Now what if I call you over there?"

She looked at him, taking a tuck of lip between her teeth. "Do you mean it?"

"I mean it. You're the one I'm going to call."

"Why me?"

He drew his chair closer to the corner of the table and put his hand in her lap. "I'm in love."

"You are," she said. "Oh."

"I've never been in love before."

"Is that right?" Keeping a wary eye on him, she turned her head toward the empty automat.

"Hold still," he said, and leaning forward put his mouth on hers before she closed it. She held still from the habit of ministering to him. She was helping him. But hold on!

"Good Lord," she said presently and to no one.

"I never thought it would be so simple," said he, musing.

"Simple?" She was caught, betwixt and between being a girl full of stratagems and a rough and ready nurse.

"That you are in love and that there is time for it and that you take the time."

"I see."

"Let's go to your house."

"What for?"

He kissed her again.

She tucked the corner of her mouth and began to nod and slap the table softly.

What he wanted to tell her but could not think quite how was that he did not propose country matters. He did not propose to press against her in an elevator. What he wanted was both more and less. He loved her. His heart melted. She was his sweetheart, his certain someone. He wanted to hold her

54

charms in his arms. He wanted to go into a proper house and shower her with kisses in the old style.

"What do you do when you also have breakfast?" she asked him.

"What? Oh," he said, seeing it was a joke. "Well, I'm not joking." He'd as soon she didn't make Broadway jokes, gags.

"I see you're not."

"I love you."

"You do." The best she could do was register it.

"Let's go to your house."

"You said you worked last night and were going to bed."

"I'm not sleepy."

"I think you need some sleep."

"I need very little sleep."

"You're pretty tough."

"Yes, I'm very strong. I can press 250 pounds and snatch 225. I can whip every middleweight at Princeton, Long Island University, and the Y.M.C.A."

"Now you're joking."

"Yes, but it's true."

"You weren't so strong in the subway."

"I blacked out for a second."

"Do you think you're going to have another spell of amnesia?"

"I don't think so. But I'd like to have you around if I do."

"For how long?"

"Let's begin with the weekend. How strange that it is Friday afternoon and that we are together now and can be together the whole weekend."

"This all seems like a conclusion you have reached entirely on your own. What about me?"

"What about you?"

"Oh boy," she said and commenced nodding and slapping again. "I don't know."

"Where do you want to go?"

"Go?"

"Now. For the weekend."

"You don't fool around, do you?"

"Don't talk like that."

"Why?"

"Because you know it's not like that."

"What is it like?"

"Where then?"

"I'm sorry," she said and put her hand on his, this time a proper girl's hand, not a nurse's. "Rita and I are going to Fire Island."

"Let Rita go and we'll stay home."

"I can't."

"Why not?"

"Rita is very dear to me. I can't hurt her feelings."

"Why is she dear to you?"

"What right have you to ask?"

"Now I'm sorry."

"No, I'll tell you. For one thing, Rita has done so much for us, for me, and we have done so badly by her."

"What has she done?"

"Oh Lord. I'll tell you. You hear about people being unselfish. She actually is—the only one I know. The nearest thing to it is my sister Val, who went into a religious order, but even that is not the same because she does what she does for a reason, love of God and the salvation of her own soul. Rita does it without having these reasons."

"Does what?"

"Helps Jamie, helps me—"

"How did she help you?"

"Mama took me up to Cleveland but I became terribly depressed and went home. I went to work in Myra's real estate office for a while, then came up here to school—and got horribly lonely and depressed again. It was then that Rita grabbed me by the scruff of the neck and began to put the pieces back together—in spite of what my brother did to her."

"What did he do to her?"

"Oh," she shrugged. "It's a long story. But what a horrible mess. Let's just say that he developed abnormal psychosexual requirements."

"I see." He frowned. He didn't much like her using the word "psychosexual." It reminded him of the tough little babes of his old therapy group, who used expressions like "mental masturbation" and "getting your jollies." It had the echo of someone else. She was his sweetheart and ought to know better. None of your smart-ass Fifty-seventh Street talk, he felt like telling her. "I was wondering," he said.

"What?"

"I love you. Do you love me?"

"If you don't kill me. I swear to goodness."

He fell to pondering. "This is the first time I've been in

love," he said, almost to himself. He looked up, smiling. "Now that I think of it, I guess this sounds strange to you."

"Not strange at all!" she cried with her actress's lilt.

He laughed. Presently he said, "I see now that it could be taken in the sense that I say it without meaning it."

"Yes, it could be taken in that sense."

"I suppose in fact that it could even be something one commonly says. Men, I mean."

"Yes, they do."

"Did you take me to mean it like that?"

"No, not you."

"Well?"

"It's time for me to leave."

"You're going to Fire Island?"

"Yes, and you're sleepy."

All of a sudden he was. "When will I see you?"

"Aren't you coming to my birthday party Monday?"

"Oh yes. In Jamie's room. I thought it was Jamie's birthday."

"We're two days apart. Monday falls between. I'll be twenty-one and Jamie sixteen."

"Twenty-one." His eyes had fallen away into a stare.

"Go to bed."

"Right." Twenty-one. The very number seemed hers, a lovely fine come-of-age adult number faintly perfumed by her, like the street where she lived.

6. WHEN HIS SOIL-BANK CHECK ARRIVED ON FRIDAY, HE, the strangest of planters, proprietor of two hundred acres of blackberries and canebrakes, was able to pay his debt to Dr. Gamow. Having given up his checking account, he cashed the check at Macy's and dropped off the money at Dr. Gamow's office on his way home Monday morning.

Sticking his head through Dr. Gamow's inner door at nine o'clock, he caught a glimpse of the new group seated around a new table. It didn't take twenty seconds to hand over the bills, but that was long enough. In an instant he sniffed out the special group climate of nurtured hostilities and calculated affronts. Though they could not have met more than two or three times, already a stringy girl with a shako of teased hair (White Plains social worker?) was glaring at a little red rooster of a gent (computer engineer?). She was letting him have it: "Don't act out at me, Buster!" The old virtuoso of groups heaved a sigh. And even though Dr. Gamow opened the door another notch by way of silent invitation, he shook his head and said goodbye. But not without regret. It was like the great halfback George Gipp paying a final visit to Notre Dame stadium.

But that left him $34.54 to buy presents for Kitty and Jamie and to eat until payday Saturday. Sunday night he sat at his console under Macy's racking his brain. What to give these rich Texas-type Southerners who already had everything? A book for Jamie? He reckoned not, because not even Sutter's book held his attention for long. It was felt, fingered, flexed, but not read. His choice finally was both easy and audacious. Easy because he could not really afford to buy a gift and himself owned a single possession. Then why not lend it to Jamie: his telescope. The money went for Kitty's present, a tiny golden ballet slipper from Tiffany's for her charm bracelet.

"I don't have any use for it right now," said he to Jamie as he clamped the Tetzlar to the window sill. "I thought you might get a kick out of it." Not for one second did he, as he fiddled with the telescope, lose sight of Kitty, who was unwrapping the little jewel box. She held up the slipper, gave him her dry sideways Lippo Lippi look, tucked in the corner of her mouth, and nodded half a millimeter. His knee leapt out of joint. What was it about this splendid but by no means extraordinary girl which knocked him in the head and crossed his eyes like Woody Woodpecker?

Jamie's bed was strewn with neckties and books—three people had given him the same funny book entitled *So You're a Crock*. The nurses bought a Merita cake and spelled out "Happy Birthday" in chart paper. The internes made a drink of laboratory alcohol and frozen grapefruit juice, as if they were all castaways and had to make do with what they had. From an upper Broadway novelty shop Mr. Vaught had obtained a realistic papier-mâché dogturd which he slipped onto the bed under the very noses of the nurses. As the latter spied it and let out their screams of dismay, the old man charged fiercely about the room, peering under appliances. "I saw him in here, a little feist dog!"

Screwing in the terrestrial ocular fitted with a prism, and focusing quickly on the Englewood cliffs, the engineer stepped aside. The patient had only to prop himself on an elbow and look down into the prism. A little disc of light played about his pupil. The engineer watched him watch: now he, Jamie, would be seeing it, the brilliant theater bigger and better than life. Picnickers they were, a family deployed on a shelf of granite above the Hudson. The father held a can of beer.

Once Jamie looked up for a second, searched his face for a sign: did he really see what he saw? The engineer nodded. Yes, he saw.

"What kind of beer is he drinking?" he asked Jamie.

"Rheingold," said Jamie.

The others took their turn, all but Rita, then Moon Mullins, who swung the Tetzlar around to the nurses' dormitory. There was no talking to Jamie this morning. He must watch the tugs on the river, the roller coaster at Palisades Park, the tollhouse on the George Washington Bridge, two housewives back-fencing in Weehawken. Now it was Jamie who became the technician, focusing on some bit of New Jersey and leaning away to let the doctors look.

Mrs. Vaught elder couldn't get over it. Her pince-nez flashed in the light and she took the engineer's arm. "Would you look at the color in that child's face!" She made her husband take a look through the telescope, but he pretended he couldn't see.

"I can't see a thing!" he cried irritably, jostling his eye around the ocular.

Presently Kitty left with Rita, giving him as she left a queer hooded brown-eyed-susan look. He sat down dizzily and blew out his lips. Why couldn't he leave with them? But when he jumped up, Mr. Vaught took him high by the arm and steered him out into the hall. He faced the younger man into a corner and for a long time did not speak but stood with his head down, nodding. The engineer thought the other was going to tell him a joke.

"Bill." The nodding went on.

"Yes sir."

"How much did that thing cost you?"

"The telescope? Nineteen hundred and eight dollars."

"How much do you make a week?"

"I take home one forty-eight."

"Did your father leave you anything?"

"Not much. An old house and two hundred acres of buckshot."

The engineer was sure he was in for a scolding—all at once the telescope seemed folly itself. But Mr. Vaught only took out his fried-up ball of a handkerchief and knocked it against his nose.

"Bill."

"Yes sir."

"How would you like to work for me?"

"I'd like it fine, sir, but—"

"We have a garage apartment, which Mrs. Vaught did over completely. You'd be independent."

"Well, I really appreciate it, but—"

"You're Ed Barrett's boy," began Mr. Vaught in an enumerating voice.

"Yes sir."

"Dolly knew your mother and said she was the sweetest little lady in the world."

"Yes sir."

"Your mother and daddy are dead and here you are up here fooling around and not knowing what in the hail you are doing. Isn't that so?"

"Well, sir, I'm a humidification engineer."

"What in the woerrrld is that?" asked the other, his mouth gone quirky and comic.

The engineer explained.

"Why, hailfire, man, you mean you're the janitor," cried Mr. Vaught, falling back and doing a jaunty little step. For the first time the engineer caught a glimpse of the shrewdness behind the old man's buffoonery.

"I guess I am, in a way."

"Tell me the truth now. You don't know what—in—the—woerrrld you are doing up here, do you?"

"Well now—" began the engineer, intending to say something about his scientific theories. But instead he fell silent.

"Where did you go to college?"

"Princeton."

"What's your religion?"

"Episcopalian," said the engineer absently, though he had never given the matter a single thought in his entire life.

"Man, there's nothing wrong with you."

"No sir."

But if there is nothing wrong with me, he thought, then there is something wrong with the world. And if there is nothing wrong with the world, then I have wasted my life and that is the worst mistake of all. "However, I do have a nervous condition—"

"Nervous! Hell, I'd be nervous too if I lived up here with all these folks." He nodded down at the moraine of Washington Heights. "All huddled up in the Y in the daytime and way up under a store all night. And peeping at folks through a spyglass. Shoot, man!"

The engineer had to laugh. Moreover, suggestible as he was, he began to think it mightn't be a bad idea to return to the South and discover his identity, to use Dr. Gamow's expression. "What would you want me to do, Mr. Vaught?"

"All right. Here's what you do. You come on down with us. Spend a year with Jamie. This will give you time to finish school if that's what you want to do, or look around for what kind of work you want. Whatever you want to do."

"I still don't exactly know what it is you want—"

"Bill, I'm going to tell you something." Mr. Vaught drew him close enough to smell his old man's sourness and the ironing-board smell of seersucker. "I need somebody to help me out. I'm taking Jamie *home*"—somebody didn't want him to!—"and I want you to come down with me."

"Yes sir. And then?"

"Jamie likes you. He dudn't like anybody else at home but he likes you. (He likes Sutter, but that sapsucker—never mind.) He's been up here four years and he's smart as a whip about some things but he doesn't know enough to come out of the rain about some others. He can't drive a car or shoot a gun! You know what he and Kitty do at home? Nothing! Sit in the pantry and pick their noses."

"How do you know I won't do the same thing?" asked the engineer, smiling.

"Do it! But also show him how folks act. I just saw what effect you had on him. That's the first time I've seen that boy perk up since I been up here. Can you drive?"

"Yes sir."

"Do you have a driver's license?"

"Yes sir." He got one to drive the Auchinclosses' Continental.

"What do you say?"

"Do I understand that you would want me to be a kind of tutor or companion?"

"Don't have to be anything. Just be in the house."

"As a matter of fact, I've had some experience along these lines," said the engineer and told him about his tutoring stints with his young Jewish charges.

"You see there! We have some of the finest Jewish people at home you'll ever find," he added, as if the engineer were himself Jewish. "Right now the main thing we need is somebody to help me drive home."

The proposal was not quite as good as it sounded. Mr. Vaught, he early perceived, was the sort of man who likes to confide in strangers. And the farther he got from home, one somehow knew, the more confidential he became. He was the sort to hold long conversations with the porter on train trips, stand out with him on dark station platforms. "How much do you make, Sam?" he might ask the porter. "How would you like to work for me?"

"I had this boy David drive us up, ahem," said Mr. Vaught, clearing his throat diffidently. "I didn't know we were going to be up here this long, so I sent him home on the bus. He couldn't drive either. He like to have scared me to death."

The engineer nodded and asked no questions, since he understood that the "boy" was a Negro and Mr. Vaught was embarrassed lest it should appear that the engineer was being offered a Negro's job.

"Mrs. Vaught is certain you'll be comfortable in Sutter's old apartment," he added quickly (you see it's not a Negro's job). For the first time the engineer began to wonder if the proposal might not be serious. "Come on, let's go get us a Coke."

7. HE FOLLOWED THE OLDER MAN TO A NICHE OFF THE corridor which had been fitted out as a tiny waiting room with a chrome sofa, a Coke machine, and a single window overlooking the great plunging battleship of Manhattan.

Mr. Vaught put his hand on the younger man's knee and

gave it a shake. "Son, when you reach my age I hope you will not wake up to find that you've gone wrong somewhere and that your family have disappointed you."

"I hope so too, sir." He was sure he would not. Because he had lived a life of pure possibility, the engineer, who had often heard older people talk this way, always felt certain he would not repeat their mistakes.

"It's something when the world goes to hell and your own family lets you down, both," said Mr. Vaught, but not at all dolefully, the engineer noticed. His expression was as chipper as ever.

The tiny room soon became so thick with cigar smoke that the engineer's eyes began to smart. Yet, as he sat blinking, hands on knees, he felt quite content.

"Ah, Billy, there's been a loss of integrity in the world, all the things that made this country great."

"Yes sir."

"But the bitterest thing of all is the ingratitude of your own children."

"It must be."

Mr. Vaught sat on the very edge of the sofa and turned around and looked back through the smoke. "Rita's the only one that's worth a damn and she's not even kin."

"Sutter's the oldest," said the engineer, nodding.

"The oldest and the smartest and still isn't worth a damn. Never was and never will be."

"He wrote some very learned articles."

"I'll tell you what he did. He went to the bad on liquor and women."

"Is that so?" All his life the engineer had heard of men who "went to the bad" on women, but he still didn't quite know what it meant. "Isn't he a good doctor?" he asked the older man.

"He had the best education money could buy and you know what he does?"

"No sir."

"He went to Harvard Medical School and made the second highest grades ever made there. After that he interned at Massachusetts General Hospital. Came home. Practiced four years with wonderful success. Was doing people a world of good. Then he quit. Do you know what he does now?"

"No sir."

"He's assistant coroner. He makes five hundred dollars a

month cutting on dead people in the daytime and chases women all night. Why, he's not even the coroner. He's the assistant. He works at the hospital but he doesn't practice. What he is is an interne. He's a thirty-four-year-old interne."

"Is that right?"

"You know that boy in there," Mr. Vaught nodded toward the room.

"Yes sir."

"He is evermore crazy about his big brother and I be dog if I know why. And smart!"

"Which one?"

"Both."

"—"

"I'll tell you what happened, though."

"What?"

"I made a mistake. Three years ago, when my other daughter Val had her twenty-first birthday, I got the idea of giving each of my children a hundred thousand dollars if they hadn't smoked till they were twenty-one. Why not enjoy your money while you're living?"

"That's true," said the engineer, who owned $7.

"Anyway I didn't want to have to look at the bunch of them tippy-toeing around and grinning like chess cats, waiting for me to die. You know what I mean."

"Yes sir," said the other, laughing.

"So what do you think happens? Sutter is older, so he gets his check the same time as Val. So Sutter, as soon as he gets his money, quits practicing medicine, goes out West, and buys a ranch and sits down and watches the birdies. And when he spends the money, do you know what he does? He takes a job at a dude ranch, like a ship's doctor, only he's taking care of five hundred grass widows. Oh, I really did him a favor. Oh, I really did him a big favor. Wait. I want to show you something. Today, you know, is Kitty's and Jamie's birthday. Kitty is twenty-one and Jamie is only sixteen, but I'm going to give him his money now."

The engineer looked at the other curiously, but he could fathom nothing.

"Maybe you and Jamie would like to take a trip around the world," said Mr. Vaught without changing his expression. He was fumbling in the back pocket of his seersucker pants and now took out a wallet as rounded off and polished as a buckeye. From it he plucked two checks and handed them to the engineer, watching him the while with a brimming expectation. They were stiff new checks, as rough as a cheese grater, bristling with red and black bank marks and punch-holes and machine printing. A row of odd Q-shaped zeros marched to the east.

"This one must be for Kitty," he said, reading the word *Katherine*. "One hundred thousand dollars." It seemed to be what the old man expected, for he nodded.

"You give it to one, you got to give it to all. I hope she dudn't mess me up too."

"Did Val mess you up?"

"Val? She was the worst. And yet she was my girlie. I used to call her that, girlie. When she was little, she used to have growing pains. I would hold her in my lap and rock her in the rocking chair, for hours."

"What did she do?"

"With the money? Gave it to the niggers."

"Sir?"

"That's what I'm telling you. She gave it to the niggers."

"But—" began the engineer, who had formed a picture of a girl standing on the front porch handing out bills to passing Negroes. "I thought Kitty told me she went into a, ah, convent."

"She did," cried the old man, peering back through the smoke.

"Then how—"

"Now she's begging from niggers. Do you think that is right?"

"I don't know, sir."

"Let me ask you something. Do you think the good Lord wants us to do anything unnatural?"

"I don't know, sir," said the engineer warily. He perceived it was an old argument and a sore subject.

"Or leave your own kind?"

"Sir?"

"I mean to go spend the rest of your life not just with niggers but with Tyree niggers—do you think that is natural?"

"I don't know, sir."

"You've heard your daddy talk about Tyree niggers?"

"I don't remember."

"Not even niggers have anything to do with Tyree niggers. Down there in Tyree County they've got three different kinds of schools, one for the white folks, one for niggers, and a third for Tyree niggers. They're speckled-like in the face and all up in the head. Some say they eat clay. So where do you think Val goes?"

"Yes sir," said the engineer.

"She went to Agnes Scott, then to Columbia and was just about to get her master's."

The engineer perceived that here was one of those families, more common in the upper South, who set great store by education and degrees.

"So what do I do? Two weeks before graduation I give her her money. So what does she do?"

"Gave it to the Tyree niggers?"

"Man, I'm telling you."

An easy silence fell between them. Mr. Vaught crossed his legs and pulled one ankle above the other with both hands. The little lobby, now swirling with cigar smoke, was something like an old-style Pullman smoker where men used to sit talking by night, pulling their ankles above their knees, and leaning out to spit in the great sloshing cuspidor.

"Let's get us another Coke, Bill."

"I'll get them, sir."

Mr. Vaught drank his Coke in country style, sticking out a little finger and swigging it off in two swallows. "Now. Here's what we'll do. The doctors say Jamie can travel in a week or so. I aim to start home about Thursday week or Friday. Mama wants to go by Williamsburg and Charleston. Now you going to quit all this foolishness up here and come on home with us. What I'm going to do is get you and Jamie a little bitty car— you know I'm in the car business. Do you play golf?"

"Yes sir."

"Hell, man, we live on the golf links. Our patio is twenty feet from number 6 fairway. You like to sail? The Lil' Doll is tied up out at the yacht club and nobody will sail her. You'd be doing me a great favor."

The engineer wished he would mention a salary.

"You and Jamie can go to college—or go round the world! Now isn't that better than being a janitor?"

"Yes sir."

"You think about it."

"I will. Sir?"

"What?"

"Here—I'm going to write down my number here in New

York." Meaning, he hoped: you didn't mention a figure and when you want to, it is for you to call me.

"Sho now," said Mr. Vaught absently, and shoved the slip of paper into the side pocket of his seersucker, a bad enough sign in itself.

8. HE STAYED ONLY LONG ENOUGH TO WATCH THE PRE-sentation of the checks. Kitty was back and without Rita!

Standing between Jamie and Kitty, Mr. Vaught crossed his arms, a check in each hand.

"When was your last cigarette?" he asked Jamie.

"There was no last cigarette," said Jamie, grinning and thrashing.

"Your last drink?"

"There was no last drink."

"Then go buy yourself a drink."

"Yes sir," said Jamie, taking his check.

"Kitty?"

"No cigarette and no drink."

"Then go buy yourself one!"

"I might," said Kitty, laughing.

"I mean it! They're certified. You can cash it right down there at the bar on the corner."

"Thank you, Poppy," said Kitty, kissing him.

The checks were passed around among family, nurses, and internes.

Once again Kitty left and once again the engineer tried to follow her, but Jamie stopped him.

"Bill."

"Yes?"

"Come here."

"What?"

"Did Poppy speak to you?" he whispered.

"Yes."

"What did you say?"

"We didn't get down to terms."

"That's Poppy. But what do you say in general?"

"I say O.K., if I can be of use to you."

"Where do you want to go?"

"Where do *I* want to go?"

Jamie waved the check. "Name it."

"No sir. You name it. And I think you'd better name a school."

"O.K.," said Jamie immediately and cheerfully.

9. DURING THE NEXT WEEK HE SET ABOUT PUTTING HIS life in order. He ate and slept regularly, worked out every day, went down to Brooks Brothers like his father and grandfather before him and bought two ten-dollar pullover shirts with a tuck in the back and no pocket in the front, socks, ties, and underwear, and dressed like a proper Princetonian. At work he read business maxims in *Living*.

The only way people are defeated by their problems is by refusing to face them.

One day, some years ago, a now famous industrial counselor walked into the office of a small manufacturing concern. "How would you like to increase sales 200% the first year?" he asked the president. The latter of course tried to get rid of him. "O.K., I'm leaving," said the counselor. "But first lend me your scratch pad." He wrote a few lines and handed the pad to the executive. "Read this. Think about it. If you put it into practice, send me a check a year from now for what it was worth to you." One year later the counselor received a check in the mail for $25,000.

The counselor had written two sentences:
(1) Make a list of your problems, numbering them in the order of priority.
(2) Devote *all* your time, one day, one month, however long it takes, to disposing of *one* problem at a time. Then go to the next.

Simple? Yes. But as a result this executive is now president of the world's third largest corporation and draws a salary of $400,000 a year.

It was no more nor less than true. You do things by doing things, not by not doing them. No more crazy upsidedownness, he resolved. Good was better than bad. Good environments are better than bad environments. Back to the South, finish his education, make use of his connections, be a business or professional man, marry him a wife and live him a life. What was wrong with that? No more pressing against girls, rassling around in elevators and automobiles and other similar monkey business such as gives you stone pains and God knew what else. What was wrong with a good little house in a pretty green suburb in Atlanta or Birmingham or Memphis and a pretty little wife in a brand-new kitchen with a red dress on at nine o'clock in the morning and a sweet good-morning kiss and the little ones off to school and a good old mammy to take care of them? The way to see Kitty is not not to see her but to see her.

But it didn't work. Kitty's phone didn't answer. Outside in the park the particles were ravening and singing. Inside he went careening around the dark Aztec corridors of the Y.M.C.A. wringing out his ear and forgetting which floor he lived on. When he lay in bed, one leg defied gravity and rose slowly of itself. His knee began to leap like a fish.

Once when he called Kitty, someone did pick up the telephone but did not speak. "Hello, hello," he said. "Who's there?" But there came only the sound of breathing and of the crepitation of skin on plastic. Presently the telephone was replaced softly.

Nor did he hear from Mr. Vaught. He went once more to visit Jamie and, coming face to face with the older man, waited upon him smilingly. But the old man pulled out his gold watch, mumbled an excuse, and was off down the hall like the white rabbit.

Very well then, said he to himself, good day. If they wanted him, let them send for him.

Wednesday when he came home from work he was handed a message with his key. It was from Kitty. Meet me in the park, at the zoo, at four thirty. He went and waited until five thirty. She did not come.

Meanwhile he was getting worse. Thursday morning he slipped another cog. It came, he hoped, from working a double shift and not eating. The day man, a fellow named Perlmutter who had a sick wife, did not show. Like an idiot, he offered to stay on, figuring, what with his new plans and his expenses at Brooks Brothers, that he needed the money.

After sixteen hours underground he came staggering out into the gorge air of Seventh Avenue. For some ten minutes he stood, finger to nose, in the thunderous blue shadow of Pennsylvania Station. A bar turned in his head. Now let me see, said he, and taking out *Living* from his pocket, read a few maxims. Hmm. The thing to do is make a list.

Somewhere in the smoky vastness of the station lanced through with late slanting cathedral beams of sunlight—late or early? was it evening or morning—and haunted by old *déjà vus* of Here-I-am-up-from-Charlotte-or-Chattanooga-or-Tuscaloosa-and-where-do-I-go-from-here, he got turned around good and proper and came down on the wrong platform, headed in the wrong direction, and took the wrong train. He must have dozed off, for when he woke up he was in New Lots Avenue, or perhaps it was Far Rockaway.

What woke him? Something. His heart was thumping, making a regular commotion. Now he knew! A pair of eyes had been looking at him, gazing into his even as he slept with eyes open. Who? Rita. Or did he dream it? The train had stopped. He looked around but there was no one. Yet somebody was following him. He knew that. Goofy as he was, his radar still swung free and there was a prickling between his shoulder blades. Somewhere in Brooklyn he changed to an old local with straw seats and came out at a seaside station.

It was dark. He found himself in a long street which was nearly black between the yellow street lights at the corners. The sea was somehow close. There was a hint of an uproar abroad in the night, a teeming in the air and the sense of coming closer with each step to a primal openness. He walked six blocks in the empty street and there it was. But it was nothing like Wrightsville or Myrtle Beach or Nag's Head, lonesome and wide and knelling. It was domesticated. There were notion shops right up to the sand and the surf was poky, came snuffling in like lake water and collapsed *plaush* on a steep little old brown beach.

He looked behind him. No one followed him in the street. The drowsiness came again. He had to sleep then and there. He lay down in the warm black sand of a vacant lot and slept two hours without moving a muscle. He woke in his right mind and went back to the Y.

10.

JOGGING HOME FROM THE RESERVOIR THE NEXT morning, he spotted Rita two hundred yards away, sitting on a bench next to the milk-fund booth, the toilet-shaped telescope case under her hand. All at once he knew everything: she had come to get rid of him. She hoped he would take his telescope and go away.

But she was, for the first time, as pleasant as could be and patted the bench next to her. And when he sat down, she came sliding smack up against him, a bit too close for comfort. He humped himself over in his sweat suit and tried to smell as good as he could.

Her fist came softly down on his knee; she looked him in the eye and spoke not eight inches away. He couldn't hear for listening.

"But you and I know better," she was saying. "He's got no business going home."

"Jamie?"

Looking into her eyes was something of a shock. Every line of her face was known to him. Yet now, with her eyes opening into his, she became someone else. It was like watching a picture toy turned one degree: the black lines come and the picture changes. Where before her face was dark and shut off as a gypsy, now her eyes opened into a girlishness.

"Bill—"

"Yes ma'am."

"Oh, come *on*. Rita."

"O.K., Rita."

Again the fist came down softly on his knee.

"I want you to do something for me."

"What?"

"The Vaughts are very fond of you."

"I'm glad to hear it."

"The extraordinary part of it is that though you are a new friend—perhaps because you are a new friend—you have more influence with them than anyone else."

"I doubt it. I haven't heard from them in several days."

71

"Oh, they carry on about you something awful. They plan to take you home with them, don't they?"

"When did you hear that?"

"Yesterday."

"Did Mr. Vaught tell you?"

"Yes."

"I'm glad to hear it."

"But never mind about Poppy. Right now it's Jamie who needs us." As gravely as she spoke, he noticed that she cast her eyes about, making routine surveys of Eighth Avenue. There was about her the air of a woman who keeps busy in a world of men. Her busyness gave her leave to be absent-minded. She was tired, but she knew how to use her tiredness.

"Why?"

"Jamie can't go home, Bill."

"Why not?"

"Let me tell you something."

"All right."

"First—how much do you care for Jamie?"

"Care for him?"

"Would you do something for him?"

"Yes."

"Would you do anything for him?"

"What do you mean?"

"If he were in serious trouble, would you help him?"

"Of course."

"I knew you would."

"What is it?" he asked after a moment.

Rita was smoothing out her skirt until it made a perfect membrane across her thighs. "Our Jamie is not going to make it, Bill," she said in a low thrilling voice and with a sweetness that struck a pang to the marrow.

There passed between them the almost voluptuous intercourse of bad news. Why is it, thought he, hunkering over and taking his pulse, I cannot hear what people say but only the channel they use?

"So it's not such a big thing," she said softly. "One small adolescent as against the thirty thousand Japanese children we polished off."

"How's that?" said the engineer, cupping his good ear.

"At Hiroshima and Nagasaki."

"I don't, ah—"

72

"But this little guy happens to be a friend of mine. And yours. He has myelogenous leukemia, Bill."

Oh, and I'm sick too, he thought anxiously, looking at his hands. Why is it that bad news is not so bad and good news not so good and what with the bad news being good, aye that is what makes her well and me sick? Oh, I'm not well. He was silent, gazing at his open hands on his knees.

"You don't seem surprised," said Rita after a moment.

"I knew he was sick," he murmured.

"What's that?" she asked quickly. He saw she was disappointed by his listlessness. She had wanted him to join her, stand beside her and celebrate the awfulness.

"Why shouldn't he go home?" he asked, straightening up.

"Why shouldn't he indeed? A very good question: because just now he is in a total remission. He feels fine. His blood's as normal as yours or mine. He's out of bed and will be discharged tomorrow."

"So?"

"So. He'll be dead in four months."

"Then I don't see why he shouldn't go home or anywhere else."

"There is only one reason. A tough little bastard by the name of Larry Deutsch up at the Medical Center. He's got a drug, a horrifyingly dangerous drug, which incidentally comes from an herb used by the Tarahumaras."

To his relief, Rita started on a long spiel about Jamie's illness. He knew the frequency of her channel, so he didn't have to listen.

"—so Larry said to me in the gentlest voice I ever heard: 'I think we're in trouble. Take a look.' I take a look, and even knowing nothing whatever about it, I could see there was something dreadfully wrong. The little cells were smudged—they looked for all the world like Japanese lanterns shining through a fog. That was over a year ago—"

Instead he was thinking of wars and death at home. On the days of bad news there was the same clearing and sweetness in the air. Families drew closer. Azaleas could be seen. He remembered his father's happiness when he spoke of Pearl Harbor—where he was when he heard it, how he had called the draft board the next morning. It was not hard to see him walking to work on that Monday. For once the houses, the trees, the very cracks in the sidewalk had not their usual minatory presence. The dreadful threat of weekday mornings was gone! War is better than Monday morning.

As his sweat dried, the fleece began to sting his skin.

"—fact number two. Jamie has the best mind I ever encountered. Better even than Sutter, my charming ex-husband. It's really quite funny. His math teacher in New Hampshire was glad to get rid of him. 'Get him out of here,' he told me. 'He wants to argue about John von Neumann's *Theory of Games*—'"

It was her silences, when they came, that he attended.

"So what is the problem?" he asked.

"He's remitted on prednisone. Poppy and Dolly refuse to admit that he is going to die. Why not give him another pill, they say. Well, there are no more pills. He's been through them all."

He was silent.

She regarded him with a fond bright eye.

"Somehow you remind me of the lance corporal in *Der Zauberberg*. Do you mind if I call you lance corporal?"

"No ma'am."

"What would you like to do if you had your choice?"

"I do have my choice. Go with Jamie."

"No, I mean if Jamie hadn't showed up."

"Oh, I'd go see Kitty."

"Leave all of us out of it. And suppose, too, money is no object."

"I guess I'd finish my education."

"In what?"

"Oh, metallurgy, I expect."

"What school would you pick?"

"Colorado School of Mines."

"You'd like to go out there?"

He shrugged. "Why not?"

"Suppose Jamie would want to go too."

"That's up to him."

"Take a look at this."

He found himself gazing at a curled-up Polaroid snapshot of a little white truck fitted with a cabin in its bed. The truck was parked on a stretch of meager shingly beach. Kitty, in long shorts, leaned against the cabin, wide-brimmed hat in hand in a burlesque of American-lady-on-safari.

"What is this?"

"Ulysses."

"Ulysses?"

"He was meant to lead us beyond the borders of the Western world and bring us home."

"I see."

"But seriously now, here's the proposition," she said. And he found that when she gave him ordinary directions he could hear her. "As of this moment you are working for me as well as for Poppy. Perhaps for both of us but at least for me. Keep Jamie up here long enough for Larry to give him a course of huamuratl. You two rascals take my apartment here in the city and here are the keys to the shack on Fire Island. Now when you get through with Larry, take Ulysses and take off. Go home. Go to Alaska. In any event, Ulysses is yours. He has been three hundred miles, cost me seven thousand dollars, and is as far as I'm concerned a total loss. Here is the certificate of ownership, which I've signed over to you and Jamie. It will cost you one dollar. Jamie has coughed up." She held out her hand. "I'll take my money, please."

"I don't have a dollar."

The articles, papers, keys, photograph she lined up on his thigh. He looked closely at the snapshot again.

"What did you get it for?" he asked her.

"To camp in Europe. Isn't that stupid? Considering that I'd have to buy gas for that monster Ulysses by the liter."

"You've already told Jamie?"

"Yes."

"And Mr. Vaught agrees to this?"

"He will if you ask him."

"What about Kitty?"

"My friend, allow me to cue you in. Perhaps you have not noticed it, but our young friend Jamie is sick to death of the women in the family. Including me. Kitty and I made him the same deal: the three of us for Long Island and the camper (it sleeps three) and he laughed in our faces and I can't say I blame him. Let me put it to you straight out."

"All right."

"Just suppose you asked him—you said, Jamie, I got Ulysses parked outside in the street—come on now, let's me and you hit the road. What would he say?"

"He wouldn't like the Ulysses part."

"Dear God, you're right." Her fist came down on his knee and stayed there. "You're right. You see, you *know*. All right, leave out the word 'Ulysses.' What then? What would he do?"

"He'd go."

"You know something: you're quite a guy."

"Thank you." He plucked at his sweat suit. It came away from him like old skin. "Then you mean Kitty will go to Europe, after all?"

"My dear young friend, hear this. I do believe you under-estimate yourself. I do not believe you realize what a hurricane you've unleashed and how formidable you yourself are. You've got our poor Kitty spinning like a top. Not that I blame her. Why is it some men can sit like Achilles sat and some men can't? But I propose to you, my lordly young sir, that we give our young friend her year abroad, which is the only one she'll ever have. Seriously, Kitty saved my life. She is the sister of that son of a bitch I married. She bucked me up when I needed it and by God I'm returning the favor. Do you have any idea what it would be like to be raised by Poppy and Dolly, who are in their own way the sweetest people in the world, but I mean—God. You have no idea what it's like down there these days, the poor bloody old South. I'll tell you what. Give her her year in Florence and then if *you* haven't forgotten all about her, I'll send her home as fast as her little legs will carry her. Or better still, when you and Jamie get through with Larry, come on over and join us!"

The next thing he knew, she was thrusting something into his pocket, but he didn't have a pocket, then inside the draw-string of his sweat suit, tucked it with a fierce little tuck like an aunt at Christmas. "Your first month's salary in advance," she said, and was on her way.

Taking the check from his loin, he read it several times. It seemed to be postdated. He scratched his head. On the other hand, what was today's date?

11. IT WAS THE FIRST HOT NIGHT. THERE WERE SIGNS of summer. Fires had broken out in Harlem. Twice there were gunshots as close as Seventieth or Eightieth Street. Police cars raced north along Central Park West. But the park was quiet. Its public space, paltry by day, was leafed out in secrecy and darkness. Lamps made gold-green spaces in the rustling leaves.

He strolled about the alp at the pond, hands in pockets and brow furrowed as if he were lost in thought. It was a dangerous place to visit by night, but he paid no attention. He felt irritable and strong and wouldn't have minded a fistfight. A few minutes earlier a damp young man had fallen in step on his deaf side.

"Didn't we take philosophy together at the Y?" the stranger murmured, skipping nimbly to get in step.

"What's that," said the engineer absently.

"I thought it unconscionably bad," murmured the other.

"Eh?" The engineer cupped his good ear.

"Are you interested in the Platonic philosophy?" the other asked him.

"In *what*," said the engineer, stopping and swinging around to hear better but also bending upon the other such an intent, yet unfocused gaze that he melted into the night.

Strong and healthy as he felt, he was, if the truth be known, somewhat dislocated. The sudden full tide of summer sent him spinning. The park swarmed with old *déjà vus* of summertime. It put him in mind of something, the close privy darkness and the black tannin smell of the bark and the cool suspiring vapors of millions of fleshy new leaves. From time to time there seemed to come to him the smell of Alabama girls (no, Mississippi), who bathe and put on cotton dresses and walk uptown on a summer night. He climbed the alp dreamily and stooped over the bench. The cul-de-sac held the same message it had held for days, a quotation from Montaigne. He read it under a lamp:

> Man is certainly stark mad. He can't make a worm, but he makes gods by the dozens.

No one had picked it up. Nor was it very interesting, for that matter: when he sniffed it, it smelled not of Montaigne but of a person who might quote Montaigne on such a night as this, an entirely different matter.

"Wait—" he stoped in a dapple of light and leaves and snapped his fingers softly. That was what his father used to say. He too quoted Montaigne on a summer night but in a greener, denser, more privy darkness than this. The young man in the park snapped his fingers again. He stood a full minute, eyes closed, swaying slightly. He raised a hand tentatively toward the West.

Yonder was not the alp but the levee, and not the lamp in the trees but the street light at Houston Street and De Ridder. The man walked up and down in the darkness under the water oaks. The boy sat on the porch steps and minded the Philco, which clanked and whirred and plopped down the old 78's and set the needle hissing and voyaging. Old Brahms went abroad into the summer night. West, atop the levee, couples sat in parked cars. East, up De Ridder, from the heavy humming ham-rich darkness of the cottonseed-oil mill there came now and then the sound of Negro laughter.

Up and down the man walked and spoke to the boy when he passed the steps. More cars came nosing discreetly up the levee, lights out and appearing to go by paws, first left then right. The man grew angry.

"The prayer meeting must be over," said the man ironically.

Out poured old Brahms, the old spoiled gorgeous low-German music but here at home surely and not in Hamburg.

"What do they expect," said the man now, westbound. He took his turn under the street light and came back.

"Now they," he went on, nodding to the east. "They fornicate and the one who fornicates best is the preacher."

The Great Horn Theme went abroad, the very sound of the ruined gorgeousness of the nineteenth century, the worst of times.

"But they," he said to the levee—"they fornicate too and in public and expect *them* back yonder somehow not to notice. Then they expect their women to be respected."

The boy waited for the scratch in the record. He knew when it was coming. The first part of the scratch came and he had time to get up and hold the tone arm just right so the needle wouldn't jump the groove.

"Watch them."

"Yes sir."

"You just watch them. You know what's going to happen?"

"No sir."

"One will pick up the worst of the other and lose the best of himself. Watch. One will learn to fornicate in public and the other will end by pissing in the street. Watch."

The man stayed, so the boy said, "Yes sir."

"Go to whores if you have to, but always remember the

difference. Don't treat a lady like a whore or a whore like a lady."

"No sir, I won't."

The record ended but the eccentric groove did not trip the mechanism. The boy half rose.

"If you do one, then you're going to be like them, a fornicator and not caring. If you do the other, you'll be like them, fornicator and hypocrite."

He opened his eyes. Now standing in the civil public darkness of the park, he snapped his fingers softly as if he were trying to remember something.

Then what happened after that? After he—

Leaning over, he peered down at the faint dapple on the path. After a long moment he held up his watch to the lamplight. After a look around to get his bearings, he walked straight to the corner of the park and down into the BMT subway.

Yet he could scarcely have been in his right mind or known exactly where he was, for what he did next was a thing one did at home but never did here. He dropped in. He walked up to Rita's apartment in the Mews and knocked on the door at eight thirty in the evening.

Kitty answered the door. Her mouth opened and closed. She could not believe her eyes. He defied the laws of optics.

"Oh," she said, fearing either to look at him or to take her eyes from him.

"Let's walk up the street," he said. "It's a nice night."

"Oh, I'd love to," she cried, "but I can't. Give me a rain check." She was managing somehow both to stand aside and to block the doorway.

"Let's go ride the ferry to Staten Island."

"Oh, I can't," she wailed like an actress.

"Aren't you going to ask me in," he said after a moment.

"What? Oh. *Oh.*" But instead of standing aside she put her head over coquettishly. *Tock*, she said, clicking her tongue and eyeing the darkness behind him. They were having a sort of date here in the doorway.

"There is something I wanted to ask you. It will not take long. Your phone didn't answer."

"It didn't?" She called something over her shoulder. It seemed that here was the issue: the telephone. If this issue could be settled, it seemed, he would take his leave like a telephone man. But it allowed her to admit him: she stood aside.

So it was at last that he found himself in the living room standing, in a kind of service capacity. He had come about the telephone. The two women smiled up at him from a low couch covered with Navaho blankets. No, only Kitty smiled. Rita eyed him ironically, her head appearing to turn perpetually away.

It was not a Barbados cottage after all but an Indian hogan. Rita wore a Chamula huipil (Kitty was explaining nervously) of heavy homespun. Kitty herself had wound a white quexquemetl above her Capri pants. Brilliant quetzals and crude votive offerings painted on tin hung from the walls.

They were drinking a strong-smelling tea.

"I've been unable to reach you by phone," he told Kitty.

The two women looked at him.

"I may as well state my business," said the engineer, still more or less at attention, though listing a bit.

"Good idea," said Rita, taking a swig of the tea, which smelled like burnt corn. He watched as the muscular movement of her throat sent the liquid strumming along.

"Kitty, I want to ask you something."

"What?"

"Could I speak to you alone?"

"You're among friends, ha-ha," said Kitty laughing loudly.

"Very well. I wanted to ask you to change your mind about going to Europe and instead go south with Jamie and me." Until the moment he opened his mouth, he had no idea what he wished to ask her. "Here is your check, Mrs. Vaught. I really appreciate it, but—"

"Good grief," said Kitty, jumping to her feet as if she had received an electric shock. "Listen to the man," she cried to Rita and smacked her thigh in a Jewish gesture.

Rita shrugged. She ignored the check.

The engineer advanced and actually took Kitty's hand. For a second her pupils enlarged and she was as black-eyed as an Alabama girl on a summer night. Then she gaped at her own hand in stupefaction: it could not be so! He was holding her hand! But instead of snatching it away, she pulled him down on the couch.

"Here. Try some hikuli tea."

"No thanks." As he lay back among the pillows, his eye fell upon a votive painting. It showed a man who had been thrown from a motorcycle and now lay in a ditch. He had apparently suffered internal injuries, for blood spurted from his mouth like a stream from a garden hose.

"That's my favorite," said Kitty. "Isn't it wonderful?"

"I guess so."

"He was cured miraculously by the Black Virgin."

"Is that right?"

As Kitty went on, no longer so nervous now but seeming rather to have hit upon a course she might steer between the two of them, he noticed a spot of color in her cheek. There was a liquid light, not a tear, in the corner of her eye.

"Ree's been giving me the most fascinating account of the hikuli rite which is practiced by the Huichol Indians. The women are absolved from their sins by tying knots in a palm-leaf string, one knot for each lover. Then they throw the string into Grandfather Fire. Meanwhile the men— Ree was just getting to the men. What do the men do, Ree?"

"I really couldn't say," said Rita, rising abruptly and leaving the room.

"Tie a knot for me," said the engineer.

"*What*," cried Kitty, craning her neck and searching the horizon like a sea bird. "Oh."

"Let us now—" he began and sought dizzily to hold her charms in his arms.

"Ah," said the girl, lying passive, eyes full of light.

"I've reached a decision," he said and leaned back uncomfortably among the pillows, head in the air.

"What is that?"

"Now you know that I need you."

"You do?"

"And that although I will be all right eventually, I still have a nervous condition, and that for some time to come I'll need you to call upon."

"You will?"

"I've loved you ever since I saw you in Central—that is, in Jamie's room."

"Ah."

Love, he thought, and all at once the word itself went opaque and curious, a little howling business behind the front teeth. Do I love her? I something her. He felt his nose.

"Let's go home, either to your home or mine, and be married."

"Married," said Kitty faintly.

81

Dander from the old blankets was beginning to bother his nose. "Would you mind taking this off," he asked her presently and took hold of her quexquemetl. "Aren't you hot?"

"Are you out of your mind," she whispered fiercely.

"I'm sorry. I didn't mean—" He hadn't meant to undress her but only to get her out of these prickly homespuns and back into decent Alabama cotton.

Kitty sat up. Her eyes were fixed in a stare upon a bowl of tiny cactus plants. "The Huichol believe that things change forms, that one thing can become another thing. An hour ago it sounded like nonsense."

"Is that right?" He had heard it before, this mythic voice of hers. One of his aunts lived in Cuernavaca.

"The hikuli plant *is* the deer. The deer *is* the corn. Look at that."

"What?"

"That color."

He looked down at the blanket between them where forked Navaho lightning clove through an old brown sky, brown as old blood.

"What about it?"

"Do you see the depths opening into depths?"

"No." He tried to blow his nose but the mucous membranes had swelled against each other like violet eiderdowns. "I think I'll be going."

"Wait," she called from the doorway as he walked rapidly off into the night, forgetful of summer now, head ducked, shouldering as if he were still bucking the winter gales. He waited.

"All right," she said. "Where do you want to go?"

He gazed vaguely about at the shuttered shops and dark brownstones.

"We can't go back there," she said. Her pale face loomed unsteadily in the darkness. He was thinking about the reciprocal ratio of love: was it ever so with the love of women that they held out until the defeat of one's first fine fervor, not merely until one feigned defeat but rather until one was in truth defeated, had shrugged and turned away and thought of other matters—and now here they came, all melts and sighs, breathing like a furnace. Her lips were parted slightly and her eyes sparkled. His nose was turning to concrete.

"And we can't go to the Y." She had taken his arm. He felt

importunate little tugs at his elbow as if he were a blind man and she wanted him to cross the street.

She pulled him close. "Do you notice anything?"

"No."

"The lampposts."

"What about them?"

"They seem alive and ominous."

He was displeased with her. Was it then the case with love that lovers must alternate, forever out of phase with one another? It did not suit her to be fanciful. Was she drunk? She gave him a kiss tasting of burnt corn. He wished she would chew Juicy Fruit like a proper Alabama girl.

"I do know a place," he said finally. "But it won't do at night."

"Why not?"

"It's in the park."

"Wait," she said and flew back to the cottage. He waited, listing at a ten-degree angle. Had he, empathic as ever, got dizzy from her dizziness?

When she returned, she wore a shirt and blouse instead of pants and quexquemetl. "Take this." She pressed something into his hand.

"What's this for?" It was a small revolver, a police special, with hardly a quarter inch of barrel.

"For the park. My brother gave it to me as a going-away present when I came to New York."

"Sutter?"

"Yes. He's a police surgeon."

He stuck the pistol into his coat pocket and allowed himself to be nudged toward the subway.

They walked from the Broadway subway exit to the park. Fifty blocks north there were more fires in Harlem and the sense of faraway soundless tumult. Police sirens kicked out, subsided to a growl.

He hesitated. "I don't know."

Again the nudge at his elbow. "Don't worry. They're all up there."

He shrugged and took her into the Ramble, a densely wooded stretch. Holding her behind him, he walked swiftly along a path, stooped and holding the girl's head down, turned into a thicket of privet whose bitter bark smelled like the dry rain gutters of his own house. Dark as it was, with no more light than a sinking gibbous moon, it didn't matter. He knew the southwest quadrant of the park as he knew his own back-yard. (Though he could not see them, he knew when he passed the Disney statuettes, could have put out a hand and touched Dopey.)

The place was down a ravine choked with dogbane and whortleberry and over a tumble of rocks into a tiny amphitheater, a covert so densely shaded that its floor was as bare as cave's dirt. By day it looked very like the sniper's den on Little Round Top which Brady photographed six weeks after the battle: the sniper was still there! a skeleton in butternut, his rifle propped peaceably against the rocks.

He set the police special in the dust beside him and drew Kitty down on the other side. They leaned into the curve of a shallow overhang of smooth rock facing the cleft where they entered. There was no sound of traffic or sight of the lighted windows of the apartment houses along Central Park West, or any sign of the city at all except, when he moved his head slightly, a chink of red sky over 110th Street.

"My Lord," said Kitty. "How could anybody find us here. I can't even see you." Her fingers brushed clumsily across his face.

He kissed her with an amiable passion, mainly concerned now to bear with her, serve her anticness as gracefully as he could. He aimed to guard her against her own embarrassment. His nose was no better.

"To answer your question," she said softly, "Yes."

"Fine," he said, nodding in the dark. What question?

"Dearest," she breathed, holding her hand to his cheek with a tenderness that struck dismay to his heart.

The puzzle is: where does love pitch its tent? in the fine fervor of a summer night, in a jolly dark wood wherein one has a bit o' fun as the English say? or in this dread tenderness of hers?

"Don't go away, darling," she whispered. "I'll be right back."

"All right."

She moved away. As he traced a finger in the dust, drawing the old Northern Pacific yin-yang symbol, he heard the rustling of clothes and the singing of zippers. She returned without a sound. He embraced her and was enveloped in turn by the warm epithelial smell of her nakedness. What a treasure, he thought, his heart beating as rapidly and shallowly as a child's. What suppleness.

"Hold me," whispered Kitty with her dismaying tenderness. "My precious."

"Right." Now holding her charms in his arms at last, he wondered if he had ever really calculated the terrific immediacy of it.

"Why don't you—" she said.

"What? Oh. Pardon," said the courtly but forgetful engineer and blushed for his own modesty, clad as he was from head to toe in Brooks Bros.' finest. Making haste to sit up, he began to unbutton his shirt.

"Now. Oh, my darling, do you love me?"

"Oh yes," said the engineer, swinging her forty-five degrees in the dust so that he could look past her toward the opening of the covert. The sky was redder. From the same direction there came a faint crepitant sound like crumpled newspaper. The cops and the Negroes were shooting it out in Harlem.

"Will you cherish me?"

"Yes, certainly," said the engineer.

"I don't mean just now. I want to be protected always. I want to be cherished."

"I will," he assured her.

"Do you know what matters most of all?"

"What?"

"Love."

"Right."

"Love is everything."

"Yes."

"Rita asked me what I believed in. I said I believed in love."

"Me too."

"Besides which I want to prove something to myself," said the girl, almost to herself.

"Prove what?"

"A little experiment by Kitty for the benefit of Kitty."

"What experiment is that?"

"Let me tell you, there is nothing wrong with Kitty," she said.

"I didn't say there was."

Holding her, he couldn't help thinking of Perlmutter, his young fresh-eyed colleague at Macy's. Though he was from Brooklyn, Perlmutter looked like an Indiana farm boy. Perlmutter spoke of his wife with a lack of reserve, though not of respect, which was startling. Making love to his wife, Perlmutter said, was like "being in heaven." Now he understood. Kitty too, he would have to say, was an armful of heaven. The astounding immediacy of her. She was more present, more here, than he could ever have calculated. She was six times bigger and closer than life. He scarcely knew whether to take alarm or to shout for joy, hurrah!

"Never mind. What about you, you big geezer?"

Geezer, thought the engineer. "What about me?"

"You were the one who was always sweeping Kitty off her feet before! What happened?" She even socked him, jokingly but also irritably. The poor girl could not get the straight of it: the engineer's alternating fits of passion and depression.

He was wondering: had the language of women, "love" and "sweeping one off one's feet," and such, meant this all along, the astounding and terrific melon immediacy of nakedness. Do women know everything?

"What about it, friend?" asked Kitty, heaving up, her pale face swimming above him. "Kitty wants to know."

"Know what?"

"Is this the same Will Barrett who swept Kitty off her feet in the automat?"

"No, but it's just as well," he said dryly.

"Tell Kitty why."

"Kitty might be too attractive," said the chivalrous but wry engineer. "So attractive that it is just as well I don't feel too well—for one thing, my sinuses are blocked—"

"Oh that's sweet," said Kitty in as guttural, as ancient and risible and unbuttoned an Alabama voice as Tallulah Bankhead. Did he know anything about women?

"Do you feel bad," she asked suddenly and touched his face. "If it is not possible now to—" she broke off.

He felt just bad enough—his head was caulked, the pressure turning him ever away into a dizzy middle distance—and so it was just possible.

"Lover," said Kitty as they hugged and kissed.

"Darling," said the engineer, not to be surpassed—was this it at last, the august secret of the Western world?

"My sweet," said Kitty, patting his cheek at the corner of his mouth.

But is love a sweetnesse or a wantonnesse, he wondered.

Yet when at last the hard-pressed but courteous and puissant engineer did see the way clear to sustaining the two of them, her in passing her test, him lest he be demoralized by Perlmutter's heaven, too much heaven too soon, and fail them both—well, I do love her, he saw clearly, and therefore I shall—it was too late.

"Dear God," said the girl to herself, even as he embraced her tenderly and strongly—and fell away from him.

"What's the matter?"

"I'm so sick," she whispered.

"Oh, that's too bad," he said, shaking his head dolefully. Even their sicknesses alternated and were out of phase.

She went to the farthest corner of the sniper's den and began to retch. The engineer held her head. After a moment she asked in a dazed voice. "What happened?"

"I think it was that tea you were drinking."

"You are so smart," she said faintly.

What with her swaying against him, he was having a hard time finding her clothes. It was too much for a man to follow, he mused, these lightning hikuli-transformations from Kitty as great epithelial-warm pelvic-upcurving-melon-immediate Maja to Kitty as waif, huddled under his arm all ashiver and sour with gastric acid. But when they were dressed, they felt better. Now trousered, collared, buttoned up, he at least was himself again. There is a great deal to be said for clothes. He touched Kitty to place her, like a blind man. To his relief she sat hugging her decent skirted knees like a proper Georgia coed.

"Do you feel better?" he asked her.

"Yes," she said, hardly audibly. "But talk to me."

"What about?"

"Anything. Anything that comes into your head."

"All right." After all, this was one thing he was good at. "I was thinking about the summer of 1864," said the engineer, who always told the truth. "My kinsman took part in the siege of Richmond and later of Petersburg. We have a letter he wrote his mother. He was exactly my age and a colonel in the infantry. Petersburg was a rats' war, as bad as Stalingrad. But do you know that even at the worst the officers would go to balls and cotillions? In the letter he thanks his mother for the buttermilk cookies and says: 'Met Miss Sally Trumbull last night. She said I danced tolerably well. She gave me her handkerchief.' He was killed later on in the Crater."

"Would you take me to a dance?" asked Kitty, her head turned away.

"Sure. But what is curious is that—"

"I've been dancing five hours a day for years and I can't remember the last dance I went to."

"—he did not feel himself under the necessity, almost moral, of making love—"

"I love to dance."

"—in order that later things be easy and justified between him and Miss Trumbull, that—"

"My grandmother composed the official ATO waltz at Mercer," said Kitty.

"—that even under the conditions of siege he did not feel himself under the necessity, or was it because it was under the conditions of siege that—"

"You're so smart," said Kitty, shivering and huddling against him. "Oh, I'm so cold."

"I must speak to your father," said the engineer absently.

The girl started nervously and stopped shivering. "What for?"

"To ask your hand in marriage," said the engineer somewhat formally.

"You know everything," said Kitty, commencing to shiver again. "You're so smart."

"No, but I know one thing."

"Tell Kitty."

"I know what you fear most."

"What?"

"People, and that is the trouble. The source of your happiness is also the source of your nightmares."

"That's true."

Even now he was at it again, scheming, establishing his credentials. Like all women, she was, he knew, forever attuned to fortune-telling, soothsaying, and such. If he told her something, she might tell him. For there was something he wanted to know.

"I know who you like to be with."

"Who?"

"Rita and me."

"That's right. Why is that?"

"You like Rita because she is among other things a woman and no threat to you. You like me and that would be enough to put you off ordinarily because I am a man but you know something is wrong with me and that neutralizes the threat."

"Yes," said the girl gloomily. "Oh, dear. I really don't feel well."

"What about Rita?"

"What about her?" He could scarcely hear her.

"What about the notes, verses, and so on, she leaves in the park for you?" He had calculated correctly. Knowing as much as he did about her, he judged that in her eyes it must appear he might know everything. She would not think to ask how he knew about the notes. For all she knew, Rita could have told him.

"The notes in the bench, yes. It is not quite what you think." Was she now smiling down at her crossed legs?

12. KITTY SAID:

The notes. You know, I have a confession to make. I led her on. It's my fault.

Here it comes again, he thought, *the sweet beast of catastrophe. Am I not like Rita after all and do I not also live by catastrophe? I can smell it out every time. Show me a strange house and I can walk straight to the door where the bad secrets are kept. The question is: is it always here that one seeks one's health, here in the sweet, dread precincts of disaster? Strange: that her disaster now enables me, that now I could love her again and more easily from the pity of it.*

No, no, no, Kitty said, I don't mean there was anything really wrong. Nothing has ever happened, not the least thing. But what I don't know is whether from the very beginning I didn't know in my heart of hearts what I was doing—the way a child knows nothing and yet knows everything. I've often wondered whether a person who found herself for the first time in her life really and truly liked by another person and having the power for the first time to make another person like her, would she not use that power every time? Rita is a remarkable person and, wonder of wonders, she liked me. I had never dreamed that anybody would like me. And I knew exactly how to make her like me! This whole thing started last summer. The notes? They're notes, that's all. Poems. Everything happened last summer in one week. Do you think there are times like that when everything comes to a head for several people and after that their lives take a different turning? Jamie and I had gone out to see Sutter and Rita in Tesuque. Val came out a little later. A few days later and everybody had gone off in different directions. First, I think Sutter found out that something was wrong with Jamie. Sutter could look at you and tell what was wrong with you—he's about shot now—but I remember he did take Jamie to the laboratory. Then he and Jamie went out into the desert and got lost etcetera etcetera. After that Val left to become a postulant or something. Then I came to New York with Rita. She and Sutter had already separated. I had never met anybody like Rita. My own life had been abnormal. I had polio as a little girl and was crippled and overcame it with ten years of toe dancing (like Glenn Cunningham, Poppy said). I had tutors and Poppy sent me to a school in Switzerland—now you talk about something peculiar: those girls were a mess. I came home. My life at home. Do you know what everybody does? We live in a country club; we are not just members, we live right there on the golf links along with a hundred other houses. The men make money and watch pro football. The women play golf and bridge at the club. The children swim in meets. The mothers of the losers hate the mothers of the winners. At night Mama always gets mad at Huntley–Brinkley, turns off the TV and gets off on the Negroes and the Jews and the Federal Reserve Bank. Sunday we go to church. That's what we do at home. Then all of a sudden I found myself with Rita. She showed me something I never dreamed existed. Two things. First, the way she devoted herself to the Indians. I never saw anything like it. They adored her. I saw one child's father try to kneel and kiss her foot. Then she showed me how a thing can be beautiful. She kept Shakespeare's sonnets by her bed. And she actually read them. Listen to this, she would say, and she would read it. And I could hear it the way she heard it! Bare ruin'd choirs, where late the sweet birds sang. Poetry: who'd have thought it? We went for walks. I listened to her but then (is this bad?) I began to see how much she was enjoying teaching me. We went to corn dances in the pueblos. I said I had a confession. My confession is this: that even though I knew Rita and Sutter were estranged, or at least were having trouble, and although I knew exactly what effect our own friendship was having, I knew how to make Rita like me and I did it. Finally when Jamie and Sutter came back there was a scene between Val and Rita and everything blew up. At the time Val was fretting about whether to go into this religious order and she was not very stable. But everybody was unstable. Anyhow Val accused Rita of destroying Carlos's faith—

Carlos?

A Zuñi boy who was Rita's servant and protégé. (I beat him too. Rita liked him but she soon liked me better.) He was her prize pupil and she'd got him into Harvard on a scholarship. She was having Carlos and me dance the Ahaiyute myths. Carlos was the Beast God and I was the Corn Woman. Val told Carlos he was trading his birthright for a mess of pottage. Rita asked her what mess of pottage she meant, the Ahaiyute myths or Harvard? This—this idolatry, said Val. But Val dear, said Rita, this *is* his birthright, the Zuñis had the Ahaiyute myths for hundreds of years before the Spanish priests came. Val stormed out. She never liked Rita.

What did Sutter say?

Nothing. Or rather he laughed. But it was then that Val made up her mind too. She came back the same night and apologized. She told Rita: "It is you who are doing the work and I who am being hateful and doing nothing. Is it possible to come to believe in Christ and the whole thing and afterwards to be more hateful than before? But at least now I know what to do, and I thank you for it, Rita." And so around she goes to each of us, kissing us and asking us to forgive her (it was that kind of summer).

What did Sutter say to that?

Oh, he said something about: now I don't know, Val, maybe there is something to be said nowadays for a theology of hatred—you know Sutter. No, you don't. But then I came on to New York with Rita. The poems in the park? They're just that. She likes to show me her favorites—she knows I can see them as she sees them. I have to get up earlier than she does and we have different lunch hours. So if she reads something the night before—she reads at all hours—she'll put it in the bench for me to read during my lunch. I owe her a great deal. Now she wants me to go to Europe with her. I owe her the pleasure she will take in showing it to me. But first I have to make sure of my own motives. I wrote Sutter that. I conceal nothing from him.

What did he say?

Nothing. He's entirely too selfish to write a letter. If Rita is the most unselfish person I know, Sutter is the most selfish. That was the real trouble all along, that Rita did all the giving and Sutter did all the taking. Do you know what he said to me? "Blankety-blank on unselfishness," said he. "I agree with Val and the Christers, it's a fornication of spirit." But that's not right either. That's not what Christ said.

Blankety-blank?

Crap.

Don't talk like that.

I'm sick. Take me home.

13. THE NEXT MORNING HE CALLED KITTY FROM Macy's. "Today," he told her, "I've got to get this business settled one way or the other."

"Don't speak to me," she said, her voice faint and cold.

"Eh?"

"You know what I'm talking about."

"No, I don't." But he thought he did—though, as it turned out, he was wrong.

"You took advantage of me."

"Ah, dearest—" he began. His heart sank: she was right.

But she broke in quickly (he was not right). "I have been out of my mind with worry the last few days, about this whole business, Jamie and Europe and everything. Then on top of everything I was allergic to the paint fumes and it was too much."

"Paint fumes," said the engineer. He looked up in time to see his old friends the Ohioans punching in at the time clock, bound for sportswear and lingerie, a lusty clear-eyed crew who had no trouble understanding each other.

"We painted Rita's attic yesterday and I turned out to be allergic to the benzene or whatever it was. I went completely out of my head. What did I say?"

"Nothing much."

"But I remember enough to know that you took advantage of me, barging in like that."

"Barging in?"

"Rita tells me that you didn't call her, you just showed up."

"Yes," he said contritely, willing, anxious to be convicted of a lesser crime. What foulness had he committed? It was not enough to lie with Kitty in Central Park like a common sailor: he must also take his pleasure, or almost take his pleasure, with a nice girl rendered defenseless by paint fumes.

"I really think it put me in a terrible position for you to come to Rita's like that. You know better than that! And then to leave without so much as a fare-you-well to Rita and walking me clear to New Jersey or wherever it was."

"Yes."

"What do you want?"

"What?"

"You called me, remember?"

"Oh yes," said the engineer, shaking his head to clear the cobwebs. "I've got to, ah, get this business settled." But he had lost his resolution.

"What business?" said Kitty coldly.

"Whether I am working for Rita or your father. But in either case—"

"Working for Rita?" she asked sharply.

"Rita wants me and Jamie to take the camper while you all go to Europe."

"I see."

"The point is," he said, gathering strength, collecting his wits at last, "I don't want you to go."

"Oh, you don't want me to go."

"No, I want you to stay here and either go south with Jamie and me or—"

"You've got your nerve."

"Kitty."

"What?"

"Do you remember that I asked you to marry me last night?"

"Oh Lord," said the girl nervously and hung up, not so much, he thought, on him as on herself.

Later, after shower and breakfast, he called Jamie from the Y.M.C.A. It was time to settle things one way or another.

Jamie surprised him by answering the phone himself.

"Why didn't you keep the telescope?" the engineer asked him.

"We're leaving, aren't we? Thanks, by the way."

"Rita spoke to me today. Do you know what she wants us to do?"

93

"Yes."

"Is that what you want to do?"

Again he heard the slight break in breathing, the little risible and incredulous sound he seemed to call forth from people.

"What would you do?" asked Jamie after a silence.

"I'd do what the doctor said."

"Me too. But in any case you're going to bum around with me for a while?"

"Sure."

"Then call Poppy and see what's what. After all, he's the boss."

"You're right. I will. Where is he?"

"At the Astor."

"How extraordinary."

"It was the only hotel they knew."

"Yello, yello." Mr. Vaught answered the telephone as eccentrically and routinely as a priest reciting the rosary.

"Sir, this is Bill Barrett."

"Who? Billy boy!"

"Yes sir. Sir—"

"Yayo."

"I would like to know exactly where we stand."

"You ain't the only one."

"Sir?"

"What is it you want to know, Bill?"

"I would like to know, sir, whether I am working for you or working for Rita or for both or for neither."

"You want to know something, Bill."

"Yes sir."

"It would be a crying shame if you didn't turn out to be a lawyer. You sound just like your daddy."

"Yes sir. But—"

"Listen to me, Bill."

"I will," said the engineer, who had learned to tell when the old man was not fooling.

"You got your driver's license?"

"Yes sir."

"All right. You be standing outside on the sidewalk at nine o'clock in the morning. We'll pick you up. Then we'll see who's going where."

"Yes sir."

"All yall be ready," he said, like Kitty, somewhat aside from the telephone, to the world around.

It was not a good sign, thought the engineer as he hung up slowly, that Mr. Vaught spoke both broadly and irritably.

14.

THE NEXT MORNING HE RESIGNED HIS POSITION AT Macy's—the chief engineer, who had heard this before and was something of a psychologist himself, nodded gravely and promised the job would be waiting for him when he felt better—checked out of the Y.M.C.A. and sat on his telescope at the curb for three hours. No one came to pick him up. Once he went inside to call the hospital, the hotel, and Kitty. Had he got the directions wrong? Jamie had been discharged, the Vaughts had left the hotel, and Kitty's telephone did not answer.

Only then, three hours later, did it occur to him that there must be a message for him. He climbed the steps again. Already the Y reentered was like a place he had lived in long ago with its special smell of earnestness and breathed air and soaped tile, the smell, as he had always taken it but only just now realized, of Spanish Protestantism. Two yellow slips were handed him across the desk. Superstitiously, he took pains to return to his perch on the street corner before reading either. The first was a garbled note, evidently from Mr. Vaught. "If plans are not finalized and you change your mind a job is always waiting. S. Vote." "Vote" could only be Vaught.

The second was from Kitty and he couldn't see for looking. "Europe out," he finally made out. "Jamie more important. Please change your mind and catch up with us at Coach-and-Four Motel, Williamsburg. Know you had cause to lose patience but please change your mind. Did you mean what you said? Kitty."

Change my mind? Mean what I said? What did I say, asked the engineer aloud. He blinked into the weak sunlight. Screwing up an eye, he tried mightily to get the straight of it. It follows, said he, diagramming a syllogism in the air, that they think I changed my mind about going with them. But I told them no such thing. Then it follows someone else did.

Another twenty minutes of squatting and musing on the telescope, not so much addled as distracted by the curiousness of sitting in the street and having no address, and he jumped suddenly to his feet.

Why, they have all left, thought he, socking himself with amazement: the whole lot of them have pulled out.

Early afternoon found him on a southbound bus counting his money. He bought a ticket as far as Metuchen. The bus was a local, a stained old Greyhound with high portholes. The passengers sat deep in her hold, which smelled of the 1940's and many a trip to Fort Dix. Under the Hudson River she roared, swaying like a schooner, and out onto old US1 with its ancient overpasses and prehistoric Sinclair stations. The green sky filtered through the high windows. In Elizabeth, when the door opened, he fancied he heard a twittering, ravening noise high in the green sky.

When the bus got clear of the factories and overpasses, he pulled the cord and alighted on the littered highway. On the corner stood a blackened stucco dollhouse with a pagoda roof, evidently a subdivision field office left over from the period between the great wars.

It began to rain, a fine dirty Jersey mizzle, and he took refuge in the pagoda, which was empty but for scraps of ancient newspapers, a sepia rotogravure section depicting Lucky Lindy's visit to Lakehurst in 1928.

The drizzle stopped but it was a bad place to catch a ride. There were few cars. The concrete underfoot trembled like an earthquake as the great tankers and tractors rolled by. Yet prudence had not failed him. Against such an occasion he had obtained certain materials in Penn Station, and, returning to the pagoda, he lettered a sign which he propped against his telescope: PRINCETON STUDENT SEEKS RIDE SOUTH.

And now once again, not entirely aware that he did so, he stuck his hands in his pockets a certain way and carried his chin in his throat. In the end he even took off his Macy's jacket (which looked more like Ohio State than Princeton), uncovering his shirt with the tuck in back and no pocket in front.

III

1. FOR AN HOUR AND A HALF THE GREAT TRUCKS ROLLED
• past, shaking the earth and exhaling clouds of blue
headache smoke. Was it possible that his Princeton placard did
more harm than good? He had in fact given up, counted his
money for the third time, and resolved to ride the bus and
waive eating; had even picked up telescope but not, fortunately, Val-Pak, which supported the placard, when a bottle-
green Chevrolet, an old '58 Junebug, passed and hesitated, the
driver's foot lifting and the carburetor sucking wind, speeded
up and hesitated again. As the engineer watched politely lest
he presume upon fortune, the Chevrolet pulled off the highway and sat interestingly on the shoulder a good hundred
yards to the south. At last it came, the sign, a hand beckoned
to him importunately and in a single swoop he caught up Val-
Pak and telescope and left placard behind.

Already, even as he stooped, smiling, to stow his gear
through the back door, which had been opened for him, he
had registered his benefactor without quite looking at him.
The driver was a light-colored high-stomached Negro dressed
in a good brown suit, no doubt a preacher or a teacher. Now
sitting beside him and taking note of the other's civil bald
bun-shaped head, of the sharp knees and thin ankles clad in
socks-with-clocks, he was sure of it: here was the sort to hold
converse at a lofty level with instant and prodigious agreement
on all subjects. He would belong to a committee on Religion
and Mental Health.

As it turned out, the driver spoke not of religion or mental
health but of Princeton and Einstein. The placard *had* worked.

97

"There was a quality of simplicity about him," said the driver, turning his head and not his eyes sociably toward his passenger, and launched at once into his own pet theory. It was his conviction that there was a balance in nature which was upset by man's attempt to improve upon it.

The engineer agreed and, casting his eye about the ruinous New Jersey flats, cited an article he had read about rivers in this very neighborhood which fairly foamed with detergents and chemical wastes.

"No no," said the driver excitedly. He explained that he was not speaking of ordinary pollution but of a far more fundamental principle. Rather was it his conviction that man's very best efforts to improve his environment, by air-conditioning and even by landscaping, upset a fundamental law which it took millions of years to evolve. "You take your modern office building, as tastefully done as you please. What does it do to a man to uproot him from the earth? There is the cause of your violence!"

"Yes," said the sentient engineer, frowning thoughtfully. Something was amiss here. He couldn't quite get hold of this bird. Something was out of kilter. It was his speech, for one thing. The driver did not speak as one might expect him to, with a certain relish and a hearkening to his own periods, as many educated Negroes speak. No, his speech was rapid and slurred, for all the world like a shaky white man's.

Obligingly, however, the engineer, who had become giddy from hunger and his long wait, set forth his own ideas on the subject of good environments and bad environments—without mentioning the noxious particles.

"Yes!" cried the driver in his damped reedy voice. He was tiring and excited and driving badly. The passenger became nervous. If only he would ask me to drive, he groaned, as the Chevy nearly ran under a great Fruehauf trailer. "That's your reaction to artificial environments in general! Wonderful! Don't you see how it dovetails?"

The engineer nodded reluctantly. He did not see. Back-to-nature was the last thing he had in mind. "Except—ahem—" said he, feeling his own voice go a bit reedy. "Except I would suspect that even if one picked out the most natural surroundings he might carry his own deprivation with him."

"Capital," cried the driver and smote the steering wheel.

The engineer could all but feel the broad plastic knurls between his knuckles. I could make this old Junebug take off, he thought. But the driver was slowing down again, rowboating badly as he did so.

"Now isn't this something," he said. "Here we are, total strangers, talking like this—" He was fairly jumping out of his skin in his nervous elation.

They passed an abandoned miniature golf links, the ancient kind with asbestos greens and gutter pipes which squirt out the ball. But no sooner had they entered the countryside of middle Jersey than the driver pulled off the highway and stopped. The hitchhiker sat as pleasant as ever, hands on knees, nodding slightly, but inwardly dismayed.

"Do you mind if I ask a question," said the driver, swinging over a sharp, well-clad knee.

"Why, no."

"I like to know what a man's philosophy is and I want to tell you mine."

Uh-oh, thought the engineer gloomily. After five years of New York and Central Park and the Y.M.C.A., he had learned to be wary of philosophers.

With his Masonic ring winking fraternally, the dignified colored man leaned several degrees nearer. "I have a little confession to make to you."

"Certainly," said the courteous engineer, cocking a weather eye at his surroundings. All around them stretched a gloomy cattail swamp which smelled like a crankcase and from which arose singing clouds of mosquitoes. A steady stream of Fruehauf tractor-trailers rumbled past, each with a *no-rider* sign on the windshield.

"I'm not what you think I am," the driver shouted above the uproar.

"You're not," said the pleasant, forward-facing engineer.

"What do you think I am? Tell me honestly."

"Um. I'd guess you were a minister or perhaps a professor."

"What *race*?"

"Why, um, colored."

"Look at this."

To the hitchhiker's astonishment, the driver shucked off his coat and pushed a jeweled cuff up a skinny arm.

"Ah," said the engineer, nodding politely, though he couldn't see much in the gathering darkness.

"Well?"

"Sir?"

"Look at that patch."

"Then you're not—?"

"I'm not a Negro."

"Is that right?"

"My name is not Isham Washington."

"No?"

"It's Forney Aiken."

"Is that so," said the interested engineer. He could tell that the other expected him to be surprised, but it was not in him to be surprised because it was no more surprising to him when things did not fall out as they were supposed to than when they did.

"Does that name ring a bell?"

"It does sound familiar," said the engineer truthfully, since his legions of *déjà vus* made everything sound familiar.

"Do you remember a picture story that appeared in July '51 *Redbook* called 'Death on the Expressway'?"

"I'm not sure."

"It was reprinted by the National Safety Council, ten million copies."

"As a matter of fact, I think I do—"

"Do you remember the fellow who interviewed Jafsie Condon in the cemetery?"

"Who?"

"Or the article in *Liberty*: 'I Saw Vic Genovese'? For forty-eight hours I was the only man alive in contact with both the F.B.I. and Vic Genovese."

"You're Forney Aiken the—"

"The photographer."

"Yes, I think I do," said the engineer, nodding but still wary. This fellow could still be a philosopher. "Anyhow I certainly do appreciate the ride." The singing hordes of mosquitoes were coming ever nearer. He wished Forney would get going.

"Forney," cried the other, holding out a hand.

"Will. Will Barrett."

The green Chevrolet resumed its journey, taking its place shakily among the Fruehauf tractors. Breathing a sigh of relief, the engineer spoke of his own small efforts in photography and took from his wallet a color snapshot of the peregrine falcon, his best.

"Tremendous," cried the photographer, once again beside

himself with delight at having fallen in with such a pleasant and ingenious young man. In return he showed his passenger a tiny candid camera concealed under his necktie whose lens looked like the jewel of a tie clasp.

It, the candid camera, was essential to his present assignment. The photographer, it turned out, was setting forth on an expedition this very afternoon, the first he had undertaken in quite awhile. It was something of a comeback, the engineer surmised. He had the shaky voice and the fitful enthusiasms of a man freshly sober.

The nature of his new project accounted for his extraordinary disguise. He wished to do a series on behind-the-scene life of the Negro. The idea had come to him in the middle of the night: why not *be* a Negro? To make a long story short, he had persuaded a dermatologist friend to administer an alkaloid which simulates the deposit of melanin in the skin, with the difference that the darkening effect could be neutralized by a topical cream. Therefore the white patch on his forearm. To complete the disguise, he had provided himself with the personal papers of one Isham Washington, an agent for a burial insurance firm in Pittsburgh.

This very afternoon he had left the office of his agent in New York, tonight would stop off at his house in Bucks County, and tomorrow would head south, under the "cotton curtain," as he expressed it.

The pseudo-Negro was even more delighted to discover that his passenger was something of an expert on American speech. "You were my first test and I passed it, and you a Southerner."

"Well, not quite," replied the tactful engineer. He explained that for one thing you don't say in*sur*-ance but *in*-surance or rather *in*-shaunce.

"Oh, this is marvelous," said the pseudo-Negro, nearly running under a Borden tanker.

You don't say that either, *mah*velous, thought the engineer, but let it go.

"What do you think of the title 'No Man an Island'?"

"Very good."

Tomorrow, the pseudo-Negro explained, he planned to stop in Philadelphia and pick up Mort Prince, the writer, who planned to come with him and do the text.

"But hold on," exclaimed the driver, smacking the steering wheel again. "How stupid can you get."

For the third time in a month the engineer was offered a job. "Why didn't I think of it before! Why don't you come with us? You know the country and you could do the driving. I'm a lousy driver." He was. His driving was like his talking. He was alert and chipper and terrified. "Do you drive?"

"Yes sir."

But the engineer declined. His services were already engaged, he explained, by a family who was employing him as tutor-companion to their son.

"Ten dollars a day plus keep."

"No sir. I really can't."

"Plus a piece of the royalties."

"I certainly appreciate it."

"You know Mort?"

"Well, I've heard of him and read some of his books."

"You know, it was Mort and I who first hit on the idea of the Writers' and Actors' League for Social Morality."

The engineer nodded agreeably. "I can certainly understand it, considering the number of dirty books published nowadays. As for the personal lives of the actors and actresses—"

The pseudo-Negro looked at him twice. "Oh-*ho*. Very good! Very ironical! I like that. You're quite a character, Barrett."

"Yes sir."

"Joking aside, though, it was our idea to form the first folk theater to travel through the South. Last summer it played in over a hundred towns. Where are you from—I bet it played there."

The engineer told him.

"My God." The pseudo-Negro ran off the road in his excitement. The hitchhiker put a discreet hand on the wheel until the Chevy was under control. "That's where we're having our festival this fall. Some of the biggest names in Hollywood and Broadway are coming down. What it is, is like the old morality plays in the Middle Ages."

"Yes sir."

"Is that where you're from?"

"Yes sir."

"Then you've got to come with us."

The engineer managed to decline, but in the end he agreed

to drive the other as far as Virginia and the "cotton curtain." When they stopped the second time to change drivers, he was glad enough to add the two ten-dollar bills, which the pseudo-Negro made a great show of paying him in advance, to his flattened wallet and to sprint around and hop into the driver's seat.

2. UNDER THE ENGINEER'S STEADY HAND, THE CHEVROlet fairly sailed down US 1. In short order it turned onto a great new westering turnpike and swept like a bird across the Delaware River not far from the spot where General Washington crossed nearly two hundred years ago.

Forney Aiken's stone cottage was also standing at the time of the crossing. Some years ago, he told the engineer, he and his wife had left New York and beat a more or less disorderly retreat to Bucks County. She was an actor's agent and had to commute. He was trying to quit drinking and thought it might help to live in the country and do chores, perhaps even farm. When farming didn't work, he took to making things, the sort of articles, firkins and sisal tote bags, which are advertised in home magazines. But this was not as simple as it looked either. There was more to it than designing an ad for a magazine. You have to have your wholesale outlet.

There were some people sitting around a lighted pool in an orchard when they arrived. The travelers skirted them in a somewhat ambiguous fashion, not quite ignoring them and not quite stopping to speak but catching a few introductions on the fly, so to speak. Mrs. Aiken looked after them with an expression which gave the engineer to understand that the photographer often showed up with strangers and skirted the pool. Even though it was dark, the photographer insisted on showing the engineer the orchard and barn. It was a pity because the engineer recognized one of the guests, a nameless but familiar actor who took the part of a gentle, wise doctor on the daytime serial which it was his habit to watch for a few minutes after lunch in the Y. But he must be shown on to the barn instead, which was stacked to the rafters with cedar firkins, thousands of them. For some eighteen months the barn had served as a firkin factory. But of the eight or nine thousand manufactured, only five hundred had been sold. "Take your pick," his host urged him, and the engineer was glad enough to do so, having a liking for well-wrought wooden things. He chose a stout two-gallon firkin of red-and-white cedar bound in copper and fitted with a top. It would be a good thing to carry country butter in or well water or just to sit on between rides.

Later he did meet the poolside group. The actor was a cheerful fellow, not at all like the sad doctor he played, even though his face had fallen into a habitual careworn expression after years in the part. But he had a thick brown merry body and a good pelt on his chest, upon which he rested his highball. No one paid any attention to Forney's disguise. They treated him with the tender apocalyptic cordiality and the many warm hugs of show-business people. Though he knew nothing about show biz, the sentient engineer had no trouble translating their tender regard for their host. It clearly signified: Forney, you're dead, done for, that's why we love you. Forney was as abrupt with them as they were tender with him. He had the manner of one going about his business. To the others, it seemed to the sentient engineer, the expedition was "something Forney was doing" and something therefore to be treated with a mournful and inattentive sympathy which already discounted failure. A rangy forty-five-year-old couple with muscular forty-five-year-old calves, burnt black as Indians, found the engineer and asked him who he was. When he told them he came with Forney, they went deaf and fond. "Forney's got more talent in his little finger than anybody here," cried the man both privately and loudly, like a proverb, and hurried away.

Though he had not eaten or slept since the day before, he drank two drinks and went swimming. Soon he was treading water in the deep dark end of the pool with Forney's daughter, the only other young person present. Everyone called her Muzh or Moosh. She had the fitful and antic manner of one used to the company of her elders. In no time the two of them had their heads together, snuffling the water like seals. It was understood between them that they were being the young folk. Muzh had just returned from her college year abroad. Her shoulders were strong and sloping from bicycling around youth hostels. In the clear yellow water her strong legs bent like pants. She told him about the guests. Her way of speaking was rapid and confidential as if they had left off only a short time earlier. She rattled off some recent history. "Coop over there—" she spoke into the lambent water, nodding toward a distinguished silver-haired gent, "—is just out of the Doylestown jail, where he served six months for sodomy, though Fra says sodomy rates two to ten." Who was Fra? (As usual, strangers expected him to know their, the strangers', friends.) And had she, for a fact, said sodomy? He wrung out his ear. Unfortunately she was at that moment on his deaf side.

She dawdled toward him, working the water to and fro through the sluice of her shoulder. On she went about the guests in her rapid, cataloguing voice, bent toward him, the waterline at his mouth, while he grew even fainter with hunger and more agitated. As her knees brushed against his and she spoke of having transcended Western values, he seized her through the thick parts, fell upon her as much from weakness as desire, fainted upon her, the fine brown berry of a girl she was. "Zut alors," she cried softly, and now perfunctorily, unsurprised, keeping herself flexed and bent away from him, she asked him about the transvaluation of values. "I couldn't say," he replied, disappointed. He had heard enough about values from Dr. Gamow. "No, really," she said. "I am in something of a value crisis and so I'm deeply concerned. What can we do?" "Let's go over yonder," he replied, fainting with hunger and desire, and nodded to the dark polygon of the barn. "Zut," she cried, but idly, and swam away. As he stood slack in the water, both lustful and shrunken with cold, she made forays in the water around him, flexing like a porpoise, came under him in the shallows, put him astride and unhorsed him in bluff youth-hostel style. "See you later," she said at last and went away, but how said she it?

Coming to himself all at once, he socked himself in the head. Swine, said he, staggering about in the shallows, white trash. Here you are in love with a certain person and bound south as a gentleman like Rooney Lee after a sojourn in the North, and at it again: pressing against girls like a horny dolphin and abusing your host besides. No more humbuggery! Leaping from the pool, he ran to the room Forney had shown him and, starved or not, threw a hundred combination punches and did thirty minutes of violent isomorphics until he dripped with sweat, took an ice-cold shower and read two pages of *Living*. Saints contemplated God to be rid of concupiscence;

he turned to money. He returned to the pool, exhausted, ravenous, but in his right mind.

"I apologize," he told Muzh formally as they stood in line for cold cuts. "As a matter of fact I've been, ahem, in something of a value crisis myself and have not eaten or slept in quite awhile. I apologize for being forward with you."

"Good God," said Muzh, brushing against him with several dorsal surfaces. "Don't," she whispered.

"Don't what?"

She didn't answer.

Damn, thought he, and had to thrust his hand through his pocket to keep his knee from leaping.

He ate three helpings of turkey and ham and rye bread and sat slack and heavy with his blood singing in his ears. Fortunately his host was brimming with plans for the morrow and put him to work after supper toting paraphernalia, cameras and insurance manuals, to the Chevrolet. Later he showed him the house.

"You're going to like Mort Prince. He's our kind of folks." They had reached the cellar, which the engineer looked at and sniffed with interest because at home the ground was too low for cellars and he'd never seen one before. "He's a sweet guy," said Forney.

"Yes sir."

"Have you read his stuff?"

"A couple of novels quite a while ago."

"You haven't read *Love*?"

"His latest? No."

"I'll get you a copy tonight."

"Thank you, but I'm very sleepy. I think I'll go to bed."

Forney came closer. "You know what that guy told me with a straight face. I asked him what this book was going to be about and he said quite seriously: it was about —ing. And in a sense it is!" They were by now back at poolside and within earshot of others, including Muzh. It made the engineer nervous. "But it is a beautiful piece of work and about as pornographic as Chaucer. Indeed it is deeply religious. I'll get you a copy."

The engineer groaned. What the devil does he mean telling me it's about —ing? Is —ing a joking matter? Am I to understand I am free to—his daughter? Or do we speak of —ing man to man, jokingly, literarily, with no thought of —ing anyone in the vicinity? His radar boggled.

"It is essentially a religious book, in the sense of being a yea-saying rather than a nay-saying," Forney went on. "Mort has one simple credo: saying Yes to Life wherever it is found."

"Yes sir," said the engineer, rising unsteadily. "I think I'll go to bed."

But no sooner had he fallen into the four-poster than a knock came at the door. It was Muzh in a shorty nightgown delivering *Love*. "You talk about randy," said she and smote her brow. "Sheesh!"

"Thank you," said the engineer, laughing heartily, and when she had left went reeling about the room like Rooney Lee after the battle of Seven Days. What saved him in the end was not only Southern chivalry but Yankee good sense. Muzh he saw all at once and belatedly, as she might have been seen by her classmates, as a horsy, good-natured, sisterly sort. She was, as they say in the North, a good kid. And so it was permitted him to leave her alone and to excuse himself. What a relief. He wiped his brow.

Worse luck, though, sleep deserted him, left him half dead from lack of it and wide awake. There was nothing to do but read *Love*. He read it straight through, finishing at three o'clock.

Love was about orgasms, good and bad, some forty-six. But it ended, as Forney had said, on a religious note. "And so I humbly ask of life," said the hero to his last partner with whose assistance he had managed to coincide with his best expectations, "that it grant us the only salvation, that of one human being discovering himself through another and through the miracle of love."

The poor engineer arose, faint with fatigue, and threw a few final combination punches to clear his head. But when he got back in bed he found himself lying at attention, his feet sticking up, his left leg tending to rise of itself. There was nothing to do but swallow two of Dr. Gamow's spansules, which induced sleep only indirectly by inhibiting the cortical influence on the midbrain—even though he knew that his sense of time and place would suffer in consequence. Though he might not know where he was tomorrow or what year it was, at least he'd feel better than this.

At any rate he went fast asleep and woke in midmorning, somewhat disoriented but feeling quite cheerful and well.

3. EARLY AFTERNOON FOUND HIM DRIVING LIKE A CAT. The bottle-green Chevrolet went roaring and banking around the many ramps and interchanges of eastern Pennsylvania. The pseudo-Negro sat beside him as alert and jumpy as ever. Presently they left the expressway and went among the sooty little hill towns. *Déjà vus* stole alongside and beckoned at the corner of his eye. How familiar were these steep streets and old 1937 brick-and-limestone high schools and the sooty monkey Pullman smell. Surely I attended that very one, he told himself, where I recall taking mechanical drawing in the basement. Two girls in summer school sat on the school steps, dumb pretty Pennsylvania girls. He waved. They waved back. Oh girls I love you. Don't let anybody mess with you till I get back because I've been here before. Where is this place? "Where is this?" he asked so abruptly that the pseudo-Negro jumped a good inch.

The pseudo-Negro kept harping on Mort Prince, whom they were presently to pick up. The writer, it seemed, had astonished his friends by moving to Levittown. He had inherited the house from an aunt and, instead of selling it, had sold his farm in Connecticut and moved in more or less, as the pseudo-Negro expressed it, for the simple heck of it. "Imagine going from Fiesole to Levittown," he said, shaking his head. The engineer could very well imagine it.

He began to look forward to meeting Mort Prince. Some years ago he had read two of his novels and remembered them perfectly—he could remember perfectly every detail of a book he had read ten years ago or a conversation with his father fifteen years ago; it was the day before yesterday that gave him trouble. After a war novel which made him famous, Mort Prince wrote a novel about a young veteran who becomes disillusioned with the United States and goes to Italy in quest of his own identity. It is in Europe that he discovers he is an American after all. The book ended on a hopeful note. Mark comes home to visit his dying father, who is a judge in Vermont. The judge is a Yankee in the old style, a man of granite integrity. Now he too, Mark, knows who he is, what he must do, and that all men are his brothers. In the last chapter he climbs High Tor overlooking the valley. If a man does nothing else in life, said Mark to himself, he can at least tell one other man (that all men are brothers) and he another and he in turn another until at last amid the hatred and the dying all men shall one day hear and hearing understand and understanding believe. Mark had come home. Arising from High Tor, he picked up his coat and turned his face to the city.

After his first return to the United States, the pseudo-Negro was saying, Mort Prince had married a hometown girl and moved to Connecticut. It was at this time, as the engineer recalled it, that he had read *The Farther Journey*, a novel about a writer who lives in Connecticut and enters into a sexual relationship with a housewife next door, not as a conventional adultery, for he was not even attracted to her, but rather as the exercise of that last and inalienable possession of the individual in a sick society, freedom. In the words of one reviewer, it was "the most nearly absolutely gratuitous act since Lafcadio pushed Fleurissoire out of the railway carriage in *Les Caves du Vatican*."

Following his divorce and his latest trip to Italy the writer, according to the pseudo-Negro, had felt the strongest compulsion to return to the United States, seek out the most commonplace environment, and there, like Descartes among the Burghers of Amsterdam, descend within himself and write the first real war novel, an absolutely unvarnished account of one day's action of one infantry platoon. When his aunt died and left him a house, he took off from Fiesole by the first plane.

The attentive engineer, at this moment skillfully piloting the green Chevrolet into the pleasant maze of Levittown, understood perfectly. If his aunt had left him such a house, he'd have moved in too and settled down in perfect contentment.

They entered Levittown. The freshly sprinkled lawns sparkled in the sunlight, lawns as beautiful as Atlanta lawns but less spectral and Druidic. Chipper little Swiss swales they were and no Negroes to cut the grass but rather Mr. Gallagher and Mr. Shean cranking up their Toros and afterward wisecracking over the fence. Here, he reckoned, housewives ran into each other's kitchens to borrow a cup of Duz. Not a bad life! Really he would like it very much. He could live here cheerfully as a Swiss with never a care for the morrow. But a certain someone was already in Old Virginny by now and his heart pressed south.

But even as they began to circle the blocks and search for house numbers, the sentient engineer began to detect unpleasant radiations. While the pseudo-Negro gabbled away and noticed nothing, it struck the engineer that more people than one might expect were standing about on their lawns and sidewalks. Indeed he could swear that some of them were shooting hostile glances in the direction of the Chevrolet! Recollecting Dr. Gamow's strong hints about certain delusions of persecution, he tried to pay no attention. But they were at it again! One group of householders in particular he noticed and one man in particular, a burly fellow with a small mustache who wore a furry alpine hat which was too small for him.

"What number did you say it was?" he asked the pseudo-Negro.

"One forty-two."

"Then here it is," said the engineer, circling the block a second time and pulling up at the same group of householders. He followed the pseudo-Negro up the walk, the latter as garrulous and shaky as ever and noticing nothing, his nerve ends firing at the slightest breeze, even nodding to the householders on the next lawn, whom he fancied to be well-wishers of some sort. They were not well-wishers. They stood about silently, hands in pockets, and kicking the turf. Next to the burly alpiner the engineer spied trouble itself: a thin fierce-eyed damp-skinned woman whose hair was done up in plastic reels, a regular La Pasionaria of the suburbs. He ventured another look. Beyond a doubt, she was glaring straight at him, the engineer!

Mort Prince met them in the deep-set cathedral door, beer in hand, a pleasant slightish fellow with twirling black hair which flew away in a banner of not absolutely serious rebellion. He wore a black leather wristlet and, as he talked, performed a few covert isometrics on the beer can. The engineer liked him at once, perceiving that he was not the mighty fornicator of his novels but a perky little bull-shooter of a certain style, the sort who stands in the kitchen during parties, suspended from himself so-to-speak, beer can in hand and matter forming at the corner of his mouth, all the while spieling off some very good stuff and very funny. One would like to get him going (and the engineer was just the one).

One glance past him into the house and he knew also how it stood with the house and how the writer lived in it. Their voices echoed on bare parquet floors. There was no furniture except a plastic dinette and an isomorphic bar in a doorway. So that was how he did it, standing clear of walls suspended within himself and disdaining chairs because chairs were for sitting and therefore cancelled themselves.

He shook hands with the engineer with a strong wiry grip, pronating his elbow.

"This is the guy that's going with us," said the pseudo-Negro, linking arms with them. "He knows everybody down there and the ones he doesn't know he's kin to."

"No," said the engineer, frowning and blushing.

"You from down South," asked Mort Prince, squeezing the beer can and not quite looking at him.

"Yes." Though the pseudo-Negro had led him to believe that Mort Prince would welcome him with open arms, he couldn't help noticing that the writer wore an indifferent, if not unfriendly, expression.

"Tell him where you're from."

The engineer told him.

But Mort Prince seemed abstracted and gloomy and did not respond. He said nothing and went back to pressing the beer can.

"That's where the festival is," said the pseudo-Negro, giving the writer several meaningful nudges.

"No, I'm sorry," said the engineer, looking at his watch. He was anxious to be on his way. He didn't like the look of things. Through the open doorway—Mort had not quite invited them in and they were standing barely beyond the sill—the engineer noticed that the householders were closer. Yes, beyond a doubt they were bearing down upon Mort Prince's house.

"I really appreciate it but as I told Mr. Aiken—" began the engineer, already nodding to the new arrivals to prepare Mort Prince and the pseudo-Negro—but it was too late.

"Hey, you," called the burly man in the alpine hat, pointing with his chin and resting his hands lightly on his hips.

The engineer looked at him twice. Beyond any question, the stranger was addressing him. His heart gave a single dread leap. Adrenalin erected his hair roots, could it have come at last, a simple fight, with the issue clear beyond peradventure? "Are you speaking to me?"

"You from Haddon Heights?"

"Sir?" The engineer cupped a hand to his ear. The burly man's T-shirt had the legend *Deep Six* printed on it. No doubt he belonged to a bowling league. He reminded the engineer of the fellows he used to see around bowling alleys in Long Island City.

"You heard me."

"Sir, I don't believe I like your tone," said the engineer, advancing a step with his good ear put forward. Perhaps the time had come again when you could be insulted, hear it aright, and have it out then and there as his grandfather used to have it out. But there must be no mistake. "You were speaking to me?" he asked again, straining every nerve to hear, for nothing is worse than being an honorable deaf man who can't be certain he is insulted.

The alpiner turned to Mort Prince. "Mae here sawr him in Haddon Heights. Her brother-in-law lives in Haddonfield."

"Haddon Heights? Haddonfield? I've never heard of either place," said the bemused engineer. "In any case I don't care for this fellow's tone." It had happened again, he knew, he had been mistaken for someone else.

The next thing he knew, another man came crowding in, a fair-skinned oldish man with a gray crew cut and tabs on his elbows like Jiggs.

"He's a Jersey agent, Mr. Prince," said the newcomer.

"What's all this about?" asked the writer, feeling his wristlet uneasily. The engineer perceived that the other set great store by getting along with his neighbors—like Descartes—and so was in a quandary.

"That's a fact, Mr. Prince," said the burly man, who had decided to take a neighborly tone toward the writer. "That's the way they do it, they come over here from Jersey like him and his friend there and they ride around the block slow like them, looking. You saw them! But we're not worried about you, Mr. Prince. I was just telling Whitey here that Mr. Prince wasn't about to sell his house."

"I'm not a Jersey agent, whatever that is," said the engineer, noticing that the pseudo-Negro was smiling a brilliant nervous rueful smile and was opening his hands first to one side and then the other.

"Fellows," the pseudo-Negro appealed to all parties, calling heaven to witness the follies and misunderstandings of men. "This is ridiculous," he cried, opening his hands, "believe me."

The engineer flushed angrily. "And furthermore I've never heard of Haddon Heights," he told them. Yet strive as he might to keep his anger pure and honorable, it was no use. The alpiner had detached himself somewhat and stood apart with an ironic expression like a man who has been in a wreck and is embarrassed by passers-by. And the engineer, up to his old tricks despite himself, began to tune him in to see how it stood with him. Damnation, he swore to himself. To make matters worse, his hay fever had returned, his nose swelled up and began to run, and he had left his handkerchiefs in the firkin. Rage leaked away.

But he had not reckoned with the woman.

"Faggot!" she cried, rushing past Jiggs and thrusting her face within inches of the engineer's. She wore a black bolero jacket over her bowling-league skirt. Her bare arms were moist and muscular like a man's.

"Faggot?" repeated the puzzled engineer, feeling his nose.

"You work for Oscar Fava, don't you?" she asked, both malignant and triumphant.

"I do not." He glanced at her uneasily. What to do with a maniac of a woman?

"As a matter of fact, I do have the place for sale," said Mort Prince, who had decided to be irritated with his neighbors after all.

"Did you sign any papers?" asked the burly man, his good nature beginning to stick in his throat.

"What is it to you?"

"Could I see the papers, Mr. Prince?" He pronounced it päpers.

"They can't break a block without you let them," said Jiggs, his face beginning to mottle Irish red and white.

"Get the hell out of my house," said Mort Prince, although the householders had not crossed the threshold. Everyone still stood in the cathedral doorway.

"Fink," said the woman, who had not taken her eyes from the engineer's face. As he watched incredulously, she balled up her fist like a man, thumb out of the way, and cocked it back.

"Hold on," said the engineer—she could hit him! And at the same moment from the corner of his eye he saw the burly man advance upon the writer, hand outstretched, perhaps for the "papers," perhaps to shake hands, but advancing nevertheless. Two other householders, he noticed for the first time, were standing in the background, speaking in low tones and swinging their arms briskly in the manner of bystanders.

"Excuse me," said the engineer to the woman, squeezing past her as if she were an irate shopper in Macy's basement. On the way he brushed against Jiggs, who immediately fell back and began to crouch and wave him in with his fingertips.

"Come on, come on," said Jiggs.

But it was the pseudo-Negro who caught his attention. He had come between the engineer and Jiggs and shook his head sadly and good-naturedly. "Hold on, fellows," he said, undoing his cuff link. "I'm afraid there's been a rather pathetic misunderstanding here—a sad commentary in fact on the fraility of us all. Fellows—"

"No," cried the engineer angrily. "Don't roll up your sleeve."

"Go ahead and roll up your sleeve," cried Jiggs, misunderstanding, dancing ominously and now waving the pseudo-Negro into him.

The engineer groaned. "No. I—" he began, taking another step toward the grinning alpiner. Here was the villain!

But in that instant, even as he was passing the woman, whom he had forgotten, she drew back her fist clear to her earlobe and, unleashing a straight whistling blow, struck the engineer on the fleshy part of his nose, which was already swollen and tender from hay fever.

Oh, hideous exploding humiliating goddamnable nose pain, the thump-thud of woe itself. Oh, ye bastards all together. "Come here," he thought he heard himself say as he struggled to get at the alpiner—did he hit him?—but the next thing he knew he was sitting on the front steps enveloped by the dreadful cordiality of misunderstandings cleared away, of debits to be balanced. The bastards, friends and foe, were all apologizing to each other. As he held his nose, he saw the pseudo-Negro rolling his sleeve down. He had shown them his white patch.

Only Mort Prince was still angry. "That's not the point," he was saying furiously to the householders, who, the engineer perceived instantly, were anxious for him to score his point. They were allowing him his anger. Everyone felt bad. The engineer groaned.

"I thought they were blockbusters, for Christ's sake," Jiggs was telling a newcomer. "They been here," he assured Mort Prince. "And they come from Jersey."

"I just want to make it damn clear I'm selling to anyone I please, regardless of race, creed, or national origin."

"Me too! That's just what I was telling Lou here."

"And hear this," said the writer, massaging his wristlet grimly. "If there is any one thing that pisses me off, its bigotry."

"You're right," cried Jiggs. "Mr. Prince, if Mae and I didn't have our savings in our house—listen, let me tell you!" But though everyone listened, he fell silent.

"We keep the lawr, Mr. Prince," said the alpiner earnestly. Then, seeing a chance to put a good face on the whole affair, he laughed and pointed his chin toward the engineer. "Tiger over there though, he was coming for me. Did you see him? I'm telling you, he was coming and I was getting out of his way. Tiger." Hand outstretched, he crossed to the engineer.

The engineer held his nose and looked at the hand. He had had enough of the whole crew.

"You not from Jersey, fella?" asked the alpiner, for some reason taking off his hat. "Mae here said—now isn't that something!" He called upon the neighborhood to witness the human comedy.

The engineer did not answer.

"You don't work for Oscar Fava?" cried the tall woman, meaning the question for the engineer, but not quite bringing herself to look at him. "You know Fava's real estate over there, next to Pik-a-Pak," she asked Jiggs and when he nodded she offered it to the engineer as a kind of confirmation, perhaps even an apology. "Over in Haddon Heights."

"I thought it was in Haddonfield," said Jiggs. They argued the point as another earnest of their good faith. "You never been over to Tammy Lanes in Haddonfield?" Jiggs asked him.

The engineer shook his head.

"Wasn't that Oscar Fava come over last night?" Jiggs asked Mae.

"And *he* was with him," said the woman. "Him or his twin brother."

"You know what I wish he would do," the alpiner told the other householders, presuming to speak of the engineer fondly—a true character was he, this engineer, another five minutes and they'd call him Rocky. "I wish he'd come on down to Tammy with us tonight, just to bug Oscar." Again he held out a hand to the engineer. "Come on down just for laughs."

"No, thank you," said the latter gloomily. He rose. "I've got to be on my way." He looked around for the pseudo-

Negro, who had vanished. Most of all he wanted to get away from Mort Prince, who was still trying to hit upon some way to use his anger, a special delayed Hemingway writer's sort of anger. It was embarrassing. This was the age of embarrassment, thought the engineer, of unspendable rage. Who to hit? No one. Mort Prince took the engineer by the arm and pulled him inside. The best Mort could do was slam the door on the householders, catching Jiggs in midsentence:

"Any time any of youse want to come down—"

Reviving now, the writer opened a fresh beer and hung suspended from himself, free and clear of the refrigerator, while he told them: "I've got it, by God. I'm going to call up this guy Oscar Fava and let him sell it. Stick around for laughs," he told the engineer.

"No, thanks," said the engineer, who was sick of them and their laughs.

Fetching his firkin, in which he had packed his medicines, he took three Chlortrimeton tablets for his hay fever and rubbed his nose with an ice cube.

"Bill," said the pseudo-Negro earnestly, "if I can't persuade you to make the tour with us, at least promise me you'll come as far as Virginia."

"No, thanks," said the engineer, politely now. "I've really got to be going. I'd be obliged if you'd take me to the bus station."

"Very well," said the pseudo-Negro, as formally as the other. Shaky as he was, he was as sentient as anyone. He knew there were times for staying and times for leaving, times for sitting and times for standing. He stood up.

"Perhaps it would be possible for us to meet you in your hometown later this summer," he said.

"Perhaps," said the engineer and picked up his firkin.

4. A WHITE MISTY MORNING IN NORTHERN VIRGINIA found a young man, pleasant of mien and moderately disoriented, dressed neatly and squatting on a stout cedar firkin beside a highway which ran between a white-oak swamp on one side and a foggy hill, flattened on top like a mesa, on the other. He sat on the firkin and counted his money several times, reviewed the contents of a notebook, and from time to time read a page or two from a small red volume. Then he unfolded an Esso map of Virginia and spread it out on an expensive case of blue leather. Opening the firkin, which was as cedarous and cool inside as a springhouse, he took out a round molding of sweet butter, a box of Ritz crackers, a plastic knife, and a quart of buttermilk. As he ate his breakfast he traced the red and blue lines on the map with his gold pencil.

Where could he have spent the night? Not even he was certain, but he must have spent it tolerably well because his Brooks Brothers shirt was still fresh, his Dacron suit unwrinkled, and his cheek smooth and fragrant with soap. Another fact may be pertinent. An hour or so earlier, a Mayflower van with two riders had turned off the highway onto the gravel road directly behind him and pulled up at a farmhouse nestled at the foot of the foggy hill. Mayflower vans, he had learned recently and already forgotten, are owned by their drivers, who usually drive them home after finishing a haul.

The sun came up and warmed his back. Sapsuckers began yammering in the swamp. He gazed at the network of red and blue lines and with his pencil circled a tiny pair of crossed swords marking a battlefield. As best he could determine, his present location lay somewhere near Malvern Hill and the James River. No doubt he was correct, because he was experiencing the interior dislocations which always afflicted him on old battlegrounds. His nose was better and he could smell. He sniffed the morning. It was white and dim and faraway as Brooklyn but it was a different sort of whiteness and dimness. Up yonder was a faraway Lapland sort of dimness, a public wheylike sunlight, where solitary youths carrying violin cases wait at bus stops. Here the dimness was private and one's own. He may not have been here before but it seemed to him that he had. Perhaps it was the place of his father's childhood and he had heard about it. From the corner of his eye he took note of the green confettilike plant which floated on the black water, of the fluted trunks and bald red knees of the cypress, of the first fall specklings of the tupelo gums.

He studied his map. He reckoned he could not be more than twenty miles from Richmond. Richmond. Yes, had he not passed through it last night? As he ate Ritz crackers and sweet butter, he imagined how Richmond might be today if the war had ended differently. Perhaps Main Street would be the Wall Street of the South, and Broad might vie with New Orleans for opera and theater. Here in the White Oak Swamp might be located the great Lee-Randolph complex, bigger than GM and making better cars (the Lee surpassing both Lincoln and Cadillac, the Lil' Reb outselling even Volkswagens). Richmond would have five million souls by now, William and Mary be as good as Harvard and less subverted. In Chattanooga and Mobile there would be talk of the "tough cynical Richmonders," the Berliners of the hemisphere.

When he finished his breakfast, he took a steel mirror from his Val-Pak and examined his nose in the morning sunlight. It was within bounds, though still lilac inside. His face reassured him. It was all of a piece, an equable lower-South Episcopal face. He began to feel better and, standing up, threw a few combinations at the rising sun. My name is Williston Bibb Barrett, he said aloud, consulting his wallet to make sure, and I am returning to the South to seek my fortune and restore the good name of my family, perhaps even recover Hampton plantation from the canebrakes and live out my days as a just man and little father to the faithful Negroes working in the fields. Moreover, I am in love with a certain someone. Or I shall marry me a wife and live me a life in the lovely green environs of Atlanta or Memphis or even Birmingham, which, despite its bad name, is known to have lovely people.

Hitchhiking in Virginia was better than New Jersey; within half an hour he had been picked up and now went roaring down historic old US 60 in a noble black Buick, a venerable four-holer. His father used to drive one and it summoned up many a *déjà vu* to hear once again the old loose-meshed roaring runaway sound of the Dynaflow transmission. It was a carful of ladies, so crowded that he had to put his Val-Pak and firkin in the trunk. Rejoicing, he climbed in and held his telescope on his lap: what good fortune to be picked up by a bevy of Virginia noblewomen. Nor did he mind when they turned out to be Texans, golfers from a Fort Worth club, fortyish and firm as India rubber and fairly bursting their seersuckers. They had just played in a tournament at Burning Tree and were out for a good time sightseeing. They laughed all the way to Williamsburg. He too. Once he caught sight of himself in the sunshade mirror grinning like a forty-pounder. They told stories on each other, on one in particular, the lady on his left, a good-looking younger one who was subject to blushing.

"Grace settin' up there," said one lady in the back seat, "acting like she's crowded and can't stand it."

"She can stand it, hooo," said another and they all hooted with laughter.

Another one said: "I peep out of my door last night and here comes Grace tippy-toeing down the hall with this little bitty man and I say what is this: look like Grace got a little blister, the way she walking."

For some reason the word "blister" set them off again. It even seemed to the engineer to mean six different things. "Hooo, she got a little blister!" The most ordinary words and objects like zippers and golf tees brought on more hoots and jabs in the ribs. Although the engineer did not quite know what the joke was—it had something to do with the good-looking one sitting next to him—he couldn't help being tickled and in fact laughed like a maniac. By the time the old howling Dynaflow Buick reached Williamsburg, his sides ached.

Though he had planned to go into town and there collect his thoughts and begin his sleuthing, it turned out not to be necessary. As the Buick sailed past the Coach-and-Four Motel on the outskirts, he spotted the two vehicles and recognized both, though he had seen neither before: the Trav-L-Aire, glittering and humped up and practical, yet somehow airy and light on its four brand-new Goodyear jumbo treads; cheek to jowl with a squirrel-gray Cadillac which was mean and low and twenty feet long. He hollered to the driver but she wouldn't let him out. When at last she did stop and he asked them to wait until he could get his firkin from the trunk, they began to hoot again, positively rolling about on the seats. He had a six-block walk back to the motel.

There was nobody in sight but a pair of listless slothlike children worming over the playground equipment. He had time to take a good look at the Trav-L-Aire. She was all she might be, a nice balance of truck heaviness, steel and stout below and cabined aluminum lightness above. She had just the faintest and rightest quilted look, her metal skin tucked down by rivets like an airplane wing. Vents and sockets and knobs made discreet excrescences, some faired against the wind, others propped out to scoop the wind. The step was down and the back door ajar and he had a peep inside: the coziest little caboose imaginable, somehow larger inside than out, yet all compact of shelf, bunk, galley, and sink.

Now here surely is a good way to live nowadays, said he and sat down on the firkin: mobile yet at home, compacted and not linked up with the crumby carnival linkage of a trailer, in the world yet not of the world, sampling the particularities of place yet cabined off from the sadness of place, curtained away from the ghosts of Malvern Hill, peeping out at the doleful woods of Spotsylvania through the cheerful Plexiglas of Sheboygan.

"Hullo!"

It was Mr. Vaught. He had come out of his motel room, scratched his seat, shot his cuff, and, spying the engineer, hailed him over as if he were just the man he was looking for.

"Got dog, man," said the old man, cocking his head direfully. "So you thought better of it."

"Thought better of what?"

"You decided to come after all."

"Sir," said the engineer, blinking. Was this the plan all along, that he was to meet them here?

"You want to see something fine?"

"Yes sir."

Mr. Vaught unlocked the trunk of the Cadillac and showed him a vast cargo of food, Quaker jams, Shaker jellies, Virginia hams. He began to give an account of each package.

"Excuse me, sir," said the engineer, interrupting him.

"Yace."

"Excuse me but I can't help but think that explanations are in order. For my part I can say—"

"That's all right," cried the old man hastily. He was actually blushing. "I'm just tickled to death to have you aboard!"

"Thank you, sir. But I think we'd better clear this up." He heard himself speak without consulting his memory. His voice had a memory of its own. "My understanding was yall were going to pick me up. I waited for three hours."

"No," cried the old man and coming close seized him under the armpit and took him aside. "Take this apple jelly."

"Thank you."

"Son, look. If it was a question of money, why didn't you say so? I'll tell you this where I wouldn't just as to say tell most folks: I got more damn money than I know what to do with and if I don't give it to you the government's going to get it anyway."

"Money," said the engineer, screwing up an eye.

"Rita said she asked you to come with us and you refused."

"No sir," he said, remembering. "What she asked was whether I wanted to be employed by her or—"

"Naturally, when I didn't hear from you to the contrary, I assumed you didn't want the job."

"No sir!"

"Son, you know what we really thought? We thought you didn't want to come with either one of us but that you would be nice enough *to* come if we asked you, just to help us, and I wasn't going to do that. Look," cried the old man joyfully.

"What?"

"It's better this way!"

"How is that, sir?"

"Now we know where we stand. Now I believe you want to come with us."

"Yes sir, that is true," said the engineer dryly. "I desire now only to have the same assurance from you."

"What! Oh! By George," said the other, shooting his cuff and calling on the high heavens. "If you're not your daddy all over again."

"Yes sir," said the engineer gloomily, wondering if the old man was slipping away again like the white rabbit. But this time Mr. Vaught took out his buckeye wallet and counted out five $100 bills, like crisp suède, freshly pollinated from the mint, into the other's hand. "One month's salary in advance. Do we understand each other now?"

"Yes sir."

"I'll tell you what we're going to do."

"What's that?"

"Rita will drive us in the Cadillac. You and Jamie take that thing." He nodded toward the camper.

"All right, sir."

"Now you and Jamie get on down the road. We'll see you at home." He counted out two more bills. "Expenses."

"Do you mean you want us to leave now and—"

But before he could finish, the rest of the family came swarming out half a dozen doors and bore down upon him. His natural shyness was almost made up for by the pleasant sensation of reunion. Perhaps he belonged here after all!

"Look who's here!"—"What in the woerrld—!"—"Well I'll be damned—!" they cried.

The side of his face was also being looked at by a pair of roguish eyes.

"Look at him blush," cried Mrs. Vaught.

For some reason his being there, hands in pockets and eyes rolled up to the eyebrows, began to be funny. They were all laughing at him. All but Kitty. She came close and touched him but at the same time it was as if she couldn't stand the sight of him. She turned him roughly by the shoulder as if she was another boy.

"What happened to your *nose*?" she asked angrily. It was somehow shameful to her that a misfortune should have befallen his *nose*.

He waved a hand vaguely toward the north. "A white lady up in New Jersey—" he began.

"*What*," Kitty cried incredulously, curling her lip and calling the others to witness. "What happened?"

"A lady from Haddon Heights hit me on the nose."

The others laughed and the engineer too. Only Kitty went on curling her lip in the most sensual and angry way. Rita laughed but her eyes were wary. She was handsome!

Jamie stood a little above them, on the motel walk, grinning and shaking his head. He looked brown and fit but a bit sooty-eyed.

"Wait a minute, Kitty," said the engineer as the girl turned away.

"What now?"

"Hold on! Don't leave."

"All right, what?"

"It seems I have not been able to make myself understood," he told them all, "or at least to prevent misunderstandings. I want to be very certain that everybody understands me now."

"I told you he wanted to come with us," said Mrs. Vaught to her husband, her pince-nez flashing.

"In any case," said the engineer, "let me state my intentions once and for all, particularly with regard to Jamie and, ah, Kitty." He almost said Miss Kitty.

"My God," said Kitty, turning red as a beet. "What is the man talking about?" She besought Rita, who in turn was watching the engineer like a hawk, her eyes wary and fine.

"I want to make clear what apparently I failed to make clear in New York, that from the beginning I accepted Mr. Vaught's offer with great pleasure and that I shall be happy to go to school with Jamie or anywhere else he wants to go."

Kitty seemed both relieved and irritated. "That's why he

was fixing to take off for Colorado," she said loudly to Rita, and hollowed out her cheek with her tongue.

"What's that," asked the engineer quickly.

"He wants to know whose idea Colorado was," she said, still addressing Rita. She actually jerked a thumb at him, angry as an umpire. What had happened to his love?

Rita shrugged.

"Have you already forgotten what you told Rita?" asked the girl, meeting his eye.

"That's possible," said the engineer slowly. The worst of it was that he could have forgotten. "Since it was Rita I told, maybe she could refresh my memory."

"Glad to, Lance Corporal," she said, shrugging and smiling. "Though it is nothing we all don't already know. What you told me, if you recall, was that what you really wanted to do was attend the Colorado School of Mines."

"Without Kitty," said Kitty.

"No," said the engineer.

"Yes," said Rita. "Don't you remember the day I returned the telescope?"

"Why yes," said the engineer, remembering something, "but I certainly did not mean that I wasn't ready and anxious to join the Vaughts. Besides that, I had already committed myself to Mr. Vaught and I always honor my obligations."

"So now we're an obligation," said Kitty, addressing all Virginia. Her eyes flashed. It crossed his mind that she was what used to be called a noble high-spirited girl.

"No no, Kitty," said the poor engineer.

"You may recall, Lance Corporal," said Rita dryly, "that I asked you straight out which of us you wanted to work for, me or Poppy. You were unable to give a clear answer and spoke instead of Colorado. Knowing that you were a gentleman and did not like wrangling with women (I don't blame you), I did not press the issue. Perhaps I was wrong."

The trouble was he could not be sure and she knew it. And as he gazed at her he fancied he caught a gleam in her eye. She was skirting with him the abyss within himself and not doing it ill-naturedly: I know, said the gleam, and you know that I know and that you are not quite sure and that I might even be right.

"Anyhow Poppy is right," said Rita, rubbing her hands briskly. "We are all here and that is what counts. Why don't we hit the road?"

They were all leaving that very day, it turned out. Another two hours and he'd have missed them.

Mrs. Vaught and Kitty had one more room in the Governor's Palace to see, one more pewter candle-snuffer to buy. The engineer stayed at the motel to help Jamie pack. But Jamie was tired and went to lie down; the engineer packed for him. Rita found him sitting on the back step of the camper counting his money.

"You can keep that," she said. He had come to her post-dated check.

"No, thanks," he said and handed it over. Now it was he who eyed her warily, but not disagreeably.

"Believe it or not, I'm very happy things worked out as they have."

"You are?"

"I'm afraid I was the cause of the misunderstanding."

He shrugged.

"Anyhow you passed your test by ordeal and here is your prize." For the second time she handed him a little hexagonal General Motors key.

"Thank you."

"You want to know why I'm glad you're here? Because you're the only one who can help Jamie. If only you will. You know sometimes I have the feeling, Lance Corporal, that you are onto all of us, onto our most private selves. Or perhaps it is rather that it is you and I who know, who really know; and perhaps it is the nature of our secret that we cannot tell our friends or even each other but must rather act for the good of our friends."

The engineer was silent. From force of habit, he looked as if he knew what she was talking about, what their "secret" was, though in truth he had not the least idea.

"Bill."

"Yes?"

"Take Jamie and get the hell out of here. Take Ulysses and go while the going is good. Go roam the byways and have a roistering good time of it. Find yourselves a couple of chicks. You're two good-looking fellows, you know!"

"Thank you," said the engineer politely.

"Drink and love and sing! Do you know what I thought as I was standing in the governor's bedroom yesterday?"

"No."

"Jamie was standing in front of me in the lovely, careless

way he gets from you or from somebody, like young golden-haired Sir Tristram, leaning on his sword, and all at once the dreadful thought occurred to me: what must it be like to live and die without ever having waked in the morning and felt the warm mouth of one's beloved on his?"

"I couldn't say," said the engineer, who had never waked in the morning and found anybody's warm mouth on his.

"Bill, have you ever been to the Golden Isles of Georgia?"

"No."

"That's where we're headed. You can meet us there or not, as you like. And if you two bums want to detour through Norfolk, that's all right too."

"O.K."

5. THEY DIDN'T, THE ENGINEER AND JAMIE, QUITE CUT loose after all, or detour through Norfolk (did Rita mean he should take Jamie to a whorehouse?) or feel any beloveds' warm mouths on theirs. But they had a good time and went their own way for a day or two at a time, wandering down the old Tidewater, sleeping in the piney woods or along the salt marshes and rendezvousing with the Cadillac in places like Wilmington and Charleston.

The camper was everything he had hoped for and more. Mornings on the road, the two young men sat together in the cab; afternoons the engineer usually drove alone. Well as he looked, Jamie tired easily and took to the bunk in the loft over the cab and either read or napped or watched the road unwind. They stopped early in the evening and went fishing or set up the telescope on a lonesome savanna and focused on the far-away hummocks where jewel-like warblers swarmed about the misty oaks.

Nights were best. Then as the thick singing darkness settled about the little caboose which shed its cheerful square of light on the dark soil of old Carolina, they might debark and, with the pleasantest sense of stepping down from the zone of the possible to the zone of the realized, stroll to a service station or fishing camp or grocery store, where they'd have a beer or fill the tank with spring water or lay in eggs and country butter and grits and slab bacon; then back to the camper, which they'd show off to the storekeeper, he ruminating a minute and: all I got to say is, don't walk off and leave the keys in it—and so on in the complex Southern tactic of assaying a sort of running start, a joke before the joke, ten assumptions shared and a common stance of rhetoric and a whole shared set of special ironies and opposites. He was home. Even though he was hundreds of miles from home and had never been here and it was not even the same here—it was older and more decorous, more tended to and a dream with the past—he was home.

A *déjà vu*: so this is where it all started and which is not quite like home, what with this spooky stage-set moss and Glynn marshes but which is familiar nevertheless. It was familiar and droll and somehow small and curious like an old house revisited. How odd that it should have persisted so all this time and in one's absence!

At night they read. Jamie read books of great abstractness, such as *The Theory of Sets*, whatever a set was. The engineer, on the other hand, read books of great particularity, such as English detective stories, especially the sort which, answering a need of the Anglo-Saxon soul, depict the hero as perfectly disguised or perfectly hidden, holed up maybe in the woods of Somerset, actually hiding for days at a time in a burrow of ingenious construction from which he could notice things, observe the farmhouse below. Englishmen like to see without being seen. They are by nature eavesdroppers. The engineer could understand this.

He unlimbered the telescope and watched a fifty-foot Chris-Craft beat up the windy Intercoastal. A man sat in the stern reading the *Wall Street Journal*. "Dow Jones, 894—" read the engineer. What about cotton futures, he wondered.

He called Jamie over. "Look how he pops his jaw and crosses his legs with the crease of his britches pulled out of the way."

"Yes," said Jamie, registering and savoring what the engineer registered and savored. *Yes, you and I know something the man in the Chris-Craft will never know.* "What are we going to do when we get home?"

He looked at Jamie. The youth sat at the picnic table where the telescope was mounted, stroking his acne lightly with his fingernails. His whorled police-dog eye did not quite look at the engineer but darted close in a gentle nystagmus of recognitions, now focusing upon a mote in the morning air just beside the other's head, now turning inward to test what he saw and heard against his own private register. This was the game they played: the sentient tutor knowing quite well how to strike the dread unsounded chords of adolescence, the youth registering, his mouth parted slightly, fingernails brushing backward across his face. *Yes, and that was the wonder of it, that what was private and unspeakable before is speakable now because you speak it.* The difference between me and him, thought the engineer and noticed for the first time a slight translucence at the youth's temple, is this: like me he lives in the sphere of the possible, all antenna, ear cocked and lips parted. But I am conscious of it, know what is up, and he is not and does not. He is pure aching primary awareness and does not even know that he doesn't know it. Now and then he, the engineer, caught flashes of Kitty in the youth, but she had a woman's knack of cutting loose from the ache, putting it out to graze. She knew how to moon away the time; she could doze.

"Why don't we go to college?" he said at last.

"It's forty miles away," said Jamie, almost looking at him.

"We can go where we please, can't we? I mean, do you want to live at home?"

"No, but—"

Ah, it's Sutter he has in mind, thought the engineer. Sutter's at home.

"We could commute," said the engineer.

"Then you'll go?"

"Sure. We'll get up early in the morning."

"What will you take?"

"I need some mathematics. What about you?"

"Yes, me too," nodded the youth, eyes focused happily on the bright mote of agreement in the air between them.

It suited them to lie abed, in the Trav-L-Aire yet also in old Carolina, listening to baseball in Cleveland and reading about set theory and an Englishman holed up in Somerset. Could a certain someone be watching the same Carolina moon?

Or they joined the Vaughts, as they did in Charlestown, where they visited the gardens even though there was nothing in bloom but crape myrtle and day lilies. Evil-tempered mockingbirds sat watching them, atop tremendous oily camellias. Sprinklers whirled away in the sunlight, leaving drops sparkling in the hairy leaves of the azaleas. The water smelled bitter in the hot sun. The women liked to stand and talk and look at houses. They were built for standing, pelvises canted, and they more or less leaning on themselves. When the men stood still for thirty minutes, the blood ran to their feet. The sun made the engineer sick. He kept close to the women, closed his eyes, and took comfort in the lady smell of hot fragrant cotton. A few years from now and we'll be dead, he thought, looking at tan frail Jamie and nutty old Mr. Vaught, and they, the women, will be back here looking at "places."

It was like home here, but different too. At home we have J. C. Penney's and old ugly houses and vacant lots and new ugly houses. Here were pretty, wooden things, old and all painted white, a thick-skinned decorous white, thick as ship's paint, and presided over by the women. The women had a serious custodial air. They knew the place was theirs. The men were not serious. They all but wore costumes. They plied their trades, butcher, baker, lawyer, in period playhouses out in the yard.

Evenings the Vaughts sat around the green chloriniferous pools of the California motels, Rita and Kitty swimming and minding their bodies, Mr. Vaught getting up often to monkey with his Cadillac (he had installed a top-oiler and claimed he got the same mileage as a Chevrolet), Mrs. Vaught always dressed to the nines and rocking vigorously in the springy pool chair and bathing her face with little paper pads soaked in cologne. When she was lucky, she found some lady from Moline who shared her views of fluoridation.

Kitty avoided him. He sought her out, but she damped him down. She must think badly of him, he decided, and quick as he was to see as others saw, was willing to believe she was right. Was it simply that she took the easy way: she was with Rita and not with him and that was that? At any rate, if she didn't love him, he discovered he loved her less.

When they met by chance in motel passageways they angled their shoulders and sidled past like strangers. At Folly Beach they collided at the ice dispenser. He stood aside and said nothing. But when she filled her pitcher, she propped it on the rim of her pelvis and waited for him, a somewhat abstracted Rachel at the well.

"It's a lovely night," she said, stooping to see the full moon through the cloister of the Quality Court.

"Yes," he said politely. He didn't feel much like waiting upon her. But he said, "Would you like to take a walk?"

"Oh yes."

They put their pitchers in the chest and walked on the beach. The moonlight curled along the wavelets. She put her hand in his and squeezed it. He squeezed back. They sat against a log. She took her hand away and began sifting sand; it was cool and dry and left not a grain on the skin.

He sat with his hands on his knees and the warm breeze flying up his pants leg and thought of nothing.

"What's the matter, Bill?" Kitty leaned toward him and searched his face.

"Nothing. I feel good."

Kitty shifted closer. The sand under her sheared against itself and made a musical sound. "Are you mad at me?"

"No."

"You act mad."

"I'm not."

"Why are you different then?"

"Different from what?"

"From a certain nut who kissed a very surprised girl in the automat."

"Hmm."

"Well?"

"I'm different because you are different," said the engineer, who always told the exact truth.

"*Me!* How?"

"I had looked forward to being with you on this trip. But it seems you prefer Rita's company. I had wanted to be with you during the ordinary times of the day, for example after breakfast in the morning. I did not have any sisters," he added thoughtfully. "So I never knew a girl in the morning. But instead we have become like strangers. Worse, we avoid each other."

"Yes," she said gravely, conscious, he could not help but notice, of saying it so: gravely. "Don't you know why?" she said at last.

"No."

She sifted the cool discrete sand into her palm, where it made a perfect pyramid, shedding itself. "You say you never had sisters. Well, I never had a date, boyfriends—except a few boys in my ballet class who had foreheads this low. Rita and I got used to living quietly."

"And now?"

"I guess I'm clinging to the nest like a big old cuckoo. Isn't that awful?"

He shrugged.

"What do you want me to do?" she asked him.

"What do I want you to do?"

"Tell me."

"How do you feel?"

"How do *you* feel? Do you still love me?"

"Yes."

"Do you? Oh, I love you too."

Why did this not sound right, here on Folly Beach in old Carolina in the moonlight?

One thing I'm sure of, thought he as he held her charms in his arms: I shall court her henceforth in the old style. I shall press her hand. No more grubby epithelial embraces in dogbane thickets, followed by accusing phone calls. Never again! Not until we are in our honeymoon cottage in a cottage small by a waterfall.

But when he kissed her and there she was again looking at him from both sides at once, he had the first inkling of what might be wrong. She was too dutiful and athletic. She worked her mouth against his (is this right, she as good as asked).

"Wonderful," she breathed, lying back. "A perfect setting."

Why is it not wonderful, he wondered, and when he leaned over again and embraced her in the sand, he knowing without calculating the exact angle at which he might lie over against her—about twenty degrees past the vertical—she miscalculated, misread him and moved slightly, yet unmistakably to get plainly and simply under him, then feeling the surprise in him stopped almost before she began. It was like correcting a misstep in dancing.

"What is it?" she whispered presently.

"Nothing," he said, kissing her tenderly and cursing himself. His heart sank. Was it not that she was right and that he made too much of it? What it was, though, was that this was the last thing he expected. It was part of his expectations of the life which lay before him that girls would be girls just as camellias were camellias. If he loved a girl and walked with her on Folly Beach by moonlight, kissed her sweet lips and held her charms in his arms, it should follow that he would be simply he and she she, she as complete as a camellia with her corolla of reticences and allurements. But she, Kitty, was no such thing. She didn't know any better than he. Love, she, like him, was obliged to see as a naked garden of stamens and pistils. But what threw him off worst was that, sentient as always, he found himself catching onto how it was with her: he saw that she was out to be a proper girl and taking every care to do the right wrong thing. There were even echoes of a third person: what, you worry about the boys as good a figure as you have, etc. So he was the boy and she was doing her best to do what a girl does. He sighed.

"What?" she asked again.

"Nothing," he said, kissing her eyes, which were, at any rate, like stars.

He sighed again. Very well, I'll be both for you, boyfriend and girlfriend, lover and father. If it is possible.

They stirred in the musical sand. "We'd better go back," said the gentlemanly engineer and kissed her somewhat lewdly so she wouldn't feel she had failed. It seemed to be his duty now to protect her non-virtue as best he could. After all, he mused, as he reckoned girls must have mused in other ages, if worst comes to worst and all else fails I can let her under me—I shan't begrudge her the sacrifice. What ailed her, him, them, he wondered. Holding her hand as they returned to the Quality Court, he flexed his wrist so that he could count his pulse against her bone.

Mainly their trouble—or good fortune, as the case might be—was that they were still out of phase, their fervors alternating and jostling each other like bad dancers. For now, back at the cooler and she then going ahead of him with her pitcher on the rim of her pelvis, desire like a mighty wind caught him from behind and nearly blew him down. He almost fainted with old motel lewd-longing. "Wait," he whispered—oh, the piercing sorrow of it, this the mortal illness of youth like death to old age. "Wait." He felt his way along the blotting-paper wall like a blind man. She took his outstretched hand.

"What is it, dearest?"

"Let's go in here," he said, opening the door to a closet which housed a giant pulsing Fedders.

"What for?" she asked. Her eyes were silvery and turned in.

"Let us go in the service room." For it is here and not by moonlight—he sighed. Her willingness and nurse-tenderness were already setting him at naught again.

"There you are," said Rita, opening the door opposite. "Where in the world was the ice machine?"

And off he went, bereft, careening down the abstract, decent, lewd Quality corridor.

The next day they went their separate ways as before, he mooning off with Jamie in the Trav-L-Aire, keeping the days empty and ears attuned to the secret sounds of summer. They met again in Beaufort. Kitty and Rita filled the day with small rites. They both took Metrecal and made a ceremony of it at every stop, lining up the wafers on a Sèvres dish, assembling a miniature stove from Lewis and Conger to heat the water for their special orange-flavored tea. Or if Kitty had a hangnail, the afternoon was spent rounding up Q-tips, alcohol, cuticle scissors.

6. ONE HOT NIGHT THEY STOPPED AT A RAW RED MOTEL on a raw red hillside in Georgia. The women had got tired of the coast and took to the upcountry in search of hooked rugs and antiques. And the engineer had to admit that it was the pleasantest of prospects: to buy a five-dollar chiffonier and come down through six layers of paint to old ribby pine from the days of General Oglethorpe.

The two youths had dawdled as usual and it was almost midnight when the Trav-L-Aire came groaning up the hill, bucket swinging under her like a Conestoga wagon, and crept into a pine grove bursting with gouts of amber rosin still fragrant from the hot afternoon. It was too hot to sleep. Jamie sat in the cab and read his *Theory of Sets*. The engineer strolled over to the cinder-block porch of the motel, propped his chair against the wall, and watched a construction gang flattening a hill across the valley. They were making a new expressway, he reckoned. The air throbbed with the machinery, and the floodlights over the hill spoiled the night like a cast in a black eye. He had noticed this about the South since he returned. Along the Tidewater everything was pickled and preserved and decorous. Backcountry everything was being torn down and built anew. The earth itself was transformed overnight, gouged and filled, flattened and hilled, like a big sandpile. The whole South throbbed like a diesel.

"—but here am I, Ree, twenty-one and never been to college!"

"Then go to a good one."

He knew now why he had left the camper. It had come over him again, the old itch for omniscience. One day it was longing for carnal knowledge, the next for perfect angelic knowledge. Tonight he was not American and horny but English and eavesdropper. He had to know without being known.

Not ten feet behind him and through the open window, Rita and Kitty lay in their beds and talked. The Trav-L-Aire had crept up the hill with its lights out—had he planned it even then? He had come onto the porch as silently as an Englishman entering his burrow in Somerset.

"Have I told you what I want to be?"

"I'm afraid you have."

"I want to be an ordinary silly girl who has dates and goes to dances."

"You're in a fair way to do it."

"I love to dance."

"Then work harder at it. You're lazy."

"You know what I mean. I mean dancing cheek to cheek. I want to be broken in on."

"They don't dance like that now."

"I want to have beaus."

"You can have beaus in Tesuque or in Salamanca and not ruin your mind while you do it."

"I want to be Tri Delt."

"Good God!"

"I want to go to dances and get a tremendous rush. That's what my grandmother used to say: I went to such and such a dance and got a tremendous rush. Did you know my grandmother composed the official ATO waltz at Mercer?"

"Yes, you told me."

"I want to talk the foolishness the girls and boys at home talk."

"You're on your way."

"I want to go to school. I want to buy new textbooks and a binder full of fresh paper and hold my books in my arms and walk across the campus. And wear a sweater."

"Very well."

"I want to go to the Sugar Bowl."

"Christ."

"But you're going to stay with us! I need you!"

Rita was silent.

"Remember our bargain, Ree."

"What bargain?" said Rita in a muffled voice. She had turned away from the window.

"That you stay till Christmas. By then I'll know. I could easily have flunked out by then just as I flunked out before. But even if I don't, I'll know. I'll know whether to go with you or not."

"We'll see," said Rita absently.

7. THEY REACHED THE GOLDEN ISLES OF GEORGIA IN time for the first tropical storm of the year. The wind whipped over the gray ocean, out of kilter with the slow rhythm of the waves, tore up patches of spume, and raised a spindrift. Georgians had sense enough to go home and so the Vaughts had the hotel to themselves, an honorable old hacienda of wide glassed-in vestibules opening into conservatories and recreation rooms, and rows of brass pots planted with ferns, great cretaceous gymnosperms from the days of Henry Grady, dry and dusty as turkey wings. They looked at stuffed birds and group photographs of Southern governors and played mahjong.

A hundred servants waited on them, so black and respectful, so absolutely amiable and well-disposed that it was possible to believe that they really were. One or two of them were by way of being characters and allowed themselves to get on a footing with you. In a day's time they had a standing joke going as if you had been there a month. One bold fellow noticed the engineer take out his red book and read a few maxims as he waited for the elevator. "Now he's gon' be the *smart* one!" he announced to the hotel and later meeting him in the hall would therefore holler: "You got your book with you?" with a special sort of boldness, even a recklessness, which he took to be his due by virtue of the very credential of his amiability. The engineer laughed politely and even cackled a bit in order to appear the proper damn fool they would have him be.

By four o'clock the afternoon had turned yellow and dark. The engineer and Jamie found some rook cards and played a game in the conservatory, which still had a magic lantern from the days when lectures were delivered to vacationers on birds and sea shells. When the wind picked up, the engineer decided to go see to the Trav-L-Aire. Jamie wouldn't come. He went out of his way to tell the engineer he was going to telephone his sister Val.

"What for?" the engineer asked him, seeing that the other wanted him to ask.

"When I feel bad, I call her and she makes me feel better."

"Is she the sister who joined the religious order?"

"Yes."

"Are you religious?"

"No."

"Then what good can she do you?" They had fallen into the abrupt mocking but not wholly unserious way of talking which people who spend a lot of time together get into.

"She is not religious either, at least not in the ordinary sense."

"What is she doing in a religious order?"

"I don't know. Anyhow that is not what I'm interested in."

"What are you interested in?" asked the engineer, sniffing the old rook cards. They smelled like money.

"I thought she might give me a job."

"Doing what?"

"Anything. Teaching, minor repairs. I am feeling very good physically."

"I'm sure it's a wonderful work she is doing."

"I'm not interested in that either," said Jamie irritably. "I'm not interested in the Negroes."

"What are you interested in?"

"Anything she wants me to do. Her place is down in Tyree County in the piney woods, ten miles from nowhere. I thought it wouldn't be bad to live there as we have been living, in the camper. We could teach, give her a hand. You may not want to. But I am feeling very strong. Feel my grip."

"Very good."

"I can put you down hand-wrestling."

"No, you can't."

"Let's see."

135

The engineer, who never faked with Jamie, put him down quickly. But Jamie was surprisingly strong.

"Why don't we work out together, Bill?"

"O.K."

"What do you think of going down to Tyree County?" asked Jamie, hiding behind his rook cards.

"I thought you wanted to go to college."

"What I don't want is to go back home to the same thing, see Mother and Poppy every morning, watch the same golfers pass on number 6 fairway."

"O.K." Then he's changed his mind about Sutter, thought the engineer.

"O.K. what? You mean you'll go?"

"Sure," said the engineer, who in truth saw how it stood with Jamie and did not think it such a bad idea himself, going to the end of nowhere, parking in the pines and doing a few humble tasks.

Jamie laughed. "You mean it, don't you? You're telling the truth, you're ready to go."

"Sure. Why shouldn't I tell the truth?"

"I don't know," said Jamie, laughing at him.

Before he left the hotel, he picked up an old crime-club selection in the library, *The Murder of Roger Ackroyd*, a light pulpy book gnawed by silverfish and smelling of the summer of 1927. Kitty saw him and wanted to go to the camper with him. He saw that she was exhilarated by the storm, and since she was, he was not. No more for him the old upside-down Manhattan monkey business of rejoicing in airplane crashes and staggering around museums half out of his head and falling upon girls in hurricanes. Henceforth, he resolved, he would do right, feel good when good was called for, bad when bad. He aimed to take Kitty to a proper dance, pay her court, not mess around.

Accordingly he proposed that they stay in the bird room and play mahjong with Poppy and Jamie and Rita but she wouldn't hear of it.

Once they were outside in the storm, however, he felt better despite himself, though he had sworn not to feel good in bad environments. It was going to be a bad storm. Under the dirty low-flying clouds the air was as yellow as electric light. His spirits rose, he told himself, because it might be possible for them to enter here and now into a new life. If they were trapped by the storm in the Trav-L-Aire, they could sit at the dinette and play gin rummy, snug as children, very like many another young couple who came down here in the days of the great Bobby Jones and had a grand time. Sit face to face and deal the cards and watch the storm, like a chapter from Mary Roberts Rinehart entitled "Trapped in the Storm: Interesting Developments"; perhaps even steal a kiss or two.

The camper was hove to in a hollow of the dunes. He had snugged her down with a hundred feet of Nylon rope which he wound around cabin and axle and lashed to iron rings set in some broken beachworks. Inside the cabin he pumped up the butane tank and lit the little ashen mantles. Soon the camper leapt against its tether; the wind sang like a harp in her rigging. She creaked in every joint like the good prairie schooner she was and wouldn't leak a drop. The sand scoured the aluminum skin like birdshot.

He got Kitty across the table fairly enough but she was not onto the game he wanted to play. Instead of dealing the ancient honorable Bicycle cards he'd brought from the hotel and playing gin rummy in good faith for itself (That was it! Ordinary things such as gin rummy had lost weight, been evacuated. Why?) and worrying about the storm in good faith and so by virtue of the good faith earning the first small dividends of courtship, a guarding of glances, a hand upon the deck and a hand upon the hand—most happy little eight of clubs to be nestled so in the sweet hollow of her hand, etc.—instead she gazed boldly at him and used up their common assets, spent everything like a drunken sailor. She gazed like she kissed: she came on at him like a diesel locomotive.

"Oh me," he sighed, already in a light sweat, and discarded the jack of clubs.

"Aren't you picking up jacks?" he reminded her.

"Am I?" she said ironically but not knowing the uses of irony.

Look at her, he thought peevishly. She had worn leotards so many years she didn't know how to wear a dress. As she sat, she straddled a bit. Once in a Charleston restaurant he had wanted to jump up and pull her dress down over her knees.

Abruptly she put her cards down and knocked up the little Pullman table between them. "Bill."

"Yes."

"Come here."

"All right."

"Am I nice?"

"Yes."

"Am I pretty?"

"Sure."

"I mean, how would I look to you if you saw me in a crowd of girls?"

"Fine. The best, in fact."

"Why don't I think so?"

"I don't know."

She stretched out her leg, clasping her dress above the knee. "Is that pretty?"

"Yes," he said, blushing. It was as if somehow it was his leg she was being prodigal with.

"Not crippled?"

"No."

"Not muscle-bound?"

"No."

"I worry about myself."

"You don't have to."

"What do you really think of me? Tell me the literal truth."

"I love you."

"Besides that."

"I couldn't say."

"Oh darling, I didn't mean that. I mean, do you also *like* me? As a person."

"Sure."

"Do you think other boys will like me?"

"I don't know," said the engineer, sweating in earnest. Great Scott, he thought in dismay. Suppose she does have a date with another "boy."

"I mean like at a dance. If you saw me at a dance, would you like to dance with me?"

"Sure."

"Do you know that I've danced all my life and yet I've never been to a regular dance?"

"You haven't missed much," said the engineer, thinking of the many times he had stood around picking his nose at Princeton dances.

"Do you realize that I've hardly ever danced with a boy?"

"Is that right?"

"What does it feel like?"

"Dancing with a boy?"

"Show me, stupid."

He switched on the Hallicrafter and between storm reports they danced to disc-jockey music from Atlanta. There was room for three steps in the camper. Even though they were sheltered by the dunes, now and then a deflected gust sent them stumbling.

She was not very good. Her broad shoulders were shy and quick under his hand, but she didn't know how close to hold herself and so managed to hold herself too close or too far. Her knees were both workaday and timid. He thought of the long hours she had spent in dusty gymlike studios standing easy, sister to the splintery wood. She was like a boy turned into a girl.

"Will I do all right?"

"Doing what?"

"Going to dances."

"Sure." It was this that threw him off, her having to aim to be what she was.

"Tell me."

"Tell you what?"

"How to do right."

"Do right?" How to tell the sweet Georgia air to be itself?

"Do you love me?" she asked.

"Yes."

The storm crashed around them. Kitty drew him down to the lower bunk, which was like the long couch in an old-style Pullman drawing room. "Hold me tight," she whispered.

He held her tight.

"What is it?" she asked presently.

"I was thinking of something my father told me."

"What?"

"When my father reached his sixteenth birthday, my grandfather said to him: now, Ed, I'm not going to have you worrying about certain things—and he took him to a whorehouse in Memphis. He asked the madame to call all the girls in and line them up. O.K., Ed, he told my father. Take your pick."

"Did he?"

"I guess so."

"Did your father do the same for you?"

"No."

"I didn't know until this minute that it was hore. I thought it was whore."

"No."

"My poor darling," said Kitty, coming so close that her two

139

eyes fused into one. "I think I understand what you mean. You've been brought up to think it is an ugly thing whereas it should be the most beautiful thing in the world."

"Ah."

"Rita says that anything two people do together is beautiful if the people themselves are beautiful and reverent and unselfconscious in what they do. Like the ancient Greeks who lived in the childhood of the race."

"Is that right?"

"Rita believes in reverence for life."

"She does?"

"She says—"

"What does Sutter say?"

"Oh, Sutter. Nothing I can repeat. Sutter is an immature person. In a way it is not his fault, but nevertheless he did something dreadful to her. He managed to kill something in her, maybe even her capacity to love."

"Doesn't she love you?"

"She is terrified if I get close to her. Last night I was cutting my fingernails and I gave her my right hand to cut because I can't cut with my left. She gave me the most terrible look and went out. Can you understand that?"

"Yes."

"Very well. I'll be your whore."

"Hore."

"Hore."

"I know," said the engineer gloomily.

"Then you think I'm a whore?"

"No." That was the trouble. She wasn't. There was a lumpish playfulness, a sort of literary gap in her whorishness.

"Very well. I'll be a lady."

"All right."

"No, truthfully. Love me like a lady."

"Very well."

He lay with her, more or less miserably, kissed her lips and eyes and uttered sweet love-murmurings into her ear, telling her what a lovely girl she was. But what am I, he wondered: neither Christian nor pagan nor proper lusty gentleman, for I've never really got the straight of this lady-and-whore business. And that is all I want and it does not seem too much to ask: for once and all to get the straight of it.

"I love you, Kitty," he told her. "I dream of loving you in the morning. When we have our house and you are in the

140

kitchen in the morning, in a bright brand-new kitchen with the morning sun streaming in the window, I will come and love you then. I dream of loving you in the morning."

"Why, that's the sweetest thing I ever heard in my life," she said, dropping a full octave to her old unbuttoned Tallulah-Alabama voice. "Tell me some more."

He laughed dolefully and would have but at that moment, in the storm's lull, a knock rattled the louvers of the rear door.

It was Rita, looking portentous and solemn and self-coinciding. She had a serious piece of news. "I'm afraid something has come up," she said.

They sat at the dinette, caressing the Formica with their fingertips and gazing at the queer yellow light outside. The wind had died and the round leaves of the sea grapes hung still. Fiddler crabs ventured forth, fingered the yellow decompressed air, and scooted back to their burrows. The engineer made some coffee. Rita waited, her eyes dry and unblinking, until he came back and she had her first swallow. He watched as the muscles of her throat sent the liquid streaming along.

"I'm afraid we're in for it, kids," she told them.

"Why is that," the engineer asked since Kitty sat silent and sullen.

"Jamie has telephoned Sutter," Rita told Kitty.

Kitty shrugged.

The engineer screwed up an eye. "He told me he was going to call his sister Val."

"He couldn't reach Val," said Rita flatly.

"Excuse me," said the engineer, "but what is so alarming about Jamie calling his brother?"

"You don't know his brother," said Rita trying to exchange an ironic glance with Kitty. "Anyhow it was what was said and agreed upon that was alarming."

"How do you know what was said?" asked Kitty, so disagreeably that the engineer frowned.

"Oh, Jamie makes no bones about it," Rita cried. "He's going to move in with Sutter."

"You mean downtown," Kitty asked quickly.

"Yes."

"I don't understand," said the engineer.

"Let me explain, Bill," said Rita. "Sutter, my ex, and Kitty and Jamie's brother, lives in a dark little hole next to the hospital. The plan of course had been for you and Jamie to take the garage apartment out in the valley."

The engineer shrugged. "I can't see that it's anybody's loss but mine if Jamie would rather live with his brother. In fact, it sounds quite reasonable."

Again Rita tried to enlist Kitty in some kind of exchange but the girl was hulkish and dull and sat gazing at the sea grapes.

"It's like this, Lance Corporal," said Rita heavily. "Kitty here can tell you how it was. I saved the man once. I loved him and pulled him out of the gutter and put him back together. And I still think he's the greatest diagnostician since Libman. Do you know what I saw him do? Kitty was there. I saw him meet a man in Santa Fe, at a party, speak with him five minutes—a physicist—ask him two questions, then turn to me and say: that man will be dead of malignant hypertension inside a year."

"Was he?" asked the engineer curiously. "Dead, I mean?"

"Yes, but that's neither here nor there."

"How did Sutter, Dr. Vaught, know that?"

"I have no idea, but that's not what concerns us now."

"What were the two questions?"

"Ask him yourself. What is important now is what's in store for Jamie."

"Yes."

"Here again Kitty will bear me out. If not, I shall be glad to be corrected. It is not that Sutter is an alcoholic. It's not that he is a pornographer. These traits, charming as they are, do not in themselves menace Jamie, or you or me—no matter what some people may say. I flatter myself that all of us are sufficiently mature. No, what concerns me is Sutter's deep ambivalence toward Jamie himself."

"What do you mean?" asked the engineer, straining his good ear. The storm had begun banging away again.

"He has every right to make away with himself but he can damn well leave Jamie alone."

"I don't believe that," said Kitty. "I mean, I don't believe he tried to harm Jamie."

"It is not a question of belief," said Rita. "It is a question of facts. Do you deny the facts?"

Kitty was silent.

"It was an experiment," she said presently.

"Some experiment. What do you think of this as an experiment, Lance Corporal. Last summer, shortly after Sutter learned of Jamie's illness, he took him camping in the desert.

They were lost for four days. Even so, it was not serious because they had plenty of water. On the fourth day the canteens were found mysteriously emptied."

"How did they get out?"

"By pure freakish chance. Some damn fool shooting coyotes from an airplane spotted them."

"He meant no harm to Jamie," said Kitty dully.

"What did he mean?" said Rita ironically.

"Val said it was a religious experience."

"Thank you all the same, but if that is religion I'll stick to my ordinary sinful ways."

"What do you mean, he is a pornographer?" the engineer asked her.

"Nothing out of the ordinary," said Rita calmly. "He likes fun and games, picture books, and more than one girl at a time."

"I don't think it's pornography," said Kitty.

"This time, by God, I know whereof I speak. I was married to him. Don't tell me."

"My brother," said Kitty solemnly to the engineer, "can only love a stranger."

"Eh?"

"It is a little more than that," said Rita dryly. "But have it any way you please. Meanwhile let us do what we can for Jamie."

"You're right Ree," said Kitty, looking at her for the first time.

"What do you want me to do?" the engineer asked Rita.

"Just this. When we get home, you grab Jamie, throw him in this thing and run for your life. He'll go with you!"

"I see," said the engineer, now falling away like Kitty and turning mindless and vacant-eyed. "Actually we have a place to go," he added. "He wants either to go to school or visit his sister Val. He asked me to go with him."

Rita looked at him. "Are you going?"

"If he wants me to."

"Fair enough."

Presently he came to himself and realized that the women had left in the storm. It was dark. The buffeting was worse. He made a plate of grits and bacon. After supper he climbed into the balcony bunk, turned up the hissing butane lamp, and read *The Murder of Roger Ackroyd* from cover to cover.

IV

1. THE SOUTH HE CAME HOME TO WAS DIFFERENT FROM the South he had left. It was happy, victorious, Christian, rich, patriotic and Republican.

The happiness and serenity of the South disconcerted him. He had felt good in the North because everyone else felt so bad. True, there was a happiness in the North. That is to say, nearly everyone would have denied that he was unhappy. And certainly the North was victorious. It had never lost a war. But Northerners had turned morose in their victory. They were solitary and shut-off to themselves and he, the engineer, had got used to living among them. Their cities, rich and busy as they were, nevertheless looked bombed out. And his own happiness had come from being onto the unhappiness beneath their happiness. It was possible for him to be at home in the North because the North was homeless. There are many things worse than being homeless in a homeless place—in fact, this is one condition of being at home, if you are yourself homeless. For example, it is much worse to be homeless and then to go home where everyone is at home and then still be homeless. The South was at home. Therefore his homelessness was much worse in the South because he had expected to find himself at home there.

The happiness of the South was very formidable. It was an almost invincible happiness. It defied you to call it anything else. Everyone was in fact happy. The women were beautiful and charming. The men were healthy and successful and funny; they knew how to tell stories. They had everything the North had and more. They had a history, they had a place

144

redolent with memories, they had good conversation, they believed in God and defended the Constitution, and they were getting rich in the bargain. They had the best of victory and defeat. Their happiness was aggressive and irresistible. He was determined to be as happy as anyone, even though his happiness before had come from Northern unhappiness. If folks down here are happy and at home, he told himself, then I shall be happy and at home too.

As he pressed ever farther south in the Trav-L-Aire, he passed more and more cars which had Confederate plates on the front bumper and plastic Christs on the dashboard. Radio programs became more patriotic and religious. More than once Dizzy Dean interrupted his sportscast to urge the listener to go to the church or synagogue of his choice. "You'll find it a rich and rewarding experience," said Diz. Several times a day he heard a patriotic program called "Lifelines" which praised God, attacked the United States government, and advertised beans and corn.

What was wrong with a Mr. and Mrs. Williston Bibb Barrett living in a brand-new house in a brand-new suburb with a proper address: 2041 Country Club Drive, Druid Hills, Atlanta, Georgia?

Nothing was wrong, but he got worse anyway. The happiness of the South drove him wild with despair.

What was wrong with marrying him a wife and living a life, holding Kitty's charms in his arms the livelong night?

Nothing, but his memory deteriorated and he was assaulted by ghostly legions of *déjà vus* and often woke not knowing where he was. His knee leapt like a fish. It became necessary to unravel the left pocket of his three pairs of pants in order to slip a hand down and keep his patella in place.

It was unsettling, too, coming among a people whose radars were as sensitive as his own. He had got used to good steady wistful post-Protestant Yankees (they were his meat, ex-Protestants, post-Protestants, para-Protestants, the wistful ones who wanted they knew not what; he was just the one to dance for them) and here all at once he found himself among as light-footed and as hawk-eyed and God-fearing a crew as one could imagine. Everyone went to church and was funny and clever and sensitive in the bargain. Oh, they were formidable, born winners (how did they lose?). Yet his radar was remarkable, even for the South. After standing around two or three days, as queer and nervous as a Hoosier, he quickly got the hang of it. Soon he was able to listen to funny stories and tell a few himself.

The Vaughts liked him fine of course and did not notice that he was worse. For he was as prudent and affable as ever and mostly silent, and that was what they expected of him. All but Sutter. He had not yet met Sutter. But one day he saw his car, as he and Jamie were sitting in the sunny quarter of the golf shelter just off number 6 fairway in front of the Vaughts' house.

Jamie was still reading *The Theory of Sets*. The engineer was pondering, as usual, the mystery of the singularity of things. This was the very golf links, he had reason to believe, where his grandfather had played an exhibition round with the great Bobby Jones in 1925 or thereabouts. It was an ancient sort of links, dating from the golden age of country clubs, with sturdy rain shelters of green-stained wood and old-fashioned ball-washers on each tee and soft rolling bunkers as peaceful as an old battlefield. Deep paths were worn through the rough where caddies cut across from green to fairway. The engineer's amnesia was now of this order: he forgot things he had seen before, but things he had heard of and not seen looked familiar. Old new things like fifty-year-old golf links where Bobby Jones played once were haunted by memory.

How bad off was he, he wondered. Which is better, to walk the streets of Memphis in one's right mind remembering everything, what one has done yesterday and must do tomorrow—or to come to oneself in Memphis, remembering nothing?

Jamie has asked him what he was thinking about. When he told him, Jamie said: "You sound like Sutter."

"Have you seen him?"

"I went to see him yesterday. Yonder he goes now."

But he saw no more than the car, a faded green Edsel which swung out of the steep driveway and disappeared down the links road. Jamie told him that Sutter drove an Edsel to remind him of the debacle of the Ford Motor Company and to commemorate the last victory of the American people over marketing research and opinion polls. The engineer wasn't sure he liked the sound of this. It had the sound of a quixotic type who admires his own gestures.

2.

THE VAUGHTS LIVED IN A CASTLE FRONTING ON A GOLF links. It was an old suburb set down in a beautiful green valley across a ridge from the city. There were other ridges, the last wrinkles of the Appalachians, which formed other valleys between them, and newer suburbs and newer country clubs.

The houses of the valley were built in the 1920's, a time when rich men still sought to recall heroic ages. Directly opposite the castle, atop the next ridge to the south, there stood a round, rosy temple. It was the dwelling of a millionaire who had admired a Roman structure erected by the Emperor Vespasian in honor of Juno and so had reproduced it in good Alabama red brick and Georgia marble. At night a battery of colored floodlights made it look redder still.

The Vaught castle was made of purplish bricks which had been broken in two and the jagged side turned out. It had beam-in-plaster gables and a fat Norman tower and casement windows with panes of bottle glass. Mr. Vaught, it turned out, was richer even than the engineer had supposed. He had made his first fortune by inventing and manufacturing a new type of journal box for coal cars. After the second war he branched out into insurance companies, real estate, and auto dealerships. Now he owned and operated the second largest Chevrolet agency in the world. His talent, as the engineer divined it, was the knack of getting onto the rhythm of things, of knowing when to buy and sell. So that was the meaning of his funny way of hopping around like a jaybird with his ear cocked but not really listening to anybody! Rather was he tuned in to the music and rhythm of ventures, himself poised and nodding, like a schoolboy waiting to go into a jump rope. The engineer soon learned to pay no attention to him either: his talk was not talk at all, one discovered, that is, a form of communication to be attended to, but rather a familiar hum such as Lugurtha the cook made when she was making beaten biscuits.

There were other persons living in the castle. The "Myra"

of whom Mrs. Vaught often spoke to the engineer as if he knew her, turned out to be Myra Thigpen, Mr. Vaught's step-daughter by an earlier marriage. The Thigpens were staying in the Vaught castle while their own house was being built across the golf links. Lamar Thigpen worked for Mr. Vaught as personnel manager. Myra ran a real estate agency. A handsome woman with strong white arms and a cloud of heavy brown hair, she reminded the engineer of the Business and Professional Women he had seen turning out for luncheons at Holiday Inns from Charleston to Chattanooga. If Mrs. Vaught had thrown him off earlier by acting as if he ought to know whom she was talking about, Myra dislocated him now by acting as if she had known him all along. Had she? "You remember that old boy Hoss Hart from Greenwood who went to Mississippi State and later moved to Ithaca?" she asked him. "You mean Mr. Horace Hart who used to sell for Checkerboard Feed?" asked the engineer, who did in fact perfectly remember such a person, having heard his name once or twice fifteen years ago. "I saw him the other day," Myra went on, "selling fruitcake for Civitan over at Boys' State. He told me about when you and he and your daddy went duck-hunting on a houseboat on the White River." "The White River?" The engineer scratched his head. Had Hoss Hart remembered something he had forgotten? "When you see Hoss," said Myra, giving him a sisterly jostle such as coeds at Mississippi State give you, "just ask him if he remembers Legs." "Yes ma'am." "Don't say Miss Homecoming of 1950, just say Legs and see what he says." "Yes ma'am, I will."

Sutter was nowhere to be seen, but the engineer made sure he would see him when he did come—as he was told Sutter occasionally did to spend the night. Sutter's old apartment was next to the quarters assigned to the two young men, on the second floor above the great four-car garage. Not two hours passed after his arrival before he explored the apartment and discovered two things. One was a bottle of three-dollar whiskey in the cupboard of the kitchenette between the two apartments. The other thing was a knot-hole in the wall of his closet which looked straight into Sutter's bedroom. He hung his Val-Pak over the hole.

I'm not well, reflected the engineer, and therefore it is fitting that I should sit still, like an Englishman in his burrow, and see what can be seen.

* * *

It was a good place to live and collect one's thoughts. In the daytime the valley echoed with the faint far-off cries of the golfers. At night a yellow harvest moon hung over the ridge and the floodlights played on the fat rosy temple of Juno. His duties were light. Indeed he had no duties. Nothing more was said after Sea Island about Jamie's plans to go live with his sister in the pine barrens or with his brother in the city. The sick youth seemed content to move into the garage apartment. Within three weeks of their arrival the two young men and Kitty had registered at the university forty miles away and two weeks later the engineer and Jamie had pledged Phi Nu and learned the grip. Kitty realized her ambition and became not a Tri Delt but a Chi Omega.

On the morning of registration they had set out for the university, the three of them, the engineer driving, Kitty in the middle, in Mrs. Vaught's Lincoln, and came home early enough to sit on the garden grass and leaf through their brand-new textbooks with the glazed glittering pages and fragrant fresh print. The engineer, who had just received his October check from Mr. Vaught, bought a $25 slide rule as thick and slick as a mahjong tile and fitted at the rear with a little window.

Later in the afternoon he played golf, borrowing Jamie's clubs and making a foursome with Mr. Vaught and two pleasant fellows, Lamar Thigpen and a man from the agency. The engineer's skill at golf stood him in good stead. (Golf he was good at, it was living that gave him trouble. He had caddied for his father and broke eighty when he was thirteen.) It was not that he was so much better than the others but rather that he was strong and had a good swing. So that when the old man, who somehow knew this, had mumbled something about "my potner" and got his bets down and waved him onto the first tee, after he and Justin and Lamar had driven, he had happened to hit a dandy. The driver sang in the air and the ball went *chack*, flattening, it seemed like, and took off low, then went high and overdrove the par four green. The two opponents exchanged great droll thunderstruck comical mid-South looks.

"Well now, what is this," said Justin, the agency man, who was a big slow easy fellow, the sort referred to in these parts as a good old boy.

"Looka here now," said Lamar.

"Sho," said Mr. Vaught, already striking out down the fairway. "Come on, potner."

He hit five more towering drives and scored a lucky-after-the-layoff 36.

"Well now goddamn," said Lamar.

They called him Bombo, the son of Tarzan, and Mr. Clean. The engineer had to laugh. They were good fellows and funny.

The sixth hole fairway of the second nine ran in front of the castle. It had got to be the custom after teeing off to mark the balls and veer over to the patio, where David, the butler, had toddies ready. Custom also required that the talk, unlike other occasions, be serious, usually about politics but sometimes even about philosophical questions. The tone of the sixth-hole break was both pessimistic and pleasurable. The world outlook was bad, yes, but not so bad that it was not a pleasant thing to say so of a gold-green afternoon, with a fair sweat up and sugared bourbon that tasted as good as it smelled. Over yonder, a respectful twenty yards away, stood the caddies, four black ragamuffins who had walked over the ridge from the city and now swung the drivers they took from the great compartmented, zippered, pocketed, studded, bonneted golf bags.

The golfers gazed philosophically into their whiskey and now and then came out with solemn *Schadenfreude* things, just like four prosperous gents might have done in old Virginny in 1774.

"The thing is, you just don't get integrity where you need it most," said Lamar Thigpen, a handsome fellow who sat slapping his bare brown arm and looking around. He was maybe forty-five and just going slack and he worried about it, pushing his sleeve up and hardening his biceps against his chest.

"I'm going to tell yall the truth," Justin might say. "If they want the country all that bad, I'm not all that much against letting them have it."

But even these dire things were not said in ill humor.

"Ain't nobody here but us niggers anyway," somebody else would say finally. "Let's play golf."

They would get up a little creakily, their sweat having cooled and muscles stiffened, and walk to their lies. Mr. Vaught always took his second shot first because he seldom drove over a hundred yards but that always straight down the middle. And now he wound up with his brassie, drawing back slowly and swaying backward too and with a ferocious deliberation; then, for all the world as if he had been overtaken by some dread mishap, went into a kind of shiver and spasm and, like a toy wound too tight and shooting its springs, came down on the ball from all directions—Poppy drives, Lamar told Justin, like a man falling out of a tree—uttering at the end of it, as he always did, a little cry both apologetic and deprecating: "Voop!", calculated to conjure away all that was untoward and out of the ordinary—and off he would march, hopping along like a jaybird.

3. LIVING AS HE DID IN THE GARAGE APARTMENT AND hanging out as he did in the pantry and not with Mrs. Vaught's coterie of patriots and anti-fluoridationists who kept to the living room, the engineer met the servants first of all. Met, not got to know. The engineer was the only white man in the entire South who did not know all there was to know about Negroes. He knew very little about them, in fact nothing. Ever since he was a child and had a nurse, he had been wary of them and they of him. Like many others, he had had a little black boy for a friend, but unlike the others, who had enjoyed perfect love and understanding with their little black friends, he had been from the beginning somewhat fuddled and uneasy. At the age of thirteen he was avoiding Negroes like a queasy middle-aged liberal.

No doubt these peculiar attitudes were a consequence of his nervous condition. Anyhow it was the oddest encounter imaginable, that between him and the Vaught servants. He baffled the Negroes and they him. The Vaught servants were buffaloed by the engineer and steered clear of him. Imagine their feeling. They of course lived by their radars too. It was their special talent and it was how they got along: tuning in on the assorted signals about them and responding with a skill two hundred years in the learning. And not merely responding. Not merely answering the signals but providing home and sustenance to the transmitter, giving him, the transmitter, to believe that he dwelled in loving and familiar territory. He must be made to make sense, must the transmitter; must be answered with sense and good easy laughter: sho now, we understand each other. But here came this strange young man who transmitted no signal at all but who rather, like them, was all ears and eyes and antennae. He actually looked at them. A Southerner looks at a Negro twice: once when he is a child and sees his nurse for the first time; second, when he is dying and there is a Negro with him to change his bedclothes. But he does not look at him during the sixty years in between. And so he knows as little about Negroes as he knows about Martians, less, because he knows that he does not know about Martians.

But here come this strange young man who act like one of them but look at you out of the corner of his eye. What he waiting for? They became nervous and jumped out of the way. He was like a white child who does not grow up or rather who grows up in the kitchen. He liked to sit in the pantry and watch them and talk to them, but they, the Negroes, didn't know what to do with him. They called him "he," just as they used to call the madam of the house "she." "Where he is?" one might say, peeping out of the kitchen door and as often as not look straight into his eyes. "Uh-oh."

"He," the engineer, usually sat in the pantry, a large irregular room with a single bay window. It was not properly a room at all but rather the space left over in the center of the house when the necessary rooms had been built. Mr. Vaught, who also did not know what he did not know, had been his own architect. The ceiling was at different levels; many doors and vestibules opened into the room. David usually sat at one end, polishing silver in the bay. The dark end of the room let into the "bar," a dusty alcove of blue mirrors and buzzing fluorescent lights and chrome stools. It was one of the first of its kind, hailing from the 1920's and copied from the swanky bars used by Richard Barthelmess and William Powell in the movies. But it had not been used as such for years and now its mirror shelves were lined with Windex bottles, cans of O-Cedar and Bab-O and jars of silver polish stuffed with a caked rag. It fell out somehow or other that both Negro and white could sit in the pantry, perhaps because it was an intermediate room between dining room and kitchen, or perhaps because it was not, properly speaking, a room at all.

David Ross was different from the other Negroes. It was as if he had not caught onto either the Negro way or the white way. A good-humored seventeen-year-old, he had grown too fast and was as raw as any raw youth. He was as tall as a basketball player and wore summer and winter the same pair of heavy damp tweeds whose cuffs were swollen as if they had a chronic infection. He was supposed to be a butler and he wore a butler's jacket with little ivory fasten-on buttons but his arms stuck out a good foot from the sleeves. He was always polishing silver, smiling as he did so a great white smile, laughing at everything (when he did not laugh, his face looked naked and strange) a hissing laugh between his teeth, *ts-ts-ts*. Something about him irritated the engineer, though. He was not cunning enough. He, the engineer, was a thousand times more cunning and he didn't have to be. He, David, was too raw. For example, he was always answering advertisements in magazines, such as *Learn Electronics! Alert Young Men Needed! Earn Fifty Dollars a Day! Send for Selling Kit!* And the selling kit would come and David would show it to everybody, but his long black-and-pink fingers could never quite work the connections and the soldering iron. He was like a rich man's son! The engineer would never have dreamed of spending such money ($10 for a selling kit!). Hell no, David, the engineer had told him, don't send off for that. Damnation, why didn't he have better sense? He should either be cunning with a white man's cunning or cunning with a black man's cunning. As it was, he had somehow managed to get the worst of each; he had both white sappiness and Negro sappiness. Why doesn't somebody tell him? One day he did tell him. "Damnation, David," said he as David showed him a selling kit for an ice-cube dispenser which was supposed to fit any kind of refrigerator. "Who do you think you're going to sell that to?"

"All the folks around here," cried David, laughing *ts-ts-ts* and waving a great limp hand in the direction of the golf links. "Folks out here got plenty money and ain't one in ten got a dispenser-type box" (he'd been reading the brochure). "It only come with GE and Servel!"

"Well, what in the world do they want it for," moaned the flabbergasted engineer.

"When the he'p gone in the evenings and folks want to fix they drinks! They ain't going to want to fool with no old-fashioned knuckle-bruising trays" (more from the brochure). "It's not S.E. on the other boxes."

"S.E.?" asked the engineer.

"Standard Equipment."

"Oh. Then you're just going to walk up to some lady's house at ten o'clock in the morning and ring the doorbell and when she comes to the door you're going to ask her to let you show this ice dispenser."

"Sho," said David and began laughing at the sour-looking engineer, *ts-ts-ts*.

"Well, you're not," the engineer would groan. Damnation, David couldn't even polish silver. There was always silver cream left in the grooves. Still, the engineer liked to watch him at work. The morning sunlight fell among the silver like fish in the shallows. The metal was creamy and satiny. The open jar of silver cream, the clotted rag, the gritty astringent smell of it, put him in mind of something but he couldn't say what.

But damn this awful vulnerability of theirs, he ranted, eyes fixed on the glittering silver. It's going to ruin us all, this helplessness. Why, David acted as if everybody was going to treat him well! If I were a Negro, I'd be tougher than that. I'd be steadfast and tough as a Jew and I'd beat them. I'd never rest until I beat them and I could. I should have been born a Negro, for then my upsidedownness would be right side up and I'd beat them and life would be simple.

But Oh Christ, David, this goddamn innocence, it's going to ruin us all. You think they're going to treat you well, you act like you're baby brother at home. Christ, they're not going to treat you well. They're going to violate you and it's going to ruin us all, you, them, us. And that's a shame because they're not that bad. They're not bad. They're better than most, in fact. But you're going to ruin us all with your vulnerability. It's God's terrible vengeance upon us, Jamie said Val said, not to loose the seven plagues upon us or the Assyrian or even the Yankee, but just to leave you here among us with this fearful vulnerability to invite violation and to be violated twenty times a day, day in and day out, our lives long, like a young girl. Who would not? And so the best of us, Jamie said she said, is only good the way a rapist is good later, for a rapist can be good later and even especially good and especially happy.

But damn him, he thought, him and his crass black inept baby-brother vulnerability. Why should I, for Christ's sake, sit here all asweat and solicitous of his vulnerability. Let him go sell his non-knuckle-bruising ice trays and if he gets hurt: well, I'm not well myself.

David's mother, Lugurtha Ross, was cook. She was respectable and black as black, with a coppery highlight, and had a straight Indian nose. She wanted no trouble with anybody. All she wanted in the world was to find fervent areas of agreement. She spoke to you only of such things as juvenile delinquency. "Chirren don't have any respect for their parents any more," she would cry. "You cain't even correck them!"—even though David was her only living child and it was impossible to imagine him as a delinquent. She made it sound as if everybody were in the same boat; if only children would have more respect, our troubles would be over. She often made beaten biscuits in the evening, and as she sifted flour on the marble and handled the mitt of dough, she sang in a high decorous deaconess voice, not spirituals but songs she made up.

> *Up in an airplane*
> *Smoking her sweet cigarette*
> *She went way up in an airplane*
> *Smoking her sweet cigarette*

John Houghton, the gardener, lived in a room under the engineer's apartment. An ancient little Negro with dim muddy eyes and a face screwed up like a prune around a patch of bristling somewhere near the middle of which was his mustache, he was at least sixty-five and slim and quick as a boy. He had come from the deep country of south Georgia and worked on the railroad and once as a hod carrier forty years ago when they built the dam at Muscle Shoals. He had been night watchman for the construction company when Mr. Vaught built his castle. Mr. Vaught liked him and hired him. But he was still a country Negro and had country ways. Sometimes Jamie and David would get him in a card game just to see him play. The only game he knew was a strange south Georgia game called pitty-pat. You played your cards in turn and took tricks but there was not much rhyme or reason to it. When John Houghton's turn came, he always stood up, drew back, and slapped the card down with a tremendous *ha-a-a-a-umph!*, just as if he were swinging a sledge hammer, but pulling up at the last second and setting the card down soft as a feather. David couldn't help laughing *ts-ts-ts*. "What game we gon' play, John," he would ask the gardener to get him to say pitty-pat. "Lessus have a game of pitty-pat," John Houghton would say, standing up also to shuffle the cards, which he did by chocking them into each other, all the while making terrific feints and knee-bends like a boxer. *"Pitty-pat,"* cried David and fell out laughing. But John Houghton paid no attention and told them instead of his adventures in the city, where, if the police caught you playing cards, they would sandbag you and take you to jail.

"What do you mean, sandbag?" asked the puzzled engineer.

"That's what I mean!" cried John Houghton. "I mean they sandbag you."

Of an evening John Houghton would don his jacket, an oversize Marine drawstring jacket with deep patch pockets, turn the collar up around his ears so that just the top of his gnarled puckered head showed above it, thrust his hands deep into the patch pockets, and take a stroll down the service road which wound along the ridge behind the big houses. There he met the maids getting off work.

At night and sometimes all night long there arose from the room below the engineer's the sounds of scuffling and, it seemed to him, of flight and pursuit; of a chair scraped back, a sudden scurry of feet and screams, he could have sworn more than one voice, several in fact, screams both outraged and risible as pursuer and quarry rounded the very walls, it seemed like.

4. THEY SAT IN THE GARDEN, THE THREE STUDENTS, ON the last day of summer and leafed through their new textbooks. The whitethroat sparrows had come back early and were scratching in the sour leaves. The October sunlight was blinding on the white glazed pages, which smelled like acetate and the year ahead. The chemistry text seemed to exhale the delicate effluvium of new compounds. From the anthology there arose a subtler smell, both exotic and businesslike, of the poet's disorder, his sweats and scribblings, and of the office order of the professor and the sweet ultimate ink. By contrast, everything else seemed untidy, the summer past, the ruined garden, one's own life. Their best hope lay in the

books themselves, the orderly march of chapter and subheading, the tables, the summaries, the index, the fine fat page of type.

The old spurious hope and elegance of school days came back to him. How strange it was that school had nothing whatever to do with life. The old talk of school as a preparation for life—what a bad joke. There was no relation at all. School made matters worse. The elegance and order of school had disarmed him for what came later.

Jamie had a queer-looking physical-chemical reference, as stubby and thick as a German handbook. Hefting it, you felt like a German: a whole body of knowledge, a *Wissenschaft*, here in your hand, a good chunky volume. Kitty had a great $15 atlas-size anthology of World Literature from Heraclitus to Robert Frost—the whole works. The engineer was content with a thin tight little volume, *The Theory of Large Numbers*, that and his slide rule, which he wore in a scabbard like a dagger. Sitting in the funky tannin smell of the fall garden, he slid the window of his rule and read off cube roots and cosines. He for artifacts, bright pretty useful objects like slide rules, and you can have your funky gardens and jaybirds crying down October.

Each believed privately that he was taking the best of course, had hit on the real thing, the meat of the university, and that the other two were deceiving themselves. Imagine what a chemistry student thinks of an anthology.

Son Junior, Lamar Thigpen's son, came out to join them and stood around fiddling with his Thunderbird keys, but they didn't like him much and nobody spoke to him and at last he went away. He was a pale glum sophomore who lived at the university and drove home to the castle on weekends. Yet strangely enough, glum as he was, he had many friends at the university who liked him despite his sullen ways. He brought them over to the castle before football games, and while everyone had a good time drinking in the pantry, he stood off and fiddled with his car keys.

The engineer, if the truth be told, was in a bad way, having been seriously dislocated by his first weeks at the university. Now feeling all at once knocked in the head, bumbly and sleepy, he excused himself and crept off to a sunny corner of the garden wall, where he curled up and went to sleep. The sparrows eyed him and hopped around in the dry crape myrtle leaves, which curled like orange peelings and seemed to burn with a clear flame in the sunlight.

What had happened was that the university had badly thrown him off with its huge pleasantness. Powerful friendship radiations came at him from all directions. It was enough to make one uneasy. By ten o'clock on the first morning he was fairly jumping with nervousness. He did believe that the campus was the pleasantest place he had ever seen. Everyone he met was happy and good-looking and victorious and kindly and at-one with themselves, and here he was, solitary and goofy and shut up in himself, eyeballs rolled up in his eyebrows. Perfect strangers in shirtsleeves spoke to him on the paths. Beautiful little flatfooted girls swinging along in fresh cotton skirts called out to him: hi! His knee leapt. The boys said: what say! and the girls said: hi! He had of course got into the Yankee way of not speaking to anyone at all. In New York it is gradually borne in upon one that you do not speak to strangers and that if you do, you are fairly taken for a homosexual. Indeed he had noticed that Northern college boys worry about being mistaken for homosexuals and take trouble to demonstrate that they are not. At Princeton one not only did not speak to strangers on the paths; one also took care which acquaintances one acknowledged. There were those, in fact, who measured their own worth by the number of people one could afford to cut in public. That was how he nearly got into a fistfight and came to take up boxing. Still used to Southern ways, he spoke to a fellow coming toward him on the path, a cool, pipe-smoking gent (it was raining and he smoked his pipe upside-down) he had been introduced to not thirty minutes earlier at an eating club. "What say," said the engineer and the fellow looked straight through him, snuffled in his pipe, and cut him dead. Now the engineer was not nearly as tense and honorable as his father but was still fairly tense and honorable and unused to slights, and after all his grandfather had been a great one for face-to-face showdowns in the street ("I told you, you bed-sheeted Ku Klux cowardly son of a bitch, to be out of town by four o'clock," etc.). Before he knew it or even thought what he was doing, he had turned back, grabbed the other by his elbow, and spun him around. "Excuse me," said the courteous engineer, "but I was introduced to you not thirty minutes ago and just now I spoke to you and furthermore I saw that you saw me speak to you and that you chose not to acknowledge my greeting. I suggest now that you do so acknowledge it." Or some such of the formal goofy language he used with strangers. "Pardon," said the other, looking at him for the maniac that he was. "I s'pose I was completely lost in my thots." And off he went, snuffling in his pipe. Later the engineer observed that he smoked the pipe upside-down even on clear days. He was a Choate man. Evidently he had discovered that the engineer graduated from Ithaca High School. Thought the latter to himself: if I'm going to be challenging these fellows on the paths, I'd better be in shape to do it. You can run into a tartar, a sure-enough thick-legged gent. And what a sad business that would be, to challenge some fellow and then get the living hell beat out of you. So he went out for boxing, became a demon middle-weight and had no more trouble with Choate snobs or anyone else for that matter.

But now it was he who had learned Yankee ways. He took to eyeing people on the path to see when they would speak. He judged the distance badly and said his "hi" and "what say" too soon. His face ached from grinning. There was something to be said after all for the cool Yankee style of going your own way and paying no attention to anyone. Here for God's sake the air fairly crackled with kinship radiations. That was it. These beautiful little flatfooted girls greeted you like your own sister! What do you do about that? He had forgotten. It made him blush to think of laying hands on them. Then he remembered: that was how you did lay hands on them!—through a kind of sisterly-brotherly joshing, messing around it was called. Everybody was wonderful and thought everybody else was. More than once he overheard one girl tell another: "She's the most wonderful girl I ever knew!"

That was how they treated the courses too: they cancelled out the whole academic side by honorifics. "Professor so-and-so? He's the second smartest professor in the United States!" "Ec 4? Universally recognized as the hardest course ever given on the subject!" Etc. And poof! out the window went the whole intellectual business, kit and caboodle, cancelled out, polished off, even when you made straight A's. Especially when you made straight A's.

Naturally in such an intersubjective paradise as this, he soon got the proper horrors. He began to skid a little and catch up with himself like a car on ice. His knee leapt so badly that he had to walk like a spastic, hand thrust through pocket and poking patella with each step. Spotting oncomers, fifty, sixty, seventy feet away, he began grinning and composing himself for the encounter. "Hi!" he hollered, Oh Lord, a good twenty feet too soon.

Under the crape myrtle in the garden the song sparrow scratched like a chicken, one foot at a time, and the yellow leaves curled in a clear flame. Close by, John Houghton trimmed the brick border with an old-fashioned spring blade. *Snick, snick snee*, went the blade scissoring along the bricks.

He was dreaming his old dream of being back in high school and running afoul of the curriculum, wandering up and down the corridors past busy classrooms. Where was his class? He couldn't find it and he had to have the credit to graduate.

Someone kissed him on the mouth, maybe really kissed him as he lay asleep, for he dreamed a dream to account for the kiss, met Alice Bocock behind the library stacks and gave her a sweet ten-o'clock-in-the-morning kiss.

There was a step behind him and presently voices. He cracked an eyelid. The song sparrow was scratching, kicking leaves and looking around like a chicken. Fireballs danced on his lashes, broke into bows and sheaves of color.

"Very well, little Hebe. Be Betty coed and have your little fun on Flirtation Walk—"

"Flirtation *Walk*!"

"And all the warm dalliance you want to. Drain your cup, little Hebe, then let me know when you want to get down to business."

"What in the world are you *talking* about?"—delivered in Kitty's new ironclad coed style, for crying out loud, her head tilted at an angle signifying mock-incredulity, eyes inattentive and going away.

Englishman that he was, he woke in his burrow without a commotion. Though his cheek was pressed into the leaves and was stinging, he did not move. The sunlight fell upon a loose screen of sasanqua. He could not see them, but he heard Kitty and Rita talking a few feet away, where they must be sitting on the grass.

A movement caught his eye. Some thirty feet away and ten feet above him a balcony of the garage overhung the garden, not a proper balcony, but just enough ledge to break the ugly wall and give a pleasant cloistered effect to the garden; not for standing on, but there stood a man anyhow, with his hands in his pockets, looking down into the garden.

He was a Vaught, with the black brow and the high color and the whorled police-dog eye, but a very finely drawn Vaught. Motionless as he was, he gave the effect of restiveness and darting. He was both merry and haggard. Sutter, the engineer was to learn, always looked as if he had just waked up, with one side of his face flushed and creased and his hair brushed up against the grain by the pillow. There was something old-fashioned about him. Perhaps it was his clothes. He was in shirtsleeves, but his shirt and pants were the kind you wear with a suit. They could be the trousers of a $35 Curlee suit. One knew at once that he would never wear slacks and a sport shirt. He put one in mind of a bachelor of the 1940's come home to his quarters and putting on a regular white shirt and regular suit pants and stepping out to take the air of an evening. Most notable was his thinness. He was thin as a child is thin, with a simple scanting of flesh on bones. The shirt, still starched and stuck together on one side, did not lay hold of his body. It was the sort of thinness a young man worries about. But this man did not. He was indifferent to his thinness. He did not hold himself in such a way as to minimize it.

Sutter's hands moved in his pockets as he watched Rita and Kitty.

"What's the story?" Rita was saying. "Why the headlong rush for anonymity?"

Kitty did not reply. The engineer could hear her hand moving against the nap of the freshly cut grass.

"Mmm?" said Rita, questioning softly.

"Nothing is *changed*, Ree," caroled Kitty.

Sutter turned his head. There was something wrong with his cheek, a shadowing, a distinguished complication like a German saber scar.

"On your way, Minnie cat," said Rita, and the women arose, laughing.

Before they could turn, Sutter, still fingering the change in his pocket, ducked through the open window. Rita looked up quickly, holding her hand against the sun.

5. "A PRETTY LINKS, ISN'T IT? YOU KNOW, I WAS ONE OF the first people to be brought up in a suburb. Aren't you Will Barrett?"

He had been watching the golfers from the patio and he turned around quickly, irritably, not liking to be surprised. There stood a woman he first took to be a Salvation Army lass and he was about to refuse her alms even more irritably. But then he noticed she was a Vaught. She must be Val.

"In the past," she went on before he could answer, "people have usually remembered their childhood in old houses in town or on dirt farms back in the country. But what I remember is the golf links and the pool. I spent every warm day of my girlhood at the pool, all day every day, even eating meals there. Even now it doesn't seem right to eat a hamburger without having wrinkled fingers and smelling chlorine." She didn't laugh but went on gazing past him at the golfers. Her musing absent-mindedness, he reckoned, was one of the little eccentricities nuns permitted themselves. He had never spoken to a nun. But perhaps she was not a proper nun after all, wearing as she did not a proper habit but a black skirt and blouse and a little cap-and-veil business. But beyond a doubt she was a Vaught, though a somewhat plumpish bad-complexioned potato-fed Vaught. Her wrist was broad and white as milk and simple: it was easy for him to imagine that if it was cut through it would show not tendon or bone but a homogenous nun-substance.

"I've been looking for you, Barrett. Once I heard your father make a speech to the D.A.R. on the subject of *noblesse oblige* and our duty to the Negro. A strange experience and a strange bunch of noblewomen. Not that I know much about *noblesse oblige*, but he gave them proper hell. He was right about one thing, of course, character. You don't hear much about that either nowadays."

"Is that why you became a nun?" he asked politely.

"Partly, I suppose. I drove up to see Jamie and now I want to see you."

"Yes ma'am."

"Jamie looks awful."

"Yes." He was about to enter with her onto the mournful ground of Jamie's illness, but she fell away again. John Houghton's scissors came snickersneeing along the brick walk behind her and flushed a towhee out of the azaleas, a dandy little cock in tuxedo-black and cinnamon vest. She gazed down at the bird with the same mild distracted eye.

"Does John Houghton still run after schoolgirls?"

"Ma'am? Oh. Well, yes."

Now freed by her preoccupation with the forgotten trophies of her past, the sentient engineer swung full upon her. What to make of it, this queer casualness of hers? Was it Catholic, a species of professional unseriousness (death and sin are our affair, so we can make light of them), almost frivolity, like electricians who make a show of leaning on high-voltage wires? Or was it an elaborate Vaught dialectic, thus: Rita and the rest of you are going to be so serious about Jamie, therefore I am not, etc. His radar boggled and couldn't get hold of her. He was obscurely scandalized. He didn't like her much.

"How long does Jamie have?"

"Eh? To live— Oh, Rita said months, four months I think she said. But I think longer. Actually he is much better."

"Jamie tells me you and he are good friends." Her gaze was still fixed on the tiny amber eye of the towhee, which crouched with its head cocked, paralyzed.

"Yes."

"He says that you and he may go somewhere together."

"Jamie changes his mind about that. He was talking earlier about living with Sutter or going down to stay with you."

"Well, now he wants to go somewhere with you."

"Do you mean, leave school?"

"Yes."

"He knows I'm ready to go any time." Presently he added: "I can understand him wanting to go away."

"Yes. That was what I want to speak to you about."

He waited.

"Mr. Barrett—"

"Yes ma'am."

"It may well happen that it will be you and not one of us who will be with Jamie during the last days of his life and even at his death."

"I suppose that is true," said the engineer, taking note of a warning tingle between his shoulder blades.

"Everyone thinks very highly of you—though for strangely diverse, even contradictory reasons. I can't help noticing. You are evidently quite a fellow. That's hardly surprising, considering whose son you are."

"Ah—" began the engineer, frowning and scratching his head.

"Though I can't say that I agree with your father on his reasons for treating Negroes well rather than beating them up, still I'd rather that he'd won over the current scoundrels even if he'd won for the wrong reasons."

"Perhaps," said the engineer uneasily, not wanting to discuss either his father's "reasons" or her even more exotic reasons.

"But in any case I too can perceive that you are a complex and prescient young man."

"I certainly appreciate—" began the engineer gloomily.

"Clearly you would do right by Jamie even if you had no affection for him, which I have reason to believe you do have."

"Yes," said the other warily. It was still impossible to get a fix on her. He had known very few Catholics and no nuns at all.

"Mr. Barrett, I don't want Jamie to die an unprovided death."

"Unprovided?"

"I don't want him to die without knowing why he came here, what he is doing here, and why he is leaving."

"Ma'am?" The engineer felt like wringing out his ear but he did not.

"It may fall to you to tell him."

"Tell him what?"

"About the economy of salvation."

"Why don't you tell him?" He was watching her as intently as the towhee watched her. There was no telling what she might do.

She sighed and sat down. The towhee, released from its spell, flew away. "I have told him."

The engineer, though standing erect, began to lean about five degrees away from her.

"It is curious, Mr. Barrett, but what I told him was absolutely the last thing on earth he would listen to. It was not simply one of a great number of things he might have listened to more or less indifferently. It was, of all things, absolutely the last thing. Doesn't that strike you as strange?"

"I couldn't say. But if you can't tell him what you believe, you his sister, how do you expect me to tell him what I don't believe?"

But she was at it again, her trick of engaging him then slipping away. "They didn't ride in carts the last time I was here," she said, gazing past him at the golfers. Do all nuns banter about salvation? "And yet, there he was, reading all that guff with relish."

"What guff?"

"That book about radio noise from the galaxies, noise which might not be noise. Did you give it to him?"

"No."

She ignored his irritation. "I've noticed," she said gloomily and not especially to him, "that it is usually a bad sign when dying people become interested in communication with other worlds, and especially when they become spiritual in a certain sense."

"Don't you believe in other worlds and, ah, spirits?"

"It is strange, but I've always distrusted so-called spiritual people," she muttered, mostly ruminating with herself. "You know how women talk about such and such a priest being spiritual?"

"No." How could he know any such thing?

"I always steer clear of those birds. But no, actually I owe spiritual people, ladies, a great deal—they're very generous with me when I beg from them. It's a strange business, isn't it? The most unlikely people are generous. Last week I persuaded the local Klonsul of the Klan to give us a Seven-Up machine. Do you think it is possible to come to Christ through ordinary dislike before discovering the love of Christ? Can dislike be a sign?"

"I couldn't say," said the sleepy engineer.

She brought herself up and looked at him for the first time. "Mr. Barrett, Jamie's salvation may be up to you."

"Eh? Excuse me, but apart from the circumstance that I do not know what the word 'salvation' means, I would refuse in any case to accept any such commission, Miss, ah—, that is, Sister—"

"Val."

"Sister Val."

"No," she said laughing. "Just Val. I am Sister Johnette Mary Vianney."

"Is that right?"

His refusal, he noticed, was delivered with a tingle of pleasure, both perverse and familiar. Familiar because—yes, he remembered his father refusing a priest and taking some satisfaction in it even though he, his father, took the Catholics' side in their troubles with the Klan. "Mr. Barrett," the priest asked him with the same jolly gall, "I don't think you realized it but you just fired one of my parishioners, heh-heh, and I want to ask you if you will take her back. She has a family and no husband—" "And who could that be," said his father, his voice ominously civil. "Souella Johnson." Souella Johnson, who, being not merely a winehead but, failing to find Gallo sherry in the house, had polished off as a poor substitute some six cases of twenty-year-old bourbon over the years. "I will not, sir," said his father and bang, down went the telephone.

"I will not," he told Val with the same species of satisfaction. Perhaps we are true Protestants despite ourselves, he mused, or perhaps it is just that the protest is all that is left of it. For it is in stern protest against Catholic monkey business that we feel ourselves most ourselves. But was her request true Catholic gall, the real article, or was it something she had hit upon through a complicated Vaught dialectic? Or did she love her brother?

He read in her eyes that he looked odd. "What is it," she asked him smiling. For a split second he saw in her his Kitty, saw it in her lip-curling bold-eyed expression. It was as if his Kitty, his golden girl of summertime and old Carolina, had come back from prison where she had got fat and white as white and bad-complexioned.

"What," she asked again.

"I was wondering," said the engineer, who always told the truth, "how you manage to come to the point where you feel free to make requests of people."

She laughed again. "Jamie was right. You're a good companion. Well, I can ask you, can't I?"

"Sure."

"It's like the story about the boy who got slapped by quite a few girls but who—well. But it's extraordinary how you can ask the most unlikely people—you can ask them straight out: say, look, I can see you're unhappy; why don't you stop stealing or abusing Negroes, go confess your sins and receive the body and blood of Our Lord Jesus Christ—and how often they will just look startled and go ahead and do it. One reason is that people seldom ask other people to do anything."

"I see."

"Now I have to go see Sutter."

"Yes ma'am."

He began nodding in ancient Protestant fuddlement and irony, not knowing whether to bow, shake hands, or look down his nose. But it didn't matter. She had left without noticing.

6. JAMIE WAS NOT IN THE APARTMENT. THERE WERE voices in the room next door. That would be Sutter and Val, he calculated, and perhaps Jamie. The old itch for omniscience came upon him—lost as he was in his own potentiality, having come home to the South only to discover that not even his own homelessness was at home here—but he resisted the impulse to eavesdrop. I will not overhear nor will I oversee, he said, and instead threw a dozen combination punches, for henceforth I shall be what I am no matter how potential I am. Whereupon he dismounted the telescope through which he and Jamie had studied the behavior of golfers who hooked their drives from number 5 tee into the creek. Some cheated. It was with a specific, though unidentified pleasure that one watched the expressions of the men who stood musing and benign and Kiwanian while one busy foot nudged the ball out of the water.

He lay on the bed, feet sticking straight up, and broke out in a cold sweat. What day is this, he wondered, what month, and he jumped up to get his Gulf calendar card from his wallet. The voices in the next room murmured away. A chair scraped back. The vacuum of his own potentiality howled about him and sucked him toward the closet. He began to lean. Another few seconds, and he was holed up as snug as an Englishman in Somerset, closet door closed behind him, Val-Pak on his back like a chasuble.

The hole commanded perhaps a 100 degree view of Sutter's room. It was furnished in rancho style with a maple couch and chair with wagonwheel arms. There were pictures of famous moments of medical history: First Use of Anesthesia, Dr. Lister Vaccinates, Tapping Ascites. Mrs. Vaught, he remembered, had fixed up the room for Sutter when he was in school.

Sutter was sitting in the wagonwheel chair, idly brandishing an automatic pistol, aiming it here and there, laying the muzzle against his cheek. Val was leaving: he caught no more than a flurry of black skirt and a shoe of cracked leather. At close range Sutter did not look so youthful. His olive skin had a yellowish cast. The high color of his cheeks resolved into a network of venules. His fingertips were wrinkled and stained by chemicals.

"—found him in New York," Val was saying. "He's Ed Barrett's son. Have you met him?"

"I saw him in the garden." Sutter aimed the pistol at something over the engineer's head.

"What did you think of him?"

Sutter shrugged. "You know. He is—" His free hand, held forth like a blade, moved back and forth across the vertical.

"Yes," said Val.

"—nice," ended Sutter with six overtones in his voice, "you know."

"Yes."

My God, thought the closeted Englishman, they already knew what he was, agreed on it, and communicated their complex agreement with hardly a word!

"Put that thing up," said Val.

"Why?"

"Some day you're going to blow your fool head off—by accident."

"That would offend you more than if I did it deliberately, wouldn't it?"

"And it would please you, wouldn't it, to die absurdly?"

The engineer heard no more. He had become extremely agitated, whether by their reference to him or by the sight of the pistol, he could not have said, but he left the closet and paced up and down the bedroom. He took his pulse: 110. A door closed and the stairs creaked under a heavy step. For some minutes he stood listening. A car started below. He went to the window. It was a Volkswagen microbus painted a schoolbus yellow and stained with red dust.

He had already started for the door, blood pounding in his ears, when the shot rang out. It was less a noise than a heavy concussion. Lint flew off the wall like a rug whipped by a broom. His ears rang. Now, hardly knowing how he came here, he found himself standing, heart pounding in his throat, outside Sutter's door on the tiny landing. Even now, half out of his mind, his first thought was of the proprieties. It had seemed better to go to Sutter's outside door than directly through the kitchenette, which with the closet separated the apartments. And now, standing at the door, knuckles upraised, he hesitated. Does one knock after a shot. With a sob of dismay, dismay less for Sutter than himself, he burst into the room.

The wagonwheel chair was empty. He went lunging about.

"You must be Barrett."

Sutter stood at a card table, almost behind the door, cleaning the pistol with a flannel disk soaked in gun oil.

"Excuse me," said the reeling engineer. "I thought I heard a noise."

"Yes."

"It sounded like a shot."

"Yes."

He waited but Sutter said no more.

"Did the pistol go off accidentally?"

"No. I shot him."

"Him?" The engineer suddenly feared to turn around.

Sutter was nodding to the wall. There hung yet another medical picture, this of The Old Arab Physician. The engineer had not seen it because his peephole was some four inches below the frame. Moving closer, he noticed that the Arab, who was ministering to some urchins with phials and flasks, was badly shot up. Only then did it come over him that his peephole was an outlying miss in the pattern of bullet holes.

"Why him?" asked the engineer, who characteristically, having narrowly escaped being shot, dispatched like Polonius behind the arras, had become quite calm.

"Don't you know who that is?"

"No."

"That's Abou Ben Adhem."

The engineer shook his head impatiently. "Now that I'm here I'd like to ask you—"

"See the poem? There in a few short, badly written lines is compressed the sum and total of all the meretricious bullshit of the Western world. And lo! Ben Adhem's name led all the rest. Why did it lead all the rest?"

"I don't know," said the engineer. His eyes were fixed vacantly on the dismantled gun barrel. The fruity steel smell of Hoppe's gun oil put him in mind of something, but he couldn't think what.

"There it is," said Sutter, loading the clip, "the entire melancholy procession of disasters. First God; then a man who is extremely pleased with himself for serving man for man's sake and leaving God out of it; then in the end God himself turned into a capricious sentimental Jean Hersholt or perhaps Judge Lee Cobb who is at first outraged by Abou's effrontery and then thinks better of it: by heaven, says he, here is a stout fellow when you come to think of it to serve his fellow man with no thanks to me, and so God swallows his pride and packs off the angel to give Abou the good news—the new gospel. Do you know who did the West in?"

"No."

"It wasn't Marx or immorality or the Communists or the atheists or any of those fellows. It was Leigh Hunt."

"Who?" repeated the engineer absently, eyes glued forever to the Colt Woodsman.

"If I were a Christian, I shouldn't hesitate to identify the Anti-Christ, Leigh Hunt."

"Leigh Hunt," said the engineer, rubbing his eyes.

"I'm glad you came down with Jimmy," said Sutter. "Come sit over here."

"Yes sir." Still not quite able to rouse himself, he allowed Sutter to lead him to the wagonwheel chair. But before he could sit down, Sutter turned him into the light from the window.

"What's the matter with you?"

"I feel all right now. I was quite nervous a few minutes ago. I've had a nervous condition for some time." He told Sutter about his amnesia.

"I know. Jimmy told me. Are you going into a fugue now?"

"I don't know. I thought perhaps that you—"

"Me? Oh no. I haven't practiced medicine for years. I'm a pathologist. I study the lesions of the dead."

"I know that," said the engineer, sitting down wearily. "But I have reason to believe you can help me."

"What reason?"

"I can tell when somebody knows something I don't know."

"You think I know something?"

"Yes."

"How can you tell?"

"I don't know how but I can. I had an analyst for five years and he was very good, but he didn't know anything I didn't know."

Sutter laughed. "Did you tell him that?"

"No."

"You should have. He could have done a better job."

"I'm asking you."

"I can't practice. I'm not insured."

"Insured?"

"The insurance company cancelled my liability. You can't practice without it."

"I'm not asking you to practice. I only want to know what you know."

But Sutter only shrugged and turned back to the Colt.

"Why did they cancel your insurance?" the engineer asked desperately. There was something he wanted to ask but he couldn't hit on the right question.

"I got the idea of putting well people in the hospital and sending the truly sick home."

"Why did you do that," asked the engineer, smiling slightly. He was not yet certain when the other was joking.

Again Sutter shrugged.

The engineer was silent.

Sutter rammed a wad through the barrel. "I had a patient once who lived under the necessity of being happy. He almost succeeded but did not quite. Since he did not, he became depressed. He became very unhappy that he was not happy. I put him in the terminal ward of the hospital, where he was surrounded by the dying. There he soon recovered his wits and became quite cheerful. Unfortunately—and by the purest bad luck—he happened to suffer a serious coronary before I sent him home. As soon as it became apparent that he was going to die, I took it upon myself to remove him from his oxygen tent and send him home to his family and garden. There he died. The hospital didn't like it much. His wife sued me for a half a million dollars. The insurance company had to pay."

The engineer, still smiling faintly, was watching the other like a hawk. "Dr. Vaught, do you know what causes amnesia?"

"Causes it? Like a virus causes chicken pox?"

"Have you seen many cases?"

"Do you regard yourself as a case?"

"I would like to know."

"You are a very persistent young man. You ask a great many questions."

"And I notice you don't answer them."

The pistol was assembled. Sutter sat down, shoved in the clip, pulled back the breach and rang up a bullet. He clicked the safety and took aim at the Arab physician. The engineer screwed up one eye against the shot, but Sutter sighed and set the pistol down.

"All right, Barrett, what's wrong?"

"Sir?"

"I'm listening. What's wrong?"

Now, strangely, the engineer fell silent for a good twenty seconds.

Sutter sighed. "Very well. How old are you?"

"Twenty-five."

Sutter was like an unwilling craftsman, the engineer perceived, a woodworker who has put on his coat and closed up shop. Now a last customer shows up. Very well, if you insist. He takes the wood from the customer, gives it a knock with his knuckles, runs a thumb along the grain.

"Are you a homosexual?"

"No."

"Do you like girls much?"

"Yes."

"How much?"

"Very much."

"Do you have intercourse with girls?"

The engineer fell silent.

"You don't like to speak of that?"

He shook his head.

"Did you speak of it with your psychiatrist?"

"No."

"Do you mean that for five years you never told him whether you had intercourse with girls?"

"No."

"Why not?"

"It was none of his business."

Sutter laughed. "And none of mine. Did you tell him that?"

"No."

"You were not very generous with him."

"Perhaps you are right."

"Do you believe in God?"

The engineer frowned. "I suppose so. Why do you ask?"

"My sister was just here. She said God loves us. Do you believe that?"

"I don't know." He stirred impatiently.

"Do you believe that God entered history?"

"I haven't really thought about it."

Sutter looked at him curiously. "Where are you from?"

"The Delta."

"What sort of man was your father?"

"Sir? Well, he was a defender of the Negroes and—"

"I know that. I mean what sort of man was he? Was he a gentleman?"

"Yes."

"Did he live in hope or despair?"

"That is hard to say."

"What is the date of the month?"

"The nineteenth."

"What month is it?"

The engineer hesitated.

"What is the meaning of this proverb: a stitch in time saves nine?"

"I would have to think about it and tell you later," said the engineer, a queer light in his eye.

"You can't take time off to tell me now?"

"No."

"You really can't tell me, can you?"

"No."

"Why can't you?"

"You know why."

"You mean it is like asking a man hanging from a cliff to conjugate an irregular verb?"

"No. I'm not hanging from a cliff. It's not that bad. It's not that I'm afraid."

"What is it then?"

The engineer was silent.

"Is it rather that answering riddles does not seem important to you? Not as important as—" Sutter paused.

"As what?" asked the engineer, smiling.

"Isn't that for you to tell me?"

The engineer shook his head.

"Do you mean you don't know or you won't tell me?"

"I don't know."

"All right. Come here."

Sutter took a clean handkerchief from his pocket and for the second time turned the other into the light. "You won't feel this." He twisted a corner of the handkerchief and touched the other's cornea. "O.K.," said Sutter and sitting down fell silent for a minute or two.

Presently the engineer spoke. "You seem to have satisfied yourself of something."

Sutter rose abruptly and went into the kitchenette. He returned with half a glass of the dark brown bourbon the engineer had noticed earlier.

"What is it?" the latter asked him.

"What is what?"

"What did you satisfy yourself about?"

"Only that you were telling the truth."

"About what?"

"About when you believe someone has something to tell you, you will then believe what he tells you. I told you you would not feel the handkerchief, so you didn't. You inhibited your corneal reflex."

"Do you mean that if you tell me to do something I will do it?"

"Yes."

The engineer told him briefly of his *déjà vus* and of his theory about bad environments. The other listened with a lively expression, nodding occasionally. His lack of surprise and secret merriment irritated the engineer. He was even more irritated when, as he finished his account, the other gave a final nod as much as to say: well, that's an old story between us—and spoke, not of him, the engineer, but of Val. Evidently her visit had made a strong impression on him. It was like going to a doctor, hurting, and getting harangued about politics. Sutter was more of a doctor than he knew.

174

"Do you know why Val came up here? This concerns you because it concerns Jimmy."

"No, I don't," said the engineer gloomily. Damnation, if I am such an old story to him, why doesn't he tell me how the story comes out?

"She wanted me to promise her something," said Sutter, keeping a bright non-medical eye on the other. "Namely, that if she were not present I would see to it that Jimmy is baptized before he dies. What do you think of that?"

"I couldn't say."

"It happened in this fashion," said Sutter, more lively than ever. "My father was a Baptist and my mother an Episcopalian. My father prevailed when Jamie was born and he wasn't baptized. You know of course that Baptist children are not baptized until they are old enough to ask for it—usually around twelve or thirteen. Later my father became an Episcopalian and so by the time Jamie came of age there was no one to put the question to him—or he didn't want it. To be honest, I think everybody was embarrassed. It is an embarrassing subject nowadays, even slightly ludicrous. Anyhow Jamie's baptism got lost in the shuffle. You might say he is a casualty of my father's ascent in status."

"Is that right," said the engineer, drumming his fingers on his knees. He was scandalized by Sutter's perky, almost gossipy interest in such matters. It reminded him of something his father said on one of his nocturnal strolls. "Son," he said through the thick autumnal web of Brahms and the heavy ham-rich smell of the cottonseed-oil mill. "Don't ever be frightened by priests." "No sir," said the startled youth, shocked that his father might suppose that he could be frightened by priests.

"Well," he said at last and arose to leave. Though he could not think what he wanted to ask, he was afraid now of overstaying his welcome. But when he reached the door it came to him. "Wait," he said, as though it was Sutter and not he who might leave. "I know what I want to ask."

"All right." Sutter drained off the whiskey and looked out the window.

The engineer closed the door and, crossing the room, stood behind Sutter. "I want to know whether a nervous condition could be caused by not having sexual intercourse."

"I see," said the other and did not laugh as the engineer

feared he might. "What did your analyst say?" he asked, without turning around.

"I didn't ask him. But he wrote in his book that one's needs arise from a hunger for stroking and that the supreme experience is sexual intimacy."

"Sexual intimacy," said Sutter thoughtfully. He turned around suddenly. "Excuse me, but I still don't quite see why you single me out. Why not ask Rita or Val, for example?"

"I'm asking you."

"Why?"

"I don't know why, but I know that if you tell me I will believe you. And I think you know that."

"Well, I will not tell you," said Sutter after a moment.

"Why not?"

Sutter flushed angrily. "Because for one thing I think you've come to me because you've heard something about me and you already know what I will say—or you think you know. And I think I know who told you."

"No sir, that's not true," said the engineer calmly.

"I'll be goddamned if I'll be a party to any such humbug."

"This is not humbug."

"I will not tell you."

"Why not?"

"Who do you think I am, for Christ's sake? I am no guru and I want no disciples. You've come to the wrong man. Or did you expect that?" Sutter looked at him keenly. "I suspect you are a virtuoso at this game."

"I was, but this time it is not a game."

Sutter turned away. "I can't help you. Fornicate if you want to and enjoy yourself but don't come looking to me for a merit badge certifying you as a Christian or a gentleman or whatever it is you cleave by."

"That's not why I came to you."

"Why then?"

"As a matter of fact, to ask what it is *you* cleave by."

"Dear Jesus, Barrett, have a drink."

"Yes sir," said the engineer thoughtfully, and he went into the kitchenette. Perhaps Kitty and Rita were right, he was thinking as he poured the horrendous bourbon. Perhaps Sutter is immature. He was still blushing from the word "fornicate." In Sutter's mouth it seemed somehow more shameful than the four-letter word.

7.

"I'VE GOT TO GO," SAID JAMIE.

"O.K. When?"

After leaving Sutter, the engineer had read a chapter of Freeman's *R. E. Lee* and was still moving his shoulders in the old body-English of correcting the horrific Confederate foul-ups, in this case the foul-up before Sharpsburg when Lee's battle orders had been found by a Union sergeant, the paper wrapped around three cigars and lying in a ditch in Maryland. I'll pick it up before he gets there, thought the engineer and stooped slightly.

"I mean leave town," said Jamie.

"Very well. When?"

"Right now."

"O.K. Where are we going?"

"I'll tell you later. Let's go."

From the pantry he could look into the kitchen, which was filled with a thick ticking silence; it was the silence which comes late in the evening after the cook leaves.

But at that moment David came over for the usual game of hearts. Rita had taken David aside for an earnest talk. In the last few days David had decided he wanted to be a sports-caster. The engineer groaned aloud. Sportscaster for Christ's sake; six feet six, black as pitch, speech like molasses in the mouth, and he wanted to be a sportscaster.

"No," he told David when he heard it. "Not a sports-caster."

"What I'm going to do!" cried David.

"Do like me," said the engineer seriously. "Watch and wait. Keep your eyes open. Meanwhile study how to make enough money so you don't have to worry about it. In your case, for example, I think I'd consider being a mortician."

"I don't want to be no mortician."

He was David sure enough, of royal lineage and spoiled rotten. He wouldn't listen to you. Be a sportscaster then.

Now he couldn't help overhearing Rita, who was telling David earnestly about so-and-so she knew at CBS, a sweet wonderful guy who might be able to help him, at least suggest a good sportscasting school. Strangest of all, the sentient engineer could actually see how David saw himself as a sportscaster: as a rangy chap (he admired Frank Gifford) covering the Augusta Masters (he had taken to wearing a little yellow Augusta golf cap Son Junior gave him).

Jamie wore his old string robe which made him look like a patient in the Veterans Hospital. While Rita spoke to David, Son Junior told the engineer and Kitty about rumors of a Negro student coming on campus next week. It was part of the peculiar dispensation of the pantry that Son Junior could speak about this "nigger" without intending an offense to David. Rita looked sternly at Son—who was in fact dull enough to tell David about the "nigger."

Sutter sat alone at the blue bar. The engineer had come in late and missed whatever confrontation had occurred between Sutter and Rita. Now at any rate they sat thirty feet apart, and Rita's back was turned. Sutter appeared to take no notice and sat propped back in a kitchen chair, whiskey in hand and face livid in the buzzing blue light. The family did not so much avoid Sutter as sequester him in an enclave of neutral space such as might be assigned an afflicted member. One stepped around him, though one might still be amiable. "What you say, Sutter," said Lamar Thigpen as he stepped up to the bar to fix a drink.

Kitty got Son off the subject by asking him what band would play for the Pan-Hellenic dance. Later Kitty whispered to the engineer, "Are you going to take me?"

"Take you to what?"

"The Pan-Hellenic."

"When is it?"

"Saturday night after the Tennessee game."

"What day is this?"

"Thursday, stupid."

"Jamie wants to go somewhere." He was thinking gloomily of standing around at a dance for seven hours drinking himself cross-eyed while Kitty danced the night away. "Where do you want to go, Jamie?"

But Jamie wouldn't tell Kitty.

"Son asked me to go with him," said Kitty.

"Isn't he your nephew?"

"Not really. Myra is no kin. She is Poppy's stepdaughter by another marriage."

"You still can't go with Son."

"Why not!" she cried, widening her eyes. Since she had become a coed, Kitty had given up her actress's lilt for a little trite sorority cry which was made with her eyes going away. She wore a cashmere sweater with a tiny gold sorority dagger pinned over her breast.

"I'm telling you, you can't." It actually made him faint to think of Kitty going anywhere with Son Junior, who was a pale glum fornicator, the type who hangs around the men's room at a dance, patting himself and talking about poontang.

"Why *not*?"—eyes going away again but not before peeping down for a glimpse of her pin.

"He's a bastard."

"Shh! He likes you."

He did. Son had discovered through intricate Hellenistic channels that the engineer had been a collegiate middleweight and had not lost a fight. "We're strong in everything but boxing," he had told the engineer, speaking of the Phi Nu's campus reputation. The engineer agreed to go out for boxing and golf. And during some hazing horseplay Son had told one of the brothers to take it easy with this one—"he can put your ass right on the Deke front porch with a six-inch punch." And so he had attached himself to the engineer with a great glum Greek-letter friendship.

Now once again Son came close, sidling up and speaking at length while he twirled his Thunderbird keys. It was the engineer's bad ear, but as best he could tell, Son was inviting him to represent the pledge class at a leadership conference next summer at the fraternity headquarters in Columbus, Ohio. "They always have outstanding speakers," Son told him. "This year the theme is Christian Hellenism."

"I really appreciate it, Son," said the engineer.

"Look, Kitty," he said when Son drifted off. He took off his own pledge pin. "Why don't you wear mine?" It was a great idea. He had only recently discovered that being pinned was a serious business at the university, the next thing to an engagement ring. If she wore his pin, Son wouldn't take her to the dance.

"Will you take me to the dance?"

"Yes. If Jamie doesn't veto it. I promised to go with him."

"Don't worry about Jamie."

As he watched, she pinned his gold shield to the same lovely soft blue mount, oh for wantonnesse and merrinesse, thought he tenderly and crossed his good knee over bad lest it leap through the card table.

Jamie punched him. He was angry because they were not paying attention to the game of hearts (here is my heart, thought the engineer sentimentally). "What do you say," whispered the youth fiercely. "Are you ready to go?"

"Yes."

"O.K. What do you think of this? We'll drive to the coast and—"

But before Jamie could tell him, the engineer caught sight of Mrs. Vaught beckoning to him from the dark doorway of the dining room. The engineer excused himself.

Mrs. Vaught had a book for him. "I saw what you were reading this afternoon in the garden!" She waggled her finger at him.

"Ma'am. Oh." He remembered the *R. E. Lee* and saw at once that the sight of it had set Mrs. Vaught off on some gambit or other.

"Here's a book on the same subject that I'm sure you'll find fascinating," she said, laughing and making rueful fun of herself, which was a sure sign she was proselytizing.

"Yes ma'am. Thank you very much. Is it about the Civil War?"

"It's the real story behind the so-called official version of General Kirby Smith's surrender at Shreveport. It's the story behind the story. We all think that General Kirby Smith wanted to surrender."

"Yes ma'am. That is true."

"No, it isn't. He was holding out until he could make a deal with the Rothschilds and the international bankers in Mexico to turn over Texas and Louisiana to Maximilian's Jewish republic."

"Ma'am?" He wrung out his good ear.

"Here's proof," she said, taking back the book and thumbing through it, still laughing ruefully at herself. She read: "At a meeting of the Rothschilds in London in 1857, Disraeli jumped to his feet and announced: 'We'll divide the United States into two parts, one for you, James Rothschild, and the other for you, Lionel Rothschild. Napoleon III will do what I tell him to do.'"

The engineer rubbed his forehead and tried to concentrate. "But don't I recall that Kirby Smith did in fact surrender at Shreveport?"

"He didn't want to! His men surrendered, fortunately for us."

She got off on the Bavarian Illuminati and he leaned down to her so he needn't look at her, looking instead at his shoes, lined up carefully with the sill of the dining-room door.

"Excuse me, Mother," said Jamie, plucking at the engineer's sleeve. Evidently he was so used to his mother's opinions that he paid no attention.

"You read this!" Again she thrust the book on him, shaking her head at her own zeal.

"Yes ma'am."

"Bill," said Jamie.

"What?"

"Let's go."

"All right. Where do you want to go?"

"Let's take the camper down to the Gulf Coast and live on the beach. Just for the weekend."

"You don't want to see the Tennessee game?"

"No."

"You mean leave after classes tomorrow?"

"No, I meant—well, all right."

"O.K."

They were headed back to the hearts game but Lamar Thigpen caught them. "Did you ever hear about this alligator who went into a restaurant?" He took them by the neck and drew them close as lovers.

"No, I didn't," said the courteous engineer, though he had. Jokes always made him nervous. He had to attend to the perilous needs of the joke-teller. Jamie dispensed himself and paid no attention: I'm sick and I don't have to oblige anybody.

"The waitress came over and brought him a menu. So this alligator says to her: do yall serve niggers in here? She says yes, we do. So he says, O.K. I'll take two."

"What about leaving tonight, Bill?" said Jamie.

"That's all right, Mr. Thigpen," said the engineer while the other held him close as a lover and gazed hungrily at his cheek. Rita had been watching Jamie and she knew something was wrong. The engineer, diverted by Lamar's terrible needs, only realized it when he heard Rita's hearty no-nonsense tone.

"Come on over here, Tiger." She took the youth's arm. Jamie flung her off angrily. He looked dog-faced. He plucked his thumb and pretended to muse.

"Hold it, Tiger," said Rita, now managing to draw him

down in David's chair but not looking at him because he was close to tears.

Jamie looked sternly about but his eyes shone and there was heat and vulnerability in the hollow of his neck. The engineer wished that Son Junior would go away. In every such situation, he had noticed, there is always one person who makes things worse.

David left quickly. Dull in some ways, he was as quick as any Negro to know when white people had white troubles. Rita drew Jamie down in David's chair.

"I can't wait for the game," cried Kitty. "You coming to see me work, Jimbo?" In the past month she had metamorphosed from ballerina to cheerleader. "We're number one! We're number one!" she would chant and set her white skirt swirling about her legs so cunningly that the engineer almost fell out of the grandstand, overcome by pride and love.

"No, it's not the game," said Rita, gazing steadfastly away but patting Jamie's arm with hard steady pats. Kitty's gambit didn't work, she was saying. But hers didn't either.

"Jamie and I are planning to go down to the Coast this weekend," said the engineer.

Everyone looked at Jamie, but he could not bring himself to say anything.

"You don't mean this weekend," cried Kitty.

"I'm going," said Jamie in a loud voice, all squeaks and horns.

"I'm with you, Tiger," said Rita, still patting.

Damn, don't pat him, thought the engineer.

Rita ran a hand through Jamie's hair (like my mother, thought the engineer in a sudden *déjà vu*, ruffling my hair for the photographer so it would look "English" and not slicked down). "Val was here today and she upset him with some of her—ideas."

"It's not that," said Jamie, losing control of his voice again.

"I think he really wants to go down to Tyree County and clear things up and I don't blame him."

"I don't."

"You said you did."

"That was before."

"Don't misunderstand me," said Rita, speaking for some reason to the engineer. "I think Val is doing a magnificent job down there. I happen to know a little about such things, having worked with Indian kids, who are just as bad off. No, my hat's off to her. But to come up here cold, so to speak, after making herself scarce for the past year as far as Jamie is concerned and to seriously propose to this guy here who despite the fact that he is a wretch and a no-good-bum"—she ruffled Jamie's hair—"nevertheless pulled down first place in the National Science competition—that a rather stupid Irishman in a black skirt pour water over his head while uttering words in a dead language (and uttering them in atrocious ecclesiastical Latin besides)—excuse me, but I think the whole affair is exceedingly curious. Though I'm frank to say I don't know why it upsets you. But listen now: if you want to go down there, Tiger, I'll drive the car for you and hold the ewer or whatever it is."

"I am *not* going there," said Jamie through his teeth. "And if I were, that would *not* be the reason." The engineer sighed with relief. Jamie's anger had got the better of his tears.

"I'm Baptist and DeMolay myself," said Son Junior, twirling his keys glumly. He had not quite got the straight of it but did perceive that the subject of religion had come up.

"That's not the point," cried Jamie, in anguish again. "I'm not interested in either—"

Mr. Vaught, who couldn't stay put anywhere for long and so made a regular tour of the house, shuttling back and forth between the pantry and the living room, where Mrs. Vaught and Myra Thigpen usually sat, happened at that moment to be circling the wall of the pantry.

"We all headed for the same place and I don't think the good Lord cares how we get there," he cried, shot his cuff, and went on his way.

"The Bible says call no man father," said Lamar Thigpen sternly, looking around for the adversary.

Sutter, whom the engineer had not for one second lost sight of, sighed and poured another glass of dark brown bourbon.

Jamie groaned and the engineer reflected that there were no clear issues any more. Arguments are spoiled. Clownishness always intervenes.

Rita waited until the Thigpens drifted away and then pulled the card players closer. "If you want to know what sets my teeth on edge and I strongly suspect Jamie here might be similarly affected"—she spoke in a low voice—"it is this infinitely dreary amalgam of Fundamentalism and racism."

"No, no, no," groaned Jamie loudly, actually holding his

head. "What do I care about that. That's not it." He glared at Rita angrily, embarrassing the engineer, who was aware of Rita's strong bid for low-pitched confidential talk and didn't mind obliging her. "This is all irrelevant," cried Jamie, looking behind him as if he was expecting someone. "I just don't care about that."

"What do you care about?" asked Rita after a moment.

"It's just that—I can't explain."

"Jamie wants to get away," said the engineer. "He would like to spend some time in a new place and live a simple life without the old associations—such as, for example, parking the camper on a stretch of beach."

"That is correct," said Jamie instantly and soberly.

"Listen who's telling me that," said Rita. "What in the world have I been saying all summer?" She spoke to them earnestly. Why didn't they finish the semester and join her in her house in Tesuque? Better still, she and Kitty could go now, since credit hours were more important to men than women— everyone made a fuss over Jamie's credit hours—get the place ready and the two young men could join them later. "I'm calling your bluff, Tiger. You can kill two birds with one stone. You can have your new life and you can get out of the closed society at the same time."

Jamie frowned irritably. He opened his mouth.

"Ah, that's fine, Rita," said the engineer. "That really sounds wonderful. But I think Jamie has in mind something right away, now, this minute." He rose. "Jamie."

"Now wait a minute," said Kitty, smoothing down her sweater, taking a final peep at the two pins (to think she is mine! rejoiced the engineer, all her sweet cashmered self!). "Whoa now. Not so fast. I think yall are all crazy. I'm going to the game and I'm going to the dance and I'm going to school tomorrow morning." She rose. "I'll meet yall in the garage at six thirty."

To the engineer's surprise, Jamie made no protest. Something had mollified him. At any rate he said no more about leaving and presently rose wearily and invited the engineer to the apartment for a bedside game of gin rummy. It pleased him to play a single snug game, pull the beds together and direct a small disk of light upon the tray between them where the cards were stacked.

Son Junior and his father started their favorite argument

about Big Ten versus Southeastern Conference football.

"The Big Ten on the whole is better," said Son glumly. "You have your ten teams, one as good as any other."

"Yes," said Lamar, "but there are always two or three teams in the Southeast which could take any of them. And don't you think the Big Ten doesn't know it. I happen to know that both Alabama and Ole Miss have been trying for years to schedule Ohio State and Michigan. Nothing doing and I don't blame them."

At that moment Myra, Lamar's wife, came into the pantry and the engineer was glad to have an excuse to leave. She would, he knew, do one of two things. Both were embarrassing. She would either quarrel with her husband or make up to Rita, whom she admired. It was a dread performance in either case, one from which, it is true, a certain amount of perverse skin-prickling pleasure could be taken, but not much.

Here she came toward Rita and as certain as certain could be she would make a fool of herself. Something about Rita made her lose her head. The night before, Kitty and Rita were talking, almost seriously, of going to Italy instead of New Mexico. Rita had lived once in Ferrara, she said, in a house where one of Lucrezia's husbands was said to have been murdered. Oh yes, broke in Myra, she knew all about Lucrezia Bori, the woman who had started St. Bartholomew's Massacre. And on and on she went with a mishmash about the Huguenots—her mother's family were Huguenots from South Carolina, etc. She had not the means of stopping herself. The engineer lowered his eyes.

"Pardon me," said Rita at last. "Who is it we are talking about? Lucrezia Bori, the opera singer, the Duchess of Ferrara, Lucrezia Borgia, or Catherine de' Medici?"

"I too often get the two of them mixed up," said the poor sweating engineer.

"But not the three," said Rita.

Why did she have to be cruel, though? The engineer sat between the two, transfixed by a not altogether unpleasant horribleness. He couldn't understand either woman: why one should so dutifully put her head on the block and why the other should so readily chop it off. And yet, could he be wrong or did he fancy that Rita despite her hostility felt an attraction for Myra? There was a voluptuousness about these nightly executions.

But tonight he wasn't up to it and he left with Jamie. He was careful not to forget his book about General Kirby Smith's surrender at Shreveport in 1865. He was tired of Lee's sad fruitless victories and would as soon see the whole thing finished off for good.

8. THE MAN WALKED UP AND DOWN IN THE DARKNESS OF the water oaks, emerging now and then under the street light, which shed a weak yellow drizzle. The boy sat on the steps between the azaleas and watched. He always imagined he could see the individual quanta of light pulsing from the filament.

When the man came opposite the boy, the two might exchange a word; then the man would go his way, turn under the light, and come back and speak again.

"Father, you shouldn't walk at night like this."

"Why not, son?"

"Father, they said they were going to kill you."

"They're not going to kill me, son."

The man walked. The youth listened to the music and the hum of the cottonseed-oil mill. A police car passed twice and stopped; the policeman talked briefly to the man under the street light. The man came back.

"Father, I know that the police said those people had sworn to kill you and that you should stay in the house."

"They're not going to kill me, son."

"Father, I heard them on the phone. They said you loved niggers and helped the Jews and Catholics and betrayed your own people."

"I haven't betrayed anyone, son. And I don't have much use for any of them, Negroes, Jews, Catholics, or Protestants."

"They said if you spoke last night, you would be a dead man."

"I spoke last night and I am not a dead man."

Through an open window behind the boy there came the music of the phonograph. When he looked up, he could see the Pleiades, which seemed to swarm in the thick air like lightning bugs.

"Why do you walk at night, Father?"

"I like to hear the music outside."

"Do you want them to kill you, Father?"

"Why do you ask that?"

"What is going to happen?"

"I'm going to run them out of town, son, every last miserable son of a bitch."

"Let's go around to the garden, Father. You can hear the music there."

"Go change the record, son. The needle is stuck in the groove."

"Yes sir."

The engineer woke listening. Something had happened. There was not a sound, but the silence was not an ordinary silence. It was the silence of a time afterwards. It had been violated earlier. His heart beat a strong steady alarm. He opened his eyes. A square of moonlight lay across his knees.

A shot had been fired. Had he dreamed it? Yes. But why was the night portentous? The silence reverberated with insult. There was something abroad.

Nor had it come from Sutter's room. He waited and listened twenty minutes without moving. Then he dressed and went outside into the moonlight.

The golf links was as pale as lake water. To the south Juno's temple hung low in the sky like a great fiery star. The shrubbery, now grown tall as trees, cast inky shadows which seemed to walk in the moonlight.

For a long time he gazed at the temple. What was it? It alone was not refracted and transformed by the prism of dreams and memory. But now he remembered. It was fiery old Canopus, the great red star of the south which once a year reared up and hung low in the sky over the cottonfields and canebrakes.

Turning at last, he walked quickly to the Trav-L-Aire, got his flashlight from the glove compartment, cut directly across the courtyard and entered the back door of the castle; through the dark pantry and into the front hall, where he rounded the newel abruptly and went up the stairs. To the second and then the third floor as if he knew exactly where he was, though he had only once visited the second floor and not once been above it. Around again and up a final closeted flight of narrow wooden steps and into the attic. It was a vast unfinished place with walks of lumber laid over the joists. He prowled through the wastes and caverns of the attic ribbed in the old heart pine of the 1920's. The lumber was still warm and fragrant from the afternoon sun. He shone the flashlight into every nook and cranny.

When he heard the sound behind him, he slid the switch of the flashlight and stepped four feet to the side (out of the line of fire?) and waited.

"Bill?"

A wall switch snapped on, lighting a row of bulbs in the peak of the roof. The girl, hugging her wrap with both arms, moved close to him and peered into his face. Her lips, scrubbed clean of lipstick, were slightly puffed and showed the violet color of blood.

"Are you all right?"

"Yes."

"I saw you outside."

He didn't answer.

"What are you looking for?"

"I heard something."

"You heard something up here from the garage?"

"I didn't know where it came from. I thought it might be from the attic."

"Why?"

"Is there a room up here?"

"A room?"

"A room closed off from the rest of the attic?"

"No. This is all."

He said nothing.

"You don't know where you are, do you?"

"Where I am?"

"Where are you?"

"I know." He did know now but he didn't mind her thinking he didn't. She was better, more herself, when he was afflicted.

"You were sleepwalking, I think."

"It's possible."

"Come on. I'll take you back."

"You don't have to."

"I know I don't."

He made her stay in the pantry. She was sweet and loving and not at all antic. It is strange, he thought as he stood in his own and Jamie's room a few minutes later: we are well when we are afflicted and afflicted when we are well. I can lie with her only if she tends my wounds.

"Was there a shot?" he asked her as he left.

She had shaken her head but smiled, signifying she liked him better for being mistaken.

The square of moonlight had moved onto Jamie's face. Arms folded, the engineer leaned against his bed and gazed down at the youth. The eye sockets were pools of darkness. Despite the strong black line of the brow, the nose and mouth were smudged and not wholly formed. He reminded the engineer of the graduates of Horace Mann, their faces quick and puddingish and acned, whose gift was the smart boy's knack of catching on, of hearkening: yes, I see. If Jamie could live, it was easy to imagine him for the next forty years engrossed and therefore dispensed and so at the end of the forty years still quick and puddingish and childlike. They were the lucky ones. Yet in one sense it didn't make much difference, even to Jamie, whether he lived or died—if one left out of it what he might "do" in the forty years, that is, add to "science." The difference between me and him, he reflected, is that I could not permit myself to be so diverted (but diverted from what?). How can one take seriously the Theory of Large Numbers, living in this queer not-new not-old place haunted by the goddess Juno and the spirit of the great Bobby Jones? But it was more than that. *Something is going to happen*, he suddenly perceived that he knew all along. He shivered. It is for me to wait. Waiting is the thing. Wait and watch.

Jamie's eyes seemed to open in their deep sockets. But they gazed back at him, not with their usual beamish expression, casting about for recondite areas of agreement in the space between them, but mockingly: ah, you deceive yourself, Jamie seemed to say. But when the engineer, smiling and puzzled, leaned closer, he saw that the eyes had not opened.

A bar of yellow light fell across the room. A figure was outlined in the doorway of the kitchenette. It beckoned to him.

It was Rita.

As soon as he was inside the tiny room, she closed the door and whispered: "Is Jamie asleep?"

"Yes."

Sutter stood gazing into the sink. The sink was dusty and still had a paper sticker in the basin.

"We want you to settle a little point," said Rita.

Sutter nodded. The engineer sniffed. The kitchenette had the close expired air of impasse. Now as if they were relieved by the diversion, its occupants turned toward him with a mild, unspecified interest.

"I want to know whether you are still prepared to go somewhere with Jamie," Rita said.

The engineer rubbed his forehead. "What time is it?" he asked no one in particular. Was this the true flavor of hatred, he wondered, this used, almost comfortable malice sustained between them, with its faint sexual reek? They turned as fondly to him as spent lovers greeting a strange child.

"Two thirty," said Sutter.

"What about it, Bill?" asked Rita crisply.

"What? Oh, Jamie," he repeated, aware that Sutter watched him. "Why, yes. But you knew all along that I would go with him. Why do you ask?"

"I have reason to believe that Jamie is getting restless and that he may ask Sutter to go off somewhere with him. I think this is too much to ask of Sutter."

He stole a glance at Sutter, but the latter's expression was still fond and inattentive.

"You are very much in demand, Bill," said he at last. "Jimmy wants you, not me."

"Then what's the difficulty?" asked the bemused engineer, feeling their apathy steal into his bones.

"The difficulty," said Sutter, "is that Rita wants to make sure Jimmy doesn't go anywhere with me."

"Why not?"

"That's a good question, isn't it, Rita," said Sutter, but still not quite looking at her (couldn't they stand the sight of each other?). "Why don't you want Jimmy to go with me?"

"Because of your deliberate cultivation of destructiveness, of your death-wish, not to mention your outhouse sexuality," said Rita, still smiling, and addressing Sutter through the engineer. "Every man to his own taste but you can bloody well leave Jamie out of it."

"What do you think I would do?" Sutter asked.

"I know what you have done."

"Jamie also spoke of going down to Val's," said the engineer for reasons of his own. He could not quite make this pair out and wished to get another fix on them. Val was his triangulation point.

"Val," said Rita nodding. "Yes, between the two of you, Sutter and Val, you could dispose of him very nicely. You'd kill him off in three weeks and Val would send his soul to heaven. If you don't mind I shall continue to minister to the living."

"Kill him off?" Sutter frowned but still could not tear his vacant eye from the engineer. "I understood he was in a remission."

"He was."

"What's his white count?"

"Eighteen thousand."

"How many immature forms?"

"Twenty percent."

"What's he on?"

"Prednisone."

"Wasn't he on Aminopterin?"

"That was a year ago."

"What's his red count?"

"Just under three million."

"Is his spleen palpable?"

"That's what I like about you and your sister," said Rita.

"What's that?"

"Your great concern for Jamie, one for his body, the other for his soul. The only trouble is your interest is somewhat periodic."

"That's what interests me," said Sutter. "Your interest, I mean."

"Put up your knife, you bastard. You no longer bother me."

They quarreled with the skillful absent-minded malice of married couples. Instead of taking offense, they nodded sleepily and even smiled.

"What is it you want this young man to do?" Sutter asked, shaking his head to rouse himself.

"My house in Tesuque is open," said Rita. "Teresita is there to cook. The Michelins are next door. I have even determined that they could transfer to the college in Santa Fe without loss of credit—at the end of this semester."

"Who are the Michelins?" asked the engineer.

"A duo piano team," said Sutter. "Why don't you take him out yourself, Rita?"

"You persuade him to go and I will," said Rita listlessly.

"Rita," said Sutter in the same mild temper which the engineer had not yet put down to ordinary friendliness or pluperfect malice, "what do you really care what happens to Jimmy?"

"I care."

"Tell me honestly what difference it makes to you whether Jimmy lives or dies."

The engineer was shocked but Rita replied routinely. "You know very well there is no use in my answering you. Except to say that there is such a thing as concern and there is such a thing as preference for life over death. I do not desire death, mine, yours, or Jamie's. I do not desire your version of fun and games. I desire for Jamie that he achieve as much self-fulfillment as he can in the little time he has. I desire for him beauty and joy, not death."

"That is death," said Sutter.

"You see, Bill," said Rita, smiling but still unfocused.

"I'm not sure," said the engineer, frowning. "But mainly what I don't understand is what you are asking me to do since you already know I will go anywhere Jamie wants to go and any time."

"I know, Bill," said Rita mournfully. "But apparently my former husband thinks you have reasons for staying."

"What reasons?" he asked Sutter.

"He cannot conceive that everyone is not as self-centered as he is," Rita put in before Sutter could reply.

"No, I can't, that's true," said Sutter. "But as to reasons, Bill, I know you are having some difficulties and it was my impression you wanted me to help you." Sutter was opening and closing cabinet doors, searching for the bottle which was in plain sight on the counter. The engineer handed it to him.

"What's number two?"

"Number two: I would not suppose that you were anxious to leave Kitty."

"Kitty?" The engineer's heart gave a queer extra thump.

"I could not help but observe her kissing you in the garden as you lay under a Governor Mouton."

He stopped his hand, which had started up to touch his lips. Then someone had kissed him, not Alice Bocock in his dream but Kitty herself, warm and flushed from the sun, tiny points of sweat glistening in the down of her lip. He shrugged. "I don't see what that has to do—"

"The question is not whether you would stay but whether Kitty would go with you."

"I don't think so," said the engineer, blushing with pleasure at the prospect. It had not occurred to him.

"The further question is, ahem, whether in case all three of you go, Rita might not go along with you after all."

"You can't reach me any more, you bastard," said Rita, but not, it seemed, angrier than before.

"You're right, of course," said Sutter cheerfully and earnestly, facing her for the first time over his drink. "You were right before and I was wrong. I couldn't stand prosperity. We were good, you and I, as good as you wanted us to be, and in the end I couldn't stand it. You were productive and so, for the first time in years, was I, and thanks to you. As you say, we were self-actualizing people and altogether successful, though somewhat self-conscious, in our cultivation of joy, zest, awe, freshness, and the right balance of adult autonomous control and childlike playfulness, as you used to call it. Though I don't mind telling you that I never really approved your using technical terms like 'penis envy' in ordinary conversation—"

"Excuse me," said the engineer, setting a foot toward the door. But Rita was squarely in the way and gave no sign of seeing him.

"I confess," Sutter went on, "that in the end it was I who collapsed. Being geniuses of the orgasm is the hardest of tasks, far more demanding than Calvinism. So I couldn't stand prosperity and had to mess around with Teresita. I longed for old-fashioned humbug in the same way other men long for the dear sights of home. You never really forgave me. And yet, now at this moment I forgive you for—"

"Don't you dare," said Rita in a strangled whisper, advancing upon Sutter and at the same time, fortuitously, upon the engineer, who saw his chance and made his escape. As he left he heard Sutter say:

"You always said I knew you backwards. Well, I'm telling you now that you are wrong about yourself and wrong about what you think you want. There is nothing wrong with you beyond a certain spitefulness and pride and a penchant for a certain species of bullshit. You're a fine girl, a fine Georgia girl—did you know Rita was from Georgia, Bill?—who got too far from home. Georgia girls have no business at Lake Chapala. Come on here—"

"Oh foul, foul, foul—" said Rita as he shut the door.

It is proof that the engineer was not in any ordinary sense an eavesdropper or a Peeping Tom that not only did he not head for the closet when he reached his room but instead closed the closet door and jumped into bed and pulled the pillow over his head so he could not hear a door close and so could not tell whether Rita stayed or left.

9. ON THE WAY TO SCHOOL FRIDAY MORNING, JAMIE leaned over and began to fiddle with the ashtray of the Lincoln. "I—ah—" said he, smiling a bit—they hardly ever spoke during this hour, the engineer drove, brother and sister watched the road as they would have from a schoolbus—"I've decided to quit school and go out west. Or rather transfer."

"How soon would you like to go?" asked the engineer.

"I'm ready now."

"Have you asked if it is all right with your parents?"

"Yes."

It was a dewy bright haunted October morning. The silvery old Rock City barns leaned into the early sunlight. Killdeers went crying along the fallow fields where tough shallow spiderwebs were scattered like saucers. Now and then the Lincoln crossed deep railroad cuts filled with the violet light of ironweed.

"Then it would be in June," said Kitty carelessly, putting her chin back to catch sight of the pledge pins on her cashmere sweater. "Could I go with you? Let's open up Rancho Merced," she cried, but in a standard coed cry, eyes going away.

But the engineer was already turning the Lincoln around. It was Mrs. Vaught's car, a good solid old glossy black four-door, rounded fore and aft in the style of the fifties and smelling inside of wax like a ship's saloon.

"What in the world," cried Kitty. "Where are you going?"

"Back to get the camper."

"The camper. What for?"

"Jamie said he wanted to go out west. The camper would be better than this car."

"My God, he didn't mean now!"

"I thought he did."

They had gotten as far as Enfield. Even after the few weeks of their commuting, every inch of the way had become as familiar to them as their own backyard: this was the place where they always ran afoul of an unlucky traffic light which detained them at an empty crossing for an endless forty-five seconds. Always when they passed at this hour a line of sun-light and shade fell across the lettering of an abandoned store-front, SALOMON, whose middle o had fallen off, leaving its outline on the brick. Enfield was a defunct coal depot on the L & N Railroad.

"Jamie, tell him to turn around. I have an eight o'clock and so do you."

But Jamie only went on with his smiling and his fiddling with the ashtray.

The engineer was smiling too, but from the pleasure of having her next to him and touching him at arm, hip, and calf. What a lovely fine fragrant Chi Omega she was in her skirt and sweater. A beautiful brown-kneed cheerleader and it was cheer to sit beside her. She saved them both from this decrepit mournful countryside. Without her he'd have jumped straight into one of these lonesome L & N gorges where old train whistles from the 1930's still echoed.

"The Tennessee game is tomorrow," she said laughing, truly shaken because now she believed them. Overnight she had turned into a fierce partisan for the Colonels, who were now ranked number two in the United States. "Tennessee is number four and if we beat them—"

"That's right," said Jamie, who, now that it was settled, sat back and took notice of the countryside. It was very different now, fifteen minutes later and what with them not going but returning with the sun in their faces. The hamlets seemed to be stirring with ordinary morning enterprise.

"How long will it take you to get ready?" Jamie asked him.

"I can have the camper stocked in thirty minutes!"

"O.K."

"I have never in my life," said Kitty, tapping her Scripto pencil on the world anthology.

He saw that she was angry. If Jamie had not been with them, he would have stopped then and there and kissed her pretty pouting lips and pressed her lovely cashmered person against him, Chi O pin and all. It was the sisterly aspect of her which excited him, big sister sweetheart at eight o'clock in the morning, her mouth not yet cleared of breakfast butter and molasses.

"Of course you're going with us," he said to her, sending the Lincoln swooping along on its limber old springs.

"Hah. Not me, boy," she cried, casting about her huffy coed glances.

"I'm serious."

"I'm serious too."

"Is it all right with you, Jamie, if your sister goes?"

"I don't care who goes. But I'm going."

"Why for God's sake?" For the first time she spoke directly to her brother.

"What do you mean, why?" he asked her irritably. "Does there have to be a why?"

When Kitty did not answer and in fact began to blink back tears Jamie said: "I am not interested in seeing the Tennessee game."

"And I happened to know how much you like Chem 2. Bubba Ray Ross was telling me. I'll bet you've heard too, haven't you Billy?"

"No."

"I am not interested in Chem 2," Jamie said, "or 3 or 4."

"Well, what in the world are you interested in?" Kitty was smiling angrily and busily tucking her skirt under her knee and squaring away the world anthology on her lap.

"I—ah. I just want to take this trip. No, to tell you the truth I'm going to transfer. I've already spoken to—it can be done."

"Transfer! Where? Where're yall going to live—in the camper?"

"I know this boy who goes to school in Albuquerque. In fact I heard from him yesterday. I correspond with him quite a bit. I could live with him, in fact." After a moment he added: "His father has a shop of some sort. Out on the highway."

"Oh, for heaven's sake. Tell him, Billy."

"All I want Jamie to tell me is whether he has made arrangements to live with somebody or whether he wants me to go with him."

"Well, I mean, if you want to."

"O.K."

"Do yall mean to tell me that you're going to jump in that little truck and go out there and park it somewhere and just start going to school?"

Jamie smiled and leaning forward spoke to both of them in a different voice. "I remember reading this novel in school last year, by a Russian writer. I think his name was Goncharov, or something like that, but he is a wonderful writer. Do you know him?"

"No," said the engineer. Kitty did not answer.

"He's really a good writer," said Jamie, going back to his ashtray. "At least in this novel. It was about this young man who was a refugee or a prisoner, I forget which. He was traveling the whole length of Russia in a cattle car, along with hundreds of others. He was sick with brain fever, whatever that is, I have only come across brain fever in Russian novels. It was summer and they were crossing Siberia, day after day, weeks even. The car was crowded and he had one tiny corner and a bit of straw and that was all. And though he was quite ill and even delirious at times, the strange thing about it was that it wasn't so bad. Through the slats of the car he could see the fields, which were covered by a little blue flower. And of course the sky. The train stopped often and peasant women would bring him bowls of blueberries and fresh warm milk— that was the peculiar thing about it, that even though he knew no one and the train only stopped for a few minutes at a time, somehow news of this young man traveled ahead of the train and they expected him. And though everybody else on the train became exhausted by the hardships of the trip, he actually got better! It was really good. I think it's the best novel I ever read."

"That's fine, Jamie, that's fine and I agree with you," said Kitty peevishly. "But I still don't see why—"

The engineer interrupted her. "Are you coming?"

"Me? No, indeed."

They were silent when the Lincoln turned up the links road. When Jamie got out into the garage, which smelled of wet concrete from David's hosing, the engineer held Kitty.

197

"What?" she said, still turned away and not quite managing a look back at him.

"I want to tell you something."

"What?"

"Or rather ask you something."

"What?"

"I want you to come with us."

"Are you kidding?"

"No, I want you to marry me."

"In the next thirty minutes?"

"Look. Jamie wants to go and I think we ought to go with him."

"*Why* does he want to go?" She was peevish still, but there was a settling under her peevishness. Though one foot was still out of the car and her book cradled in her arm, she had settled back half a millimeter.

"We can be married in Louisiana tomorrow."

"Now I have heard it all. I don't mind saying that I have heard it *all*."

"Put your book down."

"*What?*"

"Give me your book."

"What for?"

But she gave it to him and he threw it into the back seat and took hold of her while the warm Lincoln ticked away in the resounding garage. Oh, damnable straight upstanding Lincoln seat. He was almost beside himself with tenderness at the eight o'clock splendor of her. "I'm in love," he said, kissing her and taking hold of the warm pad back of her knee, which he loved best of all when she was leading cheers. But the angles were bad and contrived against him.

"Good God," cried Kitty, breaking free. "What in the world has happened to you and Jamie this morning! You're crazy!"

"Come here and let me hold you tight."

"Hold me tight, my foot."

"You didn't answer my question."

"What question?"

"Will you marry me?"

"Jeezum," she said in a new expression of hers, something she got from the Chi O's. And retrieving her world anthology from the back seat, she left him alone in the garage.

10. JAMIE BECAME CHEERFUL AND RED-CHEEKED AS they fitted out the Trav-L-Aire. While the engineer set about laying in his usual grits and buttermilk and slab bacon and filling the tank with the sweet artesian water of the valley against the day of the evil alkali water of the desert, Jamie staked out the upper forward bunk as his private domain. It was a broad bed lying athwart the trim ship, with a fine view forward over the top of the cab. There was a shelf for his radio, a recessed reading light something like the old Pullman upper berth. Jamie hit on the idea of replacing the mattress with a cot pad which not only gave him the narrow hard corner he wanted but left a gutter just wide enough to hold his books.

"Let's take plenty of fresh milk with us," said Jamie.

"O.K."

"I've drunk a lot of milk lately. I've gained three pounds."

"Good."

Jamie stretched out on the hard bed and watched the engineer store away the staples Lugurtha had given him from the kitchen. "You know I truly believe that if I could live a simple life, I could actually conserve my energy and therefore gain strength. I honestly think it's a question of living simply and conserving your energy. I'll live right here, get up, go to class, come back, get up, eat, come back, etcetera. Don't you agree?"

"Yes." To tell the truth, it didn't seem unreasonable.

"Are you really going to marry Kitty?"

"I asked her. But if I do and she does come along, it will be just the same for you. These are your quarters if we are married, yours and mine if we're not."

"What if she won't, ah—go? Will you still come?"

"If you want me to."

"O.K.," said Jamie and began to arrange his books in alphabetical order. "Where do you keep your telescope?"

"Here."

"Oh yes. I remember. Look. I'm bringing my Freylinghausen star charts along. I understand the atmosphere is a great deal clearer in New Mexico."

"That's right. Now, Jamie, I think you'd better go find your parents. It is not enough for you to tell me that you have their permission. They must tell me too."

"O.K."

"We'll drive till we get tired and start out again when we feel like it."

11. IT TURNED OUT TO BE A MORNING FOR DEALING with practical matters. Two letters awaited him on the refectory table in the castle hall. He never received mail from anywhere. They had been written more than two weeks earlier and addressed to the Y.M.C.A. in New York, forwarded to General Delivery in Williamsburg and thence to the Vaughts' home address. Both had to do with money. One was from his Uncle Fannin, who lived in Shut Off, Louisiana. His uncle wrote to remind him that although the "place" had been sold many years ago, certain mineral rights had been retained, and that he had recently received a lease offer from Superior Oil Company of California. The rights, as he must know, were jointly owned by the two surviving male Barretts. Would he, the younger, signify his intention in this matter? He, the elder, would as soon accept the offer. The share of each would come to $8,300. The letter was written in neat pencil script on ruled paper which had been torn from a pad.

The other letter had also to do with money. The First National Bank of Ithaca wished to advise him of the existence of a savings account in his name, opened for him by his father in the year 1939. What with the compounding of interest, his balance now stood at $1,715.60. The occasion of this notice was the present reorganization of the bank. He pondered—1939. That was the year of his birth.

Jamie was delayed. His clothes still lay on the bed in the garage apartment. After waiting for him a good forty minutes, the engineer returned to the house. Lugurtha was making beaten biscuits for the football picnic tomorrow. On the marble slab sifted with flour, she rolled out a soft mitt of dough.

Kitty met him in the pantry, in a secret glee, and hustled him into the "little" pantry, a dark cold closet where potatoes and onions were stored in bins. He peered at her.

"My darling," she whispered, giving him a passionate kiss and making herself free of him in an entirely new way, all joyous legs and arms. He felt a vague unease. "Guess what?"

"What?" Through two doorways he could see Lugurtha handle the dough up into the air, fingers dancing under it, giving way, yet keeping it up, setting gravity at nought.

"Jamie has decided not to go until after Christmas."

"Why?"

"Then he will have his semester credits and can transfer without losing a month's work."

"Where is he?"

"In the sun parlor. Darling, don't you see what this means?"

"Yes, but—"

"What's the matter?" Swaying, her hands clasped in the small of his back in a new conjugal way, like a French girl saying farewell to her *poilu*, she squeezed him close and leaned away from him.

"I am afraid he might be doing it for me. Us."

"He wants to!"

"I'm afraid you talked him into it."

"It was his idea!"

"Who talked to him?"

Her eyes sparkled triumphantly. "Rita!"

"Rita?" He pondered. "Did Rita know that you and I might be leaving with Jamie today?"

"Yes!" Swaying triumphantly.

"And she talked Jamie into staying?"

"She didn't talk him into anything. It was his idea. In fact, he wants more time to plan the trip." Her tongue hollowed out her cheek and made a roguish joke. "What a nut! Imagine the three of us wandering around Arkansas in the middle of the winter like a bunch of Okies." She shook her head at him fondly, wifely. "I've got news for you, you big dope."

"Eh?"

"You're among friends here, you know."

"Yes." What he could not tell her was: if I can marry, then you can travel. I can even stand this new horsy conjugal way, this sad *poilu* love with you, if you will hit the road with me. Jamie is dying, so he needs to go. But I need to go too. Now the pantry's got us, locked in, with a cold potato love, and you the chatelaine with the keys at your belt. "I'd better go see Jamie."

"He'll tell you. What's the matter?" Her fingers touched his sweating forehead.

"I'm hot."

"It's freezing in here."

His eyes were caught in a stare. Lugurtha's working of the biscuit dough, the quick kneading gathering movement of her hands against the sifted marble, put him in mind of something. She sang:

> Up in an airplane
> Smoking her sweet cigarette

Keeping his hand clasped in hers, Kitty led him to the sun parlor and showed, not him to them but them to him, as if they were trophies, the articles of her proof: Jamie stretched on the sofa with a wet handkerchief across his eyes; Mrs. Vaught waiting, hands outstretched to them: a new Mrs. Vaught, too, a genial little pony of a lady, head to one side, pince-nez flashing quick family love-flashes, Rita in a wide stance, back to the coal fire. Mrs. Vaught gave him a quick press of her hand and a kiss, a dismaying thing in itself. She said nothing, but there was an easement in the air, the tender settled sense of larger occasions.

The sun parlor itself was an unused ceremonial sort of place. He had only been inside it once before, when Mr. Vaught showed him his old Philco, a tall console glistening with O'Cedar. It had a tilted sounding board and it still worked. Mr. Vaught turned it on and presently the tubes heated up and put out regular 1932 static and the smell of hot speaker-silk such as used to attend the broadcasts of Ben Bernie and Ruth Etting and the Chase & Sanborn hour.

The cold wind pressed against the old-style double-hung windows, leaked through and set dust devils whirling along the tile under the wicker. There were lacquered Chinese boxes and miniature chests of drawers, a mahjong set, and a large gonglike table; the brass coalbox was stamped with a scene of jolly Dutch burghers. The coal grate, which had not been used, gave off a smell of burnt varnish. In one corner stood a stork five feet tall with a hollow eye and a beak which cut off the ends of cigars.

Mrs. Vaught twined her arm in his and, rocking slightly, held the two of them by the fire. "Did I tell you that I knew your mother very well one summer?"

"No'm."

"It was at the old Tate Springs Hotel. Lucy Hunicutt was the prettiest little thing I have ever seen—all dark hair and big violet eyes. And beaus! They swarmed around her like flies. She was a demon tennis player and wore a little cap like Helen Wills. In fact, everyone called her 'Little Miss Poker Face.' But there was one boy who was hopelessly in love with her— Boylston Fisk from Chattanooga (Boylston is now chairman of the board of Youngstown and Reading)—and he was the handsomest man I ever saw. But he could never dance more than three steps with her before somebody would break. So she told him if he could ever find out the name of her favorite piece she would dance it with him. Well, somehow he did. It was 'Violets.' And don't you know, he asked the orchestra to play it, not during the dance but while everyone was still at dinner. And he came across the room to her table with every eye on him and bowed and said: Miss Hunicutt, I believe this is our dance. It was like a dare, don't you see, but she got up! And they danced the whole piece out on the floor by themselves. I swear it was the most romantic thing I ever saw in my life!"

It was as if the memory of this gentler age had dispensed Mrs. Vaught from the terrible quarrels of the present. She softened. His radar sensed it without quite defining it: the connection between the past time and the present insane quarrel over fluoridation. For him it was the other way around! It was the olden time with its sweetness and its great occasions which struck a dread to his heart! It was past fathoming.

Jamie lay with the handkerchief across his eyes and said nothing. When Mrs. Vaught let him go, the engineer went over and sat on the sofa beside him.

"What happened?"

"What do you mean what happened?" said Jamie irritably.

"I thought we were leaving."

"I don't mind waiting a while. After all, what's the big hurry?"

"But it was not your idea, the postponement."

"Sure it was!"

"I'm packed and ready to go."

"I know you are."

"If you want to go, all you have to do is to get up and we'll leave. And I think Kitty will go with us. But even if she doesn't, I'm ready."

"I know you are." Jamie looked at him curiously. The engineer blushed.

"If you are staying on my account, then I don't want it. I'd truly rather leave. You understand?"

"Yes."

"So I am putting you on your honor to say whether it is on my account or anyone's account that you are staying. If it is, then let's go."

Jamie took away the wet handkerchief and wiped his mouth but did not reply. As the engineer waited, the cold air seeped into his shoes. The jaybirds called in the ragged garden outside. Above the Philco hung a great gloomy etching of Rheims cathedral depicting 1901 tourists with parasols and wide hats and bustles strolling about its portal. The three women in the parlor, he suddenly became aware, had fallen silent. Turning his head a degree, he saw that they were watching the two of them. But when he arose, Kitty and her mother had put their heads together and were talking in the most animated way, Mrs. Vaught counting off items on her fingers as if she were compiling a list of some sort. Jamie put the handkerchief across his eyes.

Rita still stood in front of the fire, feet wide apart, hands locked behind her. She watched ironically as the shivering engineer came up to get warm.

"What's the problem?"

"Ma'am?"

"You and Jamie don't seem to be very happy about things."

"Jamie told me this morning he wanted to take a trip out west—and leave immediately. I told him I would. Now I'm afraid he's delaying the trip on my account. Don't you think the trip would be a good idea?" He watched her closely.

She shrugged. "Oh, I don't know. How could a delay of a few weeks matter one way or another? Perhaps it would be better to wait at least until everyone knows what he and she really wants to do. Right now I can't help but detect a certain precipitousness in the air. I don't think it's a bad idea, once decisions are made, to live with them for a while, to see if perhaps they can be lived with."

As he watched, she set her jaw askew, made her eyes fine, and moved her chin to and fro in the web of her thumb. It was a gesture that reminded him strangely of his own father. Suddenly a thrill of recognition and of a nameless sweet horribleness ran like electricity down his spine and out along the nerves between his ribs. *She was daring him.* Very well, said the fine-eyed expression and the quirky (yes, legal) eyebrow. Let us see what we shall see. Perhaps I know something about you, you don't know. Let us see if you can do what you say you want to do, stay here and get married in the regular woman's way of getting married, marry a wife and live a life. Let us see. I dare you.

But was he being flattered or condemned? Was she saying you know better than to stay here or you don't have what it takes to stay? He cocked an eye at her and opened his mouth to say something, but at that moment Kitty plucked at his sleeve. "Let's go, Tiger."

"What?"

"I have a couple of calls to make. You want to come along?"

"Sure."

There had occurred between the people in the room, in the very air itself, a falling upward of things and into queer new place, like the patterns of a kaleidoscope. But it was his own Kitty who had been most mysteriously transformed. Her cheek was flushed and she swung her shoulders in her school blouse like a secretary sitting between three desks. She bustled. No longer was she the solitary girl on the park bench, as inward and watchful as he, who might wander with him through old green Louisiana, perch on the back step of the camper of an evening with the same shared sense of singularity of time and the excellence of place. No, she was Miss Katherine Gibbs Vaught and the next thing he knew she'd have her picture in the *Commercial Appeal*.

"Where're we going?" he asked her, trying to keep up as she sailed through the pantry.

"I am to deliver you to someone who wishes a word with you."

The next thing he knew, he was sitting in Kitty's tiny Sprite, his knees about his ears as they went roaring up and over the mountain and down into the city.

"What is this place?" he asked when they stopped in an acre or so of brand-new automobiles.

"The shop, crazy. Poppy wants to talk to you!"

He sat blinking around him, hands on his knees. The

"shop" was Mr. Vaught's Confederate Chevrolet agency, the second largest in the world. Dozens of salesmen in Reb-colonel hats and red walking canes threaded their way between handsome Biscaynes and sporty Corvettes. By contrast with their jaunty headgear and the automobiles, which were as bright as tropical birds, the faces of the salesmen seemed heavy and anxious.

"Come on," cried Kitty, already on her way.

They found Mr. Vaught in a vast showroom holding another acre of Chevrolets. He was standing in a fenced-off desk area talking to Mr. Ciocchio, his sales manager. Kitty introduced him and vanished.

"You see this sapsucker," said Mr. Vaught to Mr. Ciocchio, taking the engineer by the armpit.

"Yes sir," said the other, responding with a cordial but wary look. The sales manager was a big Lombard of an Italian with a fine head of thick curly hair. In his Reb-colonel hat he looked like Garibaldi.

"Do you know what he can do?"

"No sir."

"He can hit a golf ball over three hundred yards and he is studying a book by the name of *The Theory of Large Numbers*. What do you think of a fellow like that?"

"That's all right." Mr. Ciocchio smiled and nodded as cordially as ever. The engineer noticed that his eyes did not converge but looked at him, one past each ear.

"He is evermore smart."

The engineer nodded grimly. This old fellow, his employer, he had long since learned, had a good working blade of malice. Was this not in fact his secret: that he had it in for everybody?

"Sir," he said, politely disengaging himself from Mr. Vaught's master grip. "Kitty said you wished to see me. As a matter of fact, I wanted to see you earlier. Jamie said he wanted to take a trip out west. I told him I would take him if it met with your approval."

Mr. Ciocchio, seeing his chance, vanished as quickly as Kitty had.

"But now, it seems, plans have been changed. Jamie tells me he wishes to postpone the trip. I might add too that I asked Kitty to marry me. This seems as good a time as any to inform you of my intentions and to ask your approval. I am here, however, at your request. At least, that is my understanding."

"Well now," said the old man, turning away and looking back, eyeing him with his sliest gleam. Aha! At least he knows I'm taking none of his guff, the engineer thought. "Billy boy," he said in a different voice and hobbled over to the rail with a brand-new limp—oh, what a rogue he was. "Take a look at this place. Do you want to know what's wrong with it?"

"Yes sir."

"Do you see those fellows out there?" He nodded to a half dozen colonels weaving fretfully through the field of cars.

"Yes sir."

"I'll tell you a funny damn thing. Now there's not a thing in the world wrong with those fellows except for one thing. They want to sell. They know everything in the book about selling. But there is one thing they can't do. They can't close."

"Close?"

"Close out. They can't get a man in here where those fellows are." He pointed to more colonels sitting at desks in the fenced-off area. "That's where we sign them up. But they can't get them in here. They stand out there and talk and everybody is nice and agreeable as can be. And the man says all right, thanks a lot, I'll be back. And he's gone. Now you know, it's a funny thing but that is something you can't teach a fellow—when the time has come to close. We need a coordinator."

"Sir?"

"We need a liaison man to cruise the floor, watch all the pots, see which one is coming to a boil. Do you understand me?"

"Yes sir," said the engineer gloomily.

"I'm going to tell you the plain truth, Billy," said the old man in a tone of absolute sincerity. "You can't hire a good man for love or money. I'd pay twenty thousand a year for just an ordinary good man."

"Yes sir."

"I can't understand it."

"What's that, sir?"

"What makes those fellows so mis'able? Look at them. They are the most mis'able bunch of folks I ever saw."

"You mean they're unhappy?"

"Look at them."

They were. "What makes them miserable?"

"You figure *that* out and I'll pay you twenty-five."

"Yes sir," said the engineer absently; he had caught sight of Kitty waiting for him in her Sprite.

"Listen son," said the old man, drawing him close again. "I'm going to tell you the truth. I don't know what the hell is going on out there with those women and Jamie and all. Whatever yall want to do is all right with me. And I'm tickled to death to hear about you and Kitty. More than delighted. I know that you and I understand each other and that I'm more than happy to have you with us here any time you feel like it."

"Yes sir," said the engineer glumly.

By evening the engineer felt as uncommonly bad as he had felt good when he had set out for the university early in the morning of the same day. His knee leapt. Once he thought he heard the horrid ravening particles which used to sing in the pale sky over New York and Jersey. To make matters worse, everyone else in the pantry felt better than ever. It was the night before the Tennessee game. There was a grace and a dispensation in the air, an excitement and hope about the game on the morrow and a putting away of the old sad unaccomplished past. Tomorrow our own lads, the good smiling easy youths one met on the campus paths, but on the gridiron a ferocious black-helmeted wrecking crew, collide with the noble old single-wing of Tennessee. A big game is more than a game. It allows the kindling of hope and the expectation of great deeds. One liked to drink his drink the night before and muse over it: what will happen?

Ordinarily he too, the engineer, liked nothing better than the penultimate joys of a football weekend. But tonight he was badly unsettled. The two brothers, Jamie and Sutter, had been deep in talk at the blue bar for a good half hour. And Rita had Kitty off in the bay, Rita speaking earnestly with her new level-browed legal expression, Kitty blossoming by the minute: a lovely flushed bride. Every few seconds her eyes sought him out and sent him secret shy Mary Nestor signals. Now it was she who was sending the signals and he who was stove up and cranky. Only once had she spoken to him and then to whisper: "It may be possible to swing a sweetheart ceremony with the Chi O's as maids. I'm working on it." "Eh? What's that," cocking his good ear and holding down his knee. But she was off again before he had a chance to discover what she meant. It left him uneasy.

Something else disturbed him. Son Thigpen had brought over a carload of classmates from the university. Son, as morose as he was, and devoted exclusively to his Thunderbird and the fraternity (not the brothers themselves but the idea, Hellenism, as he called it), had nevertheless the knack of attracting large numbers of friends, lively youths and maids who liked him despite his sallowness and glumness. Now, having delivered this goodly company, he stood apart and fiddled with his Thunderbird keys. His guests were Deltans, from the engineer's country, though he did not know them. But he knew their sort and it made him uneasy to see how little he was like them, how easy they were in their ways and how solitary and Yankeefied he was—though they seemed to take him immediately as one of them and easy too. The young men were Sewanee Episcopal types, good soft-spoken hard-drinking graceful youths, gentle with women and very much themselves with themselves, set, that is, for the next fifty years in the actuality of themselves and their own good names. They knew what they were, how things were and how things should be. As for the engineer, he didn't know. I'm from the Delta too, thought he, sticking his hand down through his pocket, and I'm Episcopal; why ain't I like them, easy and actual? Oh, to be like Rooney Lee. The girls were just as familiar to him, though he'd never met them either. Lovely little golden partridges they were, in fall field colors, green-feathered and pollen-dusted. Their voices were like low music and their upturned faces were like flowers. They were no different at all from the lovely little bitty steelhearted women who sat at the end of the cotton rows and held the South together when their men came staggering home from Virginia all beaten up and knocked out of the war, who sat in their rocking chairs and made everybody do right; they were enough to scare you to death. But he for his Kitty, a little heavy-footed, yes, and with a tendency to shoulder a bit like a Wellesley girl and not absolutely certain of her own sex, a changeling (she was flushed and high-colored now just because she had found out what she was—a bride). For example, Kitty, who had worked at it for ten years, was still a bad dancer, where every last one of these Delta partridges was certain to be light and air in your arms.

They were talking about politics and the Negro, who was now rumored to be headed for the campus this weekend. "Do yall know the difference between a nigger and an ape?" said Lamar Thigpen, embracing all three Deltans. They're good chaps, though, thought the engineer distractedly, and, spying Mr. Vaught circling the walls, thought of something he wanted to ask him and took out after him, pushing his kneecap in with each step like a polio victim. They're good chaps and so very much at one with themselves and with the dear world around them as bright and sure as paradise. The game was tomorrow and they were happy about that; they knew what they wanted and who they hated. Oh, why ain't I like them, thought the poor engineer, who was by no means a liberal—never in fact giving such matters a single thought—but who rather was so mystified by white and black alike that he could not allow himself the luxury of hatred. Oh, but they were lordly in theirs, he noticed, as he hobbled along. Then forgetting what he wanted to ask Mr. Vaught, he fetched up abruptly and took his pulse. "I'm not at all well," he said to himself.

"What's the matter," asked Sutter, who had been watching him from his kitchen chair at the blue bar. Jamie, the engineer noticed, had left.

"I don't feel well. Where's Jamie?"

"He went to bed."

"I wanted to ask him what his plans were."

"Don't worry about him. He's all right. What about you?"

"I think my nervous condition is worse. I feel my memory slipping."

"What was that book you were reading earlier?"

"Freeman's *R. E. Lee*."

"Are you still strongly affected by the Civil War?"

"Not as strongly as I used to be."

"How strongly was that?"

"When I was at Princeton, I blew up a Union monument. It was only a plaque hidden in the weeds behind the chemistry building, presented by the class of 1885 in memory of those who made the supreme sacrifice to suppress the infamous rebellion, or something like that. It offended me. I synthesized a liter of trinitrotoluene in the chemistry lab and blew it up one Saturday afternoon. But no one ever knew what had been blown up. It seemed I was the only one who knew the monument was there. It was thought to be a Harvard prank. Later, in New York, whenever there was a plane crash, I would scan the passenger list to see how many Southerners had been killed."

"And yet you are not one of them." Sutter nodded toward the Thigpens.

210

"No."

"Are your nationalistic feelings strongest before the onset of your amnesia?"

"Perhaps they are," said the engineer, gazing at himself in the buzzing blue light of the mirror. "But that's not what I'm interested in."

Sutter gazed at him. "What are you interested in?"

"I—" the engineer shrugged and fell silent.

"What is it?"

"Why do they feel so good," he nodded toward the Deltans, "and I feel so bad?"

Sutter eyed him. "The question is whether they feel as good as you think, and if they do, then the question is whether it is necessarily worse to feel bad than good under the circumstances."

"That doesn't mean anything to me," said the engineer irritably.

"One morning," said Sutter, "I got a call from a lady who said that her husband was having a nervous breakdown. I knew the fellow. As a matter of fact, they lived two doors down. He was a Deke from Vanderbilt, president of Fairfield Coke and a very good fellow, cheerful and healthy and openhanded. It was nine o'clock in the morning, so I walked over from here. His wife let me in. There he stands in the living room dressed for work in his Haspel suit, shaved, showered, and in the pink, in fact still holding his attaché case beside him. All in order except that he was screaming, his mouth forming a perfect O. His corgi was howling and his children were peeping out from behind the stereo. His wife asked me for an opinion. After quieting him down and having a word with him, I told her that his screaming was not necessarily a bad thing in itself, that in some cases a person is better off screaming than not screaming—except that he was frightening the children. I prescribed the terminal ward for him and in two weeks he was right as rain."

The engineer leaned a degree closer. "I understand that. Now what I want to know is this: do you mean that in the terminal ward he discovered only that he was not so bad off, or is there more to it than that?"

Sutter looked at him curiously but did not reply.

"Did you get in trouble with him too?"

Sutter shrugged. "It was a near thing. His wife, who was a psychiatrically oriented type, put him into analysis with an old-timey hard-assed Freudian—they're only to be found down here in the South now—and he went crazy. Of course I got the blame for not putting him into treatment earlier. But she didn't sue me."

The engineer nodded toward the Deltans. "What about them?"

"What about them?"

"Would you put them in the terminal ward?"

"They're not screaming."

"Should they be screaming?"

"I should not presume to say. I only say that if they were screaming, I could have helped them once. I cannot do even that now. I am a pathologist."

The engineer frowned. He felt a stirring of anger. There was something unpleasantly ironic about Sutter's wry rapid way of talking. It was easy to imagine him ten years from now haunting a barroom somewhere and pattering on like this to any stranger. He began to understand why others made a detour around him, so to speak, and let him alone.

12. HE COULDN'T SLEEP. AS HE LAY AT ATTENTION LIS-tening to the frolic in John Houghton's room below, he began to skid a little and not recollect exactly where he was, like a boy who wakes in a strange bed. In the next bed Jamie breathed regularly. By three o'clock in the morning he was worse off than at any time since Eisenhower was President when he had worked three months for a florist in Cincinnati, assaulted by the tremendous *déjà vus* of hot green growing things.

At last he went out to the landing and, seeing a light under Sutter's door, knocked. Sutter answered immediately. He was sitting in the wagonwheel chair, dressed in the same clothes, feet flat on the floor, arms lying symmetrically on the rests. There was no drink or book beside him.

At last Sutter turned his head. "What can I do for you?" The naked ceiling bulb cast his eye sockets into bluish shadow. The engineer wondered if Sutter had taken a drug.

"I have reason to believe I am going into a fugue," said the engineer matter-of-factly. He turned up the collar of his pajamas. It was cold in here. "I thought you might be able to help me."

"Jimmy is in there dying. Don't you think I should be more concerned with helping him?"

"Yes, but I am going to live, and according to you that is harder."

Sutter didn't smile. "Why do you ask me?"

"I don't know."

"What do you want me to do?"

"Tell me what you know."

"Why don't you get married and live happily ever afterwards?"

"Why was that man screaming that you told me about? You never did say."

"I didn't ask him."

"But you knew why."

Sutter shrugged.

"Was it a psychological condition?" asked the engineer, cocking his good ear.

"A psychological condition," Sutter repeated slowly.

"What was wrong with him, Dr. Vaught?" The pale engineer seemed to lean forward a good ten degrees, like the clowns whose shoes are nailed to the floor.

Sutter got up slowly, scratching his hair vigorously with both hands.

"Come over here."

Sutter led him to the card table, which had been cleared of dirty swabs but which still smelled of fruity Hoppe's gun oil. He fetched two chrome dinette chairs and set them on opposite sides of the table.

"Sit down. Now. I think you should go to sleep."

"All right."

"Give me your hand." Sutter took his hand in the cross-palm grip of Indian wrestling. "Look at me."

"All right."

"Does it embarrass you to hold hands with a man and look at him?"

"Yes." Sutter's hand felt as dry and tendinous as broomstraw.

"Count to thirty with me. When we finish counting, you will then be able to do what I tell you."

"All right."

When they had finished counting, Sutter said: "You say you believe I know something about you. Now you will also do what I tell you."

"All right."

"When you leave this room, you will go to your room and sleep soundly for nine hours. Do you understand?"

"Yes."

"Now when you do get up tomorrow, something is going to happen. As a consequence, you are going to be in a better position to decide what you want to do."

"All right."

"For the next few days you may have a difficult time. Now I shall not tell you what to do, but I will tell you now that you will be free to act. Do you understand me?"

"Yes."

"If you find yourself in too tight a spot, that is, in a situation where it is difficult to live from one minute to the next, come and see me and I'll help you. I may not be here, but you can find me. Do you understand?"

"Yes."

"Very well. Good night." Sutter yawned, pushed back his chair, and began to scratch his head with both hands.

"Good night."

In his cold bed, the engineer curled up like a child and fell at once into a deep and dreamless sleep.

13. HE AWOKE TO A COLD DIAMOND-BRIGHT MORNING. Jamie's bed was empty. When he crossed the courtyard, the Thigpens were leaving for the game. Lamar gave John Houghton a drink, which he drained off in one gulp, little finger stuck out. In return, John Houghton did a buck-and-wing, swooping down with tremendous swoops and fetching up light as a feather, clapping his hands not quite together but scuffing the horny parts past each other. The engineer, standing pale and blinking in the sunlight, was afraid Lamar was going to say "Get hot!" or something similar, but he didn't. In fact, as the little caravan got underway and the three servants stood waving farewell on the back steps,

Lugurtha fluttering her apron, Lamar shook his head fondly. "There's nothing like the old-timey ways!" he said. The Vaught retainers seemed to remind Lamar of an earlier, more gracious time, even though the purple castle didn't look much like an antebellum mansion and the golf links even less like a cotton plantation.

Kitty was eating batter cakes in the pantry. She eyed him somewhat nervously, he thought. But when later he kissed her mouth, not quite cleared of Br'er Rabbit syrup, she kissed him back with her new-found conjugal passion, though a bit absent-mindedly.

"Rita wants to see you," she told him as she led him through the dark dining room. "Something has happened."

"Where's Jamie?"

"I'm afraid that's what it's about."

"Come over here a minute," he said, trying to pull her behind a screen of iridescent butterfly wings. He felt like a sleepy husband.

"Later, later," said Kitty absently. For the first time he saw that the girl was badly upset.

As they entered Rita's tower bedroom, Kitty, he noticed, became all at once pudding-faced and hangdog. She looked like Jamie. She hung back like a fourteen-year-old summoned to the principal's office. Her noble matutinal curves seemed to turn to baby fat.

Rita, dressed in a heavy silk kimono, lay propped on a large bed strewn with magazines, cigarettes, eyeglasses, and opened mail. She was reading a book, which she set face down on the bed. From force of habit and by way of getting at someone, he set his head over to see the title. It was *The Art of Loving*. The engineer experienced a vague disappointment. He too had read the book and, though he had felt very good during the reading, it had not the slightest effect on his life.

Getting quickly out of bed and holding an unlit cigarette to her lip, Rita strode back and forth between them. So formidable was it, this way she had of setting the side of her face into a single ominous furrow (something was up all right), that he forgot all about the book.

"Well, they've done it up brown this time," she said at last, stopping at the window and rubbing her chin in the web of her thumb. "Or rather *he* has."

"Who?" asked the engineer.

"Sutter," she said, turning to face him. Kitty stood beside

him as flat-footed and button-eyed as Betty Jo Jones in Ithaca Junior High. "Sutter has left and taken Jamie with him," said Rita quietly.

"Where, Ree?" Kitty cried, but somewhat rhetorically, her eyes in her eyebrows. The surprise was for his benefit.

Rita shrugged.

"I have an idea where they might be headed," said the engineer.

Rita rolled her eyes. "Then for pity's sake tell us."

"Jamie was determined to go either out west or to Val's."

"Then I suggest that you jump in your little truck without further ado and go get him."

"What I can't understand," said the engineer absently, putting his fist to his forehead as if to cudgel his poor wits, "is why Dr. Vaught left when he did. He told me— Well, I had no idea he was planning to make a change."

"It seems a change was made for him," said Rita dryly.

He became aware that Kitty was woolgathering. Something had happened and she knew about it.

"What change is that?" he asked.

"Sutter has been discharged from the hospital staff." Removing her glasses, she thrust them into the deep pocket of her kimono sleeve. Her pale rough face looked naked and serious and justified, like a surgeon who comes out of the operating room and removes his mask. "It was understood that if he left, he would not be prosecuted."

"Prosecuted for what?" Up to his usual tricks, the engineer took her import not from the words she said but from the signals. That the import was serious indeed was to be judged from her offhandedness, the license she allowed herself in small things. She lit a cigarette and with a serious sort of free-and-easiness cupped it inward to her palm like a Marine and hunkered over an imaginary campfire between the three of them.

"What were they going to prosecute him for?" asked the engineer again. Within himself he was fighting against the voluptuousness of bad news. Would the time ever come when bad was bad and good good and a man was himself and knew straight up which was which?

"Sutter," said Rita, warming her hands at the invisible embers and stamping her feet softly, "persuaded a ward nurse to leave her patients, some of whom were desperately ill, and accompany him to an unoccupied room, which I believe is

216

called the terminal room. There they were discovered in bed by the night supervisor, and surrounded by pictures of a certain sort. Wynne Magahee called me last night—he's chief of medicine. He told me, he said: 'Look, we wouldn't care less what Sutter does with or to the nurses on his own time, but hell, Rita, when it comes to leaving sick people—and to make matters worse, somebody on the ward found out about it and is suing the hospital.' I had to tell Wynne, 'Wynne it is not for you to make explanations to us but rather for us—'"

Beside him, Kitty had gone as lumpish and cheeky as a chipmunk. "They were *not* desperately ill, Ree," she said wearily as if it were an old argument. "It was a chronic ward."

"Very well, they were not desperately ill," said Rita, eyeing the engineer ironically.

Kitty's lower lip trembled. Poor Kitty, it remained to her, one of the last, to be afflicted. "Poor Sutter," she whispered, shaking her head. "But why in the world did he—"

"However unfortunate the situation might be," said Rita grimly, "Sutter's being discovered was not purely and simply a misfortune, that is to say, bad luck. As it happens, Sutter set the time for his rendezvous a few minutes before the night supervisor made her rounds."

"Do you mean Sutter wanted to get caught, Ree?" cried Kitty.

"There are needs, my dear," said Rita dryly, "which take precedence over this or that value system. I suspect, moreover, that our friend here knows a good deal more about the situation than we do."

But though Kitty turned to him, he felt fretful and sore and would not answer. Anyhow he didn't know what Rita was talking about. Instead he asked her: "When did this happen?"

"Thursday night."

"Then when I spoke to him last night, he already knew that he had been discharged?"

"Yes. And he also knew that he and Jamie were leaving this morning."

"But he told me I could find him if—" The engineer broke off and fell silent. Presently he asked: "Do Mr. and Mrs. Vaught know?"

"Yes."

"What did they say?"

"Poppy threw up his hands over his head, you know, and rushed out of the room. Dolly took to the bed."

He was silent.

"I had supposed that your responsibilities as his tutor and companion might include a reasonable concern for his life. The last time he went off with Sutter he was nearly killed."

The hearty thrust of her malice made him want to grin. He thought of his aunts. Malice was familiar ground. It was like finding oneself amid the furniture of one's living room. He looked at his watch. "I can leave in ten minutes. If he's in Tyree County, I'll be back tomorrow. If they've gone to New Mexico, and I think they have, it'll take longer. I'll look in Santa Fe and Albuquerque. Kitty?" He waited in the doorway without looking at her.

When she did not move, he looked up. The girl was stricken. She was wringing the fingers of one hand. He had never seen anyone wring his hands.

"Are you coming with me?"

"I can't," she said, open-mouthed and soundless like a fourteen-year-old talking past the teacher.

"Why not?"

"Bill," said Rita, brow gone all quirky, "you can't ask this child to travel with you. Suppose you do have to go to New Mexico."

"We can be married in Louisiana tomorrow. My uncle lives there and can arrange it."

She shook her head fondly. "Listen, kids. Here's what you do. Bill, go find Jamie. Then stay with him or bring him home. In either case I guarantee this girl will come a-running as fast as her little legs will carry her. Kitty, I assure you he is coming back. Look at her, Lance Corporal."

But he looked at Rita instead.

She was daring him! If you leave, said the fine gray eyes, you know that I know that you won't come back. I dare you!

And Kitty: by some queer transformation the girl, his lordly lioness of a Kitty, had been turned into a twittering bird-girl with little bitty legs.

"Kitty, I have to go to my room for a minute. Then I'm leaving."

"*Wait.*" Soundless as a little dove, she flew up to him, and still could not speak.

"What?" he said, smiling.

Rita linked arms with them and drew them together. "If it is of any interest to you, dearie," she said to Kitty, "my money is on him. Lance Corporal?"

"What?" said the puzzled engineer.

"Idiot," said Rita, giving him a dig in the ribs with her silken elbow. "The poor girl is wondering whether you are coming back."

Then, registering as he did a fine glint of appraisal in Rita's eye, he saw the two of them, Kitty and Billy, as doll-like figures tumbling before the magic wand of an enchantress. Nor, and here was the strangest part of it, did he really mind.

A note was clipped with a bobby pin to the ignition switch of the Trav-L-Aire.

Meet me in one hour. Go out 81—
Did she mean north or south 81?

Turn right near top of ridge—
Lord, which ridge and which side of it?

Watch for For Sale *sign and Mickle mailbox—*
Before or after turning off?

Pull up out of sight of the highway and wait for me. K.
Who was she afraid of?

There was time then for a stop at Sutter's apartment. For two reasons: to make sure Sutter had in fact left (for Rita was a liar), and if he had, maybe to find a clue or sign (Sutter might just leave one for him).

Straight up and over the mountain and down through deserted streets—what day was this, a holiday? No, the game! Everybody had gone to the game or in to their TV's, and the streets and cars and the occasional loiterer had the look of *not* going to the game—to the Kenilworth Arms, an ancient blackened stucco battlement, relic of the baronial years of the twenties. He went up in an elevator with a ruby glass in the door and down a narrow tile corridor hollow as a gutter. The silence and emptiness of Sutter's apartment met him at the open door, which had also been fitted with a ruby window. The apartment had a sunken living room and looked like Thelma Todd's apartment in the Hollywood Hills of 1931. There was open on the floor an old black friable Gladstone bag with a freshly ruptured handle and in the bathroom a green can of Mennen's talc. In a bureau drawer he found enclosed in a steno pad an Esso map of the Southeastern United States. A light penciled line ran southwest to an X marked in the badlands just above the Gulf Coast, turned northwest, and ran off the map past Shreveport. He cranked open a casement window. The faint uproar of the city below filled the tiled room like a sea shell. He sat on the steps of the balcony foyer and looked down into the littered well of the living room. It had an unmistakably sexual flavor. The orange candle flame bulbs, the ruby glass, the very sconces on the walls were somehow emblems of sex but of a lapsed archaic monkey-business sort of sex. Here, he reckoned, one used to have parties with flappers and make whoopee. Why did Sutter pick such a place to live in, with its echoes of ancient spectral orgies? He was not, after all, of that generation. The engineer opened the steno pad. It seemed to be a casebook of some sort, with an autopsy protocol here and there and much scribbling in between.

Sutter wrote:

A w.d. and n. white male, circa 49.

Eyes, ears, nose, mouth: neg. (upper dentures).
Skin: 12 cm. contusion rt. occipital region
Pleura: Neg.
Lungs: Neg.
Pericardium: 10 cc. pink frothy fluid
Heart: infarcted anterior wall right ventricle; coronary artery: moderate narrowing, occasional plaque; recent occlusion anterior descending branch, right c.a.
Abdomen: neg. except moderate cirrhosis of L. with texture fibrous to slice; central areas of lobules visible macroscopically.

Police report: subject found rolled in room above Mamie's on 16th St. behind old L & N depot. Traced to Jeff Davis hotel. Here from Little Rock on opticians' convention. Traced from hotel to men's smoker in warehouse (girl performer plus film, neither on opticians' schedule), thence to Mamie's, thence to room upstairs, wherein slugged or rolled; but head injury not cause of death. Mamie off hook.

Lewdness = sole concrete metaphysic of layman in age of science = sacrament of the dispossessed. Things, persons, relations emptied out, not by theory but by lay reading of theory. There remains only relation of skin to skin and hand under dress. Thus layman now believes that entire spectrum of relations between persons (e.g., a man and woman who seem to be connected by old complexus of relations, fondness, fidelity, and the like, understanding, the comic, etc.) is based on "real" substratum of genital sex. The latter is "real," the former is not. (Cf. Whitehead's displacement of the Real)

Scientist not himself pornographer in the practice of his science, but the price of the beauty and the elegance of the method of science = the dispossession of layman. Lewdness = climate of the anteroom of science. Pornography stands in a mutual relation to science and Christianity and is reinforced by both.

Science, which (in layman's view) dissolves concrete things and relations, leaves intact touch of skin to skin. Relation of genital sexuality reinforced twice: once because it is touch, therefore physical, therefore "real"; again because it corresponds with theoretical (i.e., sexual) substrata of all other relations. Therefore genital sexuality = twice "real."

Christianity is still viable enough to underwrite the naughtiness which is essential to pornography (e.g., the pornography of the East is desultory and perfunctory).

The perfect pornographer = a man who lives both in ante-room of science (not in research laboratory) and who also lives in twilight of Christianity, e.g., a technician. The perfect pornographer = lapsed Christian Southerner (who as such retains the memory not merely of Christianity but of a region immersed in place and time) who presently lives in Berkeley or Ann Arbor, which are not true places but sites of abstract activity which could take place anywhere else, a map coordinate; who is perhaps employed as psychological tester or opinion sampler or computer programmer or other para-scientific pursuit. Midwestern housewives, look out! Hand-under-dress of a total stranger is in the service both of the theoretical "real" and the physical "real."

I do not deny, Val, that a revival of your sacramental system is an alternative to lewdness (the only other alternative is the forgetting of the old sacrament), for lewdness itself is a kind of sacrament (devilish, if you like). The difference is that my sacrament is operational and yours is not.

The so-called sexual revolution is not, as advertised, a liberation of sexual behavior but rather its reversal. In former days, even under Victoria, sexual intercourse was the natural end and culmination of heterosexual relations. Now one begins with genital overtures instead of a handshake, then waits to see what will turn up (e.g., we might become friends later). Like dogs greeting each other nose to tail and tail to nose.

But I am not a pornographer, Val, like the optician, now a corpse, i.e., an ostensible liver of a "decent" life, a family man, who fancies conventions with smokers and call girls. I accept the current genital condition of all human relations and try to go beyond it. I may sniff like a dog but then I try to be human rather than masquerade as human and sniff like a dog. I am a sincere, humble, and even moral pornographer. I cultivate pornography in order to set it at naught.

Women, of course, are the natural pornographers today, because they are not only dispossessed by science of the complexus of human relations (all but the orgasm) but are also kept idle in their suburban houses with nothing to do but read pseudo-science articles in the Reader's Digest and dirty novels (one being the natural preamble of the other). U.S. culture is the strangest in history, a society of decent generous sex-ridden men and women who leave each other to their lusts, the men off to the city and conventions, abandoning their wives to the suburbs, which are the very home and habitation of lewd dreams. A dirty deal for women, if you ask me.

Don't be too hard on Rita. She is peeved, not perverted. (The major discovery of my practice: that there are probably no such entities as "schizophrenia" and "homosexuality," conceived as Platonic categories, but only peevishness, revenge, spitefulness, dishonesty, fear, loneliness, lust, and despair—which is not to say we don't need psychiatrists. You people don't seem to be doing too well, you know.)

The only difference between me and you is that you think that purity and life can only come from eating the body and drinking the blood of Christ. I don't know where it comes from.

The engineer rose unsteadily from the floor of the sunken living room, where he had been reading Sutter's casebook, and went into the bathroom. As he urinated he gazed down at the maroon toilet seat and the black tile floor. Once, he remembered, his father had visited the home of a rich Syrian to draw up a will. "They had black sheets on the bed," he confided to his son with a regular cackle. And in truth there seemed even now something Levantine and fancy about tampering with the decent white of bathrooms and bedsheets.

He folded the Esso map into the casebook and went down to the camper. Reading Sutter's casebook had a strange effect upon him. His mind, instead of occupying itself with such subjects as "American women" and "science" and "sexuality," turned with relief to the most practical matters. He drove into a filling station and while the motor was being serviced studied the Esso map, calculating almost instantly and clairvoyantly the distance to Jackson, New Orleans, and Shreveport. When the attendant brought over the dip stick, exhibiting its coating of good green Uniflow, slightly low, he savored the hot sane smell of the oil and felt in his own muscles the spring of the long sliver of steel.

14.

SURE ENOUGH, JUST OVER THE SADDLE OF THE FAR-thest ridge, the last wrinkle of the Appalachians, which overlooked a raw new golf links and a snowfield of marble-chip rooftops of five hundred G.E. Gold Medallion Homes, he found the mailbox and driveway. Up the rocky slope swarmed the sturdy G.M.C., shouldering like a badger, and plunged into a thicket of rhododendron. Thick meaty leaves swept along the aluminum hull of his ship and slapped shut behind him. He took a turn in the woods but there was no sign of Kitty. While he waited for her, he lay in Jamie's bunk and again studied the map he had found in Sutter's apartment. Sutter's casebook disturbed him; there were no clues here. But the map, with its intersecting lines and tiny airplanes and crossed daggers marking battlefields, was reassuring. It told him where to go.

The towhees whistled in the rhododendron and presently the branches thrashed. There stood Kitty in the doorway with light and air going round her arm.

"Oh, I'm glad to see you," he cried, leaping up and grabbing her, hardly able to believe his good fortune. "You are here!" And here she was, big as life, smelling of dry goods and brand-new chemical blue jeans. They were not quite right, the jeans, too new and too tight in the thigh and too neatly rolled at the cuff, like a Macy's girl bound for the Catskills, but it only made his heart leap all the more. He laughed and embraced her, held her charms in his arms.

"Whoa now," she cried, flushing.

"Eh?"

"Get the game on the radio."

"Game?"

"Tennessee is ahead."

"Right," he said and turned the game on but instead of listening told her: "Now. I can tell you that I feel very good about the future. I see now that while I was living with your family I was trying too hard to adapt myself to my environment and to score on interpersonal relationships."

"Darling," said Kitty, once again her old rough-and-ready and good-looking Wellesley self.

"Anyhow, here's what we'll do," said he, holding her on his lap and patting her. "We'll strike out for Ithaca and pick up my money, then we'll cross the mighty Mississippi and see my uncle, who lives near the town of Shut Off, Louisiana, transact another small piece of business, get married, and head west, locate Jamie in either Rita's house in Tesuque or Sutter's ranch near Santa Fe, and thereafter live in Albuquerque or perhaps Sante Fe, park the camper in an arroyo or dry wash and attend the University of New Mexico since there is bound to be such a place, and make ourselves available to Jamie in whatever way he likes. We might live at Sutter's old ranch and in the evenings sit, the three of us, and watch the little yellow birds fly down from the mountains. I don't mind telling you that I set great store by this move, for which I thank Jamie, and that I am happier than I can tell you to see that you are with me."

Kitty, however, seemed abstracted and was trying to hear the radio. But no, she changed her mind, and grabbing him, took him by her warm heavy hand and yanked him out of the Trav-L-Aire. The next thing he knew, she was showing him a house and grounds in the bustling style of a real estate agent. "Myra gave me the key. Do you know she told me she would let me work for her! She makes piles of money." It was a regular rockhouse cantilevered out over the ridge and into the treetops. She unlocked the door.

"What is this place?" he asked, wringing out his ear. The red and blue lines of the Esso map were still glimmering on his retina and he was in no mood for houses. But they were already inside and she was showing him the waxed paving stones and the fireplace and the view of the doleful foothills and the snowfield of G.E. Gold Medallion homes.

"This is the Mickle place. Myra has it listed for thirty-seven five but she'll let it go to the family for thirty-two. Isn't it lovely? Look at the stone of this fireplace."

"Thirty-seven five," said the engineer vaguely.

"Thirty-seven thousand five hundred dollars. In the summer you can't see that subdivision at all."

She took him outside to a ferny dell and a plashy little brook with a rustic bridge. When she walked with him, she slipped her hand behind him and inside his belt in a friendly conjugal style, as one sees the old folks do, John Anderson my jo John.

"Do you mean you want to come back here and live?" he asked her at last, looking around at the ferny Episcopal woods and the doleful view and thinking of feeding the chickadees for the next forty years.

"Not before we find Jamie," she cried. "Come on." She yanked him toward the Trav-L-Aire. "Wait till I get my hands on that sorry Jamie." But again she changed her mind. "Oh. I forgot to show you the foc'sle, as Cap'n Mickle used to call it, which is built into the cliff under the 'bridge.' It is soundproof and womanproof, even the doorknob pulls out, the very place for an old growl bear like you—you can pull the hole in after you for all I care."

"No, thanks. Let's be on our way," said the engineer, eyeing the Episcopal ivy which seemed to be twining itself around his ankles.

"Old Cap'n Andy," said Kitty, shaking her head fondly. "He was a bit eccentric but a dear. He used to stroll up and down the bridge, as he called it, with his telescope under his arm and peer out at the horizon and cry 'Ahoy there!'"

"Is that right," said the engineer gloomily, already seeing himself as a crusty but lovable eccentric who spied through his telescope at the buzzards and crows which circled above this doleful plain. "Come on," he said, now also eyeing her covertly. She was fond and ferocious and indulgent. It was as if they had been married five years. Ahoy there. He had to get out of here. But there would be the devil's own time, he saw clearly, in hemming her up in a dry wash in New Mexico. She was house-minded.

But he did get her in the camper at last and down they roared, down the last slope of the Appalachians, which was tilted into the autumn sun, down through the sourwood and the three-fingered sassafras.

"How much money do you have?" she asked.

He shrugged. "Somewhere around fifteen thousand—after I transact my business." A thought cheered him up. "Not nearly enough to buy Cap'n Andy's house, as good a bargain as it is."

"Will you take care of this for me?"

The Esso map was open on the dash. Squarely across old Arkansas it fell, the check, or cheque it looked more like, machine-printed, certified, punched, computed, red-inked, hatched up rough as a cheese grater. The engineer nearly ran off the mountain. A little army of red Gothic noughts marched clean to Oklahoma, leaning into the wind. It looked familiar. Had he seen it before?

"You have seen it before. Remember?"

"Yes," said the engineer. "What's it for?"

"My dowry, crazy. Turn it over."

He pulled up at a G.E. model home—what's wrong with one of these—they were much more cheerful than that buzzard's roost up on the ridge, and read aloud the lavender script: "For deposit only, to the account of Williston Bibb Barrett."

"Do you know how I got the Bibb?"

"No."

"I got Jamie to peek in your wallet."

"What do you want me to do with it?"

"Keep it. Hand me your wallet. I'll put it in."

"All right."

"It's really insurance."

"What kind of insurance?"

"Against your running out on me. I know you wouldn't steal a girl's money. Would you?"

"No."

Already the carnivorous ivy was stealing down the mountainside. Quickly he put the G.M.C. in gear and sent the Trav-L-Aire roaring down the gloomy Piedmont.

"Do we go anywhere near school?"

"Yes."

"Could we stop and pick up my books?"

"All right. But why do you want your books?"

"We have a test in Comp Lit Wednesday."

"Wednesday."

A half hour later, as dusk fell in a particularly gloomy wood, she clapped her hand to her mouth. "Oh my Lord, we forgot about the game."

"Yes."

"Turn on the radio and see if you can get the score."

"All right."

15.

TRAFFIC WAS HEAVY IN BOTH DIRECTIONS AND IT was night before they reached the campus. The engineer stopped the Trav-L-Aire under a street light and cocked an ear.

Something was wrong. Whether there was something wrong with the town or inside his own head, he could not say. But beyond a doubt, a queer greenish light flickered over the treetops. There were flat popping noises, unchambered, not like a shotgun but two-syllabled, ba-*rop*, ba-*rop*. In the next block an old car stopped and three men got out carrying shotguns and dove straight into the woods. They were not students. They looked like the men who hang around service stations in south Jackson.

"I wonder if Tennessee won," said Kitty. "Why are you stopping here?"

"I think I'll leave the camper here." His old British wariness woke in him. He backed the camper onto a vacant lot behind a billboard.

They separated at a fork in the campus walk, she bound for the Chi Omega house to fetch her books, he for his *Theory of Large Numbers*. "I'll meet you here in ten minutes," he told her uneasily.

Dark figures raced past him on the paths. From somewhere close at hand came the sound of running feet, the heavy direful sound of a grown man running as hard as he can. A girl, a total stranger, appeared from nowhere and taking him by the coat sleeves thrust her face within inches of his. "Hi," he said.

"He's here," she sobbed and jerked at his clothes like a ten-year-old. "Kill him! Kill him! Kill him!" she sobbed, jerking now at his lapels.

"Who?" he asked, looking around.

Searching his face and not finding what she wanted, she actually cast him from her and flew on her way.

"Who?" he asked again, but she was gone. Coming to a lamp, he took out his plastic Gulf Oil calendar card and held it

227

up to see what day of the month it was. He had forgotten and it made him feel uneasy.

At the Confederate monument a group of students ran toward him in ragged single file. Then he saw why. They were carrying a long flagstaff. The flag was furled—he could not tell whether it was United States or Confederate. The youth in front was a sophomore named Bubba Joe Phillips. He was known as a "con," that is, one who knows how to make money from such campus goings-on as decorating the gym for dances. Ordinarily a smiling crinkled-haired youth, he strained forward, his eyes bulging and unseeing. He was beside himself, besotted, with either fear or fury, and did not see the engineer, though he almost ran into him.

"What yall say," said the engineer amiably and stepped nimbly to the side, thinking they meant to go past him and down the path whence he came. But when they came abreast of the Confederate monument they turned toward the lights and the noise. They cleared him easily but what he did not see and they did not care about was the dark flagstaff behind them, which as they turned swept out in a wider arc and yet which he nevertheless saw a split second before the brass butt caught him at the belt buckle. "Oof," he grunted, not hurt much and even smiling. He would have sat down but for the wire fencelet, which took him by the heel and whipped him backward. He was felled, levered over, and would have killed himself if his head had struck the corner of the monument base but it struck instead the slanting face of the old pocked Vermont marble and he was sent spinning into the soft earth under an arborvitae.

The dawn of discovery, the imminent sense of coming at last upon those secrets closest to one and therefore most inaccessible, broke over him. "But why is it—?" he asked aloud, already knocked cold but raising a forefinger nevertheless, then lay down under the dark shrubbery.

228

V

1. HE AWOKE SHORTLY AFTER DAWN BUT NOT UNDER THE
arborvitae. Though he never found out how he came
to be here—perhaps he had awakened earlier, remembered
more, crawled over, and passed out again—here he was,
lying in the cab of the Trav-L-Aire, asleep on his back like a
truck driver. When he sat up, his head hurt. But he started the
truck and crept out into the street and, without noticing that he
did so, took a certain route through the back of town. The
streets were littered with broken glass. One automobile had
been set afire and burned to a cinder. He drove past an army
truck and a police car and straight out into the countryside.

Presently he heard a siren. Down the highway roared the
camper, careening like a runaway Conestoga, then topping a
rise and spying a picnic area, swerved into it and plumb
through it and dove into a copse of wax myrtle. Presently a
patrol car passed, then another, sirens lapsing to a growl.

He waited in the fragrant cave of myrtles until the sun
came up and made a dapple on the good gray hood of the
G.M.C. What is this place? Where am I going?—he asked
himself, touching his bruised head, and, as soon as he asked
himself, did not know. Noticing a map and notebook on the
seat beside him, he opened the latter.

I am the only sincere American.

Where I disagree with you, Val, is in you people's emphasis on
sin. I do not deny, as do many of my colleagues, that sin exists.
But what I see is not sinfulness but paltriness. Paltriness is the

229

disease. This, moreover, is not a mistake you are obliged to make. You could just as easily hold out for life and having it more abundantly as hold out against sin. Your tactics are bad. Lewdness is sinful but it derives in this case not from a rebellion against God (Can you imagine such a thing nowadays—I mean, who cares?)—but from paltriness.

Americans are not devils but they are becoming as lewd as devils. As for me, I elect lewdness over paltriness. Americans practice it with their Christianity and are paltry with both. Where your treasure is, there is your heart and there's theirs, *zwischen die Beinen*.

Americans are the most Christian of all people and also the lewdest. I am no match for them! Do you know why it is that the Russians, who are atheists, are sexually modest, whereas Americans, the most Christian of peoples, are also the lewdest?

Main Street, U.S.A. = a million-dollar segregated church on one corner, a drugstore with dirty magazines on the other, a lewd movie on the third, and on the fourth a B-girl bar with condom dispensers in the gents' room. Delay-your-climax cream. Even our official decency is a lewd sort of decency. Watch a soap opera on TV where everyone is decent (and also sad, you will notice, as sad as lewdness is sad; I am the only American who is both lewd and merry). Beyond any question, these people who sit and talk so sorrowfully and decently are fumbling with each other under the table. There is no other alternative for them.

Soap opera is overtly decent and covertly lewd. The American theater is overtly lewd and covertly homosexual. I am overtly heterosexual and overtly lewd. I am therefore the only sincere American.

Last night Lamar Thigpen called me un-American. That is a lie. I am more American than he is because I elect the lewdness which he practices covertly. I unite in myself the new American lewdness with the old American cheerfulness. All I lack is Christianity. If I were a Christian as well as being lewd and cheerful, I'd be the new Johnny Appleseed.

My God, what is all this stuff, thought the poor bemused shivering engineer and with a sob flung out of the cab and began running up and down and swinging his arms to keep warm when a great pain took him at the back of his head so suddenly that he almost fainted. He sat on a picnic bench and felt his skull. It had a sticky lump the size of a hamburger. "Oh, where is this place?" he groaned aloud, hoping that if he heard a question he might answer it. "Where am I bound and what is my name?" When no answer came, he reached for his wallet. But even before his hand arrived, he had felt the ominous airiness and thinness of fabric of his back pocket. It was empty and the flap unbuttoned. Jumping up, he began to slap his pockets as quickly as possible (to surprise the wallet ere it could lose itself). He searched the camper. Beyond a doubt the wallet was gone, lost or stolen. But there was $34.32 in his forward pocket. A textbook in the cabin disclosed what he seemed to know as soon as he saw it, his name.

Spying through the wax myrtles a big-shield US 87, he consulted his map. At least I am on course, he thought, noticing the penciled line. But hold! Something tugged at him, as unfinished and urgent a piece of business as leaving the bathtub running. There was something that had to be attended to RIGHT NOW. But what? He knocked his poor throbbing head on the steering wheel, but it was no use. The thing was too much in the front of his mind to be remembered, too close to be taken hold of, like the last wrenching moment of a dream.

No wonder he was confused. He had forgotten Kitty and left her at the university and now remembered nothing more than that he had forgotten. There was only the nameless tug pulling him back. But he had also forgotten what Sutter told him the night before—*come find me*—and recorded only the huge tug forward in the opposite direction. He shrugged: well, I'm not going back because I've been there.

There was nothing to do but go about his business. Taking care to remove the ignition key, he locked himself in the camper and lit the hot-water heater. After a shower in the tiny slot of the stall, he shaved carefully, took three aspirins for his headache, and two spansules for his dislocation. Then donning his Macy's slacks and Brooks Brothers shirt whose collar ran up into his hair, making him all of a piece, so to speak, and restoring his old Princeton puissance (for strangely he had forgotten the Vaughts and even the Y.M.C.A. and remembered Princeton), he cooked and ate a great bowl of minute grits and a quarter pound of slab bacon.

When he started up the camper and backed out of the myrtle thicket and went his way down US 87, the G.M.C. faltered and looked back of its shoulder like a horse leaving the barn. "Not that way!—that's where I came from," said the rider angrily and kicked the beast in the flank.

For several hours he cruised south on 87, choosing this

route as a consequence of the penciled line on the Esso map. He did not dare examine the contents of his pockets, for fear he would not recognize what he found there, or for fear rather that, confronted with positive proof of himself, he still would not know and would lose the tenuous connection he had. He was like a man shot in the bowels: he didn't dare look down.

It was a frosty morn. The old corn shucks hung like frozen rags. A killdeer went crying down a freshly turned row, its chevroned wing elbowing along the greasy disced-up gobbets of earth. The smell of it, the rimy mucous cold in his nostrils, and the blast of engine-warm truck air at his feet put him in mind of something—of hunting! of snot drying in your nose and the hot protein reek of fresh-killed quail.

In the late morning he slowed and, keeping a finger on the map, turned off the highway onto a scraped gravel road which ran for miles through a sparse woodland of post oaks and spindly pines infected with tumors. Once he passed through a town which had a narrow courthouse and an old boarded-up hotel on the square. There were still wrecks of rocking chairs on the gallery. Either I have been here before, he thought, perhaps with my father while he was trying a case, or else it was he with his father and he told me about it.

Beyond the town he stopped at the foot of a hill. A tall blackish building with fluted iron columns stood on top. He looked for a sign, but there was only an old tin arrow pointing north to: *Chillicothe Business College, Chillicothe, Ohio, 892 miles*. Halfway up the hill he stopped again and made out the letters on the pediment: *Phillips Academy*. Why, I know this place, he thought. Either I went to school here or my father did. It was one of the old-style country academies which had thirty or forty pupils and two or three teachers. Dr. so-and-so who taught Greek and Colonel so-and-so who taught military science. But perhaps it is only a *déjà vu*. But there is a way of finding out, considered the canny engineer. If he had really been here before, he should be able to recall something and then verify his recollection. Whereas a *déjà vu* only confers the semblance of memory. He put his forehead on the steering wheel and pondered. It seemed that there was a concrete slab, a court of sorts, behind the school.

But if there ever had been, there was not now. When he drove up the hill, he was disappointed to find instead a raw settlement of surplus army buildings, Quonset huts, and one geodesic dome, stretching out into the piney woods, each building fed by a silver butane sphere. It looked like a lunar installation. There was no one around, but at last he found a woman dressed in black, feeding entrails to a hawk in a chicken coop. She looked familiar. He eyed her, wondering whether he knew her.

"Aren't you—" he asked.

"Valentine Vaught," she said, continuing to feed the hawk. "How are you, Bill?"

"Not too good," he said, watching to see how she saw him. From his breast pocket he took Sutter's casebook and made a note of her name.

"Is that Sutter's?" she asked, but made no move to take it.

"I suppose it is," he said warily, "do you want it?"

"I've heard it all before, dear," she said dryly. "When he gets drunk he writes me letters. We always argued. Only I've stopped."

Tell me what is tugging at me, he wanted to say, but asked instead: "Isn't this old Phillips Academy?"

"Yes, it used to be. Did you go to school here?"

"No, it was my father. Or perhaps grandfather. Wasn't there at one time a tennis court over there or maybe an outdoor basketball court?"

"Not that I know of. I have a message for you."

"What?"

"Sutter and Jamie were here. They said I was to tell you they were headed for Santa Fe."

She seemed to expect him. Had he been on his way here? He took out the map. Who had marked the route?

"Sutter and Jamie," he repeated. Again it came over him, the terrific claim upon him, the tug of memory so strong that he broke into a sweat. "I've got to go," he muttered.

"To find Jamie?" she asked.

"I suppose," he said uneasily. But instead of leaving, he watched her. It came to him for the second time that he didn't like her, particularly her absorption with the hawk. It was a chicken hawk with an old rusty shoulder and a black nostril. She attended to the hawk with a buzzing antic manner which irritated him. It scandalized him slightly, like the Pope making a fuss over a canary. He was afraid she might call the hawk by some such name as Saint Blaise.

"This is a wonderful work you're doing here," he said,

remembering a little more, then added, for what reason God alone knew: "I've always liked Catholics."

"I wish I could say the same," she said, feeding a kidney to the hawk.

The task, he mused, was to give shape and substance to time itself. Time was turned on and running between them like the spools of a tape recorder. Was that not the nature of his amnesia: that all at once the little ongoing fillers of time, the throat-clearings and chair-scrapings and word-mumblings, stopped and the tape ran silent?

"At any rate, your bishop is a very courageous man," he heard himself say even more recklessly because he didn't know her bishop from Adam.

"I think he is chicken-hearted."

"Well, I'll be going," he said, flushing angrily. Really, he had no use for this prankish perverse manner of hers. As suggestible as ever, he began to feel it take possession of him too, a buzzing glassy-eyed inwardness.

"Why are you writing everything down?" she asked, looking at him for the first time.

He frowned. "I may have told you before that I have a nervous condition which affects my memory. Anyhow I only wrote down your name." And suddenly he remembered her religious name as well: Johnette Mary Vianney: remembered it precisely because it was difficult and barbarous. Taking note of her costume again, he reckoned she must be some sort of off-brand nun, perhaps not yet certified by the higher-ups. That's why she did not like her bishop!—he hadn't given her her license or whatever.

"If you catch up with Jamie," she said, speaking again to the hawk, "give him a good shaking."

"Why?"

"He's feeling sorry for himself and has taken to reading Kahlil Gibran, a bad sign even in healthy people. Did you give it to him—I know Sutter wouldn't."

"Who? No." *If he needed a good shaking, Sister, you should have given it to him.* But he said: "Do you like your work here?" Without knowing that he did so, he was going through his pockets. Oh my, I'm sure I had something of great value.

"We are very poor here," she said, watching him with interest.

He blushed. "I'm sorry to say that my wallet has been lost or stolen. I—" he began, and felt his sore occiput. "Otherwise I'd like very much to make a small contribution to your work."

"Say a prayer for us," she said, he thought, absently.

"Yes. Where are they now?"

"Who? Oh. The pupils don't come on weekends."

"Of course not," he said heartily. He wondered whether it was Saturday or Sunday. Something else came back to him. "I've heard the poverty here in Tyree County is abject."

"It's not that so much," she said carelessly.

"Not that? What then?"

"The children are dumb. They can't speak."

"Ah, they are mentally retarded—pellagra, no doubt."

"No, I mean they're dumb, mute. Children eleven and twelve can't speak. It took me six months to find out why. They're brought up in silence. Nobody at home speaks. They don't know thirty words. They don't know words like pencil or hawk or wallet."

"What a rewarding experience it must be to teach them."

"Yes, very," she said, and not ironically, he thought.

A complex system of scoring social debts kept him from leaving. Since he couldn't give her money, ransom himself, he had to pay her out by listening to her, since, goofy as he was, he knew two things not many people know. He knew how to listen and he knew how to get at that most secret and aggrieved enterprise upon which almost everyone is embarked. He'd give her the use of his radar.

"Is that why you came here?" he asked her. "Because of the children, I mean."

"Why I came here," she said vaguely. "No, that wasn't the reason. Somebody asked me."

"Who asked you?" he bent upon the hawk the same smiling unseeing gaze as she.

"A woman in the library at Columbia."

"A woman in the library at Columbia asked you to come down here?"

"Not directly. That is not what she asked me at first."

"What did she ask you at first?"

"I was writing a paper on Pareto. This nun and I shared the same cubicle in the stacks. She was doing her doctorate on John Dewey, whom she admired greatly—you know how

235

they've taken up with the very ones they despised a few years ago."

"No, I don't," said the engineer. His head was beginning to hurt again.

She paid no attention. "I was aware that she was eyeing me and that she had her hooks out. The strange thing was that I was not in the least surprised when she did speak." Again she lapsed.

"What did she say?" asked the engineer as gently as Dr. Gamow.

"She said, what's the matter with you? I said, what do you mean what's the matter with me? She said, you look half dead." She shook her head and fed the hawk an intricate packet of viscera.

"Yes," said the engineer after a long minute.

"I said yes, I am half dead. She said why? I said I don't know. She said how would you like to be alive. I said I'd like that. She said all right, come with me. That was it."

"That was what?" asked the engineer, frowning. "What happened?"

"I went with her to her mother house, a hideous red brick building in Paterson, New Jersey."

"Then what?"

"That was it. I received instruction, made a general confession, was shriven, baptized, confirmed, and made my first vows, all in the space of six weeks. They thought I was crazy. The Bishop of Newark required that I get a statement from my doctor that there was no insanity in the family. When all I'd done was take them at their word. They were mostly third-generation Irish from places like Bridgeport and Worcester, Mass. That's what they would say: I'm from Worcester, Mass. —never Massachusetts. They called me Alabam. You know." Again she fell silent.

"How did you get down here?"

"They asked me how I would like to work with Sister Clare in their mission down in 'Bama. I think they wanted to get rid of me. I kept telling them that I believed it all, the whole business. But try as I might, I couldn't remember the five proofs of God's existence or the difference between a substance and an accident. I flunked out. They didn't know what to do with me, so they figured six months of Sister Clare down in 'Bama would cure me. Sister Clare is a harridan, mean as hell."

"Is she here?"

"No. She had a nervous breakdown, she instead of me, as they had expected. She was sent to our rest home in Topeka. What they didn't know was that I am mean as hell too. I outlasted her. That's what I don't understand, you know: that I believe the whole business: God, the Jews, Christ, the Church, grace, and the forgiveness of sins—and that I'm meaner than ever. Christ is my lord and I love him but I'm a good hater and you know what he said about that. I still hope my enemies fry in hell. What to do about that? Will God forgive me?"

"I don't know. Why did you stay?"

"That was a fluke too." She draped two feet of gut over the perch and the hawk cocked his eye. The engineer thought about the falcon in Central Park: I could see him better at one mile than this creature face to face. Jesus, my telescope: is it still in the camper? "I think I stayed not so much out of charity as from fascination with a linguistic phenomenon—that was my field, you know. It has to do with the children's dumbness. When they do suddenly break into the world of language, it is something to see. They are like Adam on the First Day. What's that? they ask me. That's a hawk, I tell them, and they believe me. I think I recognized myself in them. They were not alive and then they are and so they'll believe you. Their eyes fairly pop out at the Baltimore catechism (imagine). I tell them that God made them to be happy and that if they love one another and keep the commandments and receive the Sacrament, they'll be happy now and forever. They believe me. I'm not sure anybody else does now. I have more influence than the Pope. Of course I'm not even supposed to be here, since I haven't taken final vows. But they haven't sent for me."

"That certainly is interesting," said the engineer, who was now leaving, actually setting a foot toward the camper. He had done his duty and was ready to be on his way. He had a fix on her at last. She struck him as an enthusiast of a certain sort who becomes wry as a countermeasure to her own outlandishness, like a collector of 1928 Model-T radiator caps who exhibits his trophies with a wry, rueful deprecation of their very oddness. He understood this. And was it not also the case that her offhandedness was a tactic and that she had *her* hooks out for *him*? He didn't mind if she had, and was even prepared to put on a thoughtful expression, as much as to say: you do give me pause, Sister; that is something to think about. But he was ready to go.

He was not to escape so easily. Changing her manner completely, she became cordial and brisk and took him on the "ten-dollar tour" of her foundation. For some fifty minutes he was towed helplessly around the outbuildings scattered through the cancerous pines. More than ever, it reminded him of a lunar installation, with silvery globes supplying nourishment to each building, a place of crude and makeshift beginnings on some blasted planet. Later there remained in his poor addled memory only a blurred impression of Seven-Up machines, plastic crucifixes, and worn, gnawed-at woodwork such as is found in old gymnasiums. Life indeed, thought he. Another hour in this gloomy cancerous wood and I'd be laid out stiff as a corpse, feet sticking up.

But she would not let him go, and when for the second or third time she led him past the wooden privies and the last time opened the door of one so that he might catch a whiff of the acuteness of the need, he got the idea. With trembling fingers he thrust hand into pocket and brought forth a disorderly clutch of bills, leaving him, as he discovered later, $1.36 in silver. "A small donation for your building fund," he murmured, blushing.

"I'll pray for you," she said absently. "Will you pray for me to receive sufficient grace in order not to hate the guts of some people, however much they deserve it?"

"Certainly," said the engineer heartily, who would have consented to anything.

She took the money with only perfunctory gratitude and, slipping it skillfully into a black-leather pouch she wore at her belt, lapsed instantly into her old smiling thrumming Papal inwardness, wherein she dispensed herself so that she might take note of God's creatures, small objects, and such. She went back to the hawk and he left.

2. DOWN FLEW THE TRAV-L-AIRE INTO THE SETTING SUN, down and out of the last of the ancient and impoverished South of red hills and Cardui signs and God-is-Love crosses. Down through humpy sugarloaves and loess cliffs sliced through like poundcake. Dead trees shrouded in kudzu vines reared up like old women. Down and out at last and onto the vast prodigal plain of the Delta, stretching away misty and fecund into the October haze. The land hummed and simmered in its own richness. Picking was still going on, great $25,000 McCormicks and Farmalls browsing up and down the cotton rows. Bugs zoomed and splashed amber against the windshield; the Trav-L-Aire pushed like a boat through the heavy air and the rich protein smells, now the sweet ferment of alfalfa, now the smell of cottonseed meal rich as ham in the kitchen. There had been the sense ever since leaving New York and never quite realized until now of tarrying in upland places and along intermediate slopes and way stations (My Lord, where had he stopped? Where had he spent the last month? He cudgeled his brain) and now at last of coming sock down to the ultimate alluvial floor, the black teeming Ur-plain. He stopped the Trav-L-Aire and got out. Buzzards circled, leaning into the heavy mothering air, three, four tiers of buzzards riding round a mile-high chimney of air. A shrike, the Negro's ghost bird, sat on a telephone wire and looked at him through its black mask. It was a heedless prodigal land, the ditches rank and befouled, weeds growing through the junk: old Maytags, Coke machines, and a Hudson Supersix pushed off into a turnrow and sprouting a crop all its own. But across the ditches and over the turnrows—here they got down to business—stretched the furrows of sifted mealy earth clean as a Japanese garden but forty miles long and going away, straight as a ruler, into the smoky distance. The cotton leaves were a dusky gray-green, as dusky as new money. Cotton wagons were on the road and the gins were humming. The little towns were squalid and rich. From the storefronts, tin roofs sagged across the sidewalk to the muddy Cadillacs.

Across the road from a decaying mustard-colored I.C. depot stretched a line of great glittering harvesters and pickers parked in echelon like a squadron of Sherman tanks.

Straight across the Delta he flew and down into the tongue of the Yazoo plain to Ithaca, so named by a Virginian who admired Pericles more than Abraham and who had had his fill of the Bethels and the Shilohs of the Scotch-Irish. Yonder in the haze rose the brownish back of the Chickasaw Bluffs, and just beyond, the old wormy concrete towers of the Vicksburg battlefield.

When he stopped at Roscoe's Servicenter, Roscoe spoke as if he had never been away.

"What you say there, Will?—" holding nozzle to spout and all the while taking in the Trav-L-Aire, acknowledging it with a quirk of his mouth but not willing to make a fuss over it or even to speak of it directly.

"All right. What you say, Roscoe."

"You been camping or going?"

"Camping? Oh, I'm going."

"Do you know those niggers over there?"

"Who? No."

"They seem to know you."

Beyond the pumps sat a bottle-green Chevrolet, a stout old Bel Aire two-door, round as a turtle and filled with Negroes and what appeared to be a couple of Syrians. Sure enough the driver, a stately bun-headed preacher-type Negro seemed to be making signs and grimaces at him. The courteous engineer, the last man on earth to inflict a snub, nodded and smiled in turn even though he didn't know them from Adam. Or did he? Ah, the dread tug of the past not quite remembered! Then, even as he nodded, an aching vista opened in his head and he remembered—not them but Kitty! The green Chevrolet sent his mind spinning back but there stood Kitty like a lion in the path. God in heaven, he groaned, I've left Kitty. Dear Jesus, he said, and began to slap his pocket again. The check for $100,000—I've lost it. Yet even as he groaned he was giving a final cheery nod and now he gunned the Trav-L-Aire out into traffic. Oh, my lovely strapping wealthy Chi O 'Bama bride, he thought, and gave his leaping knee a few hard socks. I must call her immediately.

But after half a dozen blocks he noticed that the green Chevrolet had drawn abreast of him on the left, the passengers on the front seat pressing back to clear a view for the driver, who was motioning frantically. "Barrett!" The Chevrolet began to yaw like a tender on the high seas. He still can't drive, thought the engineer, even though he did not yet know that he knew the pseudo-Negro. At the same moment he caught sight of a commotion in front of the new courthouse. Pickets bearing signs were marching on one side of the street and a crowd watched from the other. Troopers directed traffic with electric batons. Somewhere to his rear, a siren growled. Having had enough of ruckuses and police sirens and especially of this particular carload of importuning Negroes, he swung the Trav-L-Aire without slowing into a lane between Club 85 and Krystal Hamburgers. The cabin swayed dangerously, dishpans clattering into the sink. The lane was a segment of the abandoned river road which turned at this very point into the lee of the levee. Not hesitating a second, the sturdy G.M.C. swarmed straight up and over the levee out onto the batture and dove into a towhead of willows.

No one followed.

He waited in the cab until the sun set in Louisiana. When it grew dark, he walked to the highway with his firkin, emerging by dead reckoning at a haunted Piggly Wiggly and a new-old Rexall, new ten years ago and persisting stupendously in his absence.

My lovely Kitty coed, he groaned even as he stocked up on grits and buttermilk and bacon, I must call her now. The thought of her living under the same roof with Son Thigpen, a glum horny key-twiddler, set him off in a spasm of jealousy. Yet it fell out, strange to say, that when he did find himself in a phone booth, he discovered he had spent all but nine cents! Oh damnable stupidity and fiendish bad luck, but what are you going to do? I'll call her in the morning after I've been to the bank, where I will stop payment on the check, he told himself, and returned to the camper in a better humor than one might suppose.

After supper, as he lay in the balcony bunk listening to patriotic and religious programs, he heard a noise from the river, a mild sustained roar like a surf. He found a flashlight in the locker and went outside. Twenty feet away the willows were nodding and thrashing against the current. Flotsam and brown foam were caught in the leaves. He knelt and examined the thicker trunks. The water was high but falling. The sky was clear. He returned to his bunk and listened to Profit Research, a program which gave money tips for changing times, and read from Sutter's notebook:

Moderately obese young colored female, circa 13

Skin: vaccination 1. thigh; stellate keloid scar under chin.

Head: massive cmpd depressed fracture right parietal and right zygomatic arch.

Brain: frank blood in subdural space, extensive laceration right cortex; brick shards.

Thorax: comminuted cmpd fractures, right ribs 1 through 8; frank blood in pleural space; extensive lacerations RML, RLL, brick shards. Heart: neg.

Abdomen: neg. Gen.: neg.

Cops report subject discovered in basement toilet of Emmanuel Baptist Church following explosion. Church tower fell on her.

But never mind the South.

It is you who concerns me. You are wrong and you deceive yourself in a more serious way. Do you know what you have managed to do? You have cancelled yourself. I can understand what you did in the beginning. You opted for the Scandalous Thing, the Wrinkle in Time, the Jew-Christ-Church business, God's alleged intervention in history. You acted on it, left all and went away to sojourn among strangers. I can understand this even though I could never accept the propositions (1) that my salvation comes from the Jews, (2) that my salvation depends upon hearing news rather than figuring it out, (3) that I must spend eternity with Southern Baptists. But I understand what you did and even rejoiced in the scandal of it, for I do not in the least mind scandalizing the transcending scientific assholes of Berkeley and Cambridge and the artistic assholes of Taos and La Jolla.

But do you realize what you did then? You reversed your dialectic and cancelled yourself. Instead of having the courage of your scandal-giving, you began to speak of the glories of science, the beauty of art, and the dear lovely world around us! Worst of all, you even embraced, Jesus this is what tore it, the Southern businessman! The Southern businessman is the new Adam, you say, smart as a Yankee but a Christian withal and having the tragical sense, etc., etc., etc.—when the truth of it is, you were pleased because you talked the local Coca-Cola distributor into giving you a new gym.

But what you don't know is that you are cancelled. Suppose you did reconcile them all, the whites and the niggers, Yankees and the K.K.K., scientists and Christians, where does that leave you and your Scandalous Thing? Why, cancelled out! Because it doesn't mean anything any more, God and religion and all the rest. It doesn't even mean anything to your fellow Christians. And you know this: that is why you are where you are, because it means something to your little Tyree dummies (and ten years from now it won't even mean anything to them: either they'll be Muslims and hate your guts or they'll be middle-class and buggered like everybody else).

The reason I am more religious than you and in fact the most religious person I know: because, like you, I turned my back on the bastards and went into the desert, but unlike you I didn't come sucking around them later.

There is something you don't know. They are going to win without you. They are going to remake the world and go into space and they couldn't care less whether you and God approve and sprinkle holy water on them. They'll even let you sprinkle holy water on them and they'll even like you because they'll know it makes no difference any more. All you will succeed in doing is cancelling yourself. At least have the courage of your revolt.

Sutter's notebook had the effect of loosening his synapses, like a bar turning slowly in his brain. Feeling not unpleasantly dislocated, he turned off the light and went to sleep to the sound of the lashing willows and a Spanish-language broadcast to Cuban refugees from WWL in New Orleans.

3. THE NEXT MORNING HE WALKED THE LEVEE INTO ITH-aca, curving into town under a great white sky. New grass, killed by the recent frost, had whitened and curled like wool. Grasshoppers started up at his feet and went stitching away. Below where the town was cradled in the long curving arm of the levee, the humpy crowns of oaks, lobules upon lobules, were broken only by steeples and the courthouse cupola. There arose to him the fitful and compassed sound of human affairs, the civil morning sounds of tolerable enterprise, the slap of lumber, a back-door slam, the chunk of an engine, and the routine shouts of a work crew: ho; ho; *ho now!*

Here he used to walk with his father and speak of the galaxies and of the expanding universe and take pleasure in the insignificance of man in the great lonely universe. His father would recite "Dover Beach," setting his jaw askew and wagging his head like F.D.R.:

for the world which seems
To lie before us like a land of dreams,
So various, so beautiful, so new,
Hath really neither joy, nor love, nor light,
Nor certitude, nor peace, nor help for pain—

or else speak of the grandfather and the days of great deeds: "And so he looked down at him where he was sitting in his barber chair and he said to him: 'I'm going to tell you one time, you son of a bitch, and that's all, so hear me well; if anything happens to Judge Hampton, I'm not asking any questions, I'm not calling the police, I'm coming to look for you, and when I find you I'm going to kill you.' Nothing happened to Judge Hampton."

Beyond the old brown roiled water, the bindings and lacings of water upon water, the Louisiana shore stretched misty and perfunctory. When he came abreast of the quarterboat of the U.S. Engineers, his knee began to leap and he sat down in the tall grass under a river beacon and had a little fit. It was not a convulsion, but his eyes twittered around under his eyeballs. He dreamed that old men sat in a circle around him, looking at him from the corners of their eyes.

"Who's that?" he cried, jumping to his feet and brushing off his Macy's Dacron. Someone had called to him. But there was no one and nothing but the white sky and the humpy lobuled oaks of the town.

He went down into Front Street, past the Syrian and Jewish dry goods and the Chinese grocery, and turned quickly into Market and came to the iron lion in front of the bank. It was a hollow lion with a hole between his shoulders which always smelled of pee.

Spicer CoCo and Ben Huger, two planters his own age, stood in line behind him at the teller's window and began to kid him in the peculiar reflected style of the deep Delta.

"Reckon he's going to get all his money out and go on back off up there?" said Spicer CoCo.

"I notice he got his box-back coat on. I think he be here *for a while*," said Ben Huger.

He had to grin and fool with them, fend them off, while he asked the teller about the check. "Doris," he said to the pretty plump brunette, remembering her before he could forget, "can I stop payment on a certified check?"

She gave him a form to fill in. "Hello, Will. It's good to see you."

"Just fine." He scratched his head. "No, ah— You see, it's not my check and it's not on this bank. It was a check endorsed to me. I—it was misplaced." He hoped he didn't have to tell the amount.

"Then have the payer make a stop-payment order," she said, gazing at him with an expression both lively and absentminded. "How long ago did you lose it?"

"I don't remember—ah, two days."

"Same old Will."

"What?"

"You haven't changed a bit."

"I haven't?" he said, pleased to hear it. "I thought I was worse." I'll call Poppy then, he said to himself and fell to wondering: how strange that they seem to know me and that I never supposed they could have, and perhaps that was my mistake.

"You know why he taking his money out," said Spicer.

"No, why is that?" asked Ben.

The two were standing behind him, snapping their fingers and popping their knees back and forth inside their trousers. They were talking in a certain broad style which was used in Ithaca jokingly; it was something like Negro talk but not the same.

"He on his way to the game Saddy. You can tell he come on into town to get his money—look, he done took off his regular walking shoes which he hid under a bridge and done put on his town slippers"—pointing down to the engineer's suède oxfords.

"That had slipped my notice," said Ben. "But look how he still th'ows his foot out like Cary Middlecoff, like he fixin' to hit a *long ball*."

"He come over here to draw his money out and make a bet on the game and take our money because he thinks we don't know they number one."

"What are you talking about," cried the engineer, laughing and shaking his head, all but overcome by an irritable sort of happiness—and all the while trying to tell Doris Mascagni about his savings account. "Yall are number one on the U.P." he told them, turning around nervously.

"What you say there, Will." They shook hands with him, still casting an eye about in the oblique Ithaca style.

What good fellows they were, he thought, as Doris counted out his money. Why did I ever go away? Ben Huger detained him and told a story about a man who bought a golf-playing gorilla. The gorilla had been taught to play golf by the smartest trainer in the world. This man who bought the gorilla was also a hard-luck gambler but for once he seemed to have hit on a sure thing. Because when he took the gorilla out to a driving range and handed him a driver and a basket of balls, each ball flew straight down the middle for five hundred yards. So he entered the gorilla in the Masters at Augusta. On the first tee, a par five hole, the gorilla followed Nicklaus and Palmer. He addressed his ball with assurance and drove the green four hundred and ninety yards away. Great day in the morning, thought the gambler, who was acting as the gorilla's caddy, I got it made this time for sure. Already he had plans for the P.G.A. and the British Open after collecting his fifty thousand in first prize money. But when the threesome reached the green and the gambler handed the gorilla his putter to sink the one-footer, the gorilla took the same full, perfected swing and drove the ball another four hundred and ninety yards. Then—

Here's what I'll do, thought the engineer who was sweating profusely and was fairly beside himself with irritable delight. I'll come back here and farm Hampton, my grandfather's old place, long since reclaimed by the cockleburs, and live this same sweet life with these splendid fellows.

"You gon' be home for a while, Will?" they asked him.

"For a while," he said vaguely and left them, glad to escape this dread delight.

Hardly aware that he did so, he took Kemper Street, a narrow decrepit boulevard which ran as string to the bow of the river. It still had its dusty old crape myrtles and china-berries and horse troughs and an occasional tile marker set in the sidewalk: *Travelers Bicycle Club 1903*. The street changed to a Negro district. The old frame houses gave way to concrete nightclubs and shotgun cottages, some of which were converted to tiny churches by tacking on two square towers and covering the whole with brick paper. He sat on a trough which was choked with dry leaves and still exhaled the faint sunny tart smell of summer, and studied the Esso map, peering closely at the Gulf Coast, New Orleans, Houston, and points west. It came over him suddenly that he didn't live anywhere and had no address. As he began to go through his pockets he spied a new outdoor phone in a yellow plastic shell—and remembered Kitty. Lining up quarters and dimes on the steel shelf, he gazed down Kemper to the old city jail at the corner of Vincennes. Here on the top step stood his great-uncle the sheriff, or high sheriff, as the Negroes called him, on a summer night in 1928.

The telephone was ringing in the purple castle beside the golf links and under the rosy temple of Juno.

The sheriff put his hands in his back pockets so that the skirt of his coat cleared his pistol butt. "I respectfully ask yall to go on back to your homes and your families. There will be no violence here tonight because I'm going to kill the first sapsucker who puts his foot on that bottom step. Yall go on now. Go ahead on."

"Hello." It was David.

"Hello. David."

"Yes suh." He would be standing in the narrow hall between the pantry and the big front hall, the receiver held as loosely in his hand as if it had fallen into the crotch of a small tree.

"This is, ah, Will Barrett." It sounded strange because they didn't, the Negroes, know him by a name.

"Who? Yes *suh!* Mist' Billy!" David, feeling summoned, cast about for the right response—was it surprise? joy?—and hit instead on a keening bogus cheeriness, then, seeing it as such, lapsed into hilarity: *"Ts-ts-ts."*

"Is Miss Kitty there?"

"No suh. She *been* gone."

"Where?" His heart sank. She and Rita had gone to Spain. "School."

"Oh yes." Today was Monday. He reflected.

"Yes suh," mused David, politely giving shape and form to the silence. "I notice the little bitty Spite was gone when I got here. And I got here on time."

"Is anyone else there?"

"Nobody but Miss Rita."

"Never mind. Give Miss Kitty a message."

"Oh yes suh."

"Tell her I got hurt at the college, got hit in the head, and had a relapse. She'll understand. Tell her I've been sick but I feel better."

"Yes suh. I'll sho tell her. *Sick?*" David, aiming for the

famous Negro sympathy, hit instead on a hooting incredulity. David, David, thought the engineer, shaking his head, what is going to happen to you? You ain't white nor black nor nothing.

"I'm better now. Tell her I'll call her."

"Yes suh."

"Goodbye, David."

"Goodbye, Mist' Billy!" cried David, stifling his hilarity. He reached Mr. Vaught at Confederate Chevrolet.

"Billy boy!" cried the old fellow. "You still at school?"

"Sir? Well, no sir. I—"

"You all right, boy?"

"Yes sir. That is, I was hurt—"

"How bad is it down there now?"

"Down here?"

"How did you get out? They didn't want to let Kitty leave. I had to go get her myself last night. Why, they kept them down in the basement of the sorority house all night. Man, they got the army in there."

"Yes sir," said the engineer, understanding not a single word save only that some larger catastrophe had occurred and that in the commotion his own lapse had been set at nought, remitted.

"You sure you all right?"

"I was knocked out but I got away the next morning," said the engineer carefully. "Now I'm on my way to find—" He faltered.

"Jamie. Good."

"Yes. Jamie. Sir," he began again. This one thing he clearly perceived: the ruckus on the campus dispensed him and he might say what he pleased.

"Yes?"

"Sir, please listen carefully. Something has happened that I think you should know about and will wish to do something about."

"If you think so, I'll do it."

"Yes sir. You see, Kitty's check has been lost or stolen, the check for one hundred thousand dollars."

"What's that?" Mr. Vaught's voice sounded as if he had crept into the receiver. All foolishness aside: this was money, Chevrolets.

The engineer had perceived that he could set forth any facts whatever, however outrageous, and that they would be attended to, acted upon and not held against him.

"My suggestion is that you stop payment, if it is possible."

"It is possible," said the old man, his voice pitched at perfect neutrality. The engineer could hear him riffling through the phone book as he looked up the bank's number.

"It was endorsed over to me, if that is any help."

"It was endorsed over to you," repeated the other as if he were taking it down. *Very well then, it is understood this time, what with one thing and another, that it is for you to tell me and for me to listen. This time.*

"I tried to reach Kitty but couldn't. Tell her that I'll call her."

"I'll tell her."

"Tell her I'll be back."

"You'll be back."

After he hung up, he sat gazing at the old jail and thinking about his kinsman, the high sheriff. Next to the phone booth was the Dew Drop Inn, a rounded corner of streaked concrete and glass brick, a place he knew well. It belonged to a Negro named Sweet Evening Breeze who was said to be effeminate. As he left and came opposite the open door, the sound came: *psssst!*—not four feet from his ear.

"Eh," he said, pausing and frowning. "Is that you, Breeze?"

"Barrett!"

"What?" He turned, blinking. A pair of eyes gazed at him from the interior darkness.

"Come in, Barrett."

"Thank you all the same, but—"

Hands were laid on him and he was yanked inside. By the same motion a shutter of memory was tripped: it was not so much that he remembered as that, once shoved out of the wings and onto stage, he could then trot through his part perfectly well.

"Mr. Aiken," he said courteously, shaking hands with his old friend, the pseudo-Negro.

"Come in, come in, come in. Listen, I don't in the least blame you—" began the other.

"Please allow me to explain," said the engineer, blinking around at the watery darkness which smelled of sweet beer and hosed-down concrete—there were others present but he could not yet make them out. "The truth is that when I saw you yesterday I did not place you. As you may recall, I spoke to you last summer of my nervous condition and its accompanying symptom of amnesia. Then yesterday, or the day before, I received a blow on the head—"

"Listen," cried the pseudo-Negro. "Yes, right! You have no idea how glad I am to see you. Oh, boy. God knows you have to be careful!"

"No, you don't understand—"

"Don't worry about it," said the pseudo-Negro.

The engineer shrugged. "What you say, Breeze?" He caught sight of the proprietor, a chunky shark-skinned Negro who still wore a cap made of a Nylon stocking rolled and knotted.

"All right now," said Breeze, shaking hands but sucking his teeth, not quite looking at him. He could tell that Breeze remembered him but did not know what to make of his being here. Breeze knew him from the days when he, the engineer, used to cut through the alley behind the Dew Drop on his way to the country club to caddy for his father.

"Where's Mort?" asked the engineer, who began to accommodate to the gloom.

"Mort couldn't make it," said the pseudo-Negro in a voice heavy with grievance, and introduced him to his new friends. There were two men, a Negro and a white man, and a white woman. The men, he understood from the pseudo-Negro's buzzing excitement, were celebrities, and indeed even to the engineer, who did not keep up with current events, they looked familiar. The white man, who sat in a booth with a beautiful sullen untidy girl all black hair and white face and black sweater, was an actor. Though he was dressed like a tramp, he wore a stern haughty expression. A single baleful glance he shot at the engineer and did not look at him again and did not offer his hand at the introduction.

"This is the Merle you spoke of?" the actor asked the pseudo-Negro, indicating the engineer with a splendid one-millimeter theatrical inclination of his head.

"Merle?" repeated the puzzled engineer. "My name is not Merle." Though the rudeness and haughtiness of the actor made him angry at first, the engineer was soon absorbed in the other's mannerisms and his remarkable way of living from one moment to the next. This he accomplished by a certain inclination of his head and a hitching around of his shoulder while he fiddled with a swizzle stick, and a gravity of expression which was aware of itself as gravity. His lips fitted together in a rich conscious union. The sentient engineer, who had been having trouble with his expression today, now felt his own lips come together in a triumphant fit. Perhaps he should be an actor!

"You're here for the festival, the, ah, morality play," said the engineer to demonstrate his returning memory.

"Yes," said the pseudo-Negro. "Do you know the sheriff here?"

"Yes," said the engineer. They were standing at the bar under a ballroom globe which reflected watery specters of sunlight from the glass bricks. The pseudo-Negro introduced him to the other celebrity, a playwright, a slender pop-eyed Negro who was all but swallowed up by a Bulldog Drummond trenchcoat and who, unlike his white companion, greeted the engineer amiably and in fact regarded him with an intense curiosity. For once the engineer felt as powerful and white-hot a radar beam leveled at him as he leveled at others. This fellow was not one to be trifled with. He had done the impossible!—kept his ancient Negro radar intact and added to it a white edginess and restiveness. He fidgeted around and came on at you like a proper Yankee but unlike a Yankee had this great ear which he swung round at you. Already he was onto the engineer: that here too was another odd one, a Southerner who had crossed up his wires and was something betwixt and between. He drank his beer and looked at the engineer sideways. Where the actor was all self playing itself and triumphantly succeeding, coinciding with itself, the playwright was all eyes and ears and not in the least mindful of himself—if he had been, he wouldn't have had his trenchcoat collar turned up in great flaps around his cheeks. The Negro was preposterous-looking, but he didn't care if he was. The actor did care. As for the poor engineer, tuning in both, which was he, actor or playwright?

"You really did not remember him, did you?" the Negro asked the engineer.

"No, that's right."

"He's not conning you, Forney," the playwright told the pseudo-Negro.

"I knew that," cried the pseudo-Negro. "Barrett and I are old shipmates. Aren't we?"

"That's right."

"We went through the Philadelphia thing together, didn't we?"

"Yes." It seemed to the engineer that the pseudo-Negro said "Philadelphia" as if it were a trophy, one of a number of campaign ribbons, though to the best of the engineer's recollection the only campaign which had occurred was his getting hit on the nose by an irate housewife from Haddon Heights, New Jersey.

"Do you think you could prevail upon the local fuzz to do something for you?" the pseudo-Negro asked him.

"What?"

"Let Bugs out of jail."

"Bugs?"

"Bugs Flieger. They put him in jail last night after the festival, and our information is he's been beaten up. Did you know Mona over there is Bug's sister?"

"Bugs Flieger," mused the engineer.

The actor and the white girl looked at each other, the former popping his jaw muscles like Spencer Tracy.

"Tell—ah—Merle here," said the actor, hollowing out his throat, "that Bugs Flieger plays the guitar a little."

"Merle?" asked the mystified engineer, looking around at the others. "Is he talking to me? Why does he call me Merle?"

"You really never heard of Flieger, have you?" asked the playwright.

"No. I have been quite preoccupied lately. I never watch television," said the engineer.

"Television," said the girl. "Jesus Christ."

"What have you been preoccupied with?" the playwright asked him.

"I have recently returned to the South from New York, where I felt quite dislocated as a consequence of a nervous condition," replied the engineer, who always told the truth. "Only to find upon my return that I was no less dislocated here."

"I haven't been well myself," said the playwright as amiably as ever and not in the least sarcastically. "I am a very shaky man."

"Could you speak to the sheriff?" the pseudo-Negro asked him.

"Sure."

Breeze brought more beer and they all sat in the round booth at the corner under the glass bricks.

"Baby, are you really from around here?" the playwright asked the engineer.

"Ask Breeze." The engineer scowled. Why couldn't these people call him by his name?

But when the playwright turned to Breeze the latter only nodded and shrugged. Breeze, the engineer perceived, was extremely nervous. His, the engineer's, presence, disconcerted him. He didn't know what footing to get on with the engineer, the old one, the old ironic Ithaca style: "Hey, Will, where you going?" "Going to caddy." "How come your daddy pays you five dollars a round?" "He don't pay no five dollars"—or the solemn fierce footing of the others. But finally Breeze said absently and to no one and from no footing at all: "This here's Will Barrett, Lawyer Barrett's boy. Lawyer Barrett help many a one." But it was more than that, the engineer then saw, something else was making Breeze nervous. He kept opening the door a crack and looking out. He was scared to death.

But the pseudo-Negro wanted to talk about more serious matters. He asked the others some interview-type questions about racial subjects, all the while snapping pictures (only the engineer noticed) from his tie-clasp camera.

"It's a moral issue," said the actor, breaking the swizzle stick between his fingers, breaking it the way actors break swizzle sticks and pencils. The pseudo-Negro explained that the actor had flown in from Hollywood with Mona his companion to assist in the present drive at great cost to himself, both financially and emotionally, the latter because he was embroiled in a distressing custody suit in the course of which his wife had broken into his bedroom and pulled Mona's hair.

"Of course it's a moral issue," said the playwright. Now the engineer remembered seeing one of his plays with Midge Auchincloss. It was about an artist who has gone stale, lost his creative powers, until he musters the courage to face the truth within himself, which is his love for his wife's younger brother. He puts a merciful end to the joyless uncreative marriage in favor of a more meaningful relationship with his friend. The last scene shows the lovers standing in a window of the artist's Left Bank apartment looking up at the gleaming towers of Sacre-Coeur. "There has been a loss of the holy in the world," said the youth. "Yes, we must recover it," replies the artist. "It has fallen to us to recover the holy." "It has been a long time since I was at Mass," says the youth, looking at the church. "Let's have our own Mass," replies the artist as softly as Pelleas and, stretching forth a shy hand, touches the youth's golden hair.

Sweet Evening Breeze, the engineer noticed, was growing more nervous by the minute. His skin turned grayer and more sharklike and he had fallen into a complicated way of snapping his fingers. Once, after peering through the cracked door, he called the pseudo-Negro aside.

"Breeze says the fuzz is on its way over here," the pseudo-Negro told them gravely.

"How do you know?" the playwright asked Breeze.

"I know."

"How do they know we're here?"

"Ask Merle," said the actor.

"Don't be ridiculous," said the pseudo-Negro, frowning. "I pulled him in here, remember. Barrett's all right."

"The man done pass by here twice," said Breeze, rattling off a drumroll of fingersnaps. "The next time he's coming in."

"How do you know?" asked the pseudo-Negro with his lively reporter's eye.

"I knows, that's all."

"Wonderful," said the playwright. The playwright's joy, the engineer perceived, came from seeing life unfold in the same absurd dramatic way as a Broadway play—it was incredible that the one should be like the other after all.

"Bill," said the pseudo-Negro earnestly. "We've got to get Mona out of here. You know what will happen to her?"

The engineer reflected a moment. "Do you all want to leave town?"

"Yes. Our business here is finished except for Bugs."

"What about your Chevrolet?"

"They picked it up an hour ago."

"Why not get on a bus?"

"That's where they got Bugs, at the bus station."

"Here they come," said Breeze.

Sure enough, there was a hammering at the door. "Here's what you do," said the engineer suddenly. Upside down as always, he could think only when thinking was impossible. It was when thinking was expected of one that he couldn't think. "Take my camper. Here." He quickly drew a sketch of the highway and the old river road. "It's over the levee here. I'll talk to the police. Go out the back door. You drive," he said to Mona, handing her the key. The actor was watching her with a fine gray eye. "The others can ride in the back." The hammering became deafening. "Now if I don't meet you at the levee," shouted the engineer, "go to my uncle's in Louisiana.

254

Cross the bridge at Vicksburg. Mr. Fannin Barrett of Shut Off. I'll meet you there." From his breast pocket he took out a sheaf of road maps, selected a Conoco state map, made an X, and wrote a name and gave it to Mona. "Who are they?" he asked Breeze, who stood rooted at the heaving door.

"That's Mist' Ross and Mist' Gover," said Breeze eagerly, as if he were already smoothing things over with the police.

"Do you know them, Merle?" asked the actor, with a new appraising glint in his eye.

"Yes."

"How are they?"

"Gover's all right."

"Open the door, Breeze." The voice came through the door.

"Yes suh."

"No, hold it—" began the engineer.

"The man said unlock it." It was too late. The doorway was first flooded by sunlight, then darkened by uniforms.

"What do you say, Beans. Ellis," said the engineer, coming toward them.

"Where's the poontang?" asked Beans Ross, a strong, tall, fat man with a handsome tanned face and green-tinted sunglasses such as highway police wear, though he was only a town deputy.

"This is Will Barrett, Beans," said the engineer, holding out his hand. "Mister Ed's boy."

"What," said Beans, shoving his glasses onto his forehead. He even took the other's hand and there was for a split second a chance of peace between them. "What the hell are you doing here?" Beans took from his pocket a small blackjack as soft and worn as skin.

"I'll explain, but meanwhile there is no reason to hit Breeze." He knew at once what Beans meant to do.

"All right, Breeze," said Beans in a routine voice, not looking at him.

Sweet Evening Breeze, knowing what was expected of him, doffed his stocking cap and presented the crown of his head. Hardly watching but with a quick outward flick of his wrist, Beans hit Breeze on the forehead with the blackjack. Breeze fell down.

"Goddamn it, Beans," said the engineer. "That's no way to act."

"You got something to say about it?"

"Yes."

"Where's the poontang?" asked Beans, and with a gesture at once fond and conspiratorial—enlisting him—and contemptuous, he leaned across and snapped his middle finger on the engineer's fly.

"Augh," grunted the engineer, bowing slightly and seeming to remember something. Had this happened to him as a boy, getting snapped on the fly? The humiliation was familiar.

"Don't do that, Beans," said Ellis Gover, coming between them and shaking his head. "This is a real good old boy."

By the time the engineer's nausea had cleared, Beans had caught sight of Mona in the booth. Without taking his eyes from her, he pulled Ellis close and began to whisper. The engineer had time to straighten himself and to brace his foot in the corner of the jamb and sill of the front door. For once in his life he had time and position and a good shot, and for once things became as clear as they used to be in the old honorable days. He hit Beans in the root of his neck as hard as he ever hit the sandbag in the West Side Y.M.C.A. Beans's cap and glasses flew off and he sat down on the floor. "Now listen here, Ellis," said the engineer immediately, turning to the tall, younger policeman. "Yall go ahead," he told the others casually, waving them over Beans's outstretched legs and out the front door. "Catch a Bluebird cab at the corner."

"Wait a minute," said Ellis, but he did not stop them.

"Don't worry about it, Ellis. They haven't done anything. They're leaving town and that's what you want."

"But, shit, man," said Ellis, who could not take his eyes from the fallen policeman. "You done hit Beans."

"I know, but look at Breeze," said the engineer by way of answer, and nodded to the Negro, who was laid out straight as a corpse. Standing next to Ellis, he took him by the elbow just as he used to touch him in a football huddle. Ellis was all-state halfback and the engineer, who was quarterback (not all-state), had called the plays in huddle. Ellis was a bit slow in catching the signals and the engineer used to squeeze him so, just above the elbow.

"Yeah, but hailfire, Will."

"Listen, Ellis," said the engineer, already moving. "You bring charges against me to clear yourself, do you understand? Tell Beans the others got in behind you. You got it?"

"Yeah, but—"

"Now give Beans a hand and tell him to come after me,

O.K.?" He said this though Beans was still out cold, and giving Ellis a final huddle sort of squeeze and nod, the engineer walked quickly to the back door and out into Heck's Alley.

"Will," cried Ellis again, feeling that all was not well. But the other had already crossed the alley to a certain board in a fence which had been eroded into the shape of Illinois and which he knew, now fifteen years later, to swing free on a single nail, was through it and into Miss Mamie Billups' backyard. Miss Mamie was sitting on her side porch when he stooped to pass under her satsuma tree.

"How do you do, Miss Mamie," said the courteous engineer, bowing and putting his tie inside his coat.

"Who is that?" called out the old woman sharply. Everyone used to steal her satsumas.

"This is Will Barrett, Miss Mamie."

"Will Barrett! You come on up here, Will!"

"I can't right now, Miss Mamie," said the engineer, turning up Theard Street. "I'll be right back!"

4. HIS FRIENDS WAITED FOR HIM BUT NOT LONG ENOUGH. By the time he rounded the lower curve of Milliken Bend, having walked the inner shoulder of the levee out of sight of highway and town, the Trav-L-Aire had already lumbered out of the willows and started up the levee—at an angle! The cabin teetered dangerously. He forgot to tell Mona not to do this. He covered his face with his hands: Mona, thinking to spare the G.M.C. the climb straight up, was in a fair way to turn her plumb over. When he looked up, however, the levee was clear.

It was two o'clock. He was hungry. At the levee end of Theard Street he bought a half dozen tamales from a street vendor (but not the same whose cry *Rayed hot!* used to echo up and down the summer night in the 1950's). Now finding a patch of waist-high elephant grass past the towhead and out of sight of anyone standing on the levee behind him, he rolled to and fro and made a hollow which was tilted like a buttercup into the westering sun. It was warm enough to take off his coat and roll up his sleeves. He ate the tamales carefully, taking care not to stain his clothes. The meat was good but his tooth encountered a number-eight shot: rabbit or possibly squirrel. Afterwards he washed his hands in river water, which still thrashed through the lower level of the towhead, and dried them with his handkerchief. Returning to his hollow, he sat cross-legged for a while and watched a towboat push a good half acre of sulphur barges up the dead water on the Louisiana side. Then he curled up and, using his coat folded wrong-side-out for a pillow, went to sleep.

Cold and stiffness woke him. It was a moonless overcast night, but he could make out Scorpio writhing dimly over Louisiana, convulsed around great bloody Antares. Buttoning all three buttons of his jacket, he ran along the inner shoulder of the levee, out of sight of town, until he got warm. When he came abreast of the stacks of the gypsum mill, he went quickly over and down into Blanton Street and took the Illinois Central tracks, which went curving away behind the high school. It was pitch dark under the stadium, but his muscles remembered the spacing of the ties. The open rear of the bleachers exhaled a faint odor of cellar earth and urine. At the Chinaman's he took the tangent of Houston Street, which ran through a better Negro neighborhood of neat shotgun cottages and flower gardens, into the heavy humming air and ham-rich smell of the cottonseed oil mill, and out at De Ridder.

He stood in the inky darkness of the water oaks and looked at his house. It was the same except that the gallery had been closed by glass louvers and a flagpole stuck out of a second-story window. His aunts were sitting on the porch. They had moved out, television and all. He came closer and stood amid the azaleas. They were jolly and fit, were the aunts, and younger than ever. Three were watching "Strike It Rich," two were playing canasta, and one was reading *Race and Reason* and eating Whitman's Sampler. He remembered now that Sophie wrote love letters to Bill Cullen. What a tough hearty crew they were! hearty as muzhiks, and good haters, yet not ill-natured—they'd be honestly and unaffectedly glad to see him walk in, would kiss him and hold him off and make over him—rosy-skinned, easy in their consciences, arteries as supple as a girl's, husbands dead and gone these forty years, pegged out so long ago that he could not remember anyone ever speaking of them; Christian ladies every one, four Protestant, Presbyterian, and Scotch-Irish, two Catholic and

Creole, but long since reconciled, ecumenized, by bon appétit and laughter and good hearty hatred.

It was here under the water oaks that his father used to stroll of a summer night, hands in his pockets and head down, sauntering along the sidewalk in his old Princeton style of sauntering, right side turning forward with right leg. Here under the water oaks or there under the street light, he would hold parley with passers-by, stranger and friend, white and black, thief and police. The boy would sit on the front steps, close enough to speak with his father and close enough too to service the Philco which played its stack of prewar 78's but always had trouble doing it. The mechanism creaked and whirred and down came the record plop and round it went for a spell, hissing under the voyaging needle. From the open window came Brahms, nearly always Brahms. Up and down the sidewalk went his father, took his turn under the street light sometimes with a client, sometimes alone. The clients, black and white and by and large the sorriest of crews but of course listening now with every eager effort of attention and even of a special stratospheric understanding. Between records the boy could hear snatches of talk: "Yassuh, that's the way it is now! I have notice the same thing myself!"—the father having said something about the cheapness of good intentions and the rarity of good character—"I'm sho gon' do like you say"—the passer-by working him of course for the fifty cents or five dollars or what, but working him as gracefully as anyone ever worked, they as good at their trade as he at his. The boy listening: what was the dread in his heart as he heard the colloquy and the beautiful terrible Brahms which went abroad into the humming summer night and the heavy ham-rich air?

The aunts let out a holler. Bill Cullen had given away a cabin cruiser to a lady from Michigan City, Indiana.

It was on such an evening—he passed his hand over his eyes and stretching it forth touched the sibilant corky bark of the water oak—that his father had died. The son watched from the step, old Brahms went abroad, the father took a stroll and spoke to a stranger of the good life and the loneliness of the galaxies. "Yes suh," said the stranger. "I have heard tell it was so" (that the closest star was two light years away).

When the man came back the boy asked him:

"Father, why do you walk in the dark when you know they have sworn to kill you?"

"I'm not afraid, son."

To the west the cars of the white people were nosing up the levee, headlights switched first to parking, then out altogether. From the east, beyond the cottonseed oil mill, came the sound of Negro laughter.

The man walked until midnight. Once a police car stopped. The policeman spoke to the man.

"You've won," said the youth when the man came back. "I heard the policeman. They've left town."

"We haven't won, son. We've lost."

"But they're gone, Father."

"Why shouldn't they leave? They've won."

"How have they won, Father?"

"They don't have to stay. Because they found out that we are like them after all and so there was no reason for them to stay."

"How are we like them, Father?"

"Once they were the fornicators and the bribers and the takers of bribes and we were not and that was why they hated us. Now we are like them, so why should they stay? They know they don't have to kill me."

"How do they know that, Father?"

"Because we've lost it all, son."

"Lost what?"

"But there's one thing they don't know."

"What's that, Father?"

"They may have won, but I don't have to choose that."

"Choose what?"

"Choose them."

This time, as he turned to leave, the youth called out to him. "Wait."

"What?"

"Don't leave."

"I'm just going to the corner."

But there was a dread about this night, the night of victory. (Victory is the saddest thing of all, said the father.) The mellowness of Brahms had gone overripe, the victorious serenity of the Great Horn Theme was false, oh fake fake. Underneath, all was unwell.

"Father."

"What?"

"Why do you like to be alone?"

"In the last analysis, you are alone." He turned into the darkness of the oaks.

"Don't leave." The terror of the beautiful victorious music pierced his very soul.

"I'm not leaving, son," said the man and, after taking a turn, came back to the steps. But instead of stopping to sit beside the youth, he went up past him, resting his hand on the other's shoulder so heavily that the boy looked up to see his father's face. But the father went on without saying anything: went into the house, on through the old closed-in dogtrot hall to the back porch, opened the country food press which had been converted to a gun cabinet, took down the double-barrel twelve-gauge Greener, loaded it, went up the back stairs into the attic, and, fitting the muzzle of the Greener into the notch of his breastbone, could still reach both triggers with his thumbs. That was how it had to happen, the sheriff told the youth, that was the only way it could have happened.

The sound came crashing through the music, louder than twenty Philcos, a single sound, yet more prolonged and thunderous than a single shot. The youth turned off the Philco and went upstairs.

"—and Anacin does not upset your stummick," said Bill Cullen.

Again his hand went forth, knowing where it was, though he could not see, and touched the tiny iron horsehead of the hitching post, traced the cold metal down to the place where the oak had grown round it in an elephant lip. His fingertips touched the warm finny whispering bark.

Wait. While his fingers explored the juncture of iron and bark, his eyes narrowed as if he caught a glimmer of light on the cold iron skull. *Wait.* I think he was wrong and that he was looking in the wrong place. No, not he but the times. The times were wrong and one looked in the wrong place. It wasn't even his fault because that was the way he was and the way the times were, and there was no other place a man could look. It was the worst of times, a time of fake beauty and fake victory. *Wait.* He had missed it! It was not in the Brahms that one looked and not in solitariness and not in the old sad poetry but—he wrung out his ear—but here, under your nose, here in the very curiousness and drollness and extraness of the iron and the bark that—he shook his head—that—

The TV studio audience laughed with its quick, obedient, and above all grateful Los Angeles laughter—once we were lonesome back home, the old sad home of our fathers, and here we are together and happy at last.

A Negro came whistling toward him under the street light, a young man his own age. Entering the darkness of the water oaks, the Negro did not at first see him (though it had been his, the Negro's, business, until now, to see him first), then did see him two yards away and stopped for a long half second. They looked at each other. There was nothing to say. Their fathers would have had much to say: "In the end, Sam, it comes down to a question of character." "Yes suh, Lawyer Barrett, you right about that. Like I was saying to my wife only this evening—" But the sons had nothing to say. The engineer looked at the other as the half second wore on. You may be in a fix and I know that but what you don't know and won't believe and must find out for yourself is that I'm in a fix too and you got to get where I am before you even know what I'm talking about and I know that and that's why there is nothing to say now. Meanwhile I wish you well.

It was only then, belatedly, and as if it were required of him, that the Negro shuddered and went his way.

As he watched his aunts, a squad car came slowly down De Ridder and stopped not twelve feet beyond the iron horse. A policeman, not Ross or Gover, went up to the porch and spoke to Aunt Sophie. She shook her head four or five times, hand to her throat, and when the policeman left, turned off the television and in her excitement stumbled a little as she told the others. Aunt Bootie forgot the Whitman's Sampler in her lap, stood up and scattered nougats and bird eggs in all directions. No one noticed.

Without taking much care about it, he walked through the azaleas and around to the back screen door, which was locked and which he opened, without knowing that he remembered, by wedging the door back against its hinges so that the bolt could be forced free of its worn wooden mortise, and went straight up the two flights to the attic and straight into the windowless interior room built into the peak of the house. His upraised hand felt for and found the string. The old clear-glass 25-watt bulb shed a yellow mizzling light, a light of rays, actual striae. The room had not been touched, they were still here; the grandfather's army blanket, Plattsburg issue, the puttees, a belt of webbing, the Kaiser Bill helmets, the five-pound binoculars with an artillery scale etched into one lens. He picked up the Greener, broke the breech and sighted at the yellow bulb. The bore was still speckled with powder grains. And the collapsible boat: an English contraption of silvery zeppelin fabric with varnished spruce spars to spring it into shape. It lay as it had lain ten years ago, half disassembled and hastily packed from a duck hunt he and his father had taken on the White River in the early fifties. Now, as if it were the very night of their return, he knelt absently and repacked the boat, remembering the feel and fit of the spar-ends and the brass sockets and even the goofy English directions: "—Don't be discouraged if spar L does not fit immediately into socket J—patience is required."

After he repacked the boat, he lay on the cot and, propping himself against the wall, drew the hard scratchy army blanket up to his armpits. For two hours he sat so, wakeful and alert, while his eyes followed the yellow drizzle of light into every corner of the attic room.

It was eight o'clock when he went downstairs, English boat slung over one shoulder, artillery binoculars over the other. The aunts had not gotten up. Hearing D'lo shuffling about the kitchen, he took care not to startle her: he slipped out the back door and came in noisily again.

"Law, if it ain't Mr. Billy," said D'lo, rolling her eyes conventionally and noticing the wall clock as she did so. She was no more surprised by the doings of white folks than he was.

D'lo stirred steaming boilers of grits and batter, fist sunk deep into her side, knees driven together by her great weight and bare heels ridden off her old pink mules and onto the floor. It crossed his mind that D'lo had somehow known he was here. He asked her not to tell his aunts.

"I ain't gon' tell them nothing!"

"I'm surprised you're still here."

"Where I'm going!"

"They still fight?"

"Fight! You don't know, fight."

"The police are looking for me."

"Uh-oh," said D'lo. This was serious. Yet he could not have sworn she did not know all about it.

D'lo found him his father's Rolls razor and, while he washed and shaved in the downstairs bathroom, fixed him a big breakfast of grits and sausage and batter cakes. When he left, he gave her twenty dollars.

"I thank you," said D'lo formally and twisted the bill into

the stocking roll below her fat old knee, which curved out in six different arcs of rich cinnamon flesh.

A step creaked. "Here *she* come," said D'lo. Sophie was *she*, ole miss, the one who gave the orders.

"I'll be seeing you, D'lo," he said, shouldering the boat.

"All right now, Mist' Billy," she cried politely, socking down the grits spoon on the boiler and curling her lip in a rich and complex acknowledgment of his own queerness and her no more than mild sympathy and of the distance between them, maybe not even sympathy but just a good-humored letting him be. (All right now, you was a good little boy, but don't mess with me too much, go on, get out of my kitchen.)

Ten minutes later he was up and over the levee and down into the willows, where he assembled the boat and the two-bladed paddle. It was a sparkling day. The river was ruffled by glittering steel wavelets like a northern lake. Shoving off and sitting buttoned up kayak style in the aft hole, he went dropping away in the fast water, past the barrow pits and blue holes, and now beginning to paddle, went skimming over the wide river, which seemed to brim and curve up like a watchglass from the great creamy boils that shed tons of cold bottom water, down past old Fort Ste. Marie on the Louisiana side, its ramparts gone back to blackberries and honeysuckle. He knew every tunnel, embrasure, magazine room, and did not bother to look. Two Negroes in a skiff were running a trotline under the caving bank. They watched him a second longer than they might have. Now they were watching him again, under their arms as they handed the line along. He frowned, wondering how he looked in the face, then recollected himself: it was after all an uncommon sight, a man fully dressed in coat and necktie and buttoned up in a tiny waterbug of a boat and at nine o'clock of a Tuesday morning. They could not encompass him; he was beyond their reckoning. But hold on, something new! As he drifted past the fort, he rubbed his eyes. A pennant fluttered from the parapet, the Stars and Bars! And the entire fort was surrounded by a ten-foot-high hurricane fence. But of course! This very month marked the hundredth anniversary of the reduction of the fort by Admiral Foote's gunboats. It was part of the preparation for the Centennial! No doubt they would, at the proper time, imprison the "Confederates" behind the fence.

But as he dropped past the fort, he was surprised to see "sentinels" patrolling the fence and even a few prisoners inside, but as unlikely a lot of Confederates as one could imagine—men and women! the men bearded properly enough, but both sexes blue-jeaned and sweat-shirted and altogether disreputable. And Negroes! And yonder, pacing the parapet—Good Lord!—was Milo Menander, the politician, who was evidently playing the role of Beast Banks, the infamous federal commandant of the infamous federal prison into which the fort was converted after its capture. Capital! And hadn't he got himself up grandly for the occasion: flowing locks, big cigar, hand pressed Napoleonically into his side, a proper villainous-looking old man if ever there was one.

But hold on! Something was wrong. Were they not two years late with their celebration? The fort was captured early in the war, and here it was 19— What year was this? He wrang out his ear and beat his pockets in vain for his Gulf calendar card. Another slip: if Beast Banks had reduced and occupied the fort, why was the Stars and Bars still flying?

It was past figuring even if he'd a stomach for figuring. Something may be amiss here, but then all was not well with him either. Next he'd be hearing singing ravening particles. Besides, he had other fish to fry and many a mile to travel. British wariness woke in him and, putting his head down, he dropped below the fort as silently as an Englishman slipping past Heligoland.

He put in at the old ferry landing, abandoned when the bridge at Vicksburg was built and now no more than a sloughing bank of mealy earth honeycombed by cliff swallows. Disassembling and packing his boat, he stowed it in a cave-in and pulled dirt over it and set out up the sunken ferry road, which ran through loess cuts filled now as always with a smoky morning twilight and the smell of roots (here in Louisiana across the river it was ever a dim green place of swamps and shacks and Negro graveyards sparkling with red and green medicine bottles; the tree stumps were inhabited by spirits), past flooded pin-oak flats where great pileated woodpeckers went ringing down the smoky aisles. Though it was only two hundred yards from home, Louisiana had ever seemed misty and faraway, removed in time and space. Over yonder in the swamps lived the same great birds Audubon saw. Freejacks, Frenchmen, and river rats trapped muskrat and caught catfish. It was a place of small and pleasant deeds.

* * *

"Hey, Merum!"

Uncle Fannin was walking up and down the back porch, his face narrow and dark as a piece of slab bark, carrying in the crook of his arm the Browning automatic worn to silver, with bluing left only in the grooves of the etching. The trigger guard was worn as thin as an old man's wedding ring.

"Mayrom! Where's that Ma'am?"

He was calling his servant Merriam but he never called him twice by the same name.

It was characteristic of the uncle that he had greeted his nephew without surprise, as if it were nothing out of the ordinary that he should come hiking up out of nowhere with his artillery binoculars, and after five years. He hardly stopped his pacing.

"We're fixing to mark some coveys up on Sunnyside," he said, as if it were he who owed the explanations.

The engineer blinked. They might have been waiting for him.

The Trav-L-Aire was nowhere in sight and Uncle Fannin knew nothing about it or any company of "actors," as the engineer called them (calculating that a mixture of blacks and whites was somehow more tolerable if they were performers).

Merriam came round the corner of the house with two pointers, one an old liver-and-white bitch who knew what was what and had no time for foolery, trotting head down, dugs rippling like a curtain; the other pointer was a fool. He was a young dog named Rock. He put his muzzle in the engineer's hand and nudged him hard. His head was heavy as iron. There were warts all over him where Uncle Fannin had shot him for his mistakes. Merriam, the engineer perceived, was partial to Rock and was afraid the uncle was going to shoot him again. Merriam was a short heavy Negro whose face was welted and bound up through the cheeks so that he was muffle-jawed in his speech. Blackness like a fury seemed to rush forward in his face. But the engineer knew that the fury was a kind of good nature. He wore a lumpy white sweater with stuffing sticking out of it like a scarecrow.

It was not a real hunt they were setting out on. Uncle Fannin wanted to mark coveys for the season. Later in the fall, businessmen would come down from Memphis and up from New Orleans and he would take them out. The engineer refused the gun offered to him, but he went along with them. They drove into the woods in an old high-finned De Soto

266

whose back seat had been removed to make room for the dogs. A partition of chicken wire fenced off the front seat. The dogs stuck their heads out the windows, grinning and splitting the wind, their feet scrabbling for purchase on the metal seat bed. The car smelled of old bitter car metal and croker sacks and the hot funky firecracker smell of dry bird dogs.

Merriam sat with the two Barretts on the front seat, but swiveled around to face them to show he was not sitting with them, not quite on or off the seat, mostly off and claiming, in a nice deprecation, not more than an inch of seat, not through any real necessity but only as the proper concession due the law of gravity. It was not hard to believe that Merriam could have sat in the air if it had been required of him.

The De Soto plunged and roared, crashing into potholes not with a single shock but with a distributed and mediated looseness, a shambling sound like throwing a chain against a wall, knocking the dogs every whichway. When Uncle Fannin slammed on the brakes, the dogs were thrust forward, their chins pushing against the shoulders of the passengers, but already back-pedaling apologetically, their expressions both aggrieved and grinning.

They hunted from an old plantation dike long since reclaimed by the woods and now no more than a high path through thickets. The engineer, still dressed in Dacron suit and suède oxfords, followed along, hands in pockets. Rock got shot again, though with bird shot and from a sufficient distance so that it did no more harm than raise a new crop of warts.

"Meroom!"

"Yassuh."

Merriam was carrying a brand-new single-shot nickel-plated sixteen-gauge from Sears Roebuck which looked like a silver flute.

"Look at that son of a bitch."

"I see him."

Below and ahead of them the bitch Maggie was holding a point, her body bent like a pin, tail quivering. Rock had swung wide and was doubling back and coming up behind her, bounding up and down like a springbok to see over the grass. He smelled nothing.

"He's sho gon' run over her," said the uncle.

"No suh, he ain't," said Merriam, but keeping a fearful weather eye on Rock.

"What's he doing then?"

The engineer perceived that the uncle was asking the question ironically, taking due notice of the magic and incantatory faculty that Negroes are supposed to have—they know what animals are going to do, for example—but doing it ironically.

"Goddamn, he *is* going to run over her!"—joking aside now.

"He ain't stuttn it," said Merriam.

Of course Rock, damn fool that he was, did run over Maggie, landing squarely in the middle of the covey and exploding quail in all directions—it coming over him in mid-air and at the last second, the inkling of what lay below, he braking and back-pedaling wildly like Goofy. Uncle Fannin shot three times, twice at quail and once at Rock, and, like all dead shots, already beginning to talk as he shot as if the shooting itself were the least of it. "Look at that cock, one, two, and—" *Wham*. He got three birds, one with one shot and two crossing with the other shot. The third shot hit Rock. The engineer opened his mouth to say something but a fourth shot went off.

"Lord to God," groaned Merriam. "He done shot him again." Merriam went to look after Rock.

The uncle didn't hear. He was already down the levee and after a single who had gone angling off into the woods, wings propped down, chunky, teetering in his glide. Uncle Fannin went sidling and backing into the underbrush, reloading as he went, the vines singing and popping around his legs. When he couldn't find the single, even though they had seen where he landed, Merriam told the two Barretts that the quail had hidden from the dogs.

"Now how in the hell is he going to hide from the dogs," said the disgusted uncle.

"He hiding now," said Merriam, still speaking to the engineer. "They has a way of hiding so that no dog in the world can see or smell them."

"Oh, Goddamn, come on now. You hold that dog."

"I seen them!"

"How do they hide, Merriam?" the engineer asked him.

"They hits the ground and grab ahold of trash and sticks with both feets and throws theyselfs upside down with his

feets sticking up and the dogs will go right over him ever'
time."

"Hold that goddamn dog now, Mayrim!"

After supper they watched television. An old round-eyed Zenith and two leatherette recliners, the kind that are advertised
on the back page of the comic section, had been placed in a
clearing that had been made long ago by pushing Aunt
Felice's good New Orleans furniture back into the dark
corners of the room. Merriam watched from a roost somewhere atop a pile of chairs and tables. The sentient engineer
perceived immediately that the recliner he was given was
Merriam's seat, but there was nothing he could do about it.
Uncle Fannin pretended the recliner had been brought out for
the engineer (how could it have been?) and Merriam pretended
he always roosted high in the darkness. But when they, Uncle
Fannin and Merriam, talked during the programs, sometimes
the uncle, forgetting, would speak to the other recliner:

"He's leaving now but he be back up there later, don't
worry about it."

"Yes suh," said Merriam from the upper darkness.

"He's a pistol ball now, ain't he?"

"I mean."

"But Chester, now. Chester can't hold them by himself."

"That Mist' Chester is all right now," cried Merriam.

"Shoot."

Whenever a commercial ended, Uncle Fannin lifted himself and took a quick pluck at his seat by way of getting ready.

"That laig don't hold him!"

"It ain't his leg that's holding him now," said the uncle,
and, noticing that it was his nephew who sat beside him, gave
him a wink and a poke in the ribs to show that he didn't take
Merriam seriously.

Merriam didn't mind. They argued about the Western
heroes as if they were real people whose motives could be
figured out. During a commercial, Merriam told the engineer
of a program they had seen last week. It made a strong impression on him because the hero, their favorite, a black
knight of a man, both gentleman and brawler, had gotten
badly beat up. It was part one of a series and so he was still
beat up.

"I told Mist' Fanny"—Merriam spoke muffle-jawed and all
in a rush as if he hoped to get the words out before they got

bound up in his cheeks—"that the onliest way in the world they can catch him is to get in behind him. Mist' Fanny, he say they gon' stomp him. I say they got to get in behind him first. What happened, some man called his attention, like I say 'look here!' and he looked and they did get in behind him and Lord, they stomped him, bad, I mean all up in the head. He lay out there in the street two days and folks scared to help him, everybody scared of this one man, Mister errerr—, errerr—" Merriam snapped his fingers. "It slips my mind, but he was a stout man and low, lower than you or Mist' Fanny, he brush his hair up in the front like." Merriam showed them and described the man so that the engineer would recognize him if he happened to see him. "They taken his money and his gun and his horse and left him out there in the sun. Then here come this other man to kill him. And I said to Mist' Fanny, there is one thing this other man don't know and that is he got this little biddy pistol on him and they didn't take it off him because he got it hid in his bosom."

"Man, how you going to go up against a thirty-thirty with a derringer," said the uncle disdainfully, yet shyly, watchful of the engineer lest he, the engineer, think too badly of Merriam. His uncle was pleading with him!

"I'd like to see how that comes out," said the engineer. "Is the second part coming on tonight?" he asked Merriam.

"Yessuh."

"That fellow's name was Bogardus," said the uncle presently. "He carried a carbine with a lever action and he can work that lever as fast as you can shoot that automatic there."

"Yessuh," said Merriam, but without conviction.

Still no sign of the Trav-L-Aire, and at midnight the engineer went to bed—without taking thought about it, going up to the second-floor room he used to have in the summertime, a narrow cell under the eaves furnished with an armoire, a basin and ewer and chamber pot, and an old-style feather bed with bolster. The skull was still there on the shelf of the armoire, property of his namesake, Dr. Williston Barrett, the original misfit, who graduated from old Jefferson Medical College, by persuasion an abolitionist but who nevertheless went to fight in Virginia and afterwards having had enough, he said, of the dying and the dead and the living as well, the North and the South, of men in sum, came home to the country and never practiced a day in his life, took instead to his own laudanum and became a philosopher of sorts, lived another sixty years, the only long-lived Barrett male. The skull had turned as yellow as ivory and was pencil-marked by ten generations of children; it was sawed through the dome and the lid securely fastened by silver hinges; undo that and the brain pan was itself sectioned and hinged, opening in turn into an airy comb of sinus cells.

It was cold but he knew the feather bed, so he stripped to his shorts, and after washing his T-shirt in the ewer and spreading it on the marble stand to dry, he climbed into bed. The warm goosedown flowed up around him. It was, he had always imagined, something like going to bed in Central Europe. He pulled the bolster up to his shoulders and propped Sutter's casebook on its thick margin.

R.R., white male, c. 25, well-dev. but under-nour. 10 mm. entrance wound in right temporal, moderate powder tattooing and branding, right exophthalmus and hematoma; stellate exit wound left mastoidal base, approx 28 mm diam. Cops say suicide.

From Lt. B.'s report: R.R., b. Garden City, Long Island; grad LIU and MIT last June. Employed Redstone Arsenal since June 15. Drove here after work yesterday, July 3, purchased S & W .38 rev. from Pioneer Sports, rented room at Jeff D. Hotel, found on bed clothed 9 a.m., approx time of death, 1 a.m., July 4.

Lt. B.: "His life before him, etc." "One of the lucky ones, etc." "No woman trouble, liquor or drugs or money, etc." "? ? ?"

Suicide considered as consequence of the spirit of abstraction and of transcendence; lewdness as sole portal of reentry into world demoted to immanence; reentry into immanence via orgasm; but post-orgasmic transcendence 7 devils worse than first.

Man who falls victim to transcendence as the spirit of abstraction, i.e., elevates self to posture over and against world which is *pari passu* demoted to immanence and seen as examplar and specimen and coordinate, and who is not at same time compensated by beauty of motion of method of science, has no choice but to seek reentry into immanent world *qua* immanence. But since no avenue of reentry remains save genital and since reentry coterminus c̄ orgasm, post-orgasmic despair without remedy. Of my series of four suicides in scientists and technicians, 3 post-coital (spermatozoa at meatus), 2 in hotel room. Hotel room = site of intersection of transcendence and immanence: room itself, a triaxial coordinate ten floors above street; whore who comes up = pure immanence to be entered. But entry doesn't avail: one skids off into transcendence. *There is no reentry from the orbit of transcendence.*

Lt. B.: "Maybe they're so shocked by what they've turned loose on the world—" Pandora's Box theory, etc. "Maybe that's why he did it," etc.

I say: "Bullshit, Lt., and on the contrary. This Schadenfreude is what keeps them going," etc.

What I cannot tell Lt.: If R.R. had been a good pornographer, he would not have suicided. His death was due, not to lewdness, but to the failure of lewdness.

I say to Val: Re Sweden: increase in suicides in Sweden due not to increase in lewdness but to decline of lewdness. When Sweden was post-Christian but had not yet forgotten Cx (circa 1850–1914), Swedish lewdness intact and suicides negligible. But when Swedes truly post-Christian (not merely post-Christian but also post-memory of Cx), lewdness declined and suicides rose in inverse relation.

Val to me: Don't sell Sweden short. (I notice that her language has taken on the deplorable and lapsed slanginess found in many religious, priests and nuns, and in *Our Sunday Visitor*.) The next great saint must come from Sweden, etc. It is only from desolation of total transcendence of self and total descent of world of immanence that a man can come who can recover himself and world under God, etc. Give me suicidal Swede, says she, over Alabama Christian any day, etc.

I say: Very good, very good talk, but it is after all only that, that is the kind of talk we have between us.

The bar turned in his head, synapses gave way, and he slept ten hours dreamlessly and without spansules.

Still no sign of the Trav-L-Aire the next morning, but after a great steaming breakfast of brains and eggs and apple rings served in front of the Zenith. (Captain Kangaroo: Uncle Fannin and Merriam cackled like maniacs at the doings of Captain K. and Mr. Greenjeans, and the engineer wondered, how is it that uncle and servant, who were solid 3-D persons, true denizens of this misty Natchez Trace country, should be transported by these sad gags from Madison Avenue? But they were transported. They were merry as could be, and he, the engineer, guessed that was all right: more power to Captain K.)

After he had transacted his oil-lease business with his uncle, the telephone rang. It was the deputy sheriff in Shut Off. It seemed a little "trailer" had been stolen by a bunch of niggers and outside agitators and that papers and books in the name of Williston Bibb Barrett had been found therein. Did Mr. Fannin know anything about it? If he did and if it was his property or his kin's, he might reclaim the same by coming down to Shut Off and picking it up.

The uncle held the phone and told his nephew.

"What happened to the, ah, Negroes and the outside agitators?" asked the latter calmly.

Nothing, it seemed. They were there, at this moment, in Shut Off. It needed but a word from Mr. Fannin to give the lie to their crazy story that they had borrowed the trailer from his kinsman and the lot of them would be thrown in jail, if not into the dungeon at Fort Ste. Marie.

"The dungeon. So that's it," said the nephew. relieved despite himself. "And what if the story is confirmed?" he asked his uncle.

Then they'd be packed off in twenty minutes on the next bus to Memphis.

"Confirm the story," said the nephew. "And tell him I'll be there in an hour to pick up my camper." He wanted his friends free, clear of danger, but free and clear of him too, gone, by the time he reached Shut Off.

After bidding his uncle and Merriam farewell—who were only waiting for him to leave to set off with the dogs in the De Soto—he struck out for the old landing, where he retrieved his boat and drifted a mile or so to the meadows, which presently separated the river from Shut Off. So it came to be called Shut Off: many years ago one of the meanderings of the river had jumped the neck of a peninsula and shut the landing off from the river.

5. THE BOY AND THE MAN ATE BREAKFAST IN THE DINING car Savannah. The waiter braced his thigh against the table while he laid the pitted nickel-silver knives and forks. The water in the heavy glass carafe moved up and down without leaving a drop, as if water and glass were quits through usage.

A man came down the aisle and stood talking to his father, folding and unfolding his morning paper.

"It's a bitter thing, Ed. Bitter as gar broth."

"I know it is, Oscar. Son, I want you to meet Senator Oscar Underwood. Oscar, this is my son Bill."

He arose to shake hands and then did not know whether to stand or sit.

"Bill," the senator told him, "when you grow up, decide what you want to do according to your lights. Then do it. That's all there is to it."

"Yes sir," he said, feeling confident he could do that.

"Senator Underwood did just that, son, and at great cost to himself," said his father.

"Yes sir."

He awoke, remembering what Senator Underwood looked like, even the vein on his hand which jumped back and forth across a tendon when he folded and unfolded the fresh newspaper.

Dear God, he thought, pacing his five-foot aisle, I'm slipping again. I can't have met Senator Underwood, or could I? Was it I and my father or he and his father? How do I know what he looked like? What did he look like? I must find out.

Stooping, he caught sight of a forest of oil derricks. He dressed and went outside. The camper was parked in the gravel plaza of a truckers' stop. In the café he learned that he was in Longview, Texas. While he waited for his breakfast, he read from Sutter's notebook:

You're wrong about Rita, Val. She saved my life and she meant no harm to Kitty—though that does not answer your charge. I had left the old ruined South for the transcending Southwest. But there transcendence failed me and Rita picked me up for the bum I was and fed and clothed me.

The day before I left home I stood in a lewd wood by the golf links. My insurance had been canceled and I could not hospitalize patients or even treat them at home save at my own risk. The wood was the lewd wood of my youth where lovers used to come and leave Merry Widow tins and where I dreamed the lewd dreams of youth. Therefrom I spied Jackie Randolph towing her cart up number 7 fairway sans caddy and sans partner. Invited her into the woods and spoke into her ear. She looked at her watch and said she had 20 minutes before her bridge luncheon. She spread her golf towel on the pine needles, kept her spiked shoes on, and cursed in my ear.

The innocence of Mexican country women.

That evening my father gave me $100,000 for not smoking until I was 21.

Looked in J.A.M.A. classifieds, found job in Santa Fe clinic, telephoned them my credentials (which were ever good), was accepted on spot, packed my Edsel and was on my way. Clinic dreary—found my true vocation at Sangre de Cristo guest ranch.

Genius loci of Western desert did not materialize. Had hoped for free-floating sense of geographical transcendence, that special dislocatedness and purity of the Southwest which attracted Doc Holliday and Robert Oppenheimer, one a concrete Valdosta man who had had a bellyful of the concrete, the other the luckiest of all abstract men: who achieved the high watermark of the 20th century, which is to say: the device conceived in a locus of pure transcendence, which in turn worked the maximum effect upon the sphere of immanence, the world. (Both men, notice, developed weapons in the desert, the former a specially built sawed-off shotgun which he carried by a string around his neck.)

It didn't work. I found myself treating senior citizens for post-retirement anomie and lady dudes for sore rears and nameless longings. I took my money and bought a ranch, moved out and in a month's time was struck flat by an acute depression, laid out flat in the desert and assaulted by 10,000 devils, not the little black fellows of St. Anthony but wanton teen-agers who swung from the bedpost and made gestures. I stopped eating. Rita found me (she was looking for volunteer MD's for her little Indians), toted me back to her cozy house in Tesuque, fed me, clothed me, bucked me up, and stood for no nonsense. She saved my life and I married her to stay alive. We had a good time. We ate the pure fruit of transcendence. She is not, like me, a pornographer. She believes in "love" like you, though a different kind. She "falls in love." She fell in love with me because I needed her, and then with Kitty because she thought I didn't need her and because Kitty seemed to, with that Gretel-lost-in-the-woods look of hers. Now Kitty is "in love" with someone and Rita is up the creek. I told her to forget all that stuff, e.g., "love," and come on back with me to the Southwest, where we didn't have a bad time. But she is still angry with me. I forgive her sins but she doesn't mine. Hers: like all secular saints, she canonizes herself. Even her sins are meritorious. Her concern for Kitty gets put down as "broadening her horizons" or "saving her from the racists." And all she really wanted for Jamie was that he should get Barrett out of the way. She got extremely angry when I suggested it, though I told her it wasn't so bad, that she was no more guilty than everyone else. Eh, Val? You want to know the only thing I really held against her? A small thing but it got under my skin. It was an expression she used with her transcendent friends: she would tell them she and I were "good in bed." I am an old-fashioned Alabama pornographer and do not like forward expressions in a woman.

Feeling unusually elated—then I am Kitty's "someone"!— he stopped at the public library in Longview and looked up Senator Oscar W. Underwood in the *Columbia Encyclopedia*. The senator died in 1929, ten years before the engineer's birth. When he asked the librarian where he might find a picture of Senator Underwood, she looked at him twice and said she didn't know.

The same evening he called Kitty from a Dallas trailer park. To his vast relief, she sounded mainly solicitous for him. She had even supposed that he had been hurt and suffered another attack of "amnesia"—which he saw that she saw as a thing outside him, a magic medical entity, a dragon that might overtake him at any moment. Fortunately too, the events occurring that night on the campus were themselves so violent that his own lapse seemed minor.

"Oh, honey, I thought you'd been killed," cried Kitty.

"No."

"I couldn't have met you anyway. They herded us down into the basement and wouldn't let us leave till Sunday afternoon."

"Sunday afternoon," said the engineer vaguely.

"Are you all right?" asked Kitty anxiously when he fell silent.

"Yes. I'm going on now to find, ah, Jamie."

"I know. We're counting on you."

"I wish you were here with me."

"Me too."

All of a sudden he did. Love pangs entered his heart and melted his loin and his life seemed simple. The thing to do— why couldn't he remember it?—was to marry Kitty and get a job and live an ordinary life, play golf like other people.

"We will be married."

"Oh yes, darling. Just between you and I, Myra is going to take the Mickle house off the market till you get back."

"Between you and me," he said absently, "the Mickle

house?" Oh my. He'd forgotten Cap'n Andy and his lookout over the doleful plain.

"You two big dopes come on back here where you belong."

"Who?"

"You and Jamie."

"Oh yes. We will."

"You shouldn't have done it."

"Done what?"

"Told Poppy to stop payment of my dowry."

"Somebody stole it."

"Then you'll still accept it?"

"Sure."

"He wrote me another one."

"Good."

But his foreboding returned as soon as he hung up. He lay abed stiff as a poker, feet sticking up, listening to patriotic programs. When at last he did fall asleep, he woke almost immediately and with a violent start. He peeped out of the window to see what might be amiss. Evil low-flying clouds reflected a red furnace-glow from the city. Lower still, from the very treetops, he fancied he could hear a ravening singing sound. Wasting no time, he uncoupled his umbilical connections with dread Dallas, roared out onto the freeways, and by sun-up was leveled out at eighty-five and straight for the Pan-handle.

Past Amarillo the next day and up a black tundra-like coun-try with snow fences and lonesome shacks to Raton Pass. He stopped for gas at an ancient Humble station, a hut set down in a moraine of oil cans and shredded fan belts and ruptured inner tubes. The wind came howling down from Colorado, roaring down the railroad cut like a freight train. There was a meniscus of snow on the black mountainside. The attendant wore an old sheepskin coat and was as slanty-eyed as a China-man. Later the engineer thought: why he is an Indian. He steered the Trav-L-Aire out onto a level stretch of tundra, locked himself in, and slept for twenty hours.

When he woke, it was very cold. He lit the propane panel ray and, as he waited for the cabin to warm, caught sight of his own name in Sutter's casebook.

Barrett: His trouble is he wants to know what his trouble is. His "trouble," he thinks, is a disorder of such a character that if only he can locate the right expert with the right psychology, the disorder can be set right and he can go about his business.

That is to say: he wishes to cling to his transcendence and to locate a fellow transcender (e.g., me) who will tell him how to traffic with immanence (e.g., "environment," "groups," "experience," etc.) in such a way that he will be happy. Therefore I will tell him nothing. For even if I were "right," his posture is self-defeating.

(Southern transcenders are the worst of all—for they hate the old bloody immanence of the South. Southerners outdo their teachers, just as the Chinese Marxists outdo the Soviets. Did you ever talk to a female Freudian Georgia social worker? Freud would be horrified.)

Yes, Barrett has caught a whiff of the transcendent trap and has got the wind up. But what can one tell him? What can you tell him, Val?

Even if you were right. Let us say you were right: that man is a wayfarer (i.e., not transcending being nor immanent being but wayfarer) who therefore stands in the way of hearing a piece of news which is of the utmost importance to him (i.e., his salvation) and which he had better attend to. So you say to him: Look, Barrett, your trouble is due not to a disorder of your organism but to the human condition, that you do well to be afraid and you do well to forget everything which does not pertain to your salvation. That is to say, your amnesia is not a symptom. So you say: Here is the piece of news you have been waiting for, and you tell him. What does Barrett do? He attends in that eager flattering way of his and at the end of it he might even say *yes*! But he will receive the news from his high seat of transcendence as one more item of psychology, throw it into his immanent meat-grinder, and wait to see if he feels better. He told me he's in favor of the World's Great Religions. What are you going to do about that?

I am not in favor of any such thing. We are doomed to the transcendence of abstraction and I choose the only reentry into the world which remains to us. What is better then than the beauty and the exaltation of the practice of transcendence (science and art) and of the delectation of immanence, the beauty and the exaltation of lewd love? What is better than this: one works hard during the day in the front line and with the comradeship of science and at night one goes to La Fonda, where one encounters a stranger, a handsome woman. We drink, we two handsome thirty-five-year-olds, she dark-eyed, shadowy of cheek, wistful in her own transcendence. We dance. The guitar makes the heart soar. We eat hearty. Under the table a gentle pressure of the knee. One speaks into her ear at some length. "Let's go." "But we ordered dinner." "We can come back." "All right." The blood sings with voluptuousness and tenderness.

Rita says I do not love anyone. That is not true. I love all women. How lovable they are, all of them, our lovely lonely bemused American women. What darlings. Let any one of them enter a room and my heart melts. You say there is something better. *Ich warte.*

Where he probably goes wrong, mused the engineer sleepily, is in the extremity of his alternatives: God and not-God, getting under women's dresses and blowing your brains out. Whereas and in fact my problem is how to live from one ordinary minute to the next on a Wednesday afternoon.

Has not this been the case with all "religious" people?

6. DOWN, DOWN INTO THE SUNNY YELLOW CANYON OF the Rio Grande, down through the piney slopes to the ocher cliffs and the red clay bottoms. He stopped to see the famous river. When he came out of a fugue, he was in some ways like a sailor, horny and simple-minded, and with an itch to wander and see the sights, the famous places, take them in, dig every detail. But what a piddling little creek it was! A far cry from the Big Muddy: the trickle of whitish alkali water looked like the run-off from a construction site. Beside him a gold aspen rattled like foil in the sunlight. But there was no wind. He moved closer. A single leaf danced on its pedicle, mysteriously dispensed from energy laws.

Another Indian at a Phillips 66 station in Santa Fe directed him to Rancho la Merced, which he, the Indian, knew by name but not by owner. It meant leaving the highway south of the city and bumping across the desert, through scrubby junipers and fragrant piñon, up and down arroyos. Four times he had to dismount to open cattle gates.

Rancho Merced was something more than he expected. The building was not large but its lowness made it look far-flung. One almost looked down upon it: you got down into it like a sports car and with the same expectation of the chthonic dividends of living close to the ground. The windows, set in foot-thick 'dobe walls, were open. He knocked. No one answered. There were tire tracks but no car. He walked around the house. Above the piñon arose an ugly galvanized cistern and a Sears windmill. Though its tail was not folded, it did not turn. It was three o'clock.

He sat down under the cistern and sniffed a handful of soil. The silence was disjunct. It ran concurrently with one and did not flow from the past. Each passing second was packaged in cottony silence. It had no antecedents. Here was three o'clock but it was not like three o'clock in Mississippi. In Mississippi it is always Wednesday afternoon, or perhaps Thursday. The country there is peopled, a handful of soil strikes a pang to the heart, *déjà vus* fly up like a shower of sparks. Even in the Southern wilderness there is ever the sense of someone close by, watching from the woods. Here one was not watched. There was no one. The silence hushed everything up, the small trees were separated by a geometry of silence. The sky was empty map space. Yonder at Albuquerque forty miles away a mountain reared up like your hand in front of your face.

This is the locus of pure possibility, he thought, his neck prickling. What a man can be the next minute bears no relation to what he is or what he was the minute before.

The front door was unlocked. He stooped down into the house. For thirty seconds he stood blinking in the cool cellar-like darkness. The windows opened into the bright hush of the desert. He listened: the silence changed. It became a presiding and penultimate silence like the heavy orchestral tacet before a final chord. His heart began to pound. Presently it came to him: what is missing are the small hums and clicks of household motors. He went into the kitchen. The refrigerator was empty and the hot-water tank was cold but there were four cans of Chef Boy-ar-dee spaghetti on the shelf. In the bedroom the bedclothes were tied up and ready for the laundry, a pile on each bed. There was no sign of clothes or suitcases. A year-old *Life* magazine had been left on the bureau. He spotted Sutter's script running around all four edges of the Winston ad on the back cover. He held it eagerly to the light —could it be a message to him? a clue to Sutter's whereabouts?—peering intently and turning it slowly as he read. Sutter's hand was worse than usual.

Kennedy. With all the hogwash, no one has said what he was. The reason he was a great man was that his derisiveness kept pace with his brilliance and his beauty and his love of country. He is the only public man I have ever believed. This is because no man now is believable unless he is derisive. In him I saw the old eagle beauty of the United States of America. I loved him. They, the——— (unreadable: bourgeois? burghers? bastards?), wanted him dead. Very well, it will serve them right because now—

The script ran off into the brown stipple of a girl's thigh and he could make out no more.

He frowned, feeling suddenly put off and out of sorts. This was not what he was looking for and did him no good at all.

Under one bed he found a book of photographs of what appeared to him to be hindoo statuary in a jungle garden. The statues were of couples locked in erotic embraces. The lovers pressed together and their blind lozenge-eyes gazed past each other. The woman's neck arched gracefully. The man's hand sustained the globe of her breast; his pitted stone shaft pressed against the jungle ruin of her flank.

Outside he sat in the cab of the Trav-L-Aire and waited. The Sangre de Cristo range began to turn red. At five o'clock a breeze sprang up. The windmill creaked and presently little yellow flycatchers began to fly down from the mountain and line up on the rim of the cistern.

Dark fell suddenly and the stars came out. They drew in and in half an hour hung as large and low as yellow lamps at a garden party. Suddenly remembering his telescope, he fetched it from the cabin and clamped it to the door of the cab like a malt tray. Now spying the square of Pegasus, he focused on a smudge in the tail and there it was, the great cold fire of Andromeda, atilt, as big as a Catherine wheel, as slow and silent in its turning, stopped, as tumult seen from far away. He shivered. I'm through with telescopes, he thought, and the vasty galaxies. What do I need with Andromeda? What I need is my Bama bride and my cozy camper, a match struck and the butane lit and a friendly square of light cast upon the neighbor earth, and a hot cup of Luzianne between us against the desert cold, and a warm bed and there lie dreaming in one another's arms while old Andromeda leans through the night.

Returning to Santa Fe, he found a snug court in the Camino Real, in a poplar grove hard by the dry bed of the Santa Fe River, and went shopping for groceries. There was no grits to be had, and he had to buy Cream of Wheat. The next morning after breakfast he telephoned every hotel, motel, clinic, and hospital in town, but no one had heard of Dr. Sutter Vaught.

Two days later he was stamping about and hugging himself in the plaza, shivering and, for lack of anything better to do, reading the inscription on the Union monument.

> To the heroes of the Federal Army who fell at the Battle of Valverde fought with Rebels   February 21, 1862

Strangely, there occurred no stirring within him, no body English toward the reversing of that evil day at Valverde where, but for so-and-so's mistake, they might have gotten through to California. Then if they could have reached the ocean— But he felt only the cold.

At ten o'clock the sun rose over the 'dobe shops and it grew warmer. Indians began to come into the plaza. They spread their jewelry and beaded belts on the hard clay and sat, with their legs stretched out, against the sunny wall. It seemed like a good idea. He found a vacant spot and stretched out his Macy's Dacrons among the velvet pantaloons. The red Indians, their faces flat as dishes, looked at him with no expression at all. He had only just begun to read from Sutter's casebook:

> You cite the remark Oppenheimer made about the great days of Los Alamos when the best minds of the Western world were assembled in secret and talked the night away about every subject under the sun. You say, yes they were speaking *sub specie aeternitatis* as men might speak anywhere and at any time, and that they did not notice that—

when he happened to look up and catch sight of a thin man in shirtsleeves coming out of a 'dobe Rexall. He carried a paper bag upright in the crook of his arm. His shirt ballooned out behind him like a spinnaker. Without a second's hesitation the engineer was up and on his way. But when he caught up, the thin man had already gotten into a dusty Edsel and the car was moving.

"Sir," said the courteous engineer, trotting along and leaning down to see the driver.

"What?" But the Edsel kept moving.

"Wait, sir."

"Are you Philip?" asked the driver.

"Eh?" said the engineer, cupping his good ear, and for a moment was not certain he was not.

"Are you Philip and is this the Gaza Desert?" The Edsel stopped. "Do you have something to tell me?"

"Sir? No sir. I am Williston Barrett," said the engineer somewhat formally.

"I knew that, Williston," said Sutter. "I was making a joke. Get in."

"Thank you."

The hood of the car was still stained with the hackberries and sparrow droppings of Alabama. Edsel or not, it ran with the hollow buckety sound of all old Fords.

"How did you find me?" Sutter asked him. Unlike most thin men, he sat in such a way as to emphasize his thinness, craned his neck and hugged his narrow chest.

"I found a map in your room with the route traced on it. I remembered the name of the ranch. An Indian told me where it was. There was no one at the ranch, so I waited in the plaza. There was also this in your room." He handed the casebook to Sutter. "I thought you might have forgotten it."

Sutter glanced at the casebook without taking it. "I didn't forget it."

"I have pondered it deeply."

"It is of no importance. Everything in it is either wrong or irrelevant. Throw it away."

"It seems to be intended for your sister Val."

"It isn't." After a moment Sutter looked at him. "Why did you come out here?"

The engineer passed a hand across his eyes. "I—think you asked me, didn't you? I also came out to see Jamie. The family want him to come home," he said, remembering it for the first time as he spoke. "Or at least to know where he is."

"They know where he is."

"They do? How?"

"I called them last night. I spoke to Kitty."

"What did she say?" asked the engineer uneasily, and unconsciously hugged himself across the chest as if he too were a thin man.

"For one thing, she said you were coming. I've been expecting you."

The engineer told Sutter about his fugue. "Even now I am

283

not too clear about things," he said, rubbing his eyes. "But I knew that I had business here."

"What kind of business?"

He frowned. "As I told you: that I was to see you, as well as find Jamie." He waited, hoping the other would tell him something, but Sutter was silent. The engineer happened to look down and caught sight of the two bottles in the Rexall bag. It was a bourbon called Two Natural. The cork showed a pair of dice rolling a lucky seven. "How is Jamie? Where is he?"

"Jamie is very sick."

"Did you tell Kitty?"

"No."

"Why not?"

"Jamie doesn't want them to come out."

"How sick is he?"

"He got a sore throat driving out."

"That's not so bad, is it?"

"It wouldn't be if he had any leucocytes."

"I see."

"The strep also lit up an old rheumatic lesion."

"You mean in his heart?" asked the engineer, arming himself against the dread sweetness of bad news.

But Sutter merely grunted and went on driving the Edsel in his old-fashioned sporty style, forefinger curled around the spoke of the steering wheel, left elbow propped on the sill. Presently the Edsel stopped in a shady street of tall Victorian houses which flanked a rambling frame building.

"Is he in the hospital?" asked Sutter.

"Yes," said Sutter, but made no move to get out. Instead he hung fire politely, inclined sooty-eyed and civil over the wheel as if he were waiting on the engineer.

The engineer blinked. "Is Jamie in there?"

Sutter nodded and sat back with a sigh. "I'm very glad you're here," he said tapping the wheel.

"Do you wish me—"

"Go on in and see him. I have to go to work. I'll be back in a couple of hours."

"Where do you work?"

"At a guest ranch," said Sutter absently. "It's something like being a ship's doctor. It's only temporary, until—" He shrugged. "Jamie and I ran out of groceries."

When he got out, Sutter called him back.

"I forgot to tell you about the purpura."

"Purpura?"

"Like bruises. It's a new development, not particularly serious in itself but somewhat disconcerting. I thought it might bother you if you didn't know."

"Thank you." Don't worry, thought the engineer confidently. It won't bother me.

7. BUT THE PURPURA UPSET HIM BADLY. JAMIE'S FACE was covered with splotches of horrid color like oil slicks. It was as if a deep fetor, a swamp decay, had come to the surface. Speaking to him meant straining a bit as if one had to peer this way and that to see him through an evil garden of flowers.

It was an odd, unfitting business anyhow, Jamie being here. Jamie was as sick as he could be, yet he lay in a room off the street, so to speak. Could one be truly sick without proper notice and an accounting? The door was wide open and anyone could walk in. Yet no one did. He was alone. Should not some official cognizance be taken of his illness, some authorized person interposed between visitor and patient? One had only to ask the room number downstairs and walk up. The engineer could not get over the feeling that Jamie was not properly sick.

The patient was asleep. For some minutes the visitor stood about uncertainly, smiling warily, then, becoming alarmed, leaned closer to the sickbed. A sour heat radiated from the hollow of the pillow. In the triangle of Jamie's neck, a large vein pulsed in a complex rhythm. Jamie was not noticeably thinner. In fact, a deposit of new tissue, or perhaps dropsical fluid, had occurred under his skin. His face, always puddingish and ill-defined, had gone even more out of focus.

But no sooner had the engineer sat down than the patient opened his eyes and spoke to him quite naturally.

"What are you doing in these parts?" Though he was fairly goggling with fever, Jamie kept his soldierly way of lying

285

abed. He lounged like a wounded man, pushed down his thigh, made a grimace.

"Looking for you and Sutter."

"Well, you found me. What do you want?"

"Nothing," said the engineer as wryly as the other. He rose. "I'll be seeing you."

Jamie laughed and made him sit down. "What's the matter with your leg?" the engineer asked.

"Got the rheumatiz."

Jamie began to speak fondly of Sutter, catching his breath now and then in his new warrior style. "You ought to see the rascal," said Jamie, shaking his head.

The engineer listened smilingly as Jamie told of Sutter's guest ranch whose cottages had such names as O.K. Corral and Boot Hill. Sutter lived at Doc's. "Though it's called a guest ranch, it's really a way station for grass widows. Ol' Sutter is busy as a one-armed paperhanger."

"I imagine," said the engineer fondly and gloomily. Jamie, he saw, had just got onto the trick of tolerating adults in their foibles. "Where is this place?"

"On the road to Albuquerque. It's the biggest guest ranch in the world. Have you seen him?"

"Yes." The engineer told of coming upon Sutter just after he bought two fifths of Two Natural. "Does he still drink bad whiskey?"

"Oh Christ," whispered Jamie joyfully and began to thrash his legs as of old.

After a while the youth began to sweat and, quite as abruptly as he had waked up, collapsed and fell back in the hot hollow of his pillow. Dear God, I stayed too long, thought the engineer, but as he arose to leave, one hand detained him with a weak deprecatory wave.

"What," said the engineer, smiling.

But there was no reply, save the hand moving over the covers, as tentative as a Ouija. For a long ten seconds he stood so, stooped slightly and hearkening. The hand stopped. No doubt he is asleep, thought the engineer, sighing with relief. Then he noticed that the soft mound of a vein in Jamie's neck was going at it hammer and tongs.

Frankly alarmed now, he began turning on switches and pressing buttons, all the while keeping a wary eye on the sick youth. How easy was it to die? When no one came—damn, what is this place?—he rushed out into the corridor and went careening off the walls toward the nurses' station. There sat a hefty blonde with a bald forehead which curved up under a brassy cone of hair. She looked like Queen Bess. She was making notes in a chart.

"Excuse me, nurse," said the courteous engineer, when she did not look up.

She did not seem to hear, though he was not five feet away.

"Excuse me," he said loudly, but nodding and smiling to deprecate his boldness when she did look.

She did not look! She went on making notes in violet ink.

He caught sight of himself in a convex mirror, placed at a corner to show the hall, standing like a pupil at teacher's desk. He frowned and opened the gate of the station and walked in. She turned a baleful lizard eye upon him. Then her eye traveled down and came to rest upon—his hand! He was touching the metal cover of a chart. Despite himself he blushed and removed his hand: teacher had caught him doing a bad thing with his hand. She went back to her work.

"Nurse," he said in a strangled voice. "Kindly come at once to room three-two-two. The patient is having an attack."

Still she did not answer! He had clenched his fist—at least he could hit her, lay her out cold—when at last she screwed cap to pen and with every appearance of ignoring him still and going about her business got up and brushed past him. He followed, sweating with rage—if she doesn't go to Jamie I am going to strike her. And even when she did turn into Jamie's room, she managed to convey that her going had nothing to do with his summons. She was still on business of her own.

No matter! She was with him now, taking his pulse. As the visitor watched through the doorway, Jamie's head turned wearily in the hot socket of his pillow. Whew! The bolus of hatred subsided in his throat. He forgave her. And now, instead of fearing that Jamie might die, he made light of it. It was, after all, only a sore throat.

And in fact when he returned in the afternoon, Jamie felt better. The visitor brought a deck of cards and they played gin in the cheerful yellow sunlight. Death seemed out of the question. How can anyone play a six of clubs one minute and die the next? Sick as he was, Jamie asked to be cranked up straight and now sat like a very old man, weaving a bit as the artery socked away at his head.

For the next few days they played cards morning and afternoon. Sutter came at night. It was understood that the universe was contracted to enclose the two young men. If it can be kept so, Jamie as good as said and the visitor agreed, a small sunny corner where we can play a game and undertake small tasks, nothing very serious can go amiss. For the first time the engineer understood how men can spend a week playing poker, women a lifetime at bridge. The game was the thing. One became impatient with non-game happenings—a nurse coming in to empty the urinal. Time disposed itself in short tolerable stretches between the bright beads of the games. The score itself, totted up and announced, had the cheerful workaday effect of a small tidy business.

It came to be understood too that one was at the other's service and that any service could be required. As it sometimes happens between two young men, a kind of daredevil bargain was struck in which the very outrageousness of a request is itself grounds for obeying.

"Go out and buy me a quart of Monarch applesauce," said Jamie at the end of a game.

"All right."

Sutter came later in the evening. He was both affable and nervous and told them half jokingly of his two new patients, "noble intelligent women who still read Lawrence and still believed in the dark gods of the blood, why make a god of it, that was the Methodist in him, anyhow can you imagine anyone still reading Lawrence out here *now*," etc. How uneasy and talkative Sutter had become! It suddenly dawned on the engineer that Sutter, strange as it seemed, could not stand the sickroom. A hospital, of all places, made him nervous. Jamie, he noticed too, became irritable because Sutter's coming broke the golden circle of the card games. They both wished Sutter would leave. And when Jamie frowned and picked up the deck of cards, Sutter took the hint and did leave. He made a sign to the engineer, who followed him to the solarium.

"Again I can't tell you how glad I am you're here," he said, placing his feet carefully inside the black and white tiles. The hospital was old and well preserved. It looked like an army hospital from the days of Walter Reed. "He doesn't want to see me and there is no one else. Or was."

The engineer looked at him curiously. "I thought that was what you and he wanted."

288

"I didn't want him to be—sunk. I thought he might do better, though I was afraid of this all along—" Sutter trailed off.

"Isn't he sunk?"

"Your showing up has meant a great deal," said Sutter hurriedly and looked at his watch.

"What's the matter with him? Why does he have those spells?"

"Heart block," said Sutter absently. "With some right-sided failure and pulmonary edema. And you see, he can't read for long. His retina is infiltrated. You can read to him."

"What do you mean, heart block? Is that serious?"

Sutter shrugged. "Do you mean will he die today or next week?" He eyed the other. "Can you take a pulse?"

"I suppose so."

"I can't get a private nurse. If you are here when he has a syncope, take his pulse. It will almost certainly start up in a few seconds. Now I've got—"

"Wait. Good God. What are you talking about?"

"If then his pulse is steady, O.K. If it is fibrillating, call the resident."

"Good God, what do you mean, fibrillating?"

"Try to nod your head in time with his pulse. If you can't, he's fibrillating."

"Wait."

"What?"

"Nothing."

Sutter eyed him and, shoving his hands in his pockets, began to step off the tiles in an absent-minded hopscotch. With his Curlee pants down around his hips and his long-waisted shirt, Sutter looked like Lucky Lindy in the 1930's, standing in a propeller wash.

"I tell you what you do," said Sutter.

"What," said the engineer gloomily.

"Call Val. Tell her how sick Jamie is. He likes Val and wants to see her but doesn't want to send for her himself."

"Why don't you—" began the engineer.

"No, I tell you what you do," said Sutter, drawing him close in an odd little bantering confidence. "Call Rita."

"Rita," repeated the puzzled engineer.

"Yes, call Rita and Val and tell them to keep it to themselves and come on out." He held the younger man by the arm in an awkward little burlesque of Lamar Thigpen's old-buddy style.

"Why don't you call them: after all, you're the brother of one and the—"

"Because I'm like Jamie. I don't want to be the one to call either."

"I'm sorry. Jamie asked me not to call them. He trusts me."

"Then you've got nothing to worry about," said Sutter, his eyes going vacant.

"But—"

But Sutter was already on his way.

8. WITH SUTTER GONE, IT WAS POSSIBLE TO RESTORE THE golden circle of games. Jamie was dizzy and short of breath but not uncomfortable. His illness was the sort which allows one to draw in closer to oneself. Already Jamie had discovered the small privileges and warmths of invalidism. It was not a bad thing to lie back and blink at the cards lined up on the bed table, heave up on one elbow to make a play, flop down again in simple weariness. He wrapped himself snugly in his fever like a scarf. The next afternoon the engineer sat beside the bed in the sunny corner, which smelled of old wax and honorable ether. Outside in the still air, yellow as butter, the flat mathematical leaves of the aspens danced a Brownian dance in the sunlight, blown by a still, molecular wind. Jamie would play a card and talk, gaze at a point just beside the engineer's head where, it seemed, some privileged and arcane perception might be hit upon between them. Presently he fell back in the socket of his pillow and closed his eyes.

"Do me a favor."

"All right."

"Go get me a copy of *Treasure Island* and a box of soda crackers."

"All right," said the engineer, rising.

The youth explained that he had been thinking about the scene where Jim steals the dinghy and drifts offshore, lying down so he won't be seen, all the while eating soda crackers and looking at the sky.

"Also go by the post office and see if there's any mail in general delivery."

"Right."

But when he returned with the crackers and a swollen fusty

library copy of *Treasure Island* showing hairy Ben Gunn on the frontispiece, Jamie had forgotten about it.

"There was no mail?"

"No."

"I tell you what let's do."

"What?"

"Call old Val."

"All right."

"Tell her I've got a crow to pick with her."

"All right. Do you want to see any of your family?"

"No. And I don't want to see her either. Just give her a message."

"All right."

"Ask her what happened to the book about entropy."

"Entropy? Then you correspond?"

"Oh, sure. Give her a hard time about the book. She promised to send it to me. Tell her I think she lost heart in the argument. She claims there is a historical movement in the direction of negative entropy. But so what? You know."

"Yes."

The youth's eyes sought his and again drifted away to the point in the air where the two of them found delicate unspoken agreement and made common cause against Val's arguments.

"There's a phone booth downstairs, but let's finish the game."

They didn't finish the game. Jamie went out of his head with fever, though it was a minute before the engineer realized it.

"Get me a line," exclaimed the youth in an odd chipper voice.

"What? All right," said the other, rising again. He thought Jamie meant make a phone call: get a long-distance line.

"A line, a lion," Jamie called to him at the door.

"A lion?"

"Ly-in."

Then he perceived that the youth was out of his head and was hearing words according to some fashion of his own.

"I will."

He waited until Jamie closed his eyes and, returning to the bed, pressed the buzzer. This time someone came quickly, a pleasant little brunette student nurse who took Jamie's temperature and went off, but not too anxiously he was pleased to observe, to get the resident. Jamie was not dying then.

Perhaps he'd better call somebody though. Beyond a doubt Jamie was sick as a dog and also beyond a doubt Sutter had, in his own fashion, decamped. It was the inconsequence and unprovidedness of Jamie's illness which distressed him most. For the first time he saw how it might be possible for large numbers of people to die, as they die in China or Bombay, without anybody paying much attention.

As he passed the nurses' station, slapping his pockets for change, he met the eyes of the disagreeable blonde. Her malevolent expression startled him. Her bulging eye was glossy with dislike. She hated his guts! Amazing.

Thoughtfully he stacked money on the metal shelf of the phone booth. As the wires went clicking away to the East, he gazed through the open door and out into the disjunct afternoon with its simple spectrum-yellow and its flattened distance. Was it possible to call Alabama from here?

No. The line was busy.

He tried for half an hour and gave up.

When he returned to the room the pleasant student was giving Jamie an alcohol rub. Afterward the patient sat up in his right mind and began to read *Treasure Island* and eat soda crackers.

"Don't you want me to read to you?" the engineer asked him.

"No, that's all right!"

Jamie was polite but the engineer could tell he wanted to be alone.

"I'll be back after supper."

"Fine." The patient smiled his best smile because he wanted the visitor to leave. The book was the safest sunniest most inviolate circle of all.

9. THE NEXT MORNING JAMIE WAS EVEN BETTER. HIS fever was gone, but he was tired and wanted to sleep. For the first time he spoke seriously of going home, no, not home but to the Gulf Coast, where they could lie in the sand dunes and get in shape for the next semester. "I have the strongest hunch that the combination of cold salt water and the warm sunny dunes would be great!"

The engineer nodded. Sure enough it might.

Would the engineer take him?

"Let's go," said the latter rising.

Jamie laughed and nodded to signify that he knew the other meant it. "But I'll leave tomorrow, no kidding," he said as the engineer cranked him flat for his nap.

"We can make it in three days," the engineer told him. "Your monk's pad is still on the upper berth."

Jamie said no more about calling Val.

But for the present it was the engineer who lay in the upper berth and read:

Christ should leave us. He is too much with us and I don't like his friends. We have no hope of recovering Christ until Christ leaves us. There is after all something worse than being God-forsaken. It is when God overstays his welcome and takes up with the wrong people.

You say don't worry about that, first stop fornicating. But I am depressed and transcendent. In such a condition, fornication is the sole channel to the real. Do you think I am making excuses?

You are wrong too about the sinfulness of suicide in this age, at least the nurtured possibility of suicide, for the certain availability of death is the very condition of recovering oneself. But death is as outlawed now as sin used to be. Only one's own suicide remains to one. My "suicide" followed the breakdown of the sexual as a mode of reentry from the posture of transcendence.

Here is what happened. I became depressed last summer when I first saw Jamie's blood smear, depressed not because he was going to die but because I knew he would not die well, would be eased out in an oxygen tent, tranquilized and with no sweat to anyone and not even know what he was doing. Don't misunderstand me: I wasn't thinking about baptism.

The depression made me concupiscent. On a house call to the Mesa Motel to examine a patient in diabetic coma (but really only to collect blood for chemistry—I was little more than a technician that summer). Afterwards spied a chunky blonde by the pool, appraised her eye, which was both lewd and merry. She 41, aviatrix, winner of Powder Puff Derby in 1940's, raced an old Lockheed P-38 from San Diego to Cleveland. We drank two glasses of straight whiskey. I spoke in her ear and invited her to her room.

Afterwards very low. Went to ranch, shot myself, missed brain, carried away cheek.

Recovery in hospital. The purity of ordeal. The purity of death. The sweet purity of the little Mexican nurse. Did Americans become lewd when they banished death?

I saw something clearly while I had no cheek and grinned like a skeleton. But I got well and forgot what it was. I won't miss next time.

It was the last entry in Sutter's casebook. When he finished reading, the engineer left the Trav-L-Aire and threw the pad into the trashburner of Alamogordo Motor Park. As he watched it burn, glowering, his head sinking lower and lower, mouth slack and drying, he became aware that someone was speaking to him. It was a fellow Trav-L-Aire owner, a retired fire inspector from Muncie. He and his wife, the man had told him, were in the midst of their yearly swing from Victoria, B.C., to Key West. They kept just ahead of winter on the way down and just behind spring going north. It was a courtesy of the road that camper owners show their rigs to each other. The engineer invited him in. The Hoosier was polite enough—the engineer's was the most standard of all Trav-L-Aires—but it was obvious that the former had a surprise in store. After showing off his cabin, which had a tinted sun-liner roof, he pressed a button. A panel above the rear door flew open and a contraption of aluminum spars and green netting unhinged in six directions. With a final grunt of its hidden motor the thing snapped into a taut cube of a porch big enough for a bridge game. "You take off your screen door and put it here," the Hoosier told him. "It's the only thing for west Florida, where you're going to get your sand flies."

"Very good," said the engineer, nodding and thrusting his hand through his pocket, for his knee had begun to leap.

Returning to his own modest camper, he became at once agitated and lustful. His heart beat powerfully at the root of his neck. The coarsest possible images formed themselves before his eyes. But this time, instead of throwing a fit or lapsing into a fugue as he had done so often in the past, he became acutely conscious of the most insignificant sensations, the slight frying sound of the Servel refrigerator, the watery reflection on the Formica table, which seemed to float up the motes of dust. His memory, instead of failing, became perfect. He recalled everything, even a single perception years ago, one of a thousand billion, so trivial that it was not even remembered then, five minutes later: on a college field trip through the mangy Jersey woods looking for spirogyra, he had crossed a utility right-of-way. When he reached the farther woods, he had paused and looked over his shoulder. There was nothing to see: the terrain dipped, making a little swale which was overgrown by the special forlorn plants of rights-of-way, not small trees or bushes or even weeds exactly but just the unclassified plants which grow up in electric-light-and-power-places. That was all. He turned and went on.

Desolate places like Appomattox and cut-over woods were ever the occasion of storms of sexual passion. Yet now when he rushed out into the abstract afternoon to find a maid (but who?) he forgot again and instead found himself picking through the ashes of the trashburner. What was that last sentence? It had a bearing. But the notebook was destroyed.

Jumping into the cab of the G.M.C., he tore out of the poplar grove, forgetting his umbilical connections until he heard the snappings of cords and the shout of the Hoosier.

"What the—" yelled the latter like an astounded comic-strip character, Uncle Walt (so that's where the expression "What the—" comes from—Indiana).

"I'm going over to Albuquerque," shouted the engineer as if this were an explanation and as quickly changed his mind, stopped, and strode past the still-astounded Hoosier. "Pardon," he said, "I think I'll call Kitty—" and nodded by way of further explanation to a telephone hooked contingently to a telephone pole. Could he call Kitty from such a contingent telephone?

Perhaps if he could talk to a certain someone he would stop hankering for anyone and everyone, and tender feelings of love would take the place of this great butting billygoat surge which was coming over him again. He clung to the pole, buffeted by an abstract, lustful molecular wind, and might even have uttered a sound, brayed into the phone, for the Hoosier looked astounded again and rushed into his deluxe Sun-Liner.

10.

"I REMEMBER EVERYTHING NOW, DR. VAUGHT," HE said calmly, no longer agitated. "You said I was to come and find you. Very well, here I am. What was it you wished to tell me?"

So distracted had been the engineer in his headlong race across the desert that he had noticed not a single thing on the way and could not have said how he found his way here. Only now as Sutter sighed and sank into himself could he spare time to take a breath and see where he was.

Sutter was sitting in a sheriff's chair on the front porch of Doc's cottage. Doc's was one of a hundred or more such cottages fronting on a vast quadrangle of rich blue-green winter grass bordered by palm trees, a rectangular oasis in a scrabbly desert of mesquite. The evening rides were over and it was almost suppertime. Doors slammed as the dudes, mostly women, began the slow promenade to the chuck wagon. The sun was already down behind Sandia Mountain but the sky was bright and pure and empty as map space. The dudes smiled and nodded at Doc as they passed but the latter sat slumped and unresponsive, his dried-up Thom McAn shoes propped on the rail and Curlee pants hitched halfway up his skinny legs.

Sutter didn't seem to hear him. He slumped further and gazed at the bare mountain. The material of his trousers bunched up between his legs like curtain drapes.

"Then you have nothing to tell me," the engineer asked him again.

"That is correct. Nothing."

"But, sir, you wrote many things in—"

"In the first place I didn't write them to you. In the second place I no longer believe a word of it. Did you ever read the great philosopher Wittgenstein?"

"No sir," said the other gloomily.

"After his last work he announced the dictum which summarized his philosophy. He said: Whereof one cannot speak, thereof one should keep silent. And he did. He stopped teaching and went to live in a hut and said no more."

"And you believe that?"

296

"No, I don't even believe that."

They watched the women for a while. Presently the engineer said, "But you told me to come out and find you."

"I did?"

"Therefore you at least owe me the explanation of what happened to make you change your mind."

"What has happened?" Sutter looked puzzled.

"What has happened to you?"

"Nothing has happened."

From the chair beside him, where he must have held it all along and out of the other's sight, Sutter raised the Colt Woodsman and sighted it at an airliner which sparkled like a diamond in the last of the sunlight.

"But Val told me that you—"

"Val." Sutter smiled as he tracked the airliner.

"Oh, I know you don't agree with Val."

"Oh, but I do agree with her."

"You do?"

"Oh yes, in every respect. About what has happened to the world, about what God should be and what man is, and even what the Church should be."

The engineer sighed. "Yes sir. That is very interesting, but I think you know why I am here."

"You see, Barrett, Val had a dream of what the Church should come to. (And I agree! Absolutely!) For example, she did not mind at all if Christendom should be done for, stove in, kaput, screwed up once and all. She did not mind that the Christers were like everybody else, if not worse. She did not even mind that God shall be gone, absent, not present, A.W.O.L., and that no one noticed or cared, not even the believers. Because she wanted us to go the route and be like Sweden, which is not necessarily bad, but to go the route, to leave God out of it and be happy or miserable, as the case might be. She believes that then, if we go the route and run out of Christendom, that the air would be cleared and even that God might give us a sign. That's how her own place makes sense, you see, her little foundation in the pines. She conceived herself as being there with her Delco and her butane tanks to start all over again. Did you notice how much it looked like one of those surviving enclaves after the Final War, and she's probably right: I mean, who in the hell would want to bomb South Alabama? But yes, I agree with her. Absolutely! It's just that nothing ever came of it."

"Dr. Vaught. Excuse me, but—"

"Don't you see? Nothing happened. She got all dressed up for the bridegroom and the bridegroom didn't come. There she sits in the woods as if the world had ended and she was one of the Elected Ones Left to keep the Thing going, but the world has not ended, in fact is more the same than usual. We are in the same fix, she and I, only I know it and she doesn't. Here I sit in Sweden—most of those women are Swedes, spiritual Swedes, if you will notice—but I do not wait for a sign because there is no sign. I will even agree with her that when I first came to the desert I was waiting for a sign, but there was no sign and I am not waiting for one now."

"Yes sir. That is very interesting. But the reason I came, if you will recall, is that you told me—"

"But she changed, you see, and that was when we parted company. I could make some sense of her notion of being the surviving remnant of her Catholic Thing (which has to prevail, you see, in spite of all, yes, I don't mind that) set down back there in that God-forsaken place. That was fitting. But she changed, you see. *She became hopeful.* She goes to confraternity meetings in Mobile. She has dealings with the Methodist preacher, even the Baptists. She corresponds with scientists. She begs from the Seven-Up man and slips him a K.C. pamphlet. ('How many churches did Christ found?') She talks the Klonsul into giving her a gym. In short, she sold out. Hell, what she is is a Rotarian."

"Yes sir, very true, but what I want to—"

"Barrett."

"Sir?"

"Which is the best course for a man: to live like a Swede, vote for the candidate of your choice, be a good fellow, healthy and generous, do a bit of science as if the world made sense, enjoy a beer and a good piece (not a bad life!). Or: to live as a Christian among Christians in Alabama? Or to die like an honest man?"

"I couldn't say," said the engineer. He was bitterly disappointed by Sutter's refusal to take him seriously.

"How is Jamie?" asked Sutter.

"Better," said the other absently. "I am on my way there now. If you will answer my question, I'll leave."

"What question?"

"The last time I saw you you said you had something to tell me. What was it?"

"I don't remember."

The engineer, who had been pacing the tiny porch, which abutted Wells Fargo on one side and the O.K. Corral on the other, paused and fixed Sutter with a lively clairvoyant expression. Now at last he remembered everything, knew what he knew and what he didn't know and what he wished to know. He even remembered every sentence in Sutter's notebook.

"I want to know what it was you discovered while you were in the, ah, hospital out here last summer."

"What?" said Sutter, coming down hard on all four legs of the captain's chair.

The engineer was not disconcerted. "I've finished your casebook. I wish to know whether you meant only that when you're in a bad way things look better than they do ordinarily."

"Oh," said Sutter, replacing his feet. "That. I don't remember. That was a long time ago and, as I told you, I attach no importance to that stuff. It was written to be rid of it, excreta, crap, and so intended."

"I just finished speaking to Kitty." The engineer drew up another sheriff's chair. "We spoke for two hours. It cost twenty-four dollars. I had to reverse the charges."

"Good Lord. I can't imagine talking to Kitty for five minutes."

"We settled a great many things," said the engineer, frowning—who in hell was Sutter to patronize Kitty?

"Are you getting married?" asked Sutter politely, turning his chair a few degrees but keeping his pale eyes fixed on the brown schematic mountain.

"Yes. After—things are more settled. But that is not why I drove out here this afternoon. I want to know this," he said, leaning over and grabbing the rim of Sutter's chair so hard that his knuckles turned white. "I want to know why you brought Jamie out here."

Sutter tried to tear his eyes from the mountain. "You're right. It didn't work, did it?"

"Right? What do you mean? What didn't work?"

Sutter shrugged. "Jamie's little idea of a vacation."

"Jamie's? But according to what you wrote, it was your idea too. What did you expect him to do?"

"It's not what I expected."

"Then he expected something?"

"Yes."

"What?"

"He expected something to happen."

"What? Not get well?"

Sutter shrugged.

"But you brought him out. You must have hoped for something."

"Only that he might get a little better."

"Get better?" He watched the other like a hawk. "No, you mean die better, don't you?"

Sutter shrugged and said nothing.

"You didn't answer," said the engineer after a moment.

Again Sutter's feet hit the floor. "Goddamn it, Barrett, what do you mean by requiring answers from me? Why should I answer you? What are you to me? Christ, if you recall I never solicited your company in the first place."

"I am asking nevertheless," said the engineer cheerfully.

"Why me, for Christ's sake?"

"I don't know."

"What do you take me for, some pissant wise man, ole rebel Sutter whom the yokels back home can't stand and who therefore by your peculiar logic must be onto something just because they're not? You know something, Barrett? There's one thing I've never been able to get the straight of, and that is what it is you want of me. I suspect it is one of two things. You either want me to tell you to fornicate or not to fornicate, but for the life of me I can't tell which it is."

"Then tell me," said the engineer smiling.

"I will not tell you."

"Tell me to be chaste and I will do it. Yes! I will do it easily!" he said, striking the rail softly with his fists. "All you have to do is tell me."

"I will not tell you."

"Then tell me not to be chaste."

"I will not."

"Why not?"

"Barrett, since when is failure, my failure, a badge of wisdom?"

"I did not think of it that way," said the engineer, frowning. Suddenly he did see Sutter for the first time as the dismalest failure, a man who had thrown himself away. He marveled at his, the engineer's, being here.

"I know you don't," said Sutter, not unkindly. "But maybe

you better start. For both our sakes. Be done with me. Go stay with Jamie."

"That's what I'm trying to do," said the other absently.

"What?"

"Be done with you."

"I fervently wish you success."

"Yes," said the engineer, cheering up. "Yes! You're right. There is no reason why I can't just get up and go about my business, is there?"

"No reason."

"To answer your earlier question: yes, Kitty and I are getting married."

"You mentioned it."

"We spoke of many things."

"Good."

"And settled a fair proportion of them."

"Good."

"It turns out we see eye to eye on most things."

"Excellent."

"It seems that Mr. Vaught has made Lamar a vice-president and that he is going to offer me the position of personnel manager. I actually feel I might do well at it."

"I have no doubt of it."

"For the first time I feel fairly certain of what I want to do."

"I'm glad to hear it."

"We even have a house in mind. Cap'n Andy Mickle's place on South Ridge. Do you know it?"

"Very well indeed."

"You've been there?"

"A dozen times."

"Why? Oh. You mean to treat Cap'n Andy?"

"A colossal bore. He bored himself to death. But that's no reflection on the house. An ideal spot. The best view on the ridge."

The engineer frowned, thinking of the buzzards circling the doleful plain and Cap'n Andy striding the "bridge." But he quickly brightened. "We've even agreed on the same denomination."

"The same *what*?"

"Denomination. Church. Kitty has become quite religious. She is convinced of the wisdom of our having the same church home, to use her expression." The engineer laughed tolerantly, shaking his head at the ways of women, and wiped a merry tolerant little tear from his eye.

"Jesus," muttered Sutter.

"Eh?" The other cocked his good ear.

"Nothing."

"You don't fool me, Dr. Vaught. Don't forget that I've read your casebook. Though I do not pretend to understand everything, that part didn't escape me."

"What part?"

"Your awareness of the prime importance of the religious dimension of life."

"The religious dimension of life?" Sutter looked at him suspiciously. "Barrett, are you putting me on?"

"No sir."

"Then if you're not, you're doing something worse."

"Sir?" asked the engineer politely.

"Never mind."

"Dr. Vaught," said the engineer earnestly. "There is one more thing. Then I will leave."

"What is that?"

"Dr. Vaught, Kitty and I are getting married. I am going to take a good position with your father, settle down on the South Ridge, and, I hope, raise a family."

"Yes," said Sutter after a pause.

"I think I'm going to be a pretty fair member of the community. God knows the place could use even a small contribution of good will and understanding."

"Beyond a doubt. Good will and understanding. Yes. Very good."

"Well?"

"Well what?"

"What's wrong with that?"

"Nothing. I think you'll be very happy. In fact I'll go further than that. I don't think you'll have any more trouble with your fugues. And I take it back: I don't think you are kidding me."

"I see. Dr. Vaught."

"What?"

"I know you think there is something wrong with it."

"You do?"

"Yes. I know you think there is everything wrong with it."

"Nonsense." Sutter laughed. "Would you rather join me here?"

"No, but—"

"But what?"

"But nothing." The engineer rose. "There is nothing wrong with it. Truthfully I see now there is nothing wrong with such a life."

"Right!"

"It is better to do something than do nothing—no reflection, sir."

"No reflection."

"It is good to have a family."

"You are quite right."

"Better to love than be loved."

"Absolutely."

"To cultivate whatever talents one has."

"Correct."

"To make a contribution, however small."

"However small."

"To do one's best to promote tolerance and understanding between the races, surely the most pressing need before the country."

"Beyond question the most pressing need. Tolerance and understanding. Yes."

The engineer flushed. "Well, isn't it better?"

"Yes."

"Violence is bad."

"Violence is not good."

"It is better to make love to one's wife than to monkey around with a lot of women."

"A lot better."

"I am sure I am right."

"You are right."

The engineer gazed gloomily at the chuck wagon, a large red dining cottage across the quadrangle. Cookie, a Chinese with a black cap and a queue, came out and seizing the branding iron rang it around the iron triangle.

"You know, Dr. Vaught, I have lived a rather abnormal and solitary life and have tended to get things backwards. My father was a proud and solitary man. I had no other family. For a long time I have had a consuming desire for girls, for the coarsest possible relations with them, without knowing how to treat them as human beings. No doubt, as you suggested, a good part of my nervous condition stems from this abnormal relationship—or lack of relationship—"

"As I suggested? I never suggested any such goddamn thing."

"At any rate," the engineer went on hurriedly, looking down at the other, "I think I see for the first time the possibility of a happy, useful life."

"Good. So?"

"Dr. Vaught, why was that man screaming?"

"What man?"

"The man you told me about—the Deke from Vanderbilt —with the lovely wife and children—you know."

"Oh, Scotty. Christ, Barrett, for somebody with fugues, you've got quite a memory."

"Yes sir."

"Don't worry about Scotty. You won't scream. I can assure you, you will not scream."

"Then it is better not to?"

"Are you asking me?"

"Yes."

Sutter shrugged.

"You have nothing more to tell me?"

"No, Barrett, nothing." To his surprise, Sutter answered him quietly, without making a face or cursing.

The engineer laughed with relief. "For the first time I think I really might live like other men—rejoin the human race."

"I hope you'll all be happy. You and the race, I mean."

"Oh, I forgot something. It was something Kitty said to tell you. God, I'm selfish."

"But in the future you're going to be unselfish."

"What? Oh. Yes," said the engineer, smiling. He declined to conspire with Sutter's irony. "Kitty said to tell you Lamar was going to take a special course in management at the Harvard Business School."

"Good Lord, what do I care what Lamar does?"

The engineer kept a wary eye on him. "And that while he is in Boston, Myra is going to stay with Rita in New York."

"Myra Thigpen? I see. Do you want to know something? It figures."

"Rita is already gone. Myra is leaving after—afterwards."

"So Rita is gone." Sutter gazed into the empty sky, which instead of turning rosy with sunset was simply going out like a light.

As the other watched him, Sutter began idly picking off dudes, sighting the Colt at one after another of the passing women, idly yet with a regardlessness which was alarming. It was a very small thing, no more than that Sutter did not take pains to conceal the pistol from the women, but for some reason the engineer's heart began to pound against his ribs.

"On the other hand," Sutter was saying between shots, "it is also possible to die without significance and that is hardly an improvement of one's state of life. I knew a man once, not my own patient I am glad to say, who was sitting with his family one Sunday evening watching Lassie, who had befriended a crippled duck and was protecting him from varmints. During the commercial he got up and got out his old army forty-five. When his family asked him what he intended to do, he told them he was going outside to shoot a varmint. So he went outside to the garage and got into the family's second car, a Dodge Dart, and blew the top of his head off. Now that's a lot of damn foolishness, isn't it?"

"Yes sir," said the engineer, who was now more irritated than frightened by Sutter's antics with the pistol. Nor did he any longer believe Sutter's dire little case histories. "The other thing I want to tell you is that—" he said as Cookie rang second call with the branding iron. "Kitty said to tell you that the, ah, legal difficulties in your case have been cleared up and that—"

"You mean the coast is clear."

"Yes sir."

"Poppy has fixed things up and Doc Holliday can come back home to Valdosta."

"Sir, you have an enormous contribution to make—" began the engineer.

Sutter rose so suddenly that the younger man was afraid he'd made him angry again. But Sutter's attention was elsewhere.

Following his eye, the engineer alighted upon one of the guests who had left the O.K. Corral next door and was presently coming abreast of Doc's cottage. To judge from her Levis, which were stiff and blue, she was a new arrival. The old civil sorrowful air of the East still clung to her; she walked as if she still wore a dress. Though she had hooked her thumbs into her pockets, she had not yet got into the way of making herself free of herself and of swinging her legs like a man. She even wore a cowgirl hat, not at all the thing here, which had fallen down her back and was supported by a string at her throat. But she was abstracted and did not care, and instead of ambling along with the others, she went musing alone, tongue set against her teeth and hissing a solitary little tune. There was about her the wryness and ruefulness of a twenty-eight-year-old who has been staggered by a not quite mortal blow and has her own woman's way of getting over it and in fact has already done so. She knew how to muse along a path and hiss a little tune and keep herself to herself.

Sutter rose creakily but cheerfully and rubbed his dry reedy hands together. "I do believe it is time to eat. Will you join me?"

"No sir. I promised Jamie I'd be back by seven."

To his relief, Sutter left the Colt in his chair and had, apparently, forgotten about it.

"I'll be in by nine."

"Yes sir."

"Barrett, I think you'd better call the family."

"But I just—"

"Tell them they'd better get out here."

"Yes sir."

"Tell them I said so."

"All right."

"Somebody will have to be here to take care of things after Jamie's death."

"I'll be here."

"Some member of the family."

"You'll be here."

"No, Barrett, I'll not be here."

"Why not?" asked the other angrily—he had had enough of Sutter's defections.

"Barrett," said Sutter as cheerfully as ever, craning his neck to keep track of the new guest, "if you know anything at all—and, what with your peculiar gifts, you know a good deal more than that—you ought to know why not."

"I don't," said the engineer, at a total loss. He had lost his intuition!

"If I do outlive Jamie," said Sutter, putting on his Curlee jacket (double breasted!), "it will not be by more than two hours. What in Christ's name do you think I'm doing out here? Do you think I'm staying? Do you think I'm going back?"

The engineer opened his mouth but said nothing. For the first time in his life he was astonished.

"You won't join me, Barrett?"

306

"What? No. No, thanks."

Sutter nodded cheerfully, dropped the pistol in the side pocket of the jacket, and hurried down the path after the last of the dudes.

Perhaps this moment more than any other, the moment of his first astonishment, marked the beginning for the engineer of what is called a normal life. From that time forward it was possible to meet him and after a few minutes form a clear notion of what sort of fellow he was and how he would spend the rest of his life.

11. THE PLEASANT LITTLE BRUNETTE WAS COMING OUT of Jamie's room when he turned the corner. He smiled at her and experienced a pang of pleasure when she veered and he saw she meant to stop him. But she was not smiling, and instead of speaking she held out a thermometer. He couldn't see for looking, save only that the red line came dizzyingly near the top.

"Is he conscious?" he asked her.

"If you want to call it that. He's delirious."

"Do you think you should—"

"I've already notified Dr. Bice."

"How is his pulse?"

"One-thirty, but regular."

"He's not, ah, fibrillating?"

"No."

"Would you come back later, that is, from time to time when you can—as often as you can, in fact, to take his pulse."

Now she did smile. "Why, yes."

One look at Jamie and he went for the phone. The youth's face was turned to the window. His dusty dead friable hair lay on the pillow as if it had been discarded, a hank.

As he got change from the cashier—he wouldn't dare reverse the charges to Val—he began to grieve. It was the shame of it, the bare-faced embarrassment of getting worse and dying which took him by surprise and caught his breath in his throat. How is this matter to be set right? Were there no officials to deal with the shame of dying, to make suitable recompense? It was like getting badly beat in a fight. To *lose*. Oh, to lose so badly. Oh, you bastards living and well and me dying, and where is the right of that? Oh, for the bitter shame of it.

At last the circuits clicked open into the frying frazzling silence of Alabama. He fancied he could hear the creak of the cancerous pines.

"Hello," he cried after a wait. "Hello!"

"Hello," came a voice as faint and faraway as 1901.

"Who is this?"

"This here Axel." It sounded like a child standing a good two feet below a wall phone.

"Axel, let me speak to Sister Johnette Mary Vianney."

"Who?"

He repeated it.

"Who dat?"

"Sister—"

"Sister Viney?"

"Yes, Sister Viney."

"Yes suh, she here."

"Well, go get her, Axel."

"Yes suh."

The ancient Alabama silence fried away in his ear. His foot went to sleep. Twice he had to stoke the box with quarters. That black cretin Axel—

"Hello."

He gave a start. He had almost forgotten where he was. "Hello, is this Val? That is, Sister—"

"This is Val."

"Val, this is—" Christ, who? "—Will Barrett."

"Yes?" The same calculated buzzing non-surprise—he felt a familiar spasm of irritation.

"I, ah—Jamie asked me to call you."

"Yes?"

"It's about a book. A book about entropy. Actually, that is not the real reason I'm—"

"Entropy," she repeated.

"Jamie said you promised to send him a book."

"How is Jamie?"

"He asked me—"

"Never mind about the book. How is he?"

"He is very sick."

"Is he dying?"

"I think so."

"I'm leaving now. I'll get a plane in New Orleans."

"Good."

He slumped with the relief of it. She'd do, nutty as she was. It came over him suddenly: there is another use for women after all, especially Southern women. They knew how to minister to the dying! It was they all along who had set at nought the shame of it and had done it so well that he had not even known that it took doing. He'd rather have a proper Southern woman (even one of his aunts!) but he'd settle for this one. "Very good. And would you call the rest of the family. My change is gone and I have to get back to Jamie." All women come. The more women, the less shame.

"If anything happens before I get there, you'll have to attend to it."

"Yes, ma'am. Attend to what?"

"His baptism."

"Ma'am? Eh?"

"I said you'll have to see to his baptism if I don't get there in time."

"Excuse me," said the courteous but terrified engineer. "Much as I'd like to oblige you, I don't believe I can take the responsibility."

"Why not?"

"For one thing, I'm not a member of the family."

"You're his friend, aren't you?"

"Yes."

"Would you deny him penicillin if it would save his life?"

"No," he said, stiffening. None of your Catholic tricks, Sister, the little tricky triumphs of analogy. You learned more in Paterson, New Jersey, than you realize. But he said only: "Why don't you get Sutter?"

"I don't know where he is."

"As a matter of fact, he asked me to call you too."

"Good. Then you hold the fort till I get there."

"I don't believe in baptizing anybody against their will," said the sweating engineer, for lack of anything better to say.

"Then ask him if it's against his will."

"Ask him?"

"Barrett, I charge you to ask him." She sounded serious enough but he couldn't swear she wasn't laughing at him.

"It's really none of my business, Sister."

"It's my responsibility but I am giving it to you until I get there. You can call a priest, can't you?"

"I am not of your faith, Sister." Where did he get these solemn religious expressions?

"Then call a minister for God's sake. Or do it yourself. I charge you. All you have to do is—"

"But—"

"If you don't call someone, then you'll have to do it yourself."

Then God knows I'll call someone, thought the prudent engineer. But he was becoming angry. To the devil with this exotic pair, Sutter and Val, the absentee experts who would deputize him, one to practice medicine, the other to practice priestcraft. Charge him indeed. Who were they to charge anybody?

"Barrett, look. I know that you are a highly intelligent and an intuitive man, and that you have a gift for fathoming people. Isn't that true?"

"I don't know," he said glumly.

"I think you can tell when somebody is deadly serious about something, can't you?"

"I couldn't say."

"Then I am charging you with the responsibility. You will have to fathom that according to your own lights."

"You can't—" But the circuits had closed on unhappy old Alabama, frying away in its own juices.

The poor addled engineer took the steps four at a time, racing to do he knew not what. So that when he reached the sickroom and found Jamie both unconscious and unattended, he was of two minds about it: dismayed that the worst had happened, that Jamie was very likely dying here and now; yet relieved despite himself that Jamie was unconscious and so he didn't have to ask him any such question (for it was of course absolutely the last question to be tolerated by the comradely and stoic silence generated between the two of them). Here he stood, therefore, stooped over the machinery of Jamie's veins, hoist not only by the vast awkwardness of dying but now by religion too. He became angrier than ever. Where was the hospital staff? Where was the family? Where was the chaplain? Then he noticed, almost idly as if he had spied a fly on the pillow, that there was something amiss about the vein. Its machinery rhythm was out of kilter.

310

All along he had known it would come to this and that he couldn't do it. He couldn't take the pulse. The thread of artery stirred fitfully under his finger but there was no profit in it. Which stirrings to count?

Without knowing how he came there, he had fetched up again at the nurses' cage where reigned bald Queen Bess. Once again he made noises and motions and once again she annihilated him, rendered him invisible and of no account.

"Nurse," he said sternly, four feet away. He actually raised a forefinger.

She answered the telephone.

All at once time fell in, bent, and he was transported over the Dutch sort of door—it didn't seem to open—flew over it like a poltergeist and found himself inside the station. He seemed to be listening. "You hear me, goddamn it," thundered a voice terrible and strange. It was for the two of them to listen as the voice went on. "—or else I'm going to kick yo' ass down there." An oddly Southern voice, then not his surely. Yet her glossy eyes were on *him*, round as a dollar watch, the lids nictitating from below like a lizard's. Her smile, stretching open the rugae, the troughs of which he noticed were bare of lipstick, proferred a new ghastly friendship for *him*. Now as he watched, dreaming, she was using the phone again.

"Yes sir. But Mr. Barrett seems a little upset. Yes, good." She knew him! Perhaps she had known him all along. On the other hand, there seemed to have sprung up between them a brand-new friendship, a species of roguish fondness.

Again segments of time collapsed, fell away, and he was transported magically into the corridor, she at his side, squeezing his arm in a love-joke. Doors flew open. Elevators converged on the floor.

The next thing he knew he was speaking in a businesslike and considered manner to the resident and chaplain outside Jamie's closed door. He had survived the hiatus of his rage. There remained only the smell of it, strong as burnt meat; he hugged his arms to close his armpits.

The resident had just come out of Jamie's room. He spoke seriously but in a measured, relaxed way. That's what I wanted, thought the engineer, sighing—someone to give measure and form to time itself. Was that the worst of dying, dying without permission, license, so to speak?

The engineer nodded and turned to the chaplain. He explained the commission.

"Therefore it seemed proper to me," he concluded, "to pass along to you the request of his sister, who is a religious of your faith."

"I see," said the priest, who, however, instead of listening to what the engineer said, was eyeing this strange young man himself. Evidently he could not make out what kind of bird he was dealing with. Three times he asked the engineer where he came from, as if this might shed some light.

"Do you know Father Gillis from Conway, Arkansas?" the priest asked him. If only he could get a fix on him!

"No sir." Damnation, did they have to hit upon a mutual friend?

They were a curious pair, the resident and the priest. The resident was hollow-eyed and green-skinned and sunken of cheek. His hair grew down his neck in ringlets like a hyacinth. There was a rash on his throat under his loose collar. But unhealthy as he was he affected the easy nonchalance of an athlete and swung his fist softly. The priest was a neat chunky man whose thick auburn hair had been freshly cut and combed, exposing a white healthy scalp in the wide part. The gold stems of his bifocals pressed snugly against muscular temples. His hand, which he gave the engineer in a tentative interrogatory clasp (what sort of a bird are you, asked the hand), was thick through the palm and heavily freckled.

"He's fibrillating," said the haggard resident, first addressing the engineer. Then, not quite getting hold of him either, he turned to the priest, all the while making a few soft swings of fist to hand. "A heavy presystolic murmur. Temperature one-o-five point three, lungs filled up to the seventh interspace, spleen down to here."

"What does that mean?" asked the frowning engineer.

The resident shrugged, squared off with his fist for a combination punch but didn't throw it. "Pulmonary edema, for one thing. He's drowning in his own fluids."

"Will he regain consciousness?"

The resident frowned. There was a protocol here, a way of speaking-in-the-hall which the resident and priest were onto and he, the engineer, was not. The question did not pass muster, for the resident turned to the priest.

"Do you know what that joker told me last night?" (This is the way we speak.) "I always horse around with him. I wanted to take his temperature and I asked him what he wanted me to do, meaning which did he prefer, rectal or oral. So he says to

312

me: Bice, you know what you can do with it. Oh, you can't make a nickel on him," he said, trying the engineer again (Now do you see? This is the way death itself can be gotten past).

The priest hung fire, vague and fond, until he saw the resident had finished. "Now, ah," he said, touching the engineer's elbow with just the hint of interrogatory pressure, as if he meant to ask the time. But the touch was skillful. The engineer found himself guided into the solarium.

"Let me see if I understand you," said the priest, putting his head down and taking hold of a water pipe in his thick freckled hand. He watched intently as his perfect thumbnail creased a blister of paint. "This young man you say has never been baptized, and though he is unconscious now and perhaps will not regain consciousness, you have reason to believe he desires baptism?"

"No sir. His sister desires the baptism."

"But he has a Catholic background?"

"If you mean Roman Catholic, no. I'm an Episcopalian," said the engineer stiffly. Where in the world did these ready-made polemics come from? Never in his entire lifetime had he given such matters a single thought and now all at once he was a stout Anglican, a defender of the faith.

"Of course, of course. And the young man in there, is he also from a Protestant, that is, an Episcopal background?"

"No sir. His background was originally Baptist, though his family later became Episcopalian—which accounts for the delay." The engineer, who could not quite remember the explanation, fell silent. "Delay in baptism, that is," he added after a moment.

The priest examined another blister on the water pipe. "I don't quite see why I have been summoned," he said softly. "Perhaps you'd better call the Protestant chaplain."

"Oh, no, sir," said the engineer hastily, breaking out in a sweat lest the priest leave and he, the engineer, should have to go careening around the walls again. "Jamie professed no faith, so it is all the same which of you ministers, ah, ministers to him." For some reason he laughed nervously. He didn't want this fellow to get away—for one thing, he liked it that the other didn't intone in a religious voice. He was more like a baseball umpire in his serviceable serge, which was swelled out by his muscular body. "As I told you, his sister, who is a nun, made me promise to send for you. She is on her way out here. She is a religious of a modern type. Her habit is short, to about here." Then, realizing that he was not helping his case, he added nervously: "I wouldn't be surprised if she didn't found her own order. She is doing wonderful work among the Negroes. Aren't foundresses quite often saints?" He groaned.

"I see," said the priest, and actually stole a glance at the other to see, as the engineer clearly perceived, whether he was quite mad. But the engineer was past minding, as long as the priest got on with it. Evidently this was an unusual case. The priest tried again.

"Now you. Are you a friend of the family?"

"Yes, a close friend and traveling companion of the patient."

"And the other gentleman—he is the patient's brother?"

"Sutter? Is he here?" For the second time in his life the engineer was astonished.

"There is a visitor with the patient who I gather, from his conversation with Dr. Bice, is a doctor."

"That must be Sutter."

"The only thing is, I don't yet quite understand why it is you and not he who is taking the initiative here."

"He was not here when Jamie had his attack. But he told me—he must have just come."

The priest took off his glasses, exposing naked eyes and a naked nosebridge, and carefully polished the lenses with a clean handkerchief. Making a bracket of his hand, he put the glasses back on, settling the stems onto his healthy temples.

"It would help if we had some indication from the patient or at least from the immediate family. Otherwise I don't want to intrude. In fact, I would say it is a 'must.'"

"Yes sir." Unhinged as he was, the engineer was still sentient. He perceived that the priest had a certain style of talking which he no doubt shared with other priests. It was a good bet that quite a few priests liked to say such things as "It is a 'must'" or perhaps "Now that is the sixty-four-dollar question."

"Sir, could we go in and speak to the patient's brother?"

"Well, let's see what we shall see."

The resident had left. Sutter was leaning against the window in Jamie's room, his foot propped on the radiator.

"Dr. Vaught," said the engineer, handing the priest along ahead of him—the goods to be delivered at last. "This is Father—"

314

"Boomer," said the priest.

"Father Boomer," said Sutter, shaking hands but not taking his foot from the radiator.

After a glance at Jamie—the youth's head had fallen to the side and his eyes were closed—the engineer told Sutter: "Val asked me to call Father Boomer."

"You spoke to Val just now?"

"Yes."

"What did she say?"

"She's flying out."

"You called because I asked you?"

"Jamie also asked me."

Sutter put both feet on the floor and gave him an odd look. "You say Jimmy asked you?"

"He asked me to call Val about a book she promised him. That was earlier."

Sutter sank into thought. There was time for another look at Jamie. The bed had been freshly made, the seersucker counterpane drawn tightly across the youth's bony chest. It seemed to the engineer that Jamie's nose had grown sharper and that his skin clove closer to his cheekbones.

"He's developed a spruelike diarrhea and lost some fluid," said Sutter from the radiator. Was this an explanation? Sutter turned to the priest. "I refused to allow intravenous fluid, Father," he said in what struck the engineer as a challenging tone. "Even though it might prolong his life a few days. What do you think of that?"

"No objection," said the priest, scratching his fist absently. "Unless he is unconscious and you want him conscious for some reason."

Sutter's eye gleamed and he lifted an eyebrow toward the engineer. *How about this fellow?* Sutter asked him. But the engineer frowned and turned away. He wanted no humbug with Sutter.

"Of course, whether he is unconscious or not, I'll be glad to baptize him conditionally," said the priest, settling the glasses with the bracket of his hand.

"Conditionally, Father," said Sutter with a lively expression.

The priest shrugged. "I have no way of knowing whether he's been baptized before."

"Is that what the canon prescribes, Father?" Sutter's eyes roamed the ceiling.

"I think, Father—" began the engineer sternly. He would have no part of Sutter's horsing around. At the same moment he glanced at Sutter's coat pocket: it still held the pistol.

"This young man asked me to come in here," said the priest.

"That's right," said the engineer sternly.

"Therefore I should like to ask you, sir," said the priest straight to Sutter, "whether you concur in your sister's desire that I administer the sacrament of baptism to the patient. If you do not, then I shall be going about my business."

"Yes," said the engineer, nodding vigorously. He thought the priest expressed it very well in his umpire's way, taking no guff from Sutter.

"By all means stay, Father," said Sutter somewhat elaborately.

"Well?" The priest waited.

"Why don't you ask him yourself, Father." Sutter nodded to the bed behind the other two.

They turned. Jamie was getting out of bed! One hand had folded back the covers quite cogently, and the left knee had started across right leg, his eyes open and bulging slightly with seriousness of intent.

Later Sutter told the engineer that, contrary to popular notions, dying men often carry out complex actions in the last moments of life. One patient he recalled who was dying of tuberculosis had climbed out of bed, washed his pajamas in the sink, hung them out to dry, returned to the bed, pulled the covers up to his chin to hide his nakedness, and died.

"Hold it, son," Sutter stopped Jamie fondly and almost jokingly, as if Jamie were a drunk, and motioned the engineer to the cabinet. "Jamie here wants to move his bowels and doesn't like the bedpan. I don't blame him." The priest helped Sutter with Jamie. After a moment there arose to the engineer's nostrils first an intimation, like a new presence in the room, a somebody, then a foulness beyond the compass of smell. This could only be the dread ultimate rot of the molecules themselves, an abject surrender. It was the body's disgorgement of its most secret shame. Doesn't this ruin everything, wondered the engineer (if only the women were here, they wouldn't permit it, oh Jamie never should have left home). He stole a glance at the others. Sutter and the priest bent to their task as if it were nothing out of the ordinary. The priest supported Jamie's head on the frail stem of its neck. When a nurse came to service the cabinet, the engineer avoided her eye. The stench scandalized him. Shouldn't they all leave?

Sutter conducted Jamie back to bed fondly and even risibly. Suddenly the engineer remembered that this was the way Negro servants handle the dying, as if it were the oldest joke of all.

"Hold it now, son. Look out. There you go." Leaning over the bed, Sutter took hold of Jamie's chin, almost chucked it. "Listen, Jimmy. This is Father Boomer. He wants to ask you something."

But the youth goggled and closed his eyes, giving no sign of having heard. Sutter took his pulse and stepped back.

"If you have any business with him, Father," he said dryly, "I think you'd better conduct it now."

The priest nodded and leaned on the bed, supporting himself on his heavy freckled fists. He looked not at Jamie but sideways at the wall.

"Son, can you hear me?"—addressing the wall. The engineer perceived that at last the priest had found familiar territory. He knew what he was doing.

But Jamie made no reply.

"Son, can you hear me?" the priest repeated without embarrassment, examining a brown stain on the wall and not troubling to give his voice a different inflection.

Jamie nodded and appeared to say something. The engineer moved a step closer, cocking his good ear but keeping his arms folded as the sign of his discretion.

"Son, I am a Catholic priest," said Father Boomer, studying the yellow hairs on his fist. "Do you understand me?"

"Yes," said Jamie aloud. He nodded rapidly.

"I have been asked by your sister to administer to you the sacrament of baptism. Do you wish to receive it?"

The engineer frowned. Wasn't the priest putting it a bit formally?

"Val?" whispered Jamie, goggling at the engineer.

"That's right," said the engineer, nodding. "I called her as you asked me to."

Jamie looked at the priest.

"Son," said the priest. "Do you accept the truths of religion?"

Jamie moved his lips.

"What?" asked the priest, bending lower.

"Excuse me, Father," said the sentient engineer. "He said 'what.'"

"Oh," said the priest and turned both fists out and opened the palms. "Do you accept the truth that God exists and that He made you and loves you and that He made the world so that you might enjoy its beauty and that He himself is your final end and happiness, that He loved you so much that He sent His only Son to die for you and to found His Holy Catholic Church so that you may enter heaven and there see God face to face and be happy with Him forever."

Without raising his eyes, the engineer could see the curled-up toe of Sutter's Thom McAn shoe turning to and fro on the radiator trademark.

"Is that true?" said Jamie clearly, opening his eyes and goggling. To the engineer's dismay, the youth turned to him.

The engineer cleared his throat and opened his mouth to say something when, fortunately for him, Jamie's bruised eyes went weaving around to the priest. He said something to the priest which the latter did not understand.

The priest looked up to the engineer.

"He wants to know, ah, why," said the engineer.

"Why what?"

"Why should he believe that."

The priest leaned hard on his fists. "It is true because God Himself revealed it as the truth."

Again the youth's lips moved and again the priest turned to the interpreter.

"He asked how, meaning how does he know that?"

The priest sighed. "If it were not true," he said to Jamie, "then I would not be here. That is why I am here, to tell you."

Jamie, who had looked across to the engineer (Christ, don't look at me!), pulled down the corners of his mouth in what the engineer perceived unerringly to be a sort of ironic acknowledgment.

"Do you understand me, son?" said the priest in the same voice.

There was no answer. Outside in the night the engineer saw a Holsum bread truck pass under the street light.

"Do you accept these truths?"

After a silence the priest, who was still propped on his fists and looking sideways like a storekeeper, said, "If you do not now believe these truths, it is for me to ask you whether you wish to believe them and whether you now ask for the faith to believe them."

Jamie's eyes were fixed on the engineer, but the irony was shot through with the first glint of delirium. He nodded to the engineer.

The engineer sighed and, feeling freer, looked up. Sutter hung fire, his chin on his knuckles, his eyes half-closed and gleaming like a Buddha's.

Jamie opened his mouth, it seemed, to say something bright and audible, but his tongue thickened and came out. He shuddered violently. Sutter came to the bedside. He held the youth's wrist and, unbuttoning the pajamas, laid an ear to the bony chest. He straightened and made a sign to the priest, who took from his pocket a folded purple ribbon which he slung around his neck in a gesture that struck the engineer as oddly graceless and perfunctory.

"What's his name?" the priest asked no one in particular.

"Jamison MacKenzie Vaught," said Sutter.

"Jamison MacKenzie Vaught," said the priest, his fists spread wide. "What do you ask of the Church of God? Say Faith."

Jamie said something.

"What does Faith bring you to? Say Life Everlasting."

Jamie's lips moved.

The priest took the bent sucking tube from Jamie's water glass. "Go fill that over there."

"Yes sir," said the engineer. But surely it was to be expected that the priest have a kit of some sort, at least a suitable vessel. He half filled the clouded plastic glass.

As he returned with the water, Jamie's bowels opened again with the spent schleppen sound of an old man's sphincter. The engineer went to get the bedpan. Jamie tried to lift his head.

"No no," said Sutter impatiently, and coming quickly across simply bound the dying youth to the bed by folding the counterpane into a strap and pressing it against his chest. "Get on with it, Father," he said angrily.

The priest took the plastic glass. "I baptize you in the name of the Father—" He poured a trickle of water into the peninsula of fried dusty hair. "And of the Son—" He poured a little more. "And of the Holy Ghost." He poured the rest.

The three men watched as the water ran down the youth's bruised forehead. It was dammed a moment by the thick Vaught eyebrows, flowed through and pooled around the little red caruncle in the corner of his eye.

The priest bent lower still, storekeeper over his counter, and took the narrow waxy hand between his big ruddy American League paws. "Son," he said in the same flat mercantile voice, looking first at the brown stain on the wall and then down at the dying youth. "Today I promise you that you will be with our Blessed Lord and Savior and that you will see him face to face and see his mother, Our Lady, see them as you are seeing me. Do you hear me?"

The four white vermiform fingers stirred against the big thumb, swollen with blood (did they, thumb and fingers, belong to the same species?).

"Then I ask you to pray to them for me and for your brother here and for your friend who loves you."

The fingers stirred again.

Presently the priest straightened and turned to the engineer as blank-eyed as if he had never laid eyes on him before.

"Did you hear him? He said something. What did he say?"

The engineer, who did not know how he knew, was not even sure he had heard Jamie or had tuned him in in some other fashion, cleared his throat.

"He said, 'Don't let me go.'" When the priest looked puzzled, the engineer nodded to the bed and added: "He means his hand, the hand there."

"I won't let you go," the priest said. As he waited he curled his lip absently against his teeth in a workaday five-o'clock-in-the-afternoon expression.

After several minutes Sutter let go the sheet which he still held as a strap across Jamie.

"All right, Father," said Sutter in an irritable voice when the priest didn't move. "On the way out, would you send in the nurse and the resident?"

"What?" said the priest, bracketing his glasses with his free hand. "Oh, yes. Certainly." He started for the washstand, thought better of it, turned and left the room. Pausing in the doorway, he turned again. "If you need me for anything else, I'd be glad to—"

"We won't," said Sutter curtly, managing to embarrass the engineer after all.

The engineer followed the priest out into the corridor and thanked him. He wondered if one was expected to "make an offering," but he had no notion of how to hand money over except to hand it over. He contented himself with wringing the priest's hand warmly and thanking him twice.

12. IT TOOK HIM TWO BLOCKS AT TOP WALKING SPEED to overtake Sutter, who strode along with his hands in his pockets, bent forward as if he were bucking a strong wind.

"Where are you going?" the engineer asked in an unexpectedly loud voice.

"What?" said Sutter, giving a start. "Oh, to the ranch."

"The ranch," repeated the engineer absently. When Sutter started to leave, he held up his hand. "Wait."

"Wait for what?"

"What happened back there?"

"In the hospital room? You were there."

"I know, but what did you think? I could tell you were thinking something."

"Do you have to know what I think before you know what you think?"

"That does not mean that I would necessarily agree with you," said the engineer, trying to see Sutter's expression. Suddenly the engineer felt his face flush. "No, you're right. I don't need to know what you think. Wait. Did you say ranch?"

"Yes." Still he could not make out Sutter's face.

"Do you mean your ranch?"

"Yes."

"Why?"

"I have a date."

"A date?" His heart began to thud. "No, wait. Please don't go to the ranch!" Without realizing that he had done so, he had taken hold of Sutter's sleeve.

Sutter angrily shook himself free. "What in God's name do you want now?"

"Oh. I—what about the family?"

"What about them?"

"I mean, meeting them. Val should be here tonight and the rest tomorrow."

"Yes."

"They won't know. Shall I meet them? Perhaps I could even call the Vaughts and catch them before they leave."

"Good. Fine."

"Then I'll call the airport and see what the plane schedule is."

"Very good."

"What about the arrangements?"

"Arrangements? You make them. You do very well."

Sutter reached the Edsel and got into the driver's seat but made no sign that the engineer should follow.

"All right. Wait—" cried the engineer when the old buckety Ford motor caught and roared (he wondered if Sutter had ever changed the oil or whether it had oil).

"What?"

He peered down into the dark car.

"Dr. Vaught—ah—"

"What?"

"What are you going to do now?"

"I'm going to have a drink."

"No. I mean, what are you going to do?"

There was no answer. All the engineer could see was that Sutter had put his hands on the wheel at six o'clock and nine o'clock, left elbow on the window sill, a style of driving which the engineer faintly recalled from the 1940's when Delta sports used to pick up their dates and drive to the Marion Parlor on Front Street.

"Are you going home, I mean."

"I told you, Barrett, I'm going to the ranch."

"Dr. Vaught, don't leave me."

"What did you say?"

"Dr. Vaught, listen to me. I'm going to do what I told you I planned to do."

"I know. You told me."

"Dr. Vaught, I want you to come back with me."

"Why? To make this contribution you speak of?"

"Dr. Vaught, I need you. I, Will Barrett—" and he actually

pointed to himself lest there be a mistake, "—need you and want you to come back. I need you more than Jamie needed you. Jamie had Val too."

Sutter laughed. "You kill me, Barrett."

"Yes sir." He waited.

"I'll think about it. Here's some money for the arrangements, as you call them."

"Oh, no, sir." He backed away. "I have plenty."

"Anything else?"

"No sir."

But as the Edsel took off, spavined and sprung, sunk at one corner and flatulent in its muffler, spuriously elegant and unsound, like a Negro's car, a fake Ford, a final question did occur to him and he took off after it.

"Wait," he shouted in a dead run.

The Edsel paused, sighed, and stopped.

Strength flowed like oil into his muscles and he ran with great joyous ten-foot antelope bounds.

The Edsel waited for him.

About the Author

WALKER PERCY himself went to medical school and interned at Bellevue, intending to be a psychiatrist. After a three-year bout with tuberculosis, he married, converted to Catholicism, and became a writer, first of essays, then of fiction. His first novel, THE MOVIEGOER, won the National Book Award and has never been out of print since its publication in 1961. His other novels are THE THANATOS SYNDROME, LOVE IN THE RUINS, LANCELOT, and THE SECOND COMING. His nonfiction books are THE MESSAGE IN THE BOTTLE and LOST IN THE COSMOS. He and his wife, Mary Bernice, live in Covington, Louisiana.